THE HAWK AND THE HEATHER

"An utterly enchanting love story
reminiscent of Kathleen Woodiwiss
and Judith McNaught."

Katherine Sutcliffe

"Robin Leigh has penned a Cinderella story
that sparkles with the charm and flavor
of Regency England . . .
Memorable characters and a sweet romance
enhance this delightful tale."

Kathe Robin, *Romantic Times*

"Move over McNaught! . . .
A tour de force . . .
Warm, sensitive and sparkling
with characters who will win your heart . . .
Robin Leigh has captured
the true essence of romance."

Affair de Coeur

THE HAWK AND THE HEATHER

ROBIN LEIGH

AVON BOOKS ◆ NEW YORK

THE HAWK AND THE HEATHER is an original publication of Avon Books. This work has never before appeared in book form. This work is a novel. Any similarity to actual persons or events is purely coincidental.

AVON BOOKS
A division of
The Hearst Corporation
1350 Avenue of the Americas
New York, New York 10019

First Avon Books Printing: April 1992

AVON TRADEMARK REG. U.S. PAT. OFF. AND IN OTHER COUNTRIES, MARCA REGISTRADA, HECHO EN U.S.A.

Printed in the U.S.A.

RA 10 9 8 7 6 5 4 3 2 1

To Guy Webster
and the wonderful staff at
Little Professor Book Centers.
Because you love books
and you've been so good to the
authors who write them.
Especially to me.
Thanks.

Prologue

Westmorland, England, 1807

Walter FitzHugh looked up from the papers strewn across his desk. His eyes seemed dull, his face haggard, yet he was able to smile when he saw her standing in the hall outside his study. "So, pet, are you ready to leave for Beckworth House?"

Heather shook her head, feeling more lost and confused than she'd ever felt in her ten years.

The baron held out his arms to her. "Come here, child."

She ran to him and hurtled herself onto his lap, into the safety of his arms. Her hands clasped behind his neck as she buried her face against his chest.

"It won't be so terrible at your aunt Caroline's, Heather. My sister might be a trifle vain and arrogant, but she was a FitzHugh before she married the viscount. Once a FitzHugh, always a FitzHugh, I say. She'll make you a good home."

"But I don't want to leave GlenRoyal, Papa," Heather whispered. "Why do we have to leave?"

It was her brother, George, who answered her question. "Because the Duke of Hawksbury cheated at hazard." The fourteen-year-old's voice was filled with bitterness. "Isn't that right, Father?"

1

Heather turned her head toward the doorway and watched as George crossed the room, coming to stand beside her and their father. "But why does that mean we have to leave our home?"

"You're too young to understand, Heather," the baron replied. "One day we'll be able to come back. I don't know how, but one day . . ." His voice faded, the beaten expression returning to haunt his features.

"Let's make a FitzHugh oath." George stuck out his hand, palm down, toward his father and sister. Youthful idealism gleamed in his green eyes. "I swear that I shall do whatever I must to reclaim GlenRoyal for the FitzHugh family."

Heather slid from her father's lap. She stood as straight and tall as she could, not too young to understand the solemnity of taking a FitzHugh oath. She thrust her pudgy arm forward and laid her hand over her brother's. She spoke forcefully, fervently, repeating George's words. "I swear that I shall do whatever I must to reclaim GlenRoyal for the FitzHugh family."

In unison, the siblings looked toward their father, waiting expectantly.

"Children, I . . ." His gaze shifted back and forth between them. Finally, he rose from his chair. "I swear that I shall do whatever I must—" His voice broke, and he turned away from them.

Heather felt tears burning her throat at the sound of despair in her beloved father's voice. She wanted to make him laugh. She wanted to make him smile. She wanted the father she'd always known back again.

The baron moved to the window. He ran the fingers of one hand through his graying hair as he gazed outside into the bright summer sunlight. "George, take Heather outside. I won't be long."

Her brother's hand folded around hers. "Come on." His fingers squeezed hers gently. "Father wants to be alone." He led her to the door. "And don't you ever forget what we swore to do."

Insulted by his authoritarian tone, Heather lifted her chin. As if she would ever forget the importance of what they'd just promised! "A FitzHugh never breaks a FitzHugh oath," she retorted, forcing herself to sound brave and sure.

Three horses were waiting for them in the drive, their reins held by the only remaining footman at GlenRoyal.

Heather broke away from George and hurried toward her pretty chestnut mare. She stroked the horse's sleek neck as the lump returned to her throat. At least no one had taken Cathy from her. She'd been afraid when so many things had started disappearing from GlenRoyal, so many things that had meant safety and security to her. But she couldn't have stood it if someone had taken her mare. A passion for horses—for all animals, really—was something Heather shared with the baron. When she was seven, her father had given her the yearling filly, and Heather had helped to train her.

"May I give you a lift up, Miss Heather?" asked Cosgrove, the footman.

She knew that if she looked at him she would burst out crying. She didn't want to say anymore good-byes. So she shook her head. "I can do it, Cosgrove." Thus said, she led Cathy to the mounting block, hiked up her skirts, and tossed a leg over the saddle. She immediately imagined her aunt Caroline's frown of disapproval at such an unladylike act, but she didn't care. She wasn't living with Aunt Caroline yet.

A moment later, Walter FitzHugh appeared at the top of the steps. He kept his eyes straight ahead as he descended the stairs and walked to his horse.

"Good luck, my lord," the footman said as he handed the reins to the baron.

"Thank you, Cosgrove. Same to you." He swung up onto the saddle, then spun his horse away from the house and cantered down the drive, his children following close behind him.

"You know as well as I do that the duke didn't cheat at hazard," Caroline scolded. "You must make George stop saying so, or you're going to cause us no end of grief. Hawksbury is a powerful man. And that son of his is well thought of among the *ton*. They would never do anything so scandalous as cheat at cards, and well you know it. You'll find yourself called out if rumors begin because of George."

Her brother's response was to lift his glass of port and swallow several gulps.

" 'Tis your own fault, Walter. You never could stay away from the clubs and gaming hells. I'm surprised you didn't lose everything before now. Whatever would have happened to you and the children if it weren't for me? Thank heaven I had the good sense to marry a man like Frederick. He shall never leave me destitute. His daughter will never be living off someone else's charity, as your children are."

"Go away, Caroline," Walter grumbled as he refilled his glass.

"You're getting drunk."

"Go away."

His sister shot him a disgusted glance. "All right, Walter, I'll go. But you'd better spend some time deciding what you're going to do now. You haven't a home. You haven't any income left. You surely don't expect to go on living here indefinitely, being waited on hand and foot. I have my own life to lead. I have responsibilities in Society.

I can't have people gossiping behind my back about my wastrel brother."

"By George!" he shouted. "Go away and leave me in peace!"

Her face pinched with anger, Caroline twirled away from him and stormed out of the room, slamming the door behind her.

"Damn woman," Walter muttered before lifting the glass to his lips. "Never could stand her. Never could."

Now, his Victoria . . . there was a woman to love and be loved. If only she'd lived. He'd never failed at anything when Tory was alive. Since her death, life had lost its meaning for him. If it weren't for his children . . .

Heather was a lot like her mother. She had the same raven hair, curly and unruly, and the same violet eyes, big and round and expressive. Sometimes it almost hurt to look at his daughter for the sense of loss it brought him. But Heather was stronger than Tory had been. Heather was a fighter. She'd find her place in life all right, no matter what a mess her father had made of things. No, he wouldn't have to worry about Heather.

And George. George had all the best qualities of a FitzHugh and few of the weaknesses. George was well on his way to being a man. He was strong and intelligent. He wouldn't repeat his father's mistakes. He would make the FitzHugh name stand for something again. George wasn't the failure Walter had become.

He refilled his glass and let the port slide down his throat, feeling it warming all the cold parts of his body. Heaven help him, he was tired of feeling cold. He'd been cold ever since that night at Watier's.

His senses might be dulled by the alcohol, but he still remembered every detail of that night at the club at No. 81, Piccadilly, as he'd faced the

Duke of Hawksbury and his son across the hazard table. Walter had already lost a phenomenal sum of money that night. In fact, he'd known he was all but ruined. He'd had only one chance to win it back. Only one. He'd demanded that the duke accept GlenRoyal as his wager. He'd been so certain the dice would be good to him on the next roll. He'd been so sure he would nick it, that the chance would equal the main and he would win all the stakes.

But he hadn't nicked it. He'd thrown crabs. With one roll of the dice, he'd lost GlenRoyal.

God only knew why he'd allowed his son to think the duke had cheated by using dispatchers. When George had claimed the dice must have been loaded, Walter had remained silent. Perhaps it was because the truth about himself was too difficult to face. For the thrill of the game, he'd thrown away his son's future, his daughter's security. For the thrill of the game, he'd lost his family's heritage.

Caroline was right about him. He *was* a wastrel. He *was* an embarrassment to his children and his sister and his friends. Perhaps it was merciful that Tory hadn't lived to see him come to this.

"Ah, Tory, I need you with me, love. I need you."

Heather sat up suddenly, startled awake by a loud noise. Her heart hammered in her chest as she stared into the darkness of the strange room. She was frightened. Terribly frightened. She longed for her own bedchamber at GlenRoyal and her familiar bed. She didn't care that GlenRoyal wasn't as large or impressive or finely furnished as Beckworth House. She wanted her own home.

Then she heard the voices. Excited voices. Voices shouting. She heard footsteps running up and down the stairs. She heard pounding on the doors.

Her anxiety increased. Frightening forms took shape in the corners of the room, shapes that seemed to move and whisper and threaten.

"Papa," she whispered, "come find me."

A thin light appeared beneath her door. She slipped out of bed and hurried toward it, blood pounding in her ears. She yanked the door open, letting a flood of golden lamplight spill into the bedchamber, dispelling the ghosts and goblins that fear had created.

She stepped into the hallway, moving toward the commotion on the floor below. Her hand was on the banister, and she was ready to descend the stairs when George appeared.

His face was white, his green eyes eerily bright. "Stay there, Heather," he said.

"Why?"

"It's Papa. Papa's dead."

Chapter 1

London, England, 1816

To the many pairs of feminine eyes watching him covertly—and otherwise—throughout the room, Tanner Huntington Gilbert Montgomery, tenth Duke of Hawksbury, was a magnificent sight. Tall, lean, and broad of shoulder, he was dressed fashionably, yet there was something almost indolent about his appearance, as if he were mocking the gentlemen who'd spent hours at their toilet perfecting their starched cravats. His tight black trousers revealed long legs and muscular thighs. A long-tailed black coat fit him snugly at the waist. There was an aura of raw strength about him, a barely restrained power that was both frightening and fascinating.

But it was the chiseled contours of his face that drew the most attention. Ruggedly handsome, he had a wide forehead and an aquiline nose. His mouth was thin with what appeared to be a permanent cynical twist at the corners. Golden-brown hair brushed the back of his white collar, and cool blue eyes stared out at the drawing room with undisguised boredom.

Tanner sipped champagne and glanced over the rim of his glass. The Rathdrum rout was in full swing. Though the Season had only just begun, and many of the *ton* had yet to come to Town, the drawing room was packed with people. Loud voices echoed throughout the room as everyone sought to be noticed by the rest of High Society. Dandies in crisp white cravats leered at attractive young ladies in high-waisted, wide-sleeved gowns and played silly courtship games beneath the noses of their mamas.

He tossed back the rest of his drink, wondering as he did so what had possessed him to attend the gathering.

"Your grace!"

He frowned as he recognized the voice behind him.

"You are quite naughty for telling me you wouldn't be here tonight. I was frightfully disappointed."

Tanner turned dispassionate eyes upon the fresh-faced beauty. Elizabeth Sloane was in her first Season, and she'd made it clear from the moment they met that she'd set her sights on the eligible Duke of Hawksbury. He could see the hope in her attractive brown eyes as she looked at him now. She wanted much more from him than the bland indifference he'd shown her.

He nodded briefly to acknowledge her sugar-coated accusation. "My plans changed, Lady Elizabeth."

"I'm glad." Her long eyelashes brushed her flushed cheeks. "It's a gay party, isn't it?"

He knew she was waiting for an invitation to dance. Well, she would continue to wait, for he had no intention of obliging her wish. He could see Elizabeth's mother from across the crowded room. He knew what was going through the countess's mind. He'd danced with Elizabeth at the Southwicks' ball last week, giving rise to an unreasonable aspiration. If it could be seen that he preferred her daughter to all the other young women presented this Season, it would be a great feather in her cap. The countess was probably already hearing wedding bells in her head.

They wouldn't learn. None of them would ever learn. They continued to view him as some great prize, determined that he should marry one of their silly, vacuous daughters. He didn't doubt that some of them would go to great lengths to trap him into marriage.

He pictured himself being accused of sullying the reputation of some calf-eyed girl, and the self-righteous parents demanding that he do right by her. It was a preposterous image.

Suddenly he laughed—a somewhat humorless sound that echoed throughout the room.

Elizabeth looked startled and drew back from him. Heads lifted and turned, all eyes upon the strikingly handsome duke and the petite young lady at his side.

"You'll pardon me, Lady Elizabeth. It seems I have another pressing engagement to attend. You will give my best to your mother." He made an abrupt bow, then spun on his boot heel.

He walked with determined strides, glowering at anyone who didn't move instantly from his path, and reached the hall door with unusual good speed.

"My carriage," he instructed the majordomo.

"At once, your grace."

"Hawksbury ..." Althea Rathdrum's low, throaty voice caused him to turn. "You're not going so soon? You'll ruin my reputation as a hostess, leaving my party this way. They will be gossiping about it in Hyde Park on the morrow." She touched his shoulder. "Please don't go. If it's too crowded for your liking, I'm certain we could find some place more private." Her amber eyes offered far more than privacy. "You wouldn't be sorry, your grace," she whispered.

The duke lifted a scornful eyebrow. "If you're not careful, my dear Althea, they'll be gossiping about far more than my early departure. Your husband already suspects your dalliance with Lord Marsh."

Her face paled. "Kimbell couldn't possibly . . ."

Tanner's voice was low, but there was no disguising the disdain that laced each word. "Find another besotted fool to warm your bed, Althea. It would take more than you possess to tempt me into it."

Althea gasped as she stepped backward, her hand on her throat.

"Good evening, Lady Merrywood." One corner of his mouth lifted in a sardonic smile. "Give my best regards to Kimbell."

Tanner swept past the wide-eyed majordomo and out into the cool night air. He paused on the top step and drew in a deep breath, trying to clear his nostrils of Althea's sweet cologne. It angered him, the games they played. It wasn't their faithlessness that frightened the wives of polite Society. It was getting caught.

He glanced along the street, the gaslights forming two long lines of bright dots which yielded little illumination. He considered going to his club on St. James's Street.

Or, he thought, he could pay a visit to Harriette Morton, a particularly pretty cyprian of extraordinary talents. He'd first met the courtesan in Hyde Park last spring and had renewed their acquaintance upon returning to London in the fall. Now, whenever he was in Town, he often visited her house on York Place. He could relax in Harriette's company, and he found that immensely satisfying and refreshing. There was no artifice about her. She was exactly as she appeared. She wasn't out to snare a wealthy title attached to a man. She enjoyed her independence too much to want a husband. A refreshing change, Tanner thought, from the ladies of polite Society who bartered their bodies in more devious ways.

As he descended the steps toward his carriage, he dispensed with the notion of seeing Harriette tonight. She wasn't expecting him, and since by choice she had no single protector, he had no illusions about how she spent her time when he wasn't with her. He didn't want to surprise her while entertaining another member of the beau monde.

"Albany House," he told the driver as he stepped into his town coach and leaned back against the plush cushions.

He glanced out the window as the city flowed by, lost in shadows, then suddenly ablaze with light as they passed another house filled with fashionable guests, the windows unshuttered and uncurtained so all who drove by might know there was a rout going on inside.

Bloody hell! He hated it all. He was sick to death of it. The bartering of pretty faces for titles and wealthy estates in the country. Young misses, and their mothers, after proper husbands to sire their children so that one day they could sit at Almack's and see their daughters flirting with other dandies with titles to be captured. And so it would play out, year after year.

He closed his eyes, hearing his mother's soft scolding in his head. *You're two and thirty, Tanner. 'Tis time you were thinking about taking a wife. Hawksbury needs an heir.*

He knew it was true. The Montgomery estates were extensive. His income was nearly one hundred thousand pounds a year. He was the only living male in the direct Montgomery line. He had to provide a son to inherit.

But whenever he thought of it, he remembered

Judith. Judith with the laughter of an angel and the heart of the devil.

He hit the front of the carriage with his walking stick. "Crandall, take me to York Place," he shouted at the driver.

Perhaps an evening in Harriette's arms was what he needed after all. If she had company, he would see that the man decided to take his leave quickly.

Harriette poured claret into a glass, then turned toward her guest. She smiled lazily. "You should have told me you meant to come tonight."

"I didn't plan on it," Tanner answered, perhaps more sharply than he'd intended.

"Ah . . ." The soft sound was little more than a sigh. "So it's that again. You shouldn't let it trouble you so. Becoming leg-shackled needn't be the end of the world."

She moved forward, her gown whispering around her ankles as she approached the duke. She set the glass of claret on a nearby table, then lowered herself beside him on the sofa. Her fingers smoothed away his hair from his forehead before tracing a lazy path down the side of his face and cupping his chin. Leaning forward, she placed a feather-light kiss on his mouth.

Despite the calm wisdom of her words, Harriette wasn't completely dispassionate about Tanner's dilemma. She was extremely fond of the duke, in her own carefree manner, and she wished she had the means to make him happy. A foolish wish for a *fille de joie*. While she might be able to share an evening of passion with a man like Tanner, she knew her place. The most she could do was offer a piece of friendly advice.

"You should get away from London for a while, my love, before you learn to hate everyone and everything. Not all women are like—" Just in time she stopped herself from speaking Judith's name. She'd made the mistake of mentioning his deceased wife once before and had sworn never to do so again. "Not all women are alike," she amended.

Tanner gently pushed her away, then rose and walked to the window. He brushed aside the curtains to gaze down on the street below. With a frown furrowing his brow, he realized he *was* beginning to hate everyone and everything. Most of all, he hated the idea of choosing a bride.

Harriette was wrong about all women not being alike. With the exception of his charming companion, he'd seen few examples to convince him there were many honest females alive. He'd watched his sister, Emma, scheme and plot to marry the Marquess of Trent, then give birth to three daughters before her death, not one of them sired by her husband from the look of them. Even his mother, the Dowager Duchess of Hawksbury, had not been above a discreet affair while her husband was living—and he'd always considered their marriage one of the happier ones he'd known.

No, Harriette was wrong about women. He knew all too well about the majority of Society's charming, gentler half, especially those on the marriage mart. He considered them all calculating, scheming liars. They would flutter their innocent eyelashes at a man tonight, trying to win an offer of marriage, and tomorrow they would be slipping between the sheets with someone else.

He swore silently. Harriette *was* right about one thing. He *did* need to get away from London and the social whirl. He'd promised his mother he would choose a bride this year. But in six Seasons, except for Harriette, he hadn't found a girl he would care to spend more than five minutes with at any one stretch. And, of course, he couldn't marry Harriette.

That thought brought a thin smile to his lips. Marriage to Harriette Morton. Now, wouldn't that set Society on its ear!

The smile disappeared as quickly as it had come. He knew he could never be so reckless in his choice of a bride. Duty to Hawksbury demanded that she be a member of the aristocracy. His son and heir would one day be responsible for all of the Hawksbury estates. There would be many who depended upon him for their homes, their food, their incomes, perhaps their very lives. In order for his son to manage his estates well, he would have to be a part of Society, which meant Tanner had to make an acceptable match.

Besides, he didn't love Harriette.

He clenched his jaw, angered by his own thought. It didn't matter whether he loved his wife or not. He had little tolerance for such a useless sentiment. He'd wasted that emotion once before and had learned a very valuable lesson because of it. No, love would have no place in his choice of a bride.

But how was he to make that choice when they all seemed the same to him, when he couldn't bear to spend more than a few moments with any one of them?

Indeed, Harriette was right. He did need to get away from London. Perhaps if he spent some time in the country, he would find one of the lovely young ladies available to him more appealing upon his return.

Harriette touched his shoulder. "Where will you go, your grace?" she whispered as she leaned her voluptuous bosom against his back.

"I don't know. Somewhere no one will come looking for me. Somewhere I can be entirely alone."

She slipped around him, her breasts now

pressed against his chest. "And where is that, your grace?"

"I'm not sure yet."

"I'll miss you while you're gone."

The cynical smile returned as he lowered his head toward hers. "Of course you will, my sweet, but not much. Not very much."

Chapter 2

Westmorland, England, 1816

Heather FitzHugh nudged her horse, asking for more speed as they raced toward the thick hedge. As she leaned forward, she felt Cathy gathering herself for flight, and moments later, they were airborne. The instant her mare's front hooves touched the green turf, Heather eased back on the reins and drew the animal to a stop.

She gazed before her at the rear of the three-story house. It seemed to stare back at her, sad and dejected and empty. There was little one man could do to make GlenRoyal look otherwise. Years of neglect were stamped on the wide, square building that had once been her home.

But not in the gardens. There the grounds-keeper's expert touch could be seen at every turn. The hedges and bushes were neatly trimmed. The lawn was groomed to perfection. Leafy trees shaded the winding footpaths, which were kept swept free of debris. In another month or so, the roses would be in bloom.

Heather slipped from the saddle and looped the reins around a tree branch. She patted the mare's glossy chestnut neck, then started toward the barn.

She poked her head inside the open door. "Mr. Haskin?" she called.

There was no reply from his quarters above the stables. Supposing he was at work in the maze of greenery, she turned and walked toward the kennels. Immediately a cry went up from the hunting spaniels.

"Hello, pups," she greeted them.

With deft fingers, she slipped the latch of the nearest gate. A sleek red setter streaked through the opening, then raced several circles around Heather before sitting down and cocking her head to one side, leveling a curious gaze upon the young woman.

"I know, Strawberry," she said, bending to stroke the dog's head. "It has been a long time since I've come to visit. Annabella was angry with me, and Aunt Caroline said I couldn't go near the stables."

But she didn't want to think of her aunt and cousin today. It was too beautiful outside, and she was so glad to be free of the oppressive atmosphere that pervaded Beckworth House.

Patting her thigh with her fingertips to invite the dog along, she strolled toward the gardens. She moved slowly, enjoying the serenity of the place. Coming here always made her feel good.

She sank onto a stone bench near the pond and watched as a long-necked swan glided across the glossy surface. The water rippled out behind it in a V, the marks lingering like footprints in the sand, then fading away to nothing. She smiled, soothed by the tranquil scene. Seeming to sense her peace, Strawberry lay on the ground and rested her chin on the toe of Heather's worn riding boot.

Heather removed her bonnet and set it on the bench at her side, then reached into her pocket and withdrew the letter. With loving fingers, she caressed the familiar handwriting on the envelope. Nearly illegible—as always. George had never learned to handle a quill with anything bordering on dexterity. She would most likely spend the next half hour trying to decipher what he had written.

While a soft breeze rustled the leaves overhead, she opened the letter and began reading.

My dearest Heather, you are likely most distressed with me for the time that has passed since last I wrote to you . . .

It had been a long time. Almost a year since she'd received his last letter. At times she had been sick with worry, wondering what had become of him.

. . . We suffered the loss of our ship off the coast of South America. It was feared for some time that none of us would survive . . .

It wasn't the first time in the years since George had ridden away from Beckworth House that he'd been close to death. He'd nearly been killed in a duel with that lying cheat of a duke, and life as a sailor was by definition dangerous.

. . . I had hoped to return to England to see you this summer, but I am afraid I may once again disappoint you. If I do not come, please find it in your heart to forgive me. I know it is not an easy life for you with Aunt Caroline and our cousin Annabella . . .

Heather sighed. Easy? She supposed it could be worse. She had food to eat and clothes to wear. But oh, how she missed her brother. George had always been able to make her feel better. It had been George who, comforting her, had made those dark weeks following their father's death seem not quite so grim. It had been George who had made those early years in the Beckworths' home more bearable. Despite Aunt Caroline's constant reminders that they were dependent upon her charity, George had been able to make Heather forget, if only for brief periods, that they were the unwanted poor relations.

> *... Do not lose heart, dear sister. I will return to England soon, and we will be reunited.*
>> *Affectionately, your brother, George.*

Would he truly return? she wondered as she folded the letter and slipped it back into the envelope.

She sighed as her gaze returned to the pond and the elegant swan gliding across the dark water. It was nearly seven years since George had left Beckworth House, swearing he would return with the deed to GlenRoyal. He'd been only sixteen at the time and so sure of himself, so convinced that right made him invincible. He was lucky he hadn't been killed.

Nearly seven years since George had left to make good the FitzHugh oath. She remembered the day so clearly ...

Unnoticed, Heather slipped into her aunt's study and pressed herself against the wall by the door, her joy at having George home from school dimmed by the angry voices that had led her to this room.

"You'll never amount to anything, George Fitz-Hugh," Aunt Caroline snapped at the gangly youth standing opposite her. "You're as worthless as your father. I see no reason for the viscount to continue paying for your education when you behave so thanklessly."

"Father wasn't worthless," George replied in an icy voice, "and you won't say it's so."

"Don't get cheeky with me, boy. I'll not stand for it. Not as long as you're living under my roof."

George's hands formed fists at his sides. "Then maybe I won't go on living under your roof. Maybe Heather and I will go home to GlenRoyal."

"Good heavens! What makes you think you'll ever live there again?"

"Because the old Duke of Hawksbury is dead now. I'm going to see his son and demand that he do the honorable thing. I'm a FitzHugh," he said with pride, "and GlenRoyal belongs to the Fitz-Hughs."

Aunt Caroline sat down abruptly in the chair behind her desk. "You are as mad as Walter. It was a miracle we managed to keep his suicide a secret, and now you're going to stir up trouble and more gossip. What did I do to deserve such a burden? I ask you, whatever did I do to deserve it?"

Heather held her breath as she watched George and their aunt stare at each other. Suddenly, George whirled and strode out of the study, whisking past Heather without even seeming to see her. She hesitated only a moment before she followed him.

George was already saddling a horse when she caught up with him in the stables.

"What are you doing, George? Where are you going?"

"I'm going to see the duke. I'm going to get the deed to GlenRoyal or demand satisfaction. Everyone knows Nicholas Montgomery cheated Father. Even his son knows. He was there. He saw it. Everyone knows it's true."

"Aunt Caroline says we'll never live at GlenRoyal again. She says—"

"I don't care what Aunt Caroline says. GlenRoyal is ours. I swore a FitzHugh oath that I'd get GlenRoyal back, and that's what I'm going to do. If Hawksbury won't do the honorable thing, I'll call him out."

Heather grabbed her brother's arm. "Let me go with you."

"No." George swung himself up in the saddle. "When I come back, I'm going to take you to GlenRoyal. You wait for me here."

He hadn't come back, of course. The new duke had accepted a sixteen-year-old boy's challenge to a duel and then shot him. Heather had spent several agonizing weeks waiting and wondering what had happened to George.

Then his letter had come. She knew every word of it by memory, she'd read it so often. She could close her eyes and see the smudged ink even now.

My dearest sister,

I beg you to forgive me, but I shall not be returning soon to Beckworth House. My demand for satisfaction from the duke did not go quite as I had planned. I fear I took a bullet in my leg. I know, Heather, that you have worried about me, but I am nearly mended now, thanks to the care of a good doctor.

I hope you will understand why I won't be returning to Westmorland just yet. Until I am able to keep my oath to Father, until I can take you back to GlenRoyal to live, I must make my own way in the world. I can no longer bear to live off our aunt's charity.

I have signed on to go to sea with a fine captain of a merchant ship as soon as I'm fully recovered. I will send what money I can when I can, and one day, when I am able, I will return for you.

Do not despise me too much, my dearest Heather. You are often in my thoughts.

Your brother, George

Heather had been alone ever since then. And all because of the Duke of Hawksbury.

She felt a familiar surge of anger and bitterness, what she always felt when she thought of the name. It had a hateful, ugly sound. She imagined the Montgomery men as dark and swarthy with evil eyes and hearts as black as sin. The old duke would have had to be like that to steal away GlenRoyal from her father and then never once come to live here. And his son, the current duke, would have to be like that to shoot a reckless sixteen-year-old boy who'd only come to ask for justice.

Oh, how she wished she were a man. Then she would have been able to keep her oath to Papa. She didn't know how she would have gone about it, but she would have done something. She wouldn't be forced to stay at Beckworth House, waiting for George's return. She would be able to do something for herself and her beloved GlenRoyal.

Another sigh whispered between her lips. It was no use to wish such things. She couldn't change who or what she was. Besides, all of George's letters through the years had promised that he would return, and when he did, they would go home to GlenRoyal. It was that promise that gave her courage to face life at Beckworth House.

Heather rose from the bench and returned the letter to the pocket of her riding habit. The dress fit too snugly across her breasts, for she was more shapely than her cousin. But she'd learned through the years not to ask for anything new. Nearly all her clothes were secondhand, Annabella's discards. Heather could only be thankful that she and her cousin were relatively close to the same size and that Annabella tired so quickly of her clothing. Heather was especially glad for the riding habit, since she found nothing more pleasurable than being on horseback. She could escape the bonds of her small world then, racing across the rugged countryside, the wind in her hair, the earth falling away beneath flying hooves.

Besides, riding allowed her to come to GlenRoyal. Aunt Caroline would be furious if she knew where it was her niece went. Once, when Heather was eleven, she and George had ridden over to GlenRoyal and forgotten the time. It had been late in the afternoon when their uncle had found them, running through the maze. They had both received a thorough upbraiding and were told never again to trespass on the duke's property. But after George had gone to sea, Heather's loneliness had drawn her back to her home. Thus far, she had managed to keep her visits a secret, and so she'd stopped worrying that she would be found out.

She tapped her crop against her thigh as she turned her back on the pond. She wondered where Haskin was. Her old friend usually found her within minutes after she arrived. Perhaps he was working in the maze. He was always grooming the hedges.

She didn't know why he worked so hard to keep them looking grand. After all, since the day he'd been hired and sent to GlenRoyal over seven years before, Albert Haskin had never again seen his employer. As far as Heather knew, no one from the Duke of Hawksbury's family had ever come to stay, although the stables had once been stocked with fine horses and the kennels with well-trained hounds. Haskin took care of the aging animals and the grounds, but the house continued to stand empty. It seemed no one wanted the duke's ill-gotten gains.

These thoughts in mind, Heather began walking toward the maze, Strawberry trotting beside her.

* * *

Tanner stepped down from the ladder into a pile of dust-laden draperies. Faint light streamed through the grimy windows of the salon. He'd been working all morning, along with his valet, Martin Thorpe, trying to make at least a few rooms of the house livable.

Of course, he could have easily gone into the nearby village and hired servants to clean up the place, but Tanner felt a need for physical exertion. Besides, he didn't want anyone to know he was at GlenRoyal. The longer he could keep the news a secret, the better he would like it. The last thing he wanted was to have to keep up the social graces with the local gentry.

Still, as he glanced around the disorderly room, he wondered if coming to GlenRoyal had been such a good idea after all. It was bad enough to be staying in a place that seemed ready to crumble about his ears. It was worse still to find himself wondering which bedrooms Judith and her lover had used when they had rendezvoused here. He'd thought he was beyond such thoughts. Apparently he was wrong. Although his love for Judith had died long before she did, the bitterness lingered on. One night in this ramshackle manse had proved that much.

With a curse, he kicked the draperies aside and strode across the salon. "Thorpe!" he shouted. "Thorpe, get down here."

Within moments, his stouthearted valet appeared on the staircase. Thorpe's face was smudged with dirt, his normally flawlessly combed hair disheveled. "Yes, your grace?"

"Is there anything in this place to eat?"

"I'm afraid not, your grace. Perhaps Mr. Haskin left something in his quarters. I'll go have a look."

"No, I'll do it. I could use some fresh air." Tanner headed toward the rear of the house and the doorway that led to the south lawn.

It was surprising to step into the bright sunlight after the gloom of the house. He paused and inhaled deeply of the crisp April air. His gaze scanned the mist-enshrouded mountains that rose majestically in the distance.

He'd chosen to come to GlenRoyal for two reasons. First, because it was far from London. Second, because no one would think to look for him here. It had long been whispered that Judith Montgomery had used this estate in northern England to cuckold her husband in the brief months of their marriage. The fact that Tanner had never once visited GlenRoyal in all these years seemed to prove the truth of the rumors.

As he exhaled, he forced Judith and his bitter memories from his mind. He had other things to think about now, rather than faithless wives and their common lovers.

He started off in the direction of the stables. One matter he would have to see to before leaving GlenRoyal was the hiring of a proper staff. Among the first of them would be a new groundskeeper. He'd fired Haskin within minutes of his arrival yesterday. While he had to admit the grounds were immaculate and the animals well cared for, it was beyond tolerance that the man hadn't notified Tanner of the condition of the house.

As he approached the open doorway to the stables, he heard a soft nicker off to his left. A lanky chestnut stood watching him, its ears cocked forward in curiosity. He redirected his footsteps toward the animal.

"Ho, there," he said softly. "And who are you?"

He took note of the sidesaddle on the mare's back and the sweat that had dried on her neck. Apparently he was looking for a lady who had ridden either some distance or quite hard to get here.

He surveyed the grounds. There was no sign of his visitor. But she had to be around somewhere. The mare hadn't trotted in on her own and tied herself to that tree branch.

Dismayed that his presence at GlenRoyal had been discovered so soon, he glanced at the house. Was the lady in question already waiting in the withdrawing room to see him? He dispensed quickly with that notion. If she were inside, Thorpe would have called for him.

But if not in the house, where was she? And, more to the point, *who* was she?

He started down the pathway that led to the pond, his temper growing more foul with each step he took. Privacy, damn it! All he wanted was a bit of privacy. What did it take for a man to be left alone?

Except for the swan gliding effortlessly across the water, all was still in this section of the grounds. A gentle breeze whispered in the trees as sunlight filtered through the waving branches, casting a latticework of shadows across the pathway.

He heard a dog's bark first, followed by laughter. A woman's laughter, light and carefree. It came from the maze.

Frowning yet curious, he headed off in that direction.

"No, Strawberry! Bring that back, you naughty dog. Give it back."

The setter, bonnet and ribbons flapping from each side of her mouth, bounded gleefully just out of Heather's reach. With a safe distance between them, the dog dropped the bonnet and barked a challenge, her front quarters close to the ground, her hindquarters thrust in the air as her tail wagged furiously. Then, just as Heather bent forward to grasp the errant bonnet, Strawberry picked up the prize once more and darted away.

Heather knew she should sound more stern, but she couldn't help laughing at the dog's antics.

"Oh! I give up," she said breathlessly as she sank to the ground in a puddle of skirts, mindless of grass stains. "You can have the blasted thing."

Strawberry stopped. Her head came up. She dropped the bonnet again, but the play seemed to have gone out of her. Suddenly she snarled a warning.

Heather looked behind her just as a man stepped into view.

The sleeves of his once white shirt were rolled up to the elbows, revealing well-muscled forearms. He was coated from head to toe with a fine layer of dust. His face, filled with sharp angles and dominated by a pair of deep-set, cool blue eyes, was intense and angry in appearance. He seemed excessively tall and broad-shouldered, and terribly unhappy to see her.

She felt a tiny thrill of alarm. "Who are you?" she demanded as she shot to her feet, then stumbled back a step. "What are you doing here?"

"I was about to ask you the same thing," he replied. There was a hard, threatening edge to his voice.

She stiffened her spine, determined not to let him see her nervousness. "Does Mr. Haskin know you're here? He doesn't take kindly to trespassers at GlenRoyal. You'd better leave before he finds you."

"Mr. Haskin won't be finding either of us. He doesn't work here any longer."

Heather gasped. "Doesn't work here?" She didn't understand. Albert Haskin was her friend, as close to family as she had with George away. He would have told her if he were leaving

GlenRoyal. "What do you mean? Of course he works here."

"Not any longer. The old man was let go."

"Let go?" she echoed. It couldn't be. Not even the duke himself was cruel enough to turn out Albert Haskin. He'd been a faithful and good steward of the duke's property for seven years. He'd worked hard to keep the grounds well groomed and the horses and hounds cared for when not even the duke himself seemed to care about any of it.

Her skepticism obvious, she demanded, "How do you know? Were you sent here to replace him?"

"Replace ..." He paused. An odd expression crossed his face before he shook his head. "No. No, I'm just helping to clean up inside. It's in rather poor shape, you know."

Heather's hands clenched at her sides as she fought to control her anger. After all these years, the Duke of Hawksbury had finally taken notice of this property and, in doing so, had sacked his faithful servant who'd taken care of GlenRoyal for all this time. "Do you know why the duke let Mr. Haskin go?"

"I suppose because the old man let the place fall into disrepair."

There was no controlling her anger now. "And just what was he supposed to do all by himself?" Her voice rose in indignation. "Mr. Haskin wrote and told the duke what was happening here. I know he did; he told me so. Why, those wonderful horses have just grown old in the stables. And the dogs ... The puppies are a lot of scapegraces. 'Tis a crime, is what it is. But Mr. Haskin loved and cared for each and every one of them. He tried his best to keep them exercised and ready, should the duke ever come. But, of course, the duke didn't answer Mr. Haskin's letters or do anything about it. Why should a cheeseparing care-for-nobody like the Duke of Hawksbury worry about this little property so far from London?"

She stopped her tirade suddenly as a flush of embarrassment warmed her cheeks. "Excuse me, sir," she said, horrified by her outburst. "I should not have said such things to a stranger. 'Tis not your fault you work for such a man. I'm afraid I've revealed my poor manners, and if my aunt had heard me, I should have been reprimanded most diligently. I beg you to forgive me." She turned and started away.

"Wait."

She paused and glanced over her shoulder. She saw him lean forward and pick up her hat where the red setter had left it.

"Your bonnet, miss." He handed it to her.

"Thank you."

"Was Haskin a very close friend of yours?"

She nodded as she fought back hot tears. "He let me come sit in the gardens whenever I wanted. 'Tis so lovely here. GlenRoyal is . . . a very special place. I . . . I shall miss it."

"You don't have to miss it," Tanner replied, unable to stop himself. "You're welcome to come whenever you want. I won't—I'm sure his grace wouldn't mind."

She looked up at him with round violet eyes, beautiful eyes fringed with thick black lashes. Her heart-shaped face was pale, her mouth turned down in sadness. "I . . . I couldn't."

He glanced at the dog at her side. He was certain it was one of the hunters from the GlenRoyal kennel, but it was clear the dog belonged much more to the young lady than to the Duke of Hawksbury. "The dog will miss you if you don't come back," he said. A voice in the back of his head reminded him that he'd come to GlenRoyal looking for privacy, but he ignored it. There was something enjoyable about sharing a moment with a young woman who wasn't fawning over him, intent on gaining some favor.

And he had to admit it was unique for him to be confused with a servant, although he supposed he looked the part, covered with dust and sweat. It was certainly for the best that this particular lady didn't know who he was. He didn't doubt but what the chit would want to box his ears, should she learn his true identity and know that it was he who had sacked Haskin.

And just who was she? She wasn't a serving wench from a neighboring estate, or a simple villager. Her speech was too fine for that, as was the cloth of her ill-fitting gown. She was likely the daughter of some gentleman who'd run up a tick and was having trouble paying his debts. But who? If he could get her to stay a little longer, perhaps he would find out.

Looking down into her beautifully sad face, he said the first thing that popped into his head. "Perhaps I could put a word in with the duke for your Mr. Haskin. Maybe I could help him get his position back."

Her whole face lit up with her smile. "Oh! Could you? It would be so terribly wonderful of you."

"I'll do what I can, Miss . . ." He waited for her to supply a name.

Pale splotches of pink returned to her cheeks. Hastily, she turned away and tied the mauled bonnet over her ebony curls. "I must go. It was very kind of you to offer to help Mr. Haskin. I shan't forget." She hurried away from him, the red setter trotting at her side.

Tanner raised his arm, prepared to call after her to stop, but he thought better of it. Instead, he was content to watch her disappear around a corner of green hedge.

Let it go, he told himself as he turned in the opposite direction. The girl was nothing to him, nor did her opinions regarding the Duke of Hawksbury count for anything.

But perhaps he *had* been unfair, he thought as he began walking toward the house. There *might* have been a letter or two through the years from Albert Haskin reporting on the state of GlenRoyal.

He frowned in remembrance. In fact, there had been more than a couple of letters. There had been many of them. Only he hadn't wanted to have anything to do with GlenRoyal, so he'd shoved them aside.

Whoever the girl was, she was right. The duke was a "cheeseparing care-for-nobody."

His frown faded, then was replaced by a grin. When was the last time anyone had spoken an opinion of him to his face like that? Years, he supposed. Only his friend Edward Kennaway, the Earl of Mannington, had ever come close, and even Mannington hadn't had the nerve to try it again.

With quick strides, Tanner headed toward the house, his hunger forgotten. He was going to change his clothes and ride into the village to find Haskin. And then he was going to find out something about the violet-eyed miss who dared to turn his hunting hounds into pets.

Chapter 3

"I hate it here!" Annabella picked up a bottle from the dressing table and threw it across Heather's bedchamber. The glass shattered against the fireplace grate, and within moments the room was filled with the cologne's sweet fragrance. "I shouldn't have to miss the start of the Season just because Father can't get away to Town right now."

Heather bent to pick up a piece of glass lying near her foot. It had been a vial of her favorite cologne, and now it was gone, wasted in another of her cousin's angry fits. "Uncle Frederick said you'll all be able to go to London next month."

"The Season will be half over by that time." Annabella stamped her foot in vexation and gave her blond hair a saucy toss. "Why should I expect you to understand? You've never had a Season. You don't know what you're missing."

Heather pressed her lips together, refusing to acknowledge the hurt Annabella's words caused. "I didn't want one."

Annabella's mood shifted quickly. "Poor cousin," she crooned in mock sympathy. "It must be dreadful to be dished up, with no home and no prospect of ever marrying well. Of course, Mama has always done what she could for you. Terribly charitable, I've always thought, giving you a home when your own father left you in disgrace and penniless, and your brother deserted you."

Heather turned away from her cousin as her fingers tightened into a fist. A prick of pain reminded her that she was holding the broken cologne bottle. She opened her hand to see a crimson bead forming in her palm.

"Well, I would never be content to become a toad-eating tabby like you, Heather FitzHugh. You'll see. I'll get Father to go to London soon. And by the end of this Season, I'll have married a title. You see if I don't." With a swish of skirts, Annabella left the bedroom.

Heather blinked away the sting of tears.

She didn't know why her cousin felt such pleasure in making her miserable. She tried not to let the little digs and proddings bother her. Sometimes she succeeded, but not often enough.

She placed the shard of glass on a nearby table, then took a handkerchief from a drawer and tied it around her palm as she sank onto the edge of the bed, Annabella's words echoing in her head.

Penniless? True. But one day George would have his own ship and be very successful. He would return and take up his rightful place as the next Baron FitzHugh. She wouldn't ever again have to take charity from Aunt Caroline or wear another of Annabella's discarded gowns.

Deserted? No. George hadn't deserted her. He'd just gone to sea to make his own way. She understood. He couldn't come back until he'd succeeded. And he couldn't have taken her with him when he'd left. She'd understood it then, and she understood it now. Really, she did.

A toad-eating tabby? She sighed as a wistful smile curved her mouth. Perhaps she was a poor relation, subjected to the whims of the Beckworths, but she wasn't an old maid yet. She wasn't old at all. Only nineteen. And one day, she

knew, she would meet *him*. Someone very special.
She wouldn't care if he was just a simple tradesman, as long as he loved and cherished her. And
he wouldn't care that she had no dowry. Theirs
would be a love match.

Closing her eyes, she envisioned him, the man
of her dreams. Tall and ruggedly handsome and
blue-eyed, his golden-brown hair covered with
dust.

She gasped as she recognized the lover she'd
conjured up. It was the man she'd met yesterday
at GlenRoyal.

Tanner brought the tankard of ale to his lips and
drank deeply. When he set it back on the table, his
gaze returned to Albert Haskin, seated opposite
him.

"You're a hard man to find, Haskin. I've been
looking for you since yesterday. I've come to offer
you your position back. I want you to return to
GlenRoyal."

"Return, your grace?"

"I was mistaken. It was entirely my fault for letting the place go to rack and ruin. I'm going to
hire a proper staff and see that the estate is set in
order. You'll be in charge of the grounds, just as
before, but you won't be blamed for things that
aren't your responsibility."

Haskin's hands closed around his tankard. "It's
kind of you to offer, your grace . . ."

"You haven't taken another position, have you,
Haskin?"

"No, your grace. And I . . . I'd be most happy to
return to GlenRoyal."

Tanner let out a relieved sigh. "Good. Because I
promised a young lady I would bring you back."

Haskin's eyes widened. "A young lady?"

"Yes. A particularly pretty miss with violet eyes
and black hair and an affection for my dogs." He

leaned forward, his expression serious. "Do you know this girl?"

"I do, your grace," the man answered slowly, looking chagrined. "But I can promise you she's not done your dogs any harm. Has a real way with the animals, she does."

"Be that as it may, she was very upset when she learned you'd been turned out. Is she a relative of yours?"

Haskin appeared to be fighting a smile. "Lor' no, your grace. She's a lady. Real gentry. 'Twas good of her to worry about an old man like me. But that's how she is. She's a kind thing."

"Who is she?"

Haskin's grin vanished. He hesitated a moment, then said, "She lives not far from GlenRoyal."

"*Who* is she, Haskin?"

Again the old man answered evasively. "She's the niece of Viscount Moredale. She lives at Beckworth House."

"And her name?" Tanner persisted.

"You'll pardon me, your grace, but I see no reason to involve her any further. I'll make sure she doesn't come 'round to bother the dogs. There's no need to bring trouble down on her for what was my fault. I'm the one who let her come."

"Calm down, Haskin," Tanner said sharply. "I'm not angry with her. Now, tell me her name."

A long silence preceded Haskin's reply. " 'Tis FitzHugh, your grace. Heather FitzHugh."

FitzHugh? The name sounded familiar, but he couldn't place it. "She doesn't seem to have a very high regard for the Duke of Hawksbury. You wouldn't know anything about that, would you?"

Haskin shook his head.

Tanner had the feeling the old groundskeeper was keeping something from him, but he let it pass. After all, it wasn't important that he know why she disliked him. "There's one condition to

my offer of employment, Haskin. You're not to tell
Miss FitzHugh that I'm the duke. She thinks I am
in Hawksbury's employ. I'd like to leave it that
way for now. Do I have your word on it? You
won't tell her any differently?"

Haskin's bushy gray brows drew together in a
frown as he considered the duke's offer. It was obvious he was carrying on some internal battle.
Tanner began to doubt that the old man would accept his condition of employment.

Finally, Haskin nodded. "All right, your grace. I
see no harm in what you're askin', as long as
you'll tell me you're not doin' it to cause her any
grief." His expression left no doubt in Tanner's
mind what type of grief he meant. "She's an innocent lamb with a pure heart. She's had a sad enough life, and there's little joy in it but what she
makes for herself. I'd not want to be guilty of
hurtin' her."

"I promise you, Haskin, I have no designs on
the young lady. You have my solemn oath."

But as he lifted his tankard once again, he wondered if he was telling the truth. There wasn't any
reason that he should care if she knew who he
was. It shouldn't matter to him if she hated the
Duke of Hawksbury. So why was he set on changing her mind?

It was absolutely addled of her to take Cathy for
a run this afternoon. With all of Annabella's carrying on, the whole house was in an uproar, and
Aunt Caroline was in a fine temper. The viscountess would be certain to find fault with Heather for
not staying home and comforting her cousin.

But she'd had to get away. Annabella's viperous
remarks had lost their sting, but the image
Heather had conjured up afterward hadn't departed. No matter what she was doing, she kept
seeing him in her mind—tall and dusty and terri-

bly handsome. She didn't even know his name, but she wished she did. Just so she would know what to call him in her dreams.

Silly, perhaps, but she couldn't help herself.

Cathy galloped across the fields, following the usual route to GlenRoyal without guidance from Heather, who was too lost in her own thoughts to provide direction.

She couldn't go up to the door and ask him his name. Even she had better manners than that. Besides, he might not be working there any longer. He might have finished what he'd come to do and already left. Did he live nearby? In the village, perhaps?

Oh, going to GlenRoyal was a foolish thing to do. With Haskin gone, she couldn't even walk in the gardens anymore. Not without the risk of getting caught trespassing.

But who would know? The duke never came to GlenRoyal.

Or was that about to change? Why were they cleaning the house after all these years? Was the duke going to make use of it at last?

The thought left her feeling angry and confused. She didn't know if she was angry because of the neglect the duke had shown toward her old home or because he might actually come to stay there.

With her anger came a voice from the past. Her voice. So young and determined and filled with childish confidence that right would prevail. *I swear that I shall do whatever I must to reclaim GlenRoyal for the FitzHugh family.*

Oh, Papa, someday we'll get it back. Someday George and I will keep our pledge. Oh, Papa ...

Her anger drained away, replaced by a sense of piercing loss. She felt it as keenly now as she had the night her father had placed the pistol to his head and pulled the trigger.

Why, Papa? she wondered now, just as she always did. Why?

Heather had only one memory of her mother, Victoria, who had died when Heather was five. She always pictured her sitting next to the sunny windows of the salon, Victoria's watercolors and easel and canvas and paintbrushes surrounding her.

But Heather's head was filled with memories of her father. A man of easy laughter, with a zest for living. A short man, stout but not gone to fat. She'd always thought him handsome, although she supposed that was because she'd loved him so.

Walter FitzHugh had always had a passion for horses, and GlenRoyal's stables had once been filled with some of the finest bloodstock in all of England. He'd put Heather on her first pony at the age of three. He'd had her riding over fences by the time she was six.

The baron had been proud of his home. GlenRoyal wasn't large or prestigious, but it was rife with history. The house had belonged to a Baron FitzHugh since it had been built more than one hundred years before. Walter FitzHugh had been proud of the collections of paintings that adorned the walls of the salon and the stairway leading to the upper floors. He'd enjoyed entertaining, especially when his wife was still alive, and delighted in regaling his company with the exploits of FitzHughs in previous centuries.

Heather wasn't certain when the baron's interests had turned to the gaming tables of London. She didn't know how much she'd noticed at the time and how much she had learned later. She remembered his frequent absences. She remembered his frowns and the somewhat desperate look in his eyes. She remembered the way he would come to her room and hold her and tell her he would take care of her, that he wouldn't let Tory's daughter be ashamed of him. She remembered . . .

Oh, Papa. Why?

The chestnut mare lengthened her strides as they approached the final hedge separating them from GlenRoyal, drawing Heather from her memories. Instinctively, she leaned forward, her body moving in easy rhythm with the horse. Animal and rider soared as one over the thick greenery. Shortly after landing, Heather drew back on the reins and slowed Cathy to a walk, then finally to a stop.

As Heather looked toward GlenRoyal, she found herself once again wondering about the stranger she'd met in the garden. Was there any chance she might see him?

As if in answer to her thought, he walked out of the stables and turned toward the house. He took long, quick strides. Even from this distance she sensed a power, an overwhelming confidence in his movements, as if the earth and all in it would obey his every command. She wished she had the courage to call out to him. She wished he would turn and look behind him and see her sitting there. She wished . . .

Then she saw Haskin step through the doorway of the barn, and her heart trilled with surprise and relief. It couldn't be, but it was. Haskin was back. The stranger had told her he would do what he could to get the groundskeeper reinstated, and he'd done it. She didn't know how, but he'd done it.

She spurred Cathy forward, unable to hold back even for a moment.

Haskin heard her approach. His wrinkled face broke into a grin. "Miss Heather!" he called as he hurried forward.

Heather jumped down from the saddle without waiting for him to reach her. "Mr. Haskin, you're back. I can't believe it. When I was told you'd been turned out . . . It was so unfair." She grabbed his hands and squeezed. "I'm just so glad you're back."

"Thanks to you. His grace . . . well, because of what you told that fellow yesterday, I'm not turned out after all."

"How could he have managed it so quickly?" Her gaze darted toward the house. "Who *is* he, Mr. Haskin?"

"Well, ah . . . he told me his name's Tanner." Haskin rubbed his hand over his forehead, hiding his eyes for a moment, his head bent forward. "As to how, well . . . seems he's got the ear of the duke, you might say."

"I must go and thank him. I was frightfully rude to him yesterday, and he's been so kind. I must thank him." She hurried away from Haskin before she lost her courage.

She skirted around from the back of the house to the front door, and climbed the steps. Her heart was racing, and her palms felt moist inside her gloves. She hesitated, then lifted the knocker and let it fall.

It seemed forever before the door opened.

The man standing in the doorway was clad in a dark suit. Tall and bean-pole thin with a hooked nose and dark, penetrating eyes, he gazed at her with a lofty expression. "Yes?"

Heather hadn't expected to encounter anyone else. Certainly not anyone as imperious-looking as this fellow. "Excuse me. I . . . I was looking for Mr. Tanner."

"Would you care to step inside, miss?" He held the door open for her. "I shall see if . . . *he* is in."

Cautiously, Heather moved forward into the hall.

The man closed the door behind her. "Please wait here," he said, then turned and disappeared up the staircase.

It had been more than nine years since she'd been inside this house. In all the time she'd been coming to see Albert Haskin and walking in the gardens, she'd never dared to ask if she might look inside her old home. She had always been afraid it would be too painful, would remind her of how much she'd lost.

She'd been right to be afraid. It *did* hurt.

Memories came flooding back, swirling over her, sucking her back in time. George sliding down the banisters. The two of them playing hide-and-seek in the drawing room and library. Her mother working with her watercolors beside the south window of the salon. Her father's study, smelling of leather and cigar smoke.

She glanced to her left. Bare walls lined the stairway leading up to the first floor. She could see the faded marks on the crimson damask, indicating the missing portraits. Had they been among the items sold before the FitzHughs left GlenRoyal, or had the duke dispensed with them in the years since?

Through the open doors leading to the salon, she could see sheets covering most of the furniture. The draperies were gone from the windows, letting in the bright rays of the afternoon sunlight through recently washed glass. She stepped forward for a closer look.

"Good afternoon, Miss FitzHugh."

She whirled toward the sound of his voice.

He was leaning against the banister, about midway down the stairs. His simple attire was no longer covered with dust. Nor was his face. And without it, he was even more handsome than she'd imagined. One eyebrow arched above watchful eyes, and there was an amused curl in the corners of his mouth as he pushed off from the railing and descended to the ground floor.

She tried to slow her breathing and forced her voice to stay calm. "Good day, Mr. Tanner. I came to offer my thanks for what you did for Mr. Haskin."

He walked toward her. "None are necessary, Miss FitzHugh. I was only too glad to help right a wrong." He stopped a few feet away.

Her voice lowered to a near whisper. "Nonetheless, it was most kind of you to get back Mr. Haskin's position."

He merely inclined his head in acknowledgment of her thanks.

She was struck once again by his air of strength and authority. It should have been intimidating, but for some reason, she wasn't afraid. She wished she could ask him how he'd accomplished so much so quickly. She wished she could ask him where he was from and how long he would be at GlenRoyal and . . . and so much more besides.

He smiled down at her, as if knowing what she was thinking.

Heather felt her cheeks grow warm. "I'm afraid I've overstayed. I must go home." She turned toward the front entrance.

His fingers closed on her arm, stopping her. He immediately released her, but not before she'd turned to look at him.

"I hope you'll come again, Miss FitzHugh."

"I . . . I couldn't."

"But why not?" His blue eyes, so intent, so mesmerizing, commanded her to answer.

"I shouldn't want to be found by the duke trespassing on his property."

"I can assure you that you won't see the duke on your visits. There's only Thorpe and I."

Her heart made a tiny skip. "The duke isn't coming to GlenRoyal? But then why . . ."

"Why repair the house after all this time? Because his grace finally realizes it is a special place and shouldn't be allowed to go to ruin because some . . . unpleasant memories are associated with it."

Curiosity sprang to life. Unpleasant memories? What unpleasant memories could the duke have of GlenRoyal? Did he feel guilty about the way it had come into his hands? Was he ashamed of what his father before him had done to the baron? Was that why he'd avoided the estate all these years, just as his father had done?

As quickly as the questions formed in her head, she forgot them. She cared nothing for the duke or his reasons for restoring GlenRoyal after all this time. At least not now. Not while she was standing so close to Mr. Tanner.

She couldn't deny the truth. She wanted to come again. Not just to escape Aunt Caroline or Beckworth House or to sit in the gardens of GlenRoyal, but to see this man. She wanted to know everything about him.

"It wouldn't be proper for me to come again," she protested weakly, mostly because she knew it was the right thing to say, even though she didn't mean it.

"Miss FitzHugh, I promise that I won't force my company upon you. I will be kept busy with my work, and Mr. Haskin would certainly protect you, should I forget my place."

She opened her mouth to deny his insinuated reasons for her hesitation, then clamped it shut.

She turned and walked to the door. As she pulled it open, she said, "Thank you, Mr. Tanner. I should love to return to GlenRoyal sometime."

And then she hurried from the house.

Chapter 4

"**G**o on to bed, Thorpe. I'm going to be up a while."

"If you're certain you won't need me, your grace."

"I'm certain," Tanner replied as he turned his gaze toward the fire.

"Good night, then, sir."

"Good night, Thorpe."

It was past midnight, but at least the two men had made some progress in the salon today. Pale moonlight shone through the windows Thorpe had scoured that morning. The dusty sheets had been removed from the tables, chairs, and settees and piled in a corner. The floors had been swept and the rugs shaken.

His first intention had been merely to make the upstairs bedchamber fit to sleep in, and perhaps a corner of the salon clean enough for him to sit in at night. He hadn't intended to stay long. In fact, until yesterday afternoon, he'd nearly convinced himself to sell the estate, even though it had been a wedding gift from his father.

He hated to admit it, but a pair of violet eyes was making him reconsider his decision to leave Westmorland any time soon.

Zounds! He'd come here to get away from women, and here he was rearranging his schedule because of one. Poor Thorpe must think him fit for Bedlam, the way Tanner had been driving the two of them to get the place cleaned up.

Tanner pushed himself up from the chair and wandered about the salon, his way lit by the blazing fire in the hearth. It was a friendly room, sparsely furnished and not overly ornate. He liked the simplicity.

He remembered the first time he'd seen GlenRoyal nine years before, which had also been the last time he'd seen it until he'd arrived here two days ago. Nicholas Montgomery, Tanner's father, had planned to use it for a hunting retreat. The house was small, the area rugged and beautiful, a perfect escape from the excesses of London. Tanner had come here with Nicholas just weeks after his father had won the estate from Baron FitzHugh.

FitzHugh! Good Lord! Heather FitzHugh must be the baron's daughter.

So *that* was why she came here. This had been her home. She would have been a mere child when her father lost it at the gaming tables in London. And that would explain her dislike for the Duke of Hawksbury. He'd feel the same if someone else suddenly owned Hawksbury Park.

Tanner's gaze scanned the room. Silhouettes of missing paintings marred the wall coverings. Paintings sold to pay gambling debts, perhaps?

He remembered the baron well enough. A likable fellow when not playing at the tables at Brooks's or White's. But he'd been a desperate gamester, the kind who never knew when to stop, who always thought his luck would change.

Tanner imagined that most everything of value in the house had been sold off long before Walter FitzHugh had wagered his estate that fateful night more than nine years before. If memory served him, the baron had died suddenly a few weeks later.

Tanner poured himself a brandy and returned to his chair near the fire.

What was it Haskin had told him about where Heather FitzHugh lived? Oh, yes. Beckworth House. She was the niece of Viscount Moredale. Tanner was acquainted with Moredale. A faded, milk-and-water sort with a real *grande dame* for a wife. He remembered the viscountess—and their daughter—even better than Frederick Beckworth.

He shuddered. No wonder Haskin had said Heather hadn't much joy in her life. Not if she lived with Lady Moredale and Annabella.

He sipped his brandy as he envisioned Annabella Beckworth. She'd come out last Season with a flourish, but he'd seen beyond her fluttering eyes and polite phrases. He'd recognized the girl's true nature beneath her obvious beauty. Golden-haired with big brown eyes and a cute button nose. Her petite figure fashionably turned out. And anxious for a title and wealth.

A lot like Judith.

His hand tightened around the glass, and he closed his eyes. He didn't want to think of Judith . . .

He had met Judith at Theodora Southwick's soiree in June. It was a warm night. The Southwick house was ablaze with lights and filled with music, and he caught sight of Judith within minutes of his arrival. She was eighteen and beautiful. She leveled her amber eyes on him and turned his brain to mush. He pursued her throughout the remainder of the Season without respite, a young man in the throes of a grand passion. He promised her the moon and the stars and his undying love if she would only be his bride.

Time and again, Judith spurned his advances.

He'd nearly given up hope of winning her for his bride. Then suddenly, miraculously, she accepted, insisting they be married at once. By special license, they were wed before the week was out in a simple ceremony at Albany House.

Nicholas, injured two years before in a riding accident and unable to ride to the hunt, his favorite pastime, presented GlenRoyal to the couple as a wedding gift. Tanner planned a honeymoon trip to the northern estate, but Judith refused to go so far from London and the social whirl. Tanner was inclined to indulge his beautiful wife in those first weeks of their marriage.

Then tragedy struck. While engaged in a game of whist, Nicholas Montgomery slumped forward onto the table and died. Tanner inherited the dukedom and all its responsibilities. At first, Judith seemed content to remain at Hawksbury Park while he put things in order. But one morning she begged him to allow her to visit her aging parents. She said she feared she would lose them as suddenly as Tanner had lost his father. She told him she needed this time alone with them.

How could he not grant her such a request?

He had learned the reason later . . .

Tanner brought the goblet to his lips and tossed back the rest of the brandy, allowing it to burn its way down his throat. What a fool he'd been. What a besotted fool. He'd believed her when she'd played the shy, nervous bride. He'd believed her when she'd told him she loved him. He'd believed every last one of her many, countless lies.

With a vicious oath, he tossed the goblet into the fireplace and watched as the glass shattered into tiny fragments.

Never again would he believe the pretty lies that fell so easily from a woman's lips. He might have to marry and produce an heir for Hawksbury, but he wouldn't ever again play the trusting fool.

Into this dark mood intruded another image: violet eyes and short ebony curls and a sweet smile.

He shouldn't have told her she could return to GlenRoyal. She was a woman, like the rest, and not to be trusted. He was only making trouble for himself to encourage her. When she found out who he was . . .

But she needn't ever know. She was nothing to him except, perhaps, a mild diversion until he returned to London to choose the next Duchess of Hawksbury. Then he would sell GlenRoyal. He'd get rid of it and all the memories associated with this small estate in Westmorland.

Heather smiled as she drifted into consciousness. A lovely feeling lingered, the product of her dreams.

Mr. Tanner. The handsome Mr. Tanner had been with her in her dreams throughout the night.

She rolled onto her stomach and rested her chin on the back of her hand while she gave Mr. Tanner more conscious thought. Obviously, the duke held Mr. Tanner's opinion in high regard to have acted so quickly on his request to reinstate Mr. Haskin as groundskeeper. And yet Mr. Tanner seemed to have been sent to GlenRoyal merely to get rid of the cobwebs. It was a puzzle.

Oh, but what did she care! she thought as she tossed aside the covers. He'd invited her to come back whenever she liked. He'd promised she wouldn't get in trouble or run into the odious duke. And maybe, just maybe, she might see Mr. Tanner again.

She hurried to wash and change out of her nightclothes. She hated the thought of donning the same riding habit he'd already seen her wear twice, but it was the only one she owned. Perhaps if she added a bright scarf to her bonnet and a simple piece of jewelry at her collar, the gray gown would look different. Or perhaps he wasn't the sort of man to notice what a girl wore anyway.

She felt a sudden shortness of breath as she imagined his cool eyes perusing her. No, she thought. He was most likely the sort to notice *everything*.

Well, it couldn't be helped. If she was going to ride over to GlenRoyal, she'd have to wear the hand-me-down riding gown, and she'd best get on with it. It wasn't likely that any of the Beckworths were up and about this early, but she didn't want to take the chance of being stopped.

After slipping into her clothes, she ran a quick brush through her short curls. Annabella was forever telling her that short hair was terribly out of fashion, but Heather didn't care. She liked it this way. The natural curls framed her face without hours of fussing, and she had no need for hairpins.

She took the back stairway and hurried toward the north pavilion, her stomach beginning to growl with hunger.

"Looks like you're up bright an' early, miss," the cook said as Heather entered the kitchen.

"It's too beautiful outside to waste the morning in bed."

"Aye, miss, 'tis that." Mrs. Osmond pushed a wayward lock of graying brown hair away from her face with the back of her wrist, then reached into a nearby basket and retrieved a roll. "No doubt you'll be wantin' to eat in a hurry." She tossed the bread to Heather. "There's cheese over there. Help yourself."

Heather grinned. "Thank you, Mrs. Osmond."

" 'Tis naught to thank me for. The bakin' was done yesterday. You're only keepin' me from havin' t'hear her ladyship complainin' that I'm wastin' the flour."

The outside door opened, and Wesley Sykes, the Beckworth groom and Mrs. Osmond's grandson, entered the kitchen.

"Your feet had better be clean, Wes, or I'll have your head on a platter."

Heather laughed as Wesley scooted back out the door, fear written on his swarthy face. There wasn't anyone in the Beckworths' employ who didn't jump to Mrs. Osmond's tune, not even Field, the head butler. But Heather wasn't intimidated by the tall, buxom woman. Mrs. Osmond had always been kind to her, inviting her into the warmth and safety of the kitchen when, as a child, she hadn't had any place else to go where she was welcome.

The cook turned toward Heather. "And where might you be off to this mornin', as if I didn't know?"

"Just out for a ride." She cut off a chunk of cheese as she spoke. "I won't be gone long."

"See that you're not, miss. I'm afraid we're in for another day of wailin' from Miss Annabella, and her ladyship won't take kindly to you bein' gone when she wants someone to blame for her daughter's bad temper. Better to be here then than to let it simmer."

Wesley had returned before his grandmother was finished with her little speech, and he nodded as he looked at Heather. "Gram's right, Miss Heather."

"You both worry too much. I'm used to Aunt Caroline's moods." She tossed the old cook a smile as she headed for the door. Meeting Wesley's gaze, she asked, "Do you suppose Cathy is ready for another run this morning?"

"Have you ever known her not t'be?" he answered. "Give me a minute with Gram, an' I'll have her saddled for you."

"Please don't hurry because of me." Heather slipped by him and out into the morning sunshine.

She felt excitement building in her chest as she walked toward the stables. She had lied to Wesley when she'd said she wasn't in a hurry. She was in a great hurry. She wanted to be on her way *now*.

Of course, it was far too early to go calling, but then, she wasn't going calling. She was just riding over to GlenRoyal to stroll through the gardens, as she'd been doing for years. She didn't intend to meet anyone.

Oh, but how very much she hoped she would.

"I'm not sure 'tis the right thing I've done," Albert Haskin muttered as he ran the brush over the shiny black coat of the duke's sleek gelding. "But where's an old man t'go for a job these days? An' maybe I'm wrong about his grace. Could be he's a real nob and a gentleman to boot. He promised he'd do Miss Heather no harm. Then again, could be I'm borrowin' trouble. Maybe she won't come 'round now that he's here."

He dropped the brush, then lifted the gelding's front leg. " 'Twould be wrong for the girl to form an attachment to such a man. You can see well enough the bitterness in him. He'd only go about hurtin' an innocent lamb like Miss Heather." He straightened as he set the hoof back on the ground. " 'Course, a man can't blame his lordship for bein' bitter after what the duchess did to him. A regular witch, she was."

Haskin shook his head as he remembered the three visits the Duchess of Hawksbury had made to GlenRoyal. She and that lover of hers. An Irishman by birth and a painter of portraits by trade. Not many months later, Haskin had heard the

duchess had died. GlenRoyal hadn't seen any of
the Montgomerys in all the years since then.

And Haskin had to admit he'd liked it that way.
Oh, he'd written to the duke to tell him what re-
pairs were needed, but he rather enjoyed the solitude. He liked puttering in the gardens and
keeping the lawns well groomed without anyone
saying whether he'd done it right or wrong. And
the animals weren't any problem. He just fed them
and turned them out to run every day. Of course,
the horses were getting a bit long in the tooth, and
he doubted the oldest of the hounds remembered
how to hunt.

Maybe that was why they got on so well. The
animals were all old, like him.

"Nothin' old about you, is there, Rebellion," he
said as he focused on the tall black again.

As if in response, the horse tossed his head and
danced sideways.

"Oh, Mr. Haskin! He's beautiful."

He turned to find Heather standing in the stable
doorway, her eyes wide and admiring. His heart
sank. He'd known all along that she would come
today.

"I've never seen a horse so fine. Rebellion? Is
that what you called him?" She walked toward the
stall. "Is he Mr. Tanner's horse?"

Haskin nodded. *But he's not Mr. Tanner*, he
wanted to say. *He's the duke himself. Now get on back
to Beckworth House and forget you ever seen him.*

But, of course, he'd given his word he wouldn't
tell, and so he held his tongue, sending up a silent
prayer that the duke would keep himself indoors
until Heather had the good sense to go home.

An hour later, feeling disappointed but hating to
admit why, Heather rode Cathy away from
GlenRoyal. She didn't hurry the mare this time.
What was the point? There wasn't anyone at

Beckworth House whom she was hoping to see, not as there had been at GlenRoyal.

She frowned, pursing her lips. She wasn't merely disappointed because she hadn't seen Mr. Tanner. She was irritated with herself for not asking Mr. Haskin more about him. She would wager the groundskeeper knew a lot more about the man than just his name. Mr. Haskin had a shrewd eye and sharp ears.

She sighed, imagining Mr. Tanner astride his magnificent black gelding. Rebellion. What an appropriate name. And how well they would fit each other. Both were tall and strong and elegant. Mr. Tanner was so handsome, so noble, so . . .

Heather stopped Cathy, horrified by her sudden inspiration. How could she have been so foolish? He was obviously more than a common laborer. He had the ear of the duke, Mr. Haskin had said, and he could afford to own a horse like Rebellion. Mr. Tanner was certainly no man's lackey.

Oh, what a silly fool she must have appeared to him!

Her cheeks grew warm with embarrassment. Had he been laughing at her? she wondered. Oh, it would be too terrible if he had.

She nudged the mare forward once again, trying to remember everything they'd said the day they met. He hadn't denied he worked for the duke, but then again, he hadn't said he did either. He'd merely told her he was helping to clean the house. He could even be a friend of the duke's. But what nobleman would spend his time cleaning a house when he could hire dozens of servants to do it for him?

It didn't make sense. Could she be wrong? Could Mr. Tanner simply have a regal bearing even though he was just a common tradesman?

She was so engrossed in her private dilemma she almost didn't hear the frantic meowing coming from the tree branches overhead. When the sound penetrated her thoughts, she stopped Cathy and looked up into the leafy maze. It took her a while to spy the small kitten, clinging to the tree trunk high above.

"How did you get up there?" Heather asked.

The kitten's response was to caterwaul even louder.

"Where's your mother?"

Heather slipped down from the saddle and walked over to the tree. Her sharp gaze searched everywhere, but she saw no sign of the missing tabby.

"Well, I can't just leave you up there."

The first branch looked sturdy, she decided, and it was within easy enough reach. It wouldn't be too terribly hard to rescue the kitten. She could bring it to Mr. Haskin. He was always willing to take in the strays she found.

Quickly, she sat down on the ground and removed her riding boots, followed by her stockings. Then she drew up the hem of her habit and tucked it into the waistline of her riding trousers. She untied the burgundy scarf that held her bonnet in place and tossed them both on the ground.

The moment she jumped up to grab hold of the lower branch, she felt a surge of pleasure. It had been years since she'd climbed a tree. She'd almost forgotten how good it felt to be high above the ground, surrounded by leafy branches, hidden from the rest of the world. The last time she'd done it, Aunt Caroline had given her a thorough lecture on the proper etiquette of a young lady and then taken away her riding privileges for a month.

Gripping the thick limb with her toes and holding onto another branch above her head, Heather reached for the frightened kitten. As she closed her hand around its belly, its howls increased to a fever pitch. She tried to pull it away from the tree, but its claws were sunk deeply into the bark.

"Let go, little one," she said through clenched teeth.

She slipped her fingers beneath one of the kitten's front legs and pried it free, wincing as the sharp claws penetrated her hand. By the time she lowered the kitten to her chest, her hand was crisscrossed with tiny scratches, and a fine sweat beaded her forehead.

"Now all we have to do is get you down," she whispered as she brushed the kitten's soft fur against her cheek.

"Hand him to me, Miss FitzHugh. It will make things easier."

Heather gasped and teetered on the branch, grasping hold of the tree to steady herself before looking down at the ground below.

For a moment, he thought he was going to have to catch her as she tumbled to the ground. Not that he wouldn't enjoy feeling her in his arms. Still, he was glad when she regained her balance.

Her face turned a delightful shade of pink. "Sir, I . . . Please turn around. I'm not decent."

Tanner couldn't contain his grin. "I've seen trousers before. And bare feet."

"Not mine," she replied in a small voice.

He laughed. "No, not yours. Here, hand me that kitten, and I shall gladly turn around while you come down."

Her cheeks grew brighter as she sat down on the limb and lowered the kitten into his grasp. Still grinning, he turned his back toward her.

"You're certain you don't need my help?" he asked.

"I'm certain."

He heard her land on the ground. "May I turn around?"

"Not until I'm properly dressed. If you're a gentleman, you will stay where you are."

He couldn't resist teasing her. "Where on earth did you get the notion that I was a gentleman?" But he kept his back to her, all the while stroking the tiny kitten in his hands, trying to still its protests.

He wasn't sure what had possessed him to follow after the lady when he'd seen her riding away from GlenRoyal, but he was glad now that he had. It had been a long time since he'd witnessed anything so amusing as Heather FitzHugh, dress tucked up in her waistband, scrambling up the trunk of a tree.

He had quite a wait before he heard her soft permission to turn around.

"All right, Mr. Tanner. I'm presentable."

He turned and gave her a long, slow perusal. She was wearing the same gray riding habit he'd seen before, the skirt now properly in place, her slender legs once again hidden from view. She had brightened the drab gown with a gold-and-rose brooch at the throat. A burgundy scarf was wrapped around her bonnet and tied beneath her chin. A faint pink blush lingered on her cheeks, but there was an amused curl to her mouth and a twinkle of mischief in her eyes. For some reason, it pleased him that her embarrassment had vanished.

"Do you often climb trees, Miss FitzHugh?"

"Not usually when there is a gentleman present, sir."

"But you do climb them?"

She reached to take the kitten from him. "Only if someone needs me to."

"And what are you going to do with the little fellow now that you have him?"

"I'll take him to Mr. Haskin. He'll make sure he's all right until he's old enough to be on his own." She glanced up at Tanner. Her smile disappeared. "But I must hurry. I'm already late returning home."

"Allow me to take him to Mr. Haskin for you."

She seemed to be weighing his offer, studying him to see whether or not she should accept. He felt as if he could read her every thought through those round, clear eyes of hers. He got a strange feeling when she looked at him that way. He couldn't recall ever seeing a face that seemed so fresh, so innocent, so totally without guile or subterfuge.

"I promise the kitten will not come to any harm," he said softly as he took a step toward her.

Heather found it difficult to breathe with him standing so close. When he reached forward and placed his large hand over hers, she felt as if she'd been shocked. In truth, it wasn't an altogether unpleasant feeling.

It seemed next to impossible to tear her gaze away from him. His hair gleamed golden in the morning sunlight. His eyes were the sharpest of blues. His mouth . . .

She felt a tightening in her stomach as she stared at his mouth, imagining for a moment what it might be like to press her lips against his.

"The kitten, Miss FitzHugh?"

She felt the flush of embarrassment returning as she handed the kitten quickly into his grasp, then turned and hurried toward Cathy. Once there, she felt a flash of irritation. She wasn't about to hike her skirts and swing up onto the saddle as she'd been known to do. Mr. Tanner had seen more than enough of her trousers for one day. Nor did she want to ask the gentleman for assistance.

"Allow me," he said.

Heather glanced over her shoulder to find him standing close by. Peeking at her over the hem of his coat pocket, was the kitten, silent now and seemingly quite content. Before she could accept or refuse Mr. Tanner's offer, he'd closed his hands about her waist and lifted her onto the back of her mare.

Once again she found herself looking into his commanding gaze. It left her feeling weak, confused, and very disoriented. Not at all the way she usually felt.

"Who are you, Mr. Tanner?" she asked suddenly.

He raised an eyebrow but didn't reply.

She felt some of her courage return. "You weren't sent to GlenRoyal merely to clear the dust," she persisted. "Even a simple country girl like me can see that, sir. Just who *are* you, Mr. Tanner?"

One corner of his mouth curved upward. "If I tell you about me, Miss FitzHugh, I will expect the same courtesy in return. I would like to know who you are."

Exhilaration made her feel light-headed. He wanted to know her. He was interested in who she was. She swallowed and tried to calm her racing heart. "Pray, sir. You would find yourself bored to tears with my story."

"I'll take the risk." He strode toward the sleek black horse grazing not far away. He stepped up into the saddle, then turned the gelding toward Heather.

His gaze seemed to challenge her, and she nodded in response, apparently helpless to do otherwise.

"We have an agreement, sir," she replied in a low voice.

"You have found me out, Miss FitzHugh. I didn't come here to repair the house, nor am I in the duke's employ. I . . . I know Hawksbury quite well. Better than any man, I suppose." He paused, a slight smile reappearing, then nodded. "Yes, quite well indeed. And the rest of the Montgomerys, too." The hint of a smile vanished, and his voice became more stern. "I wanted to get away from London, spend some time alone, and it was suggested that I come here. So I brought my man with me for a short stay. I wanted solitude, so I chose not to have a lot of servants hanging around. Thorpe and I have done our best to make the place livable."

He had a very noble face. How could she have ever thought he was a mere workman? She should have recognized him immediately as a member of the aristocracy, no matter what he'd been wearing. He was no doubt related to a duke or an earl. Probably a younger son, with no title but plenty of breeding.

"Are you disappointed, Miss FitzHugh?"

"Disappointed?" She straightened in her saddle, brought up from her musings. "No, Mr. Tanner. I was thinking how foolish I must have appeared to ever have believed you were anyone's servant."

"Well, now that you know, I have a favor to ask."

"A favor?"

"Yes. I don't want it known that I'm staying here. I came for some peace and quiet. You would do me a great service if you would refrain from telling the Beckworths or anyone else that I'm at GlenRoyal."

"You needn't fear that, Mr. Tanner. I have never told my aunt that I ride over to GlenRoyal. She wouldn't be pleased to know I was trespassing on the duke's property."

He nudged his horse forward. "Very well, then.

Now it is your turn." He guided Rebellion in a close arc behind the mare's rump, then brought the gelding to a halt when his Hessian boot drew level with Heather's stirrup. "Tell me about Heather FitzHugh."

"I warned you, 'tis not very interesting." Heather laughed as the two horses stepped forward. "My mother died when I was five and my father when I was ten. That's when I went to live at Beckworth House. Aunt Caroline is my father's sister. I have a brother, but he no longer lives in England. I haven't seen him in seven years."

"I'm surprised we didn't meet when you were in London last Season."

"Oh, I've never been to London. At least, not since I was six or seven." She felt his eyes upon her but didn't turn her head to confirm it. She knew what he was thinking.

He cleared his throat. "Miss FitzHugh, am I mistaken in assuming you are—"

"I will be twenty on my next birthday, Mr. Tanner. I assure you, although I may still climb trees, you are not escorting a child in short skirts back to her home."

A lengthy pause stretched between them before he said, "I never thought that for a moment."

His deep voice sent a chill up her spine, his words forcing her head to turn so that their eyes could meet. Beneath the power of his gaze, she felt a new awareness of her femininity, an enormously enjoyable sensation.

"One more question, Miss FitzHugh." His voice was still low, controlled. "Why is it you dislike the Duke of Hawksbury?"

For just a moment, she considered telling him that GlenRoyal had once been her home, but she dispensed with the notion. It would serve no purpose. At most, it would make him feel sorry for her, and she didn't want his pity. But her natural honesty demanded an honest response.

"I do not highly regard a man who would cheat a family out of its home."

"Cheat? The duke did no such thing. GlenRoyal was a gift to him from his father. Nicholas Montgomery gave it to his son just before he died."

It was on the tip of her tongue to tell him just what she thought of both Nicholas Montgomery and his son. They not only cheated at the gaming tables, they shot down hotheaded boys.

"Besides," her companion continued, "no matter how the duke came by GlenRoyal, you can hardly blame him for what his father might have done, now, can you?"

That freed her tongue. "Oh, but I *can* blame him, sir. The duke has neglected the place shamefully. It was once someone's home, a warm place filled with laughter. He let it sit empty and useless. It was nothing to him, yet he wouldn't let it be something to someone else."

Tanner saw the anger flash in those violet eyes and felt a stirring of guilt in response. The young lady certainly didn't mince words.

Her hand flew up to cover her mouth. When it fell away, she wore a chagrined expression. "I've done it again. I have said far too much. The duke is a friend of yours."

"I asked for your reasons. You have done no more than answer honestly."

"Pray, let us forget what I've said. The day is too bright for angry thoughts, and 'tis time I was returning home."

Before he knew what she was about, she'd pressed her horse into a gallop. Her laughter trailed behind her.

"I'll race you to the giant pine tree," she called back to him.

In an instant he was after her, unaware of the smile on his face.

Chapter 5

For the next three days, Heather obediently remained at Beckworth House as her aunt demanded, listening to her cousin bemoaning the disaster of going to London after the Season had begun. Annabella's complaints fell on deaf ears, eliciting no sympathy from Heather. What did Heather care about London when Mr. Tanner was staying at GlenRoyal? Her only concern was when she might see him again.

"Why don't you say something to Papa?" Annabella asked as they entered the dining room that morning.

Heather glanced over at her cousin, her eyes wide with surprise. "Me?"

"He might listen to you. He certainly doesn't care a fig what Mama and I want."

It would be nice to have them gone, she thought. She wouldn't have to be so careful about her comings and goings then. She wouldn't have to worry about what she wore or being home for dinner on time or who among the local gentry might come calling. She wouldn't have to listen to Aunt Caroline's constant nagging or Annabella's ridicule. She could look forward to nearly three months of peace and solitude.

And she could see Mr. Tanner as often as she dared.

"I'll do what I can," she said softly.

Moments later, her aunt and uncle walked into the dining room. She could tell by the dark look on Aunt Caroline's face that the two had shared words about their delayed departure for London. Her uncle looked weary and battle-worn. Not for the first time, she felt a twinge of pity for him.

The meal was taken in complete silence. Aunt Caroline shot frequent angry glances at her husband, and Annabella sniffed back tears several times. The theatrics were fruitless. Uncle Frederick was clearly determined to ignore his wife and daughter. He didn't linger at the table once he had finished eating.

As he walked out of the room, Heather felt a sharp kick against her shin. Her cousin jerked her head toward the doorway and pressed her lips together in a silent command for Heather to keep her word.

Heather bit back her anger. She reminded herself of what she would gain once the family withdrew from Beckworth House. She excused herself from the table and hurried after her uncle. She found him in his study.

"Uncle Frederick? May I speak with you?"

He glanced up from his desk, wearing a harried expression. "What is it, Heather?"

She closed the door behind her. "Well, I ... I was wondering if there might be something I could do to help you. Aunt Caroline and Annabella are so set on going to London, and I know you said you couldn't leave Westmorland yet. I just thought ... well ... perhaps I could be of some help to you."

"No, my dear," he answered with a deep sigh. "But it's kind of you to offer. I'm afraid there's nothing you can do. My wife and daughter will just have to be patient."

Heather searched for something else to say, but

words eluded her. She suspected finances had something to do with his decision to shorten his daughter's Season. If so, there truly wasn't anything she could do except offer a bit of sympathy.

Her own reasons for wishing them off to London were quickly forgotten as compassion for the man returned. Uncle Frederick had never been unkind to her, or made her feel the poor relation. True, he'd never done much to protect her from the viperish tongues of the others in the family either, but perhaps that was because he'd been seeking safety from those same tongues himself. She secretly thought herself much more capable of surviving Aunt Caroline's and Annabella's treatment than her uncle was, and woe to him should he find himself without blunt to pay for the things they required.

She walked across the study, skirting the desk, and laid a hand on her uncle's shoulder. "Perhaps I could help with the housekeeping. You could let one of the maids go, and I—"

Uncle Frederick patted her hand. "You're an unusual young woman, Heather FitzHugh. I wish Annabella—" He stopped himself, then shook his head. His voice was stronger when he spoke again. "You've listened to enough of Annabella's wailing. Why don't you take that horse of yours out for a run?"

"But Aunt Caroline said I wasn't to . . ."

"I'll take care of your aunt. Go on with you."

She didn't have to be told again. For three days she'd wanted nothing more than to take Cathy for a gallop—and she knew exactly in what direction. "Thank you, Uncle Frederick." She dropped a quick kiss on his balding pate, then hurried from his study.

* * *

Rebellion moved restlessly beneath him. Tanner spoke softly to the horse, calming the impatient gelding. Waiting in the long grass, shaded by the tall pine tree, Strawberry sat with ears alert and eyes watchful.

Although he wouldn't admit it to himself, Tanner felt a certain disappointment as he stared across the empty fields. He'd thought for certain Heather would have returned to GlenRoyal by now. It appeared he'd been wrong.

"Guess we'd best go back," he said to himself as he tightened the reins and prepared to turn the horse around.

At that moment Strawberry jumped to her feet and barked several times. Then she was off and running, a red streak across the green meadow. Tanner raised his eyes to see the familiar chestnut mare sailing over a low hedge.

He held Rebellion back, remaining in the shadows of the tree as he watched Heather rein in the mare. Strawberry darted up to her, barking gleefully. He heard her laughing cry of greeting to the dog, saw her slip from the saddle and kneel on the ground, watched as she ruffled the dog's ears and nuzzled the animal's head with her nose. Then, when Strawberry had quieted, she straightened, her head held high, her eyes searching.

Tanner nudged the black gelding out of the shade and into the sunlight. He couldn't see her smile, but he knew it was there as she raised her arm and waved to him. His own mouth curved gently as he returned the wave.

Tanner eased up on the reins, and Rebellion broke quickly into a canter. Heather rose to her feet as horse and rider approached.

She was wearing that same tiresome gray gown, and it occurred to him that it must be the only riding outfit she owned. It shouldn't be so, he thought. A girl as gay and lovely as Heather Fitz-

Hugh should have a half-dozen riding habits at the very least. If it were up to him ...

Her jerked back on the reins, a reflex action to stop the direction of his thoughts as much as to halt Rebellion. By gad, he wasn't about to lose his head over some country chit! Amusing company during his brief stay in the north—that was all she was to him.

"Good morning, Mr. Tanner," she said, her violet eyes sparkling with pleasure, her smile as bright as he'd suspected it would be.

The look of genuine joy on her face made him forget his determination to remain cool and aloof. "Good morning, Miss FitzHugh. Fine day for a ride, is it not?"

"Indeed, sir."

"Were you, by chance, going toward GlenRoyal? If so, I would ask the pleasure of riding with you."

An attractive splash of pink colored each cheek as she gazed up at him. "It just so happens I *was* riding in that direction, kind sir, and I would enjoy your company."

Tanner vaulted from the back of his horse and strode toward the girl. She tilted her head back, looking up at him from beneath the brim of her straw bonnet. A delicate, flowery scent reached his nostrils, teasing him with its fresh fragrance. Light and honest. It suited her well.

As he closed his hands about her waist to lift her onto the mare's back, he ignored the sudden urge to kiss her instead. He knew by the look in her eyes that she wouldn't resist him, at least not for long.

Thankfully for them both, he still retained some small shred of decency. He wasn't going to toy with this girl and then leave her in disgrace. No, theirs would be a platonic friendship. If he needed more, he could very well get himself back to the more decadent salons of London.

By the time he released her, his thoughts had brought a scowl to his face. He moved swiftly back to his horse, feeling his good mood slipping away.

"I'm glad you brought Strawberry with you," Heather said as she guided her mare up beside him. "She loves nothing so much as a good run. She's a wonderful dog."

Tanner nudged Rebellion into a walk, not bothering to look at his companion. "Too much of a pet to be a decent hunter," he replied in a low voice.

"No one's ever tried her." From her tone, it was clear Heather had taken his statement as a personal insult. "She's smart enough to learn anything you might want to teach her."

Despite himself, the slight upward curve returned to his mouth as he looked at her. Her head was held high, her back straight, her expression mutinous and resolute.

"If the hounds in the GlenRoyal kennels are worthless, 'tis the duke's fault. He's the one who let them sit idle for so long." Her impassioned words demanded his full attention. It was clear that she was determined to convince him of the truth of what she said. "Mr. Haskin quit breeding them about four years ago 'cause he only had to sell the pups. They weren't being used or trained." Her gaze moved to the dog trotting beside her mare, and her expression softened. "Strawberry was the runt of the last litter born, but I knew right away she was the smartest of the lot. I convinced Mr. Haskin to keep her."

The curve of Tanner's mouth became a full-fledged grin. "And I'm sure his grace will appreciate that you saved the best of the litter for him."

Heather made an unladylike sound in the back of her throat. "I didn't do it for that rakeshame. If he were here right now, I suspect Strawberry would as soon bite him on the leg as obey his commands. He'll probably never know he owns the dogs in that kennel unless you tell him." Her eyes widened as she glanced his way. "You don't think he'll sell them all if he knows they're just going to waste, do you? You won't tell him to get rid of them, will you?"

He'd been enjoying watching her indignation and hadn't even minded her insults upon his good name, but he found no pleasure in her sudden apprehension.

"You needn't worry, Miss FitzHugh. The duke has no intention of selling off the hounds in the GlenRoyal kennels. I can assure you of that."

Relief lit her face like a candle brightens the darkness. The smile returned. "I'll race you to the stables," she said just before the chestnut mare leaped forward into an all-out gallop.

That was twice the little minx had gotten a head start on him.

Heather leaned sideways on the stone bench beside the pond and traced circles on the surface of the water. She was surrounded by dogs. Two black-and-white setters lay at her feet. Three others chased after birds that flitted between the trees. Strawberry sat on her left side, her muzzle in Heather's lap. The red dog's parents lay beneath the stone bench, their heads resting on their paws.

"No," she said in answer to Mr. Tanner's question, straightening on the bench as she did so. "I haven't minded not going to London for the Season too terribly much. 'Tis frightfully expensive. Uncle Frederick isn't exactly plump in the pocket these days, and Aunt Caroline and Cousin Annabella do insist that they be all the crack for the Season. 'Tis not easy for him." She shrugged. "I don't know what I would do in Town anyway. I'm not acquainted with Society's ways. Besides, I'm a poor conversationalist." She idly stroked

Strawberry's head. "I haven't the foggiest notion what I would say to anyone at one of their routs."

"There's nothing much to it," he said as he stepped away from the shade tree and came to stand before her. He bowed low. As he straightened, he reached out to take hold of her hand. "You are looking exceedingly lovely this afternoon, Miss FitzHugh. London must agree with you."

He really had captivating eyes, she thought as her breath caught in her throat.

"May I join you?" Without waiting for a reply, he sat beside her.

He had such an aristocratic face. Such a strong jaw and fine forehead. A ripple of expectancy ran through her as her gaze moved to his mouth. She wondered what it might be like to touch his lips with hers, to feel his warm breath against her skin, to . . .

"Have you heard the latest about Lady Thornback?"

Her gaze darted to his. She caught the teasing twinkle and smiled in response. "No, my lord. Pray, do tell me."

" 'Tis said she has formed a *tendre* for Lord Thatchgallows. The two were seen having a rather indiscreet tête-à-tête at Vauxhall."

"Oh, dear." She sighed dramatically, getting into the spirit of the game. "Such a match would never do. Lord Thatchgallows has pockets to let. He could never provide for a wife."

"And what about Lady Gabbler? Have you seen what she's done to her hair? Outrageous. Simply outrageous."

His amusement spread from his eyes to his mouth. Heather wondered what it would be like to see him *really* smile. Not one of his half smiles or the dubious grins she'd noticed, but a real, full-fledged smile that came from the heart. She thought it might be very nice, indeed.

Tanner wanted very much to kiss her. Not as a prelude to lovemaking, but for the simple enjoyment of feeling her lips against his, of tasting the sweetness he suspected he would find there.

He knew when she realized the teasing had stopped. Her eyes rounded, and she pulled her hand from his. She turned her head away as she nervously folded her hands in her lap.

"See," he said, trying to revive the lighthearted mood they'd been enjoying, "there's nothing to the fine art of conversation, at least not in most gatherings. You simply pass on the gossip you heard from the other ladies over your afternoon scandal broth, whether it is true or not, cast aspersions on anyone who is not a close friend, and never think more highly of anyone else than you do of yourself."

She didn't smile, as he'd expected her to. "I cannot imagine that that would be a very enjoyable way to spend one's time, sir. I think I am right to want to stay here in the country. I should never fit with the *ton*."

Her refreshing honesty stunned him into momentary silence. It was followed by a renewed desire to hold her and kiss her. A sixth sense warned him that he would regret it if he followed through on that desire. Somehow he knew, enjoy it though he would, he would not be satisfied for long with a simple chaste kiss in the garden.

He rose abruptly from the bench and took several steps away before turning to face her again. "Where *do* you fit, Miss FitzHugh? What is it you like to do, if not buy new gowns or dance at balls or gossip with the other ladies over tea?"

"I like to ride, of course," she answered, meeting his gaze, "and climb trees." She teased him with a grin.

Something inside him tightened in response to her smile. He felt drawn to her but again resisted his own impulse.

"And I always liked to go fishing."

"Fishing?"

Heather laughed at his surprised tone. "Yes. My father used to take my brother and me fishing in the mountain streams. We would leave very early in the morning and ride up to our special place." Her eyes took on a faraway look, and her voice softened to a near whisper. "Papa always made such a fuss over the fish I caught. He always made me feel as if no one had ever hooked anything bigger or finer than the one I'd just caught."

At times like this, he wished her face weren't so open. It was all too easy to see how much she missed her father, too easy to read the loneliness in her beautiful eyes.

"I know what it's like," he said unexpectedly, feeling his own loss. "My father died several years ago."

Mr. Tanner's sad tone brought her out of her memories. Realizing they had both lost their fathers made her feel closer to him. She rose from the bench and moved toward him. Tenderly, she took hold of his hand and squeezed, then immediately released it.

She felt his questioning gaze and merely smiled in return, hoping he would understand the special way she felt. And as she stood there, so close to him, she felt as if the rest of the world had faded away to nothing. There were just the two of them, standing there, so close she imagined she could feel the heat of his body, so close she thought she could hear the beat of his heart. So close. So very close.

She stepped suddenly backward, frightened by the strange and unusual feelings that swirled in her head and her heart, alarmed by her own rapid pulse. She groped for something to say, anything to return them to the lighthearted banter of only moments before.

"Well, sir, you can see why I should remain here. A young lady who prefers fishing to gossip would never meet with approval in London."

"And what about marriage, Miss FitzHugh?"

"Marriage?" she echoed breathlessly.

His blue eyes seemed inordinately intense. "Yes. Marriage."

The thundering of her heart made it difficult for her to think, let alone reply. "I'm not all that anxious to find myself a husband." He couldn't possibly be suggesting . . .

"But surely the viscount wants to see you well married. It would be much easier to find a husband for you in Town. You might meet someone there for whom you would form a fondness. You might change your mind about marriage."

Heather let the disappointment wash through her, then laughed lightly at her own foolishness. "I doubt Uncle Frederick gives much thought to me at all. Living with Aunt Caroline, one tries only to do what will please her to avoid her wrath."

Mr. Tanner shook his head slowly. "It would seem Lady Moredale could do more for her niece. At the very least, another riding habit would seem in order."

Embarrassment flooded her, hot and sudden. She'd so hoped he hadn't noticed she'd had to wear the same gown every time they'd been together. But he *had* noticed. Not just noticed, but commented upon it. She stared down at her hands, now clenched in front of her.

"Miss FitzHugh . . ." His voice rang tender in her ears.

Hesitantly, she raised her eyes to him.

"On you, 'tis a tremendously attractive gown."

Her heart did a funny skip, as if it had lost track

of its own rhythm. "I fear I have no fashion sense at any rate, Mr. Tanner. 'Tis better that I leave that to Annabella. As long as I'm able to ride Cathy and come occasionally to GlenRoyal, I haven't any need for fancy clothes."

"You're an unusual young woman, Miss Fitz-Hugh," he replied softly.

It was the second time today she'd heard those words, and coming from Mr. Tanner, they sounded like the most wonderful compliment in the world. She smiled, then turned her gaze once more upon the water, glad that she'd come, glad that he found her unusual.

Chapter 6

Tanner wasn't sure when the idea first came to him. Maybe it was the day Heather so hastily thanked him for getting Haskin's job back. Or maybe it was the day he caught her rescuing that kitten in the tree. Or maybe it was a few days later, when she sat on the bench beside the pond, surrounded by all the hounds from the kennels, and told him about going fishing with her father.

Most likely it was this afternoon, at this very moment, when she was nearly beating him at a game of chess.

Why not Heather FitzHugh?

The barony of the FitzHughs was two hundred years old, so there was no disputing Heather's claim to the aristocracy. Impoverished she might be, but she was quality. The dowager duchess could have no objections in that regard.

She was an innocent to the machinations and conspiracies of Society. She was warm, bright, and gay, and totally without affectation. She was quick to laugh and equally quick to anger, but her anger never turned shrewish.

She was beautiful and intelligent. It wouldn't be difficult for a man to spend time in her company, nor would it be unpleasant to sire a child with her. Perhaps several children, just to ensure that an heir survived to adulthood.

She seemed genuinely fond of him, not because he was a duke, but despite the fact that she thought he wasn't. She'd made it clear she hadn't any aspirations to marry a title or obtain great wealth through a successful alliance. In fact, she seemed in no hurry to marry at all. The girl was surprisingly satisfied with her lot, not even complaining over the miserly treatment she'd received at the hands of the Beckworths.

Yes, Tanner Huntington Gilbert Montgomery, tenth Duke of Hawksbury, thought Heather Fitz-Hugh would do rather well as his duchess. Now all he had to do was decide how and when to reveal his intentions to her.

"Check!" Heather clapped her hands together in excitement as she leaned back in her chair.

Tanner frowned down at the chess set. "Who taught you to play chess, Miss FitzHugh?"

"My brother. We used to sit in his bedchamber and play for hours." A trace of sadness darkened her eyes. "But that was a long time ago. I haven't played chess in years."

There were many things he'd like to ask her, much more he wanted to know, but mostly he wished to understand how she remained so cheerful despite what seemed to him an austere existence. "Besides riding, fishing, and playing chess," he said, leaning forward slightly, "what else do you like to do? For fun, I mean."

"I love to read. When I was a girl, I'd hide in a tree and read for hours."

"Ah . . . trees again." He twirled a pawn between his thumb and forefinger. "You do seem addicted to them."

"It wasn't the trees," she retorted with mock indignation. "It was the privacy. No one ever thought to look for me there. I could read a long time without being disturbed."

"You're not a blasted bluestocking, are you, Miss FitzHugh?"

Her laughter was light and airy. "I assure you not, sir. I confess my weakness is for novels."

"Along with every other woman in England," he muttered as he returned his attention to the chessboard. Then, one eyebrow cocked, a half smile curving his mouth, he moved his knight. "Check." It was his turn to lean back, arms folded across his chest.

Her face fell. "Oh. However did I miss that?" She studied the game pieces carefully, the fingertips of her right hand moving back and forth across her lips.

Lovely lips, he thought. A very kissable mouth. Smooth and full and inviting.

She smiled and lifted her face toward him, an impish expression twinkling in her eyes. "I won't forget your strategy, Mr. Tanner." She took her hand away from her lips and slid her queen into position. "Checkmate."

Tanner was scarcely aware of the move she'd made. He'd suddenly lost interest in the chess game. He was much more cognizant of the delightful fullness of her lower lip, the delicate arch of her brows, the graceful curve of her throat.

Their gazes met and held, and her smile began to fade.

Yes, indeed. A very kissable mouth.

"I'm afraid it's grown late." Her voice was soft and quivery. "Aunt Caroline has been perturbed by my frequent absences. I never meant to stay so long. I must leave at once."

He rose with her from the table, quickly taking hold of her arm as he walked her toward the door. Without warning, he stopped, his grip on her arm propelling her around to face him. With a single step forward, he drew her into his embrace.

She fit quite nicely in his arms. Despite their

clothing, he could feel the firm suppleness of her breasts against his chest. Hers was a body ripe for picking, youthful and innocent and vibrant. It was easy to imagine her lying naked in his arms, warming to his touch.

"Mr. Tanner . . ." she protested softly.

He ignored her.

The first touch of his lips upon hers sent a fire of desire searing through his veins. He fought to keep the kiss light and unthreatening, but it was almost more than he could manage, especially when her mouth seemed so welcoming, so pliable beneath his.

It was dangerous, this flash of wanting, this desire to make her his, to become a part of her. It was dangerous when all he wanted was to carry her to his bed and remove her clothes and bury himself in her. He'd thought of all the reasons it made sense to make Heather his bride, but he wouldn't allow her to become an obsession. The fires of their lovemaking would burn hot and furious, of that he had no doubt, and he knew the pleasures would be many. But he was determined to control his feelings of desire as rigidly as he controlled all others.

It took a will of iron to break the kiss and set her back from him.

Her eyes seemed a shade darker as she gazed up at him, her cheeks more pale. Her mouth parted as if to speak, but no words were uttered.

"I think you were right after all." His voice was deep and hoarse. " 'Tis time for you to go."

"I fear it wasn't wise for me to come inside, Mr. Tanner," she whispered.

"You're wrong, Miss FitzHugh. I think it was very wise. I look forward to our next game of chess." He opened the door.

"You needn't walk me to my horse, sir. I can find my own way." With that, she slipped from his grasp and disappeared around the corner of the house.

Heather's heart was pounding so hard she feared it would explode inside her chest. As she galloped Cathy toward home, she kept replaying in her mind that moment when their lips had touched and his arms had held her close against him. It had been everything she'd ever dreamed, ever hoped a kiss could be.

Better still, *he* was everything she'd ever hoped he'd be. Mr. Tanner . . . She didn't even know his first name, yet she was certain she was falling in love with him.

Imagine. Heather FitzHugh in love. She'd always believed she would one day meet someone special and fall in love, yet there'd been a element of fear that it wouldn't come true.

Wouldn't Annabella be pea-green with envy if she knew about Mr. Tanner? Of course, *she* wouldn't want anything to do with him. He hadn't a title, and Annabella insisted on a title. Heather supposed he had money. One wasn't usually friends with a wealthy duke without having substantial blunt of one's own. But she wouldn't care if he hadn't a brass farthing. She wouldn't have cared if he was in the duke's employ, just as she'd thought him at first.

Oh, it was positively grand to be in love!

She replayed the scene over and over in her mind, reliving the warm pressure of his hand on her back, the hard feel of his chest against her breasts. She could still taste his kiss on her lips, still smell the warm scent of his cologne. She remembered the husky sound of his voice when he'd admitted it was time for her to leave. She would swear his words were the very opposite of what he'd wanted. He'd wanted her to stay.

He wanted her. Perhaps he loved her, too.

Surely he wouldn't have kissed her if he didn't love her, at least a little.

Oh, yes. It was grand to be in love.

Heather's head was still in the clouds as she trotted her chestnut mare into the stables. Wesley was there to take the reins from her the moment she dismounted.

"Miss Heather—" he began.

"Thank you, Wes. See that Cathy gets an extra scoop of grain, will you?"

"Yes, miss, but—"

"I'll want her again in the morning." She turned away, still smiling, and began humming a gay tune as she walked toward the stable door.

"Miss Heather, wait."

She glanced back over her shoulder, finally seeing the groom's troubled expression. She felt a quiver of apprehension. "What is it, Wes? Is something wrong?"

" 'Fraid so. The viscountess herself came down to the stables an' told me you're t'see her the instant you come back."

"Oh." Her joyful mood disintegrated. Her song was forgotten. "Thank you, Wes."

She was in for it now. Aunt Caroline had forbidden her to ride this week. But it had been several days since her last visit to GlenRoyal, several days since she'd seen Mr. Tanner, and she just couldn't help herself. She'd only meant to ride over and say hello and return home at once. If she'd kept to her intention, her aunt never would have known she'd left Beckworth House.

But Mr. Tanner had invited her to play chess, and she hadn't been able to make herself refuse. The game had gone on and on. It had been so much fun, such a tremendous challenge, and she'd lost all track of time.

Well, she'd have the devil to pay now. There'd be no getting around it.

Lifting her chin, she marched resolutely toward the house and her interview with Aunt Caroline.

"You are the most ungrateful child, Heather FitzHugh. Heaven knows what I ever did to deserve such thoughtlessness. I expressly forbade you to go riding today, did I not?"

"Yes, Aunt Caroline."

"Now, I demand to know where you were."

"Just riding and walking and enjoying the beauty of the day." That was true. She had done all three of those things before Mr. Tanner had invited her inside for that game of chess.

Her aunt drew herself up to her full, imposing height. She was standing before the tall windows of her study, making it difficult for Heather to see her face. Her fingers thrummed against the surface of her desk. "I'm waiting for the truth."

"The truth?" Heather repeated in a small voice.

"You've been to GlenRoyal, haven't you? And this isn't the first time. Cough up, girl. How long has this been going on?"

"Aunt Caroline, I haven't hurt anything by—"

"Good gracious! It's true." Aunt Caroline sat down suddenly. "I didn't credit it when Lady Lister told me she'd seen you jumping the hedges onto the estate. You little hoyden! Running around wild on the duke's property. Do you know what people will be saying of us because of you?"

"I cannot imagine why they should say anything of you. 'Tis I who went there. And really, Aunt Caroline, I've done nothing amiss. Merely looked at the gardens."

"Be silent and sit down."

Heather promptly obeyed.

Caroline Beckworth turned toward the window, the palms of her hands pressed together, her fingers splayed. Her expression was thoughtful as she gazed out the window.

In her youth, Aunt Caroline had probably been considered handsome, but time and the excesses she enjoyed had broadened her figure and made her complexion sallow. Her golden hair was still free of gray, however, and her brown eyes remained sharp and shrewd. But the Aunt Caroline whom Heather knew seemed forever to be wearing a scowl, and her mouth was nearly always pursed with displeasure.

The woman's gaze returned to Heather. "Well, if we are fortunate, the duke shan't hear of your mischief. Thank goodness he has never seen fit to have anything to do with that disreputable place. I will simply implore Lady Lister not to repeat what she thinks she saw and swear that you were nowhere near GlenRoyal. She won't believe me, of course, but it might cast some doubt on any rumors."

Aunt Caroline rose slowly from her chair, her hand pressed against the shiny wood surface of her writing desk. "As for you, Heather, I can see I shall have to be more firm. You must be punished. I will instruct Sykes to sell that mare of yours. You are not to go near the stables until I tell you differently. Do you understand me?"

"Sell Cathy?" Heather jumped to her feet. "But, Aunt Caroline—"

"Enough!" her aunt shouted, one hand slamming against the desk. "I've had my fill of your impudence, you ungrateful chit. Now go to your room and think of how much we've done for you out of the goodness of our hearts and how appallingly you've treated us in return."

Heather's eyes were swimming with unshed tears, her throat burning. "Please, Aunt Caroline," she whispered hoarsely. "I promise I won't disobey you again. I won't think about riding until you tell me I may. But please don't sell Cathy. Papa gave her to me when she was still a filly, and

George helped me train her. She's all I have left of them. She's all the—"

"Sentimental rubbish," the woman muttered in response. But then she nodded. "All right, Heather. I will give it more thought. I have your word you won't go near the stables? Not until I say you may?"

"I promise." Tears trickled down her cheeks.

"Then go to your room. I will let you know when I've made my decision."

Heather choked back the rest of her tears as she turned toward the door. Head held high, she walked out of her aunt's study, hiding her inner turmoil. She made her way up to the second floor and the small bedchamber that had been hers ever since she'd come to Beckworth House with her father and George.

"Oh, George," she whispered, "why aren't you here?"

Sudden anger filled her even as hot tears burned her eyes and the back of her throat. She was angry at her father for wasting his inheritance and gambling away the family estates and taking his own life. She was angry with George for leaving her here with Aunt Caroline while he escaped to the excitement of foreign lands. She was angry with Annabella for never allowing them to become friends. She was angry with Aunt Caroline for being spiteful when all Heather had ever wanted was to love and be loved in return.

Then, as quickly as the anger had come, it vanished, leaving only loneliness and frustration in its wake. Her heart aching, she flung herself onto her bed and wept as she hadn't wept in a very long time.

Tanner swung into the saddle just as sunrise was lighting the eastern sky. With a low command, he calmed Rebellion's prancing. "Expect the workmen within the week, Haskin. Thorpe will remain to hire the household staff. I should return by the end of the month."

"Your Grace?" Haskin glowered as he looked up at Tanner. "Is there ... is there anything I should say to Miss Heather when she comes next?"

Tanner would consider the groundskeeper's protectiveness amusing if he didn't know how sincere Haskin was. Despite knowing Tanner could discharge him in the blink of an eye, Haskin had never hesitated to let his disapproval show over the goings-on between Tanner and Heather.

"Just tell her I was called to London on business," he replied.

Haskin grumbled and turned his eyes toward the ground.

"Nothing else, Haskin. Is that understood?"

"Aye, your grace. 'Tis understood."

Tanner didn't wait for the old man to think of something else to say. He spun Rebellion around and cantered down the drive. It would take him several days to reach Hawksbury Park in Essex by horseback, and he was anxious to start the journey.

There was much to be done before he could return to GlenRoyal, much to be done before he would see Heather again. And when he returned, it wouldn't be with secrecy.

When he returned, it would be as the Duke of Hawksbury.

Chapter 7

"I cannot believe it, Tanner. You've finally decided on a bride?" Sophia Montgomery, the Dowager Duchess of Hawksbury, sat forward as she looked at her tall and handsome son. Her sharp gray eyes noted that he looked rested despite the journey he'd just completed.

He grinned. "It's true, Mother. I intend to offer for Miss FitzHugh as soon as I return to GlenRoyal."

"Miss FitzHugh? Do I know her?"

"She's the daughter of Baron FitzHugh. Yes," he said when he saw her eyes widen, " 'tis the same FitzHugh. Heather was born at GlenRoyal. She hasn't had a Season, and I can say with confidence that you've never met her. The baron, as you probably know, is deceased, and his daughter has been raised by Viscount Moredale and his wife."

Sophia inhaled sharply. "Lord-a-mercy! Tanner, have you taken complete leave of your senses? I know I have pressed you to do your duty by Hawksbury, but I would not wish you to marry a girl who has been influenced by Lady Moredale."

He threw back his head, and his deep laughter filled the room.

She wasn't amused. "I'm serious, Tanner."

"I know you are, Mother," he replied as he composed himself. "But you needn't worry. Miss Fitz-Hugh is nothing like her cousin Annabella."

Sophia hid a shudder. "I pray not."

She fixed a stern gaze on her son. She had been after him for several years to marry and provide an heir. But most of all, she wanted her son to be happy, as happy as he once had been, all too long ago. She'd seen too clearly what Judith's betrayal had done to him. While Sophia was sensible enough not to hope for a love match after the fiasco of his last marriage, she did want him to find a wife who would at least make a tolerable companion.

Sophia leaned back in her chair once again and folded her hands in her lap. "Tell me something about this girl you think you want to marry. Why hasn't she had a Season? Is she so very young? Or is there another reason?"

"She'll be twenty on her next birthday. As to why no Season, I suspect it's because Miss Beckworth doesn't want the competition. Heather FitzHugh is quite lovely. And she's intelligent. She's clever enough to best me at a game of chess, and she's not trying to better her lot in life by snaring me for a husband, because she doesn't know who I am."

"Doesn't know ... Confound it, Tanner, you aren't making sense. How could she not know who you are?"

Tanner rose from his chair and crossed the room. "It's a long story, Mother, but if you must hear it, I'll tell it to you over supper. I'm famished."

He took hold of her elbow and drew her up from the chair. His smile disappeared as he met her gaze. "I believe I could be content enough with Miss FitzHugh while making sure Hawksbury has an heir, and she's the first lady I've thought that about in years."

"Then I'm sure I shall like her," Sophia responded softly as her fingers tightened on his arm. Together they strolled toward the dining room.

The dowager duchess retired for the night shortly after supper. Tanner kissed her cheek, then watched as she made her way toward the family apartments in the east wing of the ground floor.

Alone, Tanner returned to the drawing room. His thoughts, however, were nearly three hundred miles away. He wondered what the crew of workmen he'd hired to renovate GlenRoyal had managed to accomplish in their first few days. He wondered if Thorpe had hired a staff yet. He wondered if Heather had come visiting, and if she'd been disappointed by his absence.

He imagined her round violet eyes misty with unshed tears and found himself wanting to hold her in his arms.

With firm resolve, he squashed the desire. He realized he was dangerously close to forming a real affection for the girl, and that wouldn't do at all. He'd allowed himself to fall in love once and had gained nothing from it but pain. He would marry Miss FitzHugh, but he wouldn't be foolish enough to allow more between them than mutual friendship.

And she would be a fool not to be happy with the arrangement. After all, he was thought to be a pleasant companion for the ladies, both in the company of others and in private. She would find herself not only a duchess but one with a beautiful, stately home and great wealth. He would be more than fair with her. He would settle a comfortable allowance on her. She would have all the gowns and bonnets and fripperies a woman's heart could ever desire.

Of course, there was the small matter of her resentment toward the Duke of Hawksbury, but that could be overcome. He had already explained to her that he himself had had no hand in the Fitz-Hughs' loss of GlenRoyal. Besides, it wasn't the fault of Nicholas Montgomery that the baron had been a gamester and a wastrel. She was intelligent and couldn't help but see the truth.

He envisioned her again. Not with tears this time, but with her eyes sparking with anger. His confidence wavered. Perhaps she wouldn't be quite so easy to convince. Especially when she discovered he'd been misleading her.

He shook off the doubts as quickly as he'd suppressed thoughts of a growing attachment for Heather. If the young lady should decide to be stubborn in the matter, he knew he could depend on the viscountess to help his cause. Caroline Beckworth would never allow Heather to turn down his offer. The viscountess would most assuredly have preferred him for a son-in-law, but she would settle for this arrangement rather than allow him to slip away completely. She would see too many advantages for herself that were to be found in an association by marriage to the Montgomery family. If nothing else, greed for the handsome settlement he planned to offer would seal the bargain.

That settled in his mind, Tanner turned from the drawing room and headed for his own bedchamber. Tomorrow he would look up Edward Kennaway, and together they could plan a little excursion to Westmorland. He would invite his mother's friend, Lynette Moberly, to come as well. Lynette would be the perfect chaperon for this particular occasion.

Heather felt like a caged lion. She had spent the endless days of her captivity in her room, pacing much of the time. She thought often of Mr. Tanner and the strange feelings he had stirred in her heart. She contemplated the confused emotions and could only conclude time and again that she had fallen in love with him. She longed to see him, longed for him to take her in his arms and kiss her as he had the last time they'd been together. She wondered if he might even now be missing her, wondering why she didn't return.

The days stretched into one week and then into two, and still she was forbidden to leave the house or go near the stables. She was glad whenever it rained. At least when the weather was bad, she was able to console herself with the thought that she couldn't have gone riding anyway.

Heather also took comfort in Aunt Caroline's silence regarding her niece's visits to GlenRoyal. Nor had her aunt mentioned any further punishment. Nothing more had been said about selling Cathy. For that alone, Heather was willing to endure her confinement without complaint.

The same couldn't be said for Annabella. She continued to complain bitterly about the delay in going to Town. When not badgering her father or mother, she bemoaned her fate in Heather's room.

So it was with some degree of dread that Heather heard Annabella calling her name, moments before the door to her bedchamber flew open. She looked up from her place in the window seat and set the book she'd been reading facedown in her lap as Annabella hurried across the room.

"Heather! You won't believe what has happened. Right in the midst of the Season. To come here. I cannot believe it. And he's going to give a ball. The guest list will be very select, of course. You cannot expect such a man to invite just *anyone* to his home. Papa received the invitation today. The footman's taking our acceptance back even now. Mama has sent for the modiste so we might have new gowns."

Heather watched as Annabella flung herself

onto her back across the bed. Her brown eyes sparkled with glee. Splashes of pink colored her cheeks. Heather couldn't begin to understand whom her cousin was babbling about, but it was obviously someone of great importance to have dragged Annabella from her doldrums.

Annabella sat up and twisted around to face Heather. "I promise I shall wake you the moment we return, and tell you all about it." Again she flopped back on the bed, staring up at the ceiling while her hands drummed against the counterpane. "Oh, I can't wait until Thursday night. However shall I bear the wait? Do you suppose he came here just to see me? We met last year in London. Perhaps, when I wasn't there this Season . . . Oh, that must be it."

Heather couldn't hide her amused smile, even as her own curiosity got the better of her. "*Who* are you talking about, Annabella?"

"His grace," her cousin said with a sigh, her eyes fluttering closed. "The Duke of Hawksbury. He's come to Westmorland. Even now he's settling into the dreadful little place where you used to live."

Heather felt cold wash over her. Her smile seemed frozen in place. "The duke?" she whispered. "At GlenRoyal? Are you certain?"

"Of course I'm certain. Do you think an impostor would dare send out invitations in his name? Oh, Heather, you're such a complete chaw-bacon. No wonder Mama won't take you to Town with us. You would embarrass us all."

She was too numb to feel the sting of Annabella's insult.

The duke was at GlenRoyal. Her father's enemy had come to stay there after all. And then another thought invaded her mind. She wouldn't be able to see Mr. Tanner again. Not as long as the duke remained.

"Why, Heather, you're as white as a goose. Are you ill?"

She focused her eyes on her cousin. "No, Annabella, I'm not ill. And I'm very happy for you to be going to the duke's ball. 'Tis an honor, I'm sure."

"I will never understand you," Annabella said, rising from the bed, smoothing the skirt of her gown as she did so. "You don't mind at all that you weren't invited."

"Why should I mind?" Heather's voice was cool and controlled, masking the storm of confusion that raged within. "It doesn't signify. I wouldn't have gone regardless."

Frustrated by Heather's lackluster reaction, Annabella headed for the door. "You're hopeless," she tossed over her shoulder as she left the bedchamber.

When the door closed, Heather turned toward the window with unseeing eyes, blinded by her own fury.

The Duke of Hawksbury at GlenRoyal. The duke sitting in her father's salon, perhaps even in his favorite chair. The duke sleeping in her father's bedchamber. The duke looking over the horses in the stable and the hounds in the kennels, perhaps even telling Haskin to sell the lot of them.

Oh, how she would love to see him get what he deserved. Being thrown into a dank dungeon would be too good for him. Perhaps being flayed with a cat-o'-nine-tails would be more appropriate.

She remembered herself at ten, standing so bravely before her father and brother, her hand solemnly lying atop George's as she swore a Fitz-Hugh oath. Then she imagined herself facing the dark and brooding Duke of Hawksbury on the field of honor. Pacing out the appropriate steps, she would turn, raise her pistol, and fire a hole through his black heart.

He was giving a ball at GlenRoyal. He was giving a ball, and she wasn't going.

Sudden tears burned her eyes as she sank onto the window seat. The unfairness of it all rushed over her. She wasn't immune to the things her cousin said to her. She was as normal as any other young woman her age. Despite her protests to the contrary, she would have liked to have a Season. She would love to go to parties and balls and wear pretty dresses.

And it was the Duke of Hawksbury's fault that she didn't have those things. Perhaps not the current duke, but his father. If not for him, the baron wouldn't have given up on life. He might still be alive, and George never would have left England. She wouldn't have been denied a Season in London because her father's last days had been spent in penniless disgrace. She might have fallen in love and married . . .

Fallen in love . . . Mr. Tanner . . .

She closed her eyes, squeezing back the fresh wave of tears. The duke was even keeping her away from Mr. Tanner. As long as he remained, even if she were allowed to ride, she couldn't go to GlenRoyal to see Mr. Tanner. How long would he wait to see her again?

Perhaps he hadn't stayed after the duke had arrived. Perhaps he'd already left, and she would never see or hear from him again.

If that happened, that too would be the duke's fault. Always the Duke of Hawksbury. His father had destroyed her father. This duke had nearly killed her brother. And now he was keeping her from finding happiness.

The tears dried, replaced by renewed resentment.

I swear I shall do whatever I must to reclaim GlenRoyal for the FitzHugh family.

"Oh, Papa, I haven't forgotten my promise," she whispered. "I'll find some way to keep it. I don't know how, but I'll find a way."

Tanner gazed around the salon with satisfaction. It was miraculous what had been accomplished in so short a time. New draperies hung at the windows. New carpets covered the floor. Polished wood gleamed everywhere. Portraits once again adorned the walls.

"I say, Hawk. You should have brought us here years ago. Although I'd find your invitation more enticing in the fall."

Tanner turned as Edward Kennaway, the Earl of Mannington, strolled into the salon. His friend was cut from much the same cloth as Tanner himself—tall, lean and handsome. Although Edward's hair was a darker brown and his eyes a deeper blue, his aquiline nose and wide forehead attested to the shared blood that had filtered down to the two men from some distant relative.

Edward settled into a wing chair and retrieved his pipe. "You're bloody fortunate anyone came from London at this time of year. 'Tis a sign of our regard for you that we're here."

Tanner didn't bother to answer. He'd invited only a select few from London. He wanted Heather's introduction to Society to be a pleasant one. He knew he could trust Edward and the others to be kind to her.

"When do I get to meet her?" Edward asked.

Tanner turned, his gaze meeting the earl's. "Meet who?"

"Come now, Hawk. You think I can't see through you?"

He cocked an eyebrow, fixing his friend with a disbelieving glare.

Edward sighed, then smiled sheepishly. "All right. So you're not so easy to read, my friend. I confess the dowager duchess had a word or two with me before we left Essex."

"I thought as much." Tanner returned a wry grin. He should have known his mother would want Edward's opinion of the lady he'd chosen for the next duchess. He imagined Sophia had asked the same of Lynette Moberly. Not that his mother would interfere with his decision. Sophia Montgomery had never been the meddling sort, but she would be most interested in what Edward had to tell her.

"Well?" the earl prompted.

Tanner sat in a matching wing chair. It was easy to conjure up Heather's image. She'd never been far from his thoughts during the weeks he'd been away from GlenRoyal.

"Not until the ball," he responded. "She's been invited along with the other members of the gentry hereabout." His smile faded. "You may as well know something, Mannington. Miss FitzHugh doesn't know I'm the Duke of Hawksbury. She thinks I'm merely a friend of the family. And she has no idea I intend to ask for her hand in marriage."

"Good Lord!" Edward's whispered exclamation was followed by a lengthy silence while he puffed on his pipe.

Tanner turned his gaze out the window. The late afternoon sun was casting long shadows across the gardens. Sunlight glittered upon the pond, and he could barely see the swan that floated amidst the bright reflections. He thought perhaps that was where he enjoyed seeing Heather most, sitting next to the pond, the elegant birds in the background, dogs lying near her feet.

He supposed she would have heard by now that the duke was in residence in her old home. He knew she wouldn't come visiting of her own accord. But he'd been a bit puzzled to learn from Haskin that she hadn't returned to GlenRoyal since the day before Tanner had left for London. Since the day he'd kissed her.

He frowned as he rubbed his chin.

He could *not* have been mistaken. She *had* responded to his kiss. Surely she hadn't stayed away all this time to avoid a repeat of his actions. But what other reason could there be?

"Your grace?"

Tanner turned from the window.

Seton, GlenRoyal's new butler, crossed the salon, an envelope on the silver tray in his hand. "This was just delivered, your grace. It's from Viscount Moredale."

Tanner opened the envelope and pulled out the folded stationery. It was the acknowledgment he'd expected. No. Not quite what he'd expected. The viscount stated that he and his wife and daughter would be at the ball. There was no mention of his niece.

Tanner felt his temper flaring. He'd be damned if he would give this ball and not have Heather in attendance. It was for her benefit, after all.

He rose from the chair. "Has Moredale's servant left yet?"

"I'm afraid so, your grace. Shall I send a footman after him?"

"No. Tomorrow will be soon enough to send another message."

Seton nodded, then left the salon.

"Bad news, Hawk?" Edward asked, his keen eyes on Tanner.

"Just a slight misunderstanding," the duke answered in a tone that promised the problem would be quickly rectified.

* * *

Heather wasn't certain why her aunt's summons was making her so anxious. It unquestionably wasn't the first time she'd had a maid appear at her bedchamber door with a message from Aunt Caroline demanding her immediate appearance.

Perhaps it was because of the blue funk she'd been in ever since Annabella had come to her room yesterday. She couldn't seem to shake the depression that had settled over her. And it wasn't like her. Not like her by half. She'd never spent much time feeling sorry for herself, and she certainly didn't want to start such a practice now.

She paused at the bottom of the staircase and squared her shoulders, silently scolding herself. It was all this blasted inactivity. She wasn't used to so much idleness. That was all that was causing her present mood. Once she was allowed to ride again, she'd stop thinking of balls and parties and the like. She'd decided long ago that she didn't want anything to do with Society, not if it was peopled with the likes of Annabella and her friends. She would be glad when the Beckworths departed for London and she had the house to herself.

Her gaze moved ahead of her to the drawing room doors as she walked slowly across the hall.

It could be that Aunt Caroline had decided her punishment had gone on long enough. It could be that the duke's invitation had brightened her spirits as much as it had Annabella's. Perhaps her aunt was inclined to be forgiving, now that Annabella was so sure she was bait for a duke.

Pausing to draw in a deep breath, she grasped the doorknob and pulled open the door.

She saw their gazes turn upon her. Uncle Frederick was standing near the fireplace, his elbow resting on the mantel. Aunt Caroline was seated on the green brocade settee. Annabella was in a nearby chair, her hands folded in her lap, her pretty faced pinched with anger.

It was instantly clear that Heather's hopeful thoughts about the reason for this meeting were fantasy rather than fact. Whatever it was she had done, it had involved the entire family, and none of them looked at all pleased with her.

Heather unconsciously lifted her chin in a show of courage, then moved across the drawing room toward the threesome.

"You sent for me, Aunt Caroline?"

"I most certainly did. I hope you are pleased with yourself, Heather FitzHugh. You've managed to ruin our standing with our neighbors. We shall soon be the subject of everyone's gossip."

She blinked but forced herself to keep her gaze fastened on her aunt. "I don't understand."

"No. Of course you don't. You don't understand anything. You never have. You are every bit your father's child. Never mindful of what scandal your actions might bring down upon your head or your family's. Well, Heather, your trespassing at GlenRoyal has been found out by his grace, the duke."

A shiver ran up her spine.

"There can be no other reason for this." Aunt Caroline waved a slip of paper in the air. "The duke is demanding that you come to his ball with us. He wants to meet you."

"Come to his . . ." She felt the color drain from her face, then return in a blaze. "No. I won't go. I shall send him my regrets."

"Mama!" Annabella exclaimed.

"Be quiet, Annabella!" the viscountess snapped. She rose from the settee, her brown eyes flashing with anger. "You will do no such thing. His grace has made it clear that he desires an audience with you, and he shall most certainly have it. Perhaps he will be forgiving if you do nothing more to bring disgrace upon us."

"I don't have a ball gown," Heather replied stubbornly.

"You have a wardrobe full of clothes, you ungrateful chit."

Bitterness rose like bile, suddenly overwhelming her. "But none of them fit. They were made for Annabella, not for me. Surely you would be mortified for me to be seen in public in such clothes. What would people say about you, raising a niece with absolutely no taste in clothing?" She turned and started to leave the room. "No, I shall simply not go."

"Heather."

The tone of her uncle's voice stopped her in her tracks. She turned to look back at him, knowing already that she'd lost.

As Heather's gaze met his, she felt that same flicker of pity she'd felt before. She knew that he needed her cooperation. Although Frederick Beckworth had never shown her any real affection, neither had he been truly unkind to her. Perhaps he didn't express affection because he never received any. Certainly not from his wife or daughter, at any rate. They were only concerned with their clothing allowances and what routs they could give and attend while in London.

But the Moredale estates were not vast, the coffers not bottomless. Of the women of the house, only Heather sensed that the financial condition was strained and growing more so. Neither Aunt Caroline nor Annabella would have considered such a thing plausible, and neither of them gave any thought to Uncle Frederick.

The bitterness that had burned so hotly in Heather's chest only moments before disappeared. She was helpless to deny her uncle's silent plea. It wasn't in her to turn away from anyone in need.

With a sigh, she said, "I'll ask Mary to help me alter one of the dresses. I'm sure we can make one presentable by tomorrow night."

Without waiting to hear if anyone responded, she hastily returned to her room.

Chapter 8

Tanner stopped on the landing and glared down at the crush of guests filling the small country house. This sort of thing wasn't much to his liking. It reminded him too much of the crowded salons and drawing rooms in London, a scene he'd never been particularly fond of and one he'd grown to dislike even more with the passing of every Season. But he hadn't wanted to offend his new neighbors, just in case any were friends of Heather's, so he'd invited them all.

As he watched the milling crowd, Lady Moberly appeared in the doorway of the salon on the arm of her current suitor. An attractive widow in her early forties, Lynette Moberly was not only a close friend of the dowager duchess but one of the leading hostesses among the *ton* as well. Unlike many of her ilk, she'd earned Tanner's grudging admiration. She had a quick mind, and she'd proved it by increasing her annual income severalfold, through sound investments, since the death of her husband. She wasn't cowed by greater wealth or titles, nor did she seem inclined to become leg-shackled a second time. Most importantly in Tanner's mind, Lynette was a shrewd judge of character.

Her companion, Thomas Sainsbury, younger than the widow by a good five or more years, was a likable chap. Tanner was convinced that his feelings for Lynette were genuine and that he was no mere fortune hunter. A refreshing arrangement, he thought. Rare, indeed, judging from his own observations and experience.

With them was Lynette's godchild, Lady Celeste Andermont. Tanner had been pleased when Lynette had suggested that Celeste accompany her to GlenRoyal. The girl was about the same age as Heather and might prove helpful to his cause should Heather decide to be stubborn about his offer of marriage. He was inclined to like Lady Celeste despite himself, perhaps because Edward liked her.

As Tanner watched, Edward made his way through the crowd and moments later bowed over the hand of the pretty strawberry blonde. Celeste smiled sweetly as Edward straightened and looked into her eyes. It was painfully clear to Tanner that his friend would find himself buckled before long. The fool. He had three younger brothers who could provide an heir for Mannington. He needn't be in such a rush to give up his freedom.

The same couldn't be said for Tanner.

Thus reminded of his purpose, he moved his gaze over the gathering once again, looking for that familiar crop of black curls, waiting to gaze into an uplifted pair of violet eyes, listening for the bright tinkle of laughter that was so uniquely hers. He didn't find her and was surprised by his sharp disappointment.

Bloody hell! he thought, irritated by these unfamiliar feelings.

With a determined step, he continued down the stairs. He knew he might as well get the formalities over with and meet his neighbors. Members of the local gentry, most were strangers to him. Which was understandable, he thought. If they'd had the money or connections, they would be in

Town for the Season. The fact that they were here
in Westmorland at this time of year spoke elo-
quently about their finances, their low standing in
Society, or a combination of both. He didn't even
consider that they might not like the London Season any more than he did. Society demanded that
the *ton*—the most fashionable of its members—be
in Town for the Season, and so they went, like it or
not. Even the Duke of Hawksbury was not entirely
immune to Society's requirements.

Edward and the three others he'd invited up
from London were different from his other guests.
They were in Westmorland because they were his
friends. They'd come because he had asked them,
and for no other reason.

"You know, Hawksbury," Lord Sainsbury said
as they came face-to-face near the bottom of the
stairs, "only you could have coaxed Lynette from
Town in May."

"I promise you an entertaining few days for
your trouble, Sainsbury." He turned toward the
woman on Lord Sainsbury's arm. "I'm honored
you chose to come, Lady Moberly."

"How could I resist?" Lynette responded with a
smile. "Especially after Sophia hinted that you
were going to be introducing your intended. Is it
true, Hawk? Is the future duchess going to be here
this evening?"

His answer was an enigmatic smile before he
moved on, continuing to greet his guests, but always surreptitiously watching the front door for
her entrance.

As the Beckworth carriage rocked along the
country road, the interior cloaked in darkness,
Heather sat rigidly against the seat, her hands
folded in her lap, her eyes closed. Her stomach
was balled as tightly as her hands, and she won-

dered if she would cast up her accounts before they reached GlenRoyal.

She was going to see the Duke of Hawksbury. Face-to-face, she was going to see him. He knew about her visits to GlenRoyal. He'd summoned her to this ball tonight. Why? To shame her in front of his friends and neighbors? Would he be shaming her in front of Mr. Tanner as well?

She felt light-headed as her stomach did another somersault, and she squeezed her hands even tighter together, trying to force the sick feeling away.

"We're here!" Annabella exclaimed. "Oh, Mama, can you imagine? If we'd gone to London, we should have missed this."

"Remember yourself, Annabella," the viscountess whispered. "Not many young ladies are afforded such a wonderful opportunity. There's no other eligible woman in Westmorland as properly suited for the duke as you. If you make a good impression tonight, he's sure to remember you once we all return to Town."

Heather opened her eyes. From the blaze of lights pouring through the windows of GlenRoyal, she could see the excitement written on Annabella's pretty face. How appropriate that her cousin should be set on winning Heather's enemy for a husband.

As the carriage drew to a halt before the front door of the house, Heather ran her hands over the folds of her lavender gown. It was the prettiest of any of the hand-me-downs she owned, and the one most easily altered. But there was no disguising the fact that the dress had been meant for a woman with smaller breasts. Heather felt indecently exposed by the unaccustomed décolletage.

Aunt Caroline turned abruptly toward her niece. "Hold your tongue and let me do the talking. If the duke mentions your intrusions upon his land, I'll expect you to apologize and mean it. Do you understand me?"

"Yes."

"Good."

The carriage door opened, and the party alighted with the help of the footman.

Heather remained beside the carriage and stared at the house. Was it merely the bright lights that had brought the place alive? She couldn't recall it ever looking so lovely. Surely Mr. Tanner and Thorpe hadn't accomplished so much by themselves.

Mr. Tanner . . .

Her heart did its usual flip-flop at the thought of him. Would he be here? Would he like her ball gown? Would he think her pretty? Perhaps seeing him would make the rest of this dreadful event worthwhile.

"Heather!"

Her aunt's sharp voice forced her to hurry up the steps to the front door.

Tanner was standing at the opposite side of the hall when the door opened again. Across the sea of heads, he saw her enter.

It was the first time he'd seen her in anything besides drab gray, and he was surprised to find she looked even more beautiful than he'd remembered. Her ebony curls framed a face of flawless ivory skin. There was an impudent look about her petite, buttonlike nose, a stubborn aspect in the straight line of her jaw.

High, firm breasts filled the bodice of the lavender silk gown to perfection. In fact, perhaps it was a little too perfect. He was not the only man in the room able to see the delightful glimpse of cleavage. But he was the only one to know what she felt like, pressed against him. How perfectly she fit next to his body. The narrowness of her waist. The gentle rounding of her hips.

Tanner curbed his rising desire as he returned his gaze to her face. He noticed then that her eyes seemed wider than usual. Her pretty mouth was drawn, her cheeks colorless. It was clear she didn't want to be here.

He wondered if he'd made a mistake. Perhaps this wasn't the best way he could have let her know who he was. But it was done now. There was no going back.

With determined steps, he made his way across the hall.

As he stepped into the entranceway, their eyes met briefly. He saw the tiniest smile lift her mouth and took courage from it. Then he turned to her uncle.

"Welcome to GlenRoyal, Moredale," Tanner said as the two men shook hands.

Frederick Beckworth nodded, then glanced at the women at his side. "It is we who should welcome you to Westmorland, your grace. I trust you remember my wife and daughter."

Tanner heard Heather's tiny intake of air even as he bowed over Lady Moredale's hand. He gave Annabella only a cursory nod before turning to Heather. If he'd thought she looked pale before, it was nothing compared to now. She was staring at him with a look of abhorrence in her violet eyes.

"And this must be your niece," he said in a low, controlled voice.

"Ah ... yes. My wife's niece, Miss FitzHugh."

Tanner took hold of her hand, which was hanging limply at her side. Her fingers were as cold as ice. He squeezed them lightly. "A pleasure to meet you, Miss FitzHugh."

Her eyes rolled back in her head, and she wilted like a hothouse flower exposed to the cold, falling toward him in a dead faint.

Annabella's indignant exclamation was followed by sudden silence throughout the hall. Tanner ignored the staring faces as he lifted Heather in his arms and carried her toward the withdrawing room. The throng of people parted like the waters of the Red Sea before his determined gaze.

She seemed so small and helpless in his arms. He'd never thought of her as being fragile. He'd always admired her strength. He'd seen her laughter, her anger, her beauty, but it was her strength of spirit he'd admired most. Now, as she lay cradled in his embrace, he realized how truly vulnerable she was. He could very well be to blame if she was hurt.

Once inside the withdrawing room, he laid the unconscious girl on a couch, then knelt beside her. He heard the mumbling voices behind him and glanced over his shoulder to see his guests peering through the doorway. His valet slipped into the room at just that moment.

"Close the door, Thorpe," he commanded.

He immediately turned his attention back to Heather. He took one of her small hands in his and gently rubbed it, trying to bring some warmth back into her cold body.

Tanner had witnessed numerous young ladies swoon in his day. He was convinced it was a practiced art. But Heather hadn't rehearsed this reaction. There had been nothing delicate or artful about it.

Lord, what a fool he was. What a bloody, blasted fool. He should have thought of a better way to reveal himself to her.

At last her eyelids fluttered, then opened. For a moment, she stared at him with glazed, unseeing eyes.

"Miss FitzHugh?" he said softly. "Are you feeling better?"

"What happened?" she whispered.

"You . . . ah . . . you had a case of the vapors."

"You mean I fainted? But I've never fainted in my life." She sounded highly skeptical. She blinked, then looked at him again. The glazed look disappeared, replaced by one that could only be described as utter horror. "You're *him*. You're the duke."

"I'm afraid so."

A strangled cry rose from her chest as she turned her head away and pressed her face against the sofa cushions.

He tightened his grasp on her fingers. "I beg you to forgive me my little masquerade, Miss Fitz-Hugh. If you'll allow me to explain, I hope you'll understand.'

"Understand?" She jerked her hand free. "Understand why you lied to me and played me for a fool?"

Color returned to her cheeks, and when she met his gaze again, he saw the blaze of anger in her enormous violet eyes. He couldn't contain the smile that went with his satisfaction at seeing the return of fire. It was *this* Heather he enjoyed the most.

"Go on and laugh, your grace." She sat up. " 'Tis a fine joke. I'm sure your friends shall appreciate it."

Tanner forced the smile from his lips as he rose to his feet. "I assure you, my friends will not think it a joke any more than do I."

"Let me through, I say!"

The door burst open, revealing an irate Lady Moredale, followed by her daughter.

"Your grace, you cannot imagine how humiliated—" Caroline turned suddenly. "Close that door," she snapped at Thorpe.

Tanner's eyes narrowed.

"Oh, good heavens! I cannot bear the shame." The viscountess sank onto a nearby chair and began to fan herself. "Whatever must your grace think of us? I knew she shouldn't have been allowed to come. Heather hasn't the least notion how to behave in Society. You see what she has done. She has embarrassed us all."

"Miss FitzHugh is not the first young lady to swoon at a crowded ball, Lady Moredale." There was no mistaking the severe tone of his voice. "If fainting was a social blunder, half the young ladies of the *ton* wouldn't be able to show their faces in public."

He held out his hand to Heather, and his voice softened. "Now, since I believe Miss FitzHugh is feeling herself again, I should like to escort her into the salon. 'Tis time for the music to begin. Shall we, Miss FitzHugh?"

Heather stared at him. Not Mr. Tanner, but the Duke of Hawksbury. He looked so gloriously, wonderfully handsome in his evening attire. He was incredibly tall, his hair touched with gold, his blue eyes sharp and penetrating.

This man, her enemy.

She couldn't dance with him. If she did, she would be betraying her father, her brother, every FitzHugh who had ever lived. She had to refuse. She had to leave GlenRoyal before her nerves shattered completely.

Then she glanced at her aunt and cousin. She saw their haughty, horrified expressions, and something in her reacted more strongly to them than to the hated identity of the man before her.

She reached out and took his hand.

She was rewarded with another of his half smiles as he escorted her across the withdrawing room. Thorpe moved quickly to open the door for his master and the lady on his arm.

Heather was filled with fear as she faced the crowd of people in the hall. For a moment, she felt totally out of her depth. She was afraid she might faint again. Then she recognized several faces. They were members of the local gentry. A baronet. A few lords and ladies. The vicar and his wife. She'd seen them now and again at Beckworth House.

She glanced around the hall as her courage returned. This was GlenRoyal, her home. She needn't be afraid here. She held her head high as the duke guided her toward the salon, stopping frequently to introduce her to his other guests.

"I can't tell you how happy I am to meet you, my dear," Lynette Moberly said following their introduction. "I'm glad you're not ill. I was afraid you wouldn't be able to spend the evening with us."

"I have embarrassed myself beyond measure, Lady Moberly. I assure you, I'm not prone to suffering the vapors in public. Or in private, for that matter. I don't know what came over me."

The woman smiled knowingly. "You wouldn't be the first young lady to swoon over Hawksbury," she whispered.

Heather felt a flash of anger. "I think a more likely explanation is my failure to eat since breakfast."

Lynette answered with jubilant laughter.

Heather would have sworn she heard the duke chuckle, too, but when she glanced up at him, his face was composed and unreadable. He nodded slightly as their eyes met; then he led her into the salon.

Heather had only a brief moment to look around the room. The rugs had been rolled up and the furniture pushed back against the walls to accommodate dancing, but she could still see the changes that had been wrought in the salon since her last visit. New paintings hung on the walls. New drapes framed the windows. Gold and silver sconces held blazing candles. With a nod from the duke, the orchestra began to play, and he led her into the center of the room. He bowed formally, then held her hand as they began to move to the music.

At first, she had to concentrate too hard on the steps of the minuet to worry about her partner. Through the years, she'd received dance lessons along with Annabella, but this was the first opportunity she'd had to put those lessons to use. She could only pray her memory would serve her and her feet wouldn't betray her.

"Relax, Miss FitzHugh. I'd hoped you would enjoy yourself."

"Enjoy myself, your grace? When you have lied to me from the very start? When you let me tell you how I feel about you and your family without ever revealing yourself? You are no gentleman, and I shall not enjoy myself until I am far away from you."

"I am truly sorry you feel that way. Would it make any difference if I told you *why* I didn't tell you I was the Duke of Hawksbury?"

She refused to look at him. She would never forgive him for the deception. Never. She had begun to fancy herself in love with a man who didn't exist. She could not forgive him for that.

The steps of the minuet carried her away from his side, then back to him once again.

"Very well, Miss FitzHugh," he continued as if there had been no break in their conversation, "but I'm going to tell you anyway. You may not believe this, given your predilection to despise the house of Montgomery, but there are many people who try to form alliances with me simply because of my name, because of what I might be able to do for them. You see, Miss FitzHugh, the house of Montgomery is a wealthy one, the Hawksbury title quite powerful."

Despite herself, she was listening to him.

"Responsibilities come with wealth and power. One such responsibility is to provide an heir to carry on. It is time I took a wife, and all Society is aware of it. I must take a bride soon."

"I pity the poor lady you choose."

His smile seemed to mock her. "Don't pity her too much."

"You are betrothed?" She felt a cold chill seeping through her veins.

"No. That's one reason I came to GlenRoyal. To escape the many young ladies of the *ton* who are trying to help me decide."

Heather sniffed. "You have an elevated opinion of your charms, your grace."

"Perhaps." His voice deepened; his grip on her hand tightened. The blue of his eyes seemed to turn to ice. "But I have been played the fool by a woman before, and everyone knew it. It won't happen again. When I choose a bride, I will know that the same mistakes won't be repeated."

She didn't think he even knew he was holding her, dancing with her. For a terrible moment, she seemed able to see inside the man. He didn't look so imposing, so threatening. For now, he wasn't the vile Duke of Hawksbury, her sworn enemy. He was more the wounded warrior.

"I'm sure you will find someone who'll love you very much, your grace," she whispered.

He looked at her as if she'd just grown a second head. "Love?" The sardonic half smile returned to his lips. "That's a notion for your novels, my dear. Not real life." He shook his head. "I came here to rest and think, Miss FitzHugh, but I confess that meeting you was even more refreshing. I rather liked being mistaken for a carpenter or a simple footman or whatever you thought me. I've enjoyed making the acquaintance of a woman who didn't know I was the Duke of Hawksbury, someone who wasn't out to snare me for a husband."

"Believe me, your grace, I have no interest in you as a husband or anything else."

"I believe you." He actually chuckled. "That's another reason why I enjoy your company. You, Miss FitzHugh, are refreshingly honest. I doubt you could tell a lie if you tried. Besides, your eyes would give you away if you did."

"The same cannot be said of you, your grace," she retorted hotly. "You lie *extremely* well." She scowled up at him as they circled, first to the left and then to the right. "Why did you let me think your name was Mr. Tanner when we met? You had no cause to lie. You could have just sent me away."

"I told you why I didn't send you away. And the name was not a lie. Not exactly. My name *is* Tanner. Tanner Montgomery. 'Twas you who added the 'mister.' "

Heather stared into his eyes, hating to admit that he spoke the truth. Mr. Haskin had simply said his name was Tanner. She had assumed the rest. But he could have set her straight. He could have corrected her the first time she called him Mr. Tanner.

He stopped in the middle of the dance floor. He held her hand and stared down into her eyes as he spoke softly. "Miss FitzHugh, may I introduce myself once again? Tanner Huntington Gilbert Montgomery, tenth Duke of Hawksbury, Earl of Albany, Viscount Stafford, at your service."

And then with expert skill he guided her into the steps of the minuet once again, so precisely that she wondered if they'd actually ever stopped moving.

She was filled with so many conflicting emotions, she couldn't sort them through. She wished the music could cease so she could escape his presence. Maybe then she could think straight. No woman could think straight when she was looking into those mysteriously powerful blue eyes of his. Eyes that begged her to draw closer, to discover the man behind them. Eyes that at times seemed so cold and distant, and then so warm and filled with laughter, laughter he kept bottled up inside. Eyes that made her feel so ... so confused.

As if in answer to her wish, the melody ended. Tanner led her across the salon, bowed to her, and turned away, leaving her standing beside her aunt.

Heather was vaguely aware of Aunt Caroline's simmering anger and the petulant look on Annabella's face, but her own swirling emotions were more than enough for her to deal with now. She would worry about her aunt and cousin later.

"I should like to call upon you at Beckworth House, if you would allow it, Miss FitzHugh."

The duke's parting words echoed over and over in her head as the carriage rolled toward home. To her horror, Heather realized that she had not refused him. She had said nothing at all.

Well, if he did come, she would send him her regrets. He knew how she felt about him, about his father, about GlenRoyal's neglect. Thank heaven she'd never told him that GlenRoyal had once been her home. Her humiliation at his hand would have been complete then.

She caught her breath. What a ninny she was! Of course he knew. He would know how his own father had come to own GlenRoyal, and it wouldn't have taken much to deduce the rest.

A new fury burned hot in her chest. Even now he must be laughing at her, the country bumpkin, the naive fool. What a lark he'd been having all evening at her expense. Did his friends from London know? Were they even now sitting in the salon and sharing the laughter?

The moment she stepped down from the carriage, Heather beat a hasty retreat to her room. She wanted to get out of this horrid dress.

"Lavender is your color, Miss FitzHugh," he'd whispered to her the second time they'd danced. "You should wear it often."

She'd burn the thing. She would rather wear rags than ever put on this dress again.

She didn't wait for Mary's help to begin undressing. She was tugging at the ribbons beneath her breasts before the door had closed behind her, all the while fighting back hot tears of rage.

She had just slipped her nightgown over her head when her bedchamber door opened. She turned as Annabella sailed into the room.

Her cousin's brown eyes regarded her with disdain. "You made a perfect fool of yourself tonight, Heather, and don't think Mama will forgive you for it. Nor will I."

Suddenly drained of all emotion, Heather sank onto the bed. She hadn't the strength to deal with Annabella now. She couldn't even summon up her anger. "I didn't *want* to go to his ball," she answered in a monotone.

"You may have fooled the duke, but you didn't fool me. I know you didn't really faint. You aren't the first woman who's employed such a device. But he'll forget you soon enough when he returns to London. I'll make sure he does. I've decided *I'm* going to marry him."

"Believe what you want." Heather sighed deeply, wishing her cousin would just go away. "You are welcome to him."

Annabella smiled. "That's the problem with your side of the family, cousin. You all give up so easily. Your father died to escape his debts. Your brother ran away in shame and left you on Mama's hands. And you . . ." She shrugged dismissively. "I, on the other hand, will find a way. He will be obliged to marry me, if nothing else." Her expression, even more than her words, revealed her determination. Then she shrugged again. "Of course, it won't make a bit of difference if you do want the duke. I will win him in the end."

"I *don't* want him," Heather repeated.

"Naturally you don't. You wouldn't know what to do with such a man. Hawksbury will need a real lady for his duchess, not some little hoyden who hasn't the least idea how to behave in Society. He's one of the richest men in England and must soon take a wife or there will be no heir. I plan to give him that heir." Her smile thinned. "Stay out of my way, Heather. The duke might dally with you, but he would never marry a little nobody."

Heather's temper was rising. "And I would never marry a scoundrel like the Duke of Hawksbury. He's a beast. A liar and a cheat."

"Good." The confident smile returned. "Then we understand each other. Good night, cousin." With that, Annabella swept out of the room.

"Papa was cheated out of GlenRoyal," Heather whispered toward the closed door. "And George didn't desert me. He'll be back. You'll see."

She walked to the window and stared out at the ink-black sky. The moon had long since completed its nightly trek. It wouldn't be long before the first streaks of dawn painted the horizon a lighter shade.

Keen disappointment pierced Heather's chest as she remembered the times she'd shared with Mr. Tanner. Then the memories were shattered as she visualized him once again, the tall and handsome Duke of Hawksbury. Bitterness swallowed any happiness that had come before.

"You can have him, Annabella," Heather whispered. "He deserves you."

She left the window and lay back on the bed, then rolled onto her stomach, giving in to the hurt that gnawed at her heart. She didn't look up when Mary entered the room, picking up the clothes she'd left on the floor. She made no sound as the maidservant pulled a comforter over her, extinguished the light, and left the room.

As the minutes crawled by, she realized that Annabella had given her the key, had at last made her understand the real importance of her Fitz-Hugh oath. She would prove her cousin wrong. The FitzHughs *didn't* give up easily. At least not *this* FitzHugh.

Perhaps she couldn't get GlenRoyal back just yet, but she could make the duke regret he'd ever heard the name FitzHugh. She could make him regret even more the day he'd met Heather Fitz-Hugh.

She would harden her heart against his lopsided smile, against the cool blue of his eyes, against the breadth of his shoulders, against the sound of his voice. She would harden her heart against everything he said and did, and she would find a means for revenge.

If it meant she had to lie and mislead and manipulate, then she would do all those things and more. He thought she would be a poor liar. Perhaps that had been true yesterday, but today Tanner had shown her how easily it could be done. She was a good student. She would not fail to take this lesson to heart. She would, indeed, do whatever she had to do.

Daylight had invaded her room by the time she had formulated the perfect course for revenge against Tanner Montgomery, Duke of Hawksbury.

She knew now how to make him regret what his family had done to the FitzHughs. She knew how to make him pay for what he had done to her.

And knowing it, she slept.

Chapter 9

He'd chosen well, Tanner thought as he cantered Rebellion across the fields toward Beckworth House. Heather FitzHugh was as easy to read as any book. She hadn't been trained by her mama in the beau monde arts of subterfuge and guile. She would never be able to lie to him, at least not without him seeing it clearly written in her eyes.

She had manners as well and knew how to conduct herself, even when in a dither. After her initial shock last night, there'd been no hiding the fury in her eyes, but she'd conducted herself with decorum. She was truly to the manor born, an aristocrat in the very best sense of the word.

Yes, he'd chosen well.

She would come round to seeing his point of view. She would soon understand that he wasn't a bad sort. He would treat her well, and they would have a quite tolerable marriage.

Of course, she would have to understand that his views on marriage were a bit different from those of many others among the *ton*. Even after she'd provided him with an heir, he would never countenance his wife taking a lover, no matter how discreet she was. He would not be played the fool again, even with Society's tacit permission. When Heather married him, it would be with the understanding that she remain faithful to her vows until death parted them.

He pushed away such thoughts, certain that Heather would never stray. She would need no reminders from him in that regard.

Then he remembered her anger and found himself grinning. Never had he seen such a beautiful fury. Her violet eyes grew so dark, they nearly became black. Bright color infused her smooth cheeks. Her nostrils flared ever so slightly, and she held her head as if she were the bloody Queen of England herself.

His life would never be boring with Heather for a wife.

He thought of the way she'd looked in that lavender gown, her firm, rounded breasts held precariously beneath the scooped bodice. He remembered how he'd longed to cup them in his hands, to free them from the fabric so he could see their fullness, to tease the dark nipples with his tongue.

Boring? By gad, having Heather for a wife might be heaven on earth.

He slowed Rebellion as Beckworth House came into view. He wondered if Heather was watching for him from one of those windows even now. Of course, when he'd asked permission last night to come calling on her, he hadn't indicated he would present himself so soon. He hadn't expected to act so quickly either. But when he'd awakened this morning, he'd found he was eager to get on with the business of courting her.

Perhaps it was the memory of the kiss they'd shared when he was simply Mr. Tanner and she had no reason to despise him. Perhaps it was because he wanted to know if her kisses would be as sweet now that she knew he was the Duke of Hawksbury.

He trotted the black gelding down the long

drive toward the viscount's sprawling estate, taking note of the slightly shabby exterior and the less than perfectly groomed lawn. Clearly, Heather's assessment of her uncle's financial condition was accurate. Walter FitzHugh hadn't been the only one in her family who couldn't manage his funds. Lord Moredale was clearly a bit short in the pocket.

Tanner had already dismounted when a footman appeared to take hold of Rebellion's reins. The same tardiness wasn't shown at the door, however. Before he had a chance to knock, it opened, held by an austere-looking butler in a dark livery that had seen better days.

Tanner handed the man one of his cards. "Kindly see if Miss FitzHugh is receiving," he said.

The butler raised an eyebrow. "At once, your grace. Please step into the drawing room while I speak with the lady." He ushered Tanner to the drawing room door, then disappeared into the bowels of the house.

It wasn't long until Tanner heard the rustle of skirts and watched as Caroline Beckworth entered the room.

"Your grace, what a pleasant surprise."

"The pleasure is mine, Lady Moredale," he lied politely. "I hope I have not come at an inopportune time."

"Not at all, your grace. I have asked for some tea to be sent in. Please, won't you join me?" She motioned toward a gathering of chairs.

Before he moved, he said, "I trust Miss Fitz-Hugh will be down shortly."

Caroline hesitated, then replied, "Yes. I'm sure it shan't be long."

His glance didn't fail to note that the viscountess was dressed in the highest fashion. A gold-and-emerald choker circled her throat, and matching jewels adorned her ears. It seemed that Lord Moredale's income was spent first upon his wife, then upon his lands.

And never, Tanner thought with a bite of displeasure, upon his niece.

"You sent for me, Mama."

He wasn't surprised to see Annabella enter the drawing room.

"Oh, your grace," the girl said, sounding surprised. "I didn't know you were here." She smiled prettily.

The coy look only increased his annoyance. It was obvious what they were up to. They hoped he would be so impressed with Annabella's charms that he would forget her cousin.

"Do come join us, Annabella," her mother replied, her tone sugary-sweet.

Annabella was wearing an amber-colored gown which nicely set off her blond hair and brown eyes. The silky fabric fell toward the floor in an almost straight line.

The sardonic smile returned to his lips as he stood and welcomed her. He wondered how long it would be before Annabella tired of the gown she was wearing, how long before Heather would be trying to modify it to fit her more feminine curves.

"Your ball was ever so wonderful, your grace," Annabella gushed as she settled onto the settee beside her mother.

"I'm glad you enjoyed yourself."

"Will you be remaining in Westmorland long?" Caroline asked.

"Not if my business at GlenRoyal proceeds as planned." He glanced toward the door, but it was only the maidservant he'd heard, carrying in the tea tray.

"May I pour for you, your grace?" Annabella asked.

The maid set the silver tray on the low table before Annabella.

"Thank you, Miss Beckworth, but I think I shall wait for Miss FitzHugh. I'm sure she won't be much longer."

Caroline's voice shook slightly as she spoke to the maid. "Maude, see what is keeping Heather. Tell her we are awaiting tea with her."

"Yes, m'lady."

Tanner suspected it would be the first message that had been sent to Heather, and his dislike for Lady Moredale and her daughter increased accordingly.

"We shall be going to Town soon," Annabella continued as if there hadn't been an interruption. "Perhaps we shall have the opportunity to see one another again."

She was a forward piece of baggage, and he recognized the eager look in her eyes. Oh, yes. He knew that look all too well.

Caroline cleared her throat. "I believe I hear Heather coming now. Annabella, will you pour the tea? I fear I'm a trifle parched. We don't normally keep such late hours as we had last night, your grace. The country life is much quieter."

"And much more pleasant," he replied. "I believe it would be easy for me to remain forever in the country if not for my seat in Parliament. And, of course, the running of my estates sometimes demands that I conduct business in Town."

"You can't mean you would forgo the Season?" Annabella's brown eyes were filled with abhorrence. "Surely you can't mean it, your grace?"

"I'm afraid I do, Miss Beckworth."

The inhabitants of the room fell into an awkward silence. Tanner turned his eyes toward the doorway and kept them there, thereby stopping any attempt to renew a conversation. He heard the rattle of Caroline's teacup and the nervous tapping of Annabella's shoe on the floor, but he refused to make it easy on either of them.

Heather entered the room in a hurry, coming to an abrupt halt the moment their gazes met.

As he rose from his chair, his attentive eyes noted the sassy black curls that framed her face, the way her eyes widened when she saw him, the way her breasts so delightfully filled out the bodice of her sunshine-yellow gown, the way the shiny fabric swayed about her ankles, offering him a glimpse of her matching slippers and a bit of ankle.

"Good afternoon, Miss FitzHugh." He allowed himself a full smile.

She was fighting an internal battle. She was still angry with him, but not too angry, he thought. Ah, it was refreshing to see such honesty on a woman's face.

He knew the moment the battle ended in his favor.

Heather moved slowly across the drawing room. She didn't return his smile, but her voice carried a note of welcome. "Good afternoon, your grace."

"We were just about to take tea, Heather," her aunt said. "Do sit down and join us before it grows cold."

Tanner motioned toward a chair next to his. Heather tilted her head to one side, slanting a glance in his direction, then took her seat where he'd indicated.

For the next twenty minutes, Tanner endured Annabella's and Caroline's chatter without offering much response. Heather didn't participate. She simply sipped her tea and kept her gaze sedately on the carpet near her feet. Tanner was wondering how he was going to have an opportunity to speak with her when Caroline Beckworth offered a solution.

"Did you know, your grace, that Beckworth House has one of the finest art galleries north of London? I'm sure Annabella would—"

"Is that true, Lady Moredale? Why, I should love to see your paintings. Perhaps Miss FitzHugh would be kind enough to show them to me." He stood quickly and held out his hand to Heather.

For the first time since she'd sat down beside him, Heather lifted her eyes to meet his. Tanner wished she would honor him with one of her smiles, the same sweet smile she'd turned on him the afternoon of their chess game.

"Miss FitzHugh?"

She set down her teacup and rose gracefully from her chair. "I would be happy to show you the gallery."

His warm hand enveloped hers as he tucked it in the crook of his arm. She watched as he nodded briefly to his hostess and Annabella, then turned with her toward the drawing room door.

Heather's heart was hammering in her chest, so hard she feared he must be able to hear it. She wondered if the duke was still able to read her thoughts so clearly in her eyes. If so, he would realize how much she despised him.

But he didn't despise her, she reminded herself. He liked her company because she was "refreshingly honest," even innocent and naive. He enjoyed being with her because she wanted nothing from him.

Well, he was wrong on all accounts, and he would one day discover the error of his thinking.

She remembered the harsh look of his face last night, the icy tone of his voice. *I have been played the fool by a woman before . . . It won't happen again.*

How wrong you are, my lord duke, she thought. *And I am the one who will make it happen.*

Her plan of revenge was so delightfully simple. The Duke of Hawksbury needed a wife. He found her refreshing and fun to be with. It could not be too difficult to convince him that the innocent, naive, refreshingly honest Heather FitzHugh would be just the sort of wife he needed. And the marriage proposal would only be the beginning.

She wanted nothing from him? How wrong he was. She would require much to become a proper duchess. Gowns and hats and gloves and jewelry and cloaks. There must be a hundred ways she could spend his money, and all she needed was to make him give it to her.

It would be important that his friends like her. She needed to be accepted by the *ton*. She wanted Tanner to be envied by other men, and for him to know just how much she was desired by others. For that, she would need a Season in London.

Most important of all, she needed Tanner himself to want and desire her. She wanted him to be driven half mad by the wanting, just like the heroes in the novels she read. Remembering the kiss they had shared, she was certain she could accomplish this goal as well.

And then, after she had all these things, when she walked down the aisle of the church and the reverend asked if she would take this man for her wedded husband, she would say no. In front of all his friends and peers, she would reject him. She would publicly prove him a fool a second time.

Heather glanced at the man beside her as they walked toward the gallery. Her plan had seemed simple enough last night. Wasn't his presence here now proof that he liked her company and was earnest about gaining her affections? Still, Heather sensed these were dangerous waters lapping at her feet. She knew nothing of men like the Duke of Hawksbury.

It didn't signify, she reminded herself. She would learn about men like Tanner. She would learn everything she could and do whatever she had to do. She would not give up, nor would she give in to fear or uncertainty. She would make her plan work. Somehow, she would make it work.

The duke stopped suddenly. His arm tightened against his side, pressing her hand between his elbow and body. "Miss FitzHugh, I would be greatly honored if you would consent to go riding with me and a few of my friends tomorrow. Lady Moberly will be in attendance, so I see no reason your aunt could find fault with my invitation. We shall be taking a picnic beside the brook beyond GlenRoyal's north border."

She remembered the times they had ridden together and felt her pulse quicken at the memory. She loved to see him astride Rebellion, his golden-streaked hair flying back from his face, his blue eyes intent. It was on horseback that she was most apt to catch a glimpse of a real smile. Not the lopsided, ironic grin he so often wore, but a smile that came up from somewhere deep inside him.

"Well, Miss FitzHugh?" he prompted.

She shoved away her memories. Those were not the reasons she needed to be with him. She had to remember the role she played from this moment on.

She shook her head and gave him a sad look. "I must decline your kind invitation, your grace. I am unable to ride at present."

His brows drew together in a frown. "You are injured?"

"No." She shrugged helplessly. "I'm afraid I've been forbidden to ride."

"Ah ... I see."

Was he giving up so easily? she wondered. Her disappointment was keen, but only because of her plan to even the score with him, she told herself. It surely wasn't because she wanted to spend time in his company.

She stared up into his eyes and suddenly

thought how appropriately he was titled. Like the hawk, he seemed to soar above her, his crown golden, his eyes piercing, unwavering, and intent upon his prey. At any moment he might swoop down and capture her ...

"I will speak to Lady Moredale. Perhaps she will relent."

She swallowed and looked away, breaking the spell he'd cast upon her. Slipping her hand from his arm, she walked into the center of the gallery. She didn't turn to look at him when she spoke. "I should be happy to join you, should my aunt give her permission, your grace." She pointed at a nearby portrait. "Have you seen this? At one time it belonged to Lady Wentworth in London."

Caroline Beckworth was not pleased. In fact, Tanner feared she might burst a vessel in her head before she found her tongue. But he meant to have his way in this matter. He would give her no opportunity to deny him Heather's company. He didn't allow his gaze to stray from Caroline's face for even a moment.

"Well ..." Caroline moistened her lips, then began again. "I suppose if Lady Moberly is acting as chaperon, I can find no reason to deny your request." She stiffened her back. "However, I'm afraid Heather doesn't have a proper mount. Our stables are inadequately stocked at present. 'Tis a sad state, which will be rectified before we return from London."

"But, Aunt Caroline," Heather interrupted, "whatever do you mean? Cathy has always been a well-mannered mount."

Caroline looked quickly at her niece, her face turning from pink to scarlet. "Cathy is not ... available."

"Not availa—" The word was strangled in Heather's throat.

For just a moment, Tanner wondered if she was about to faint again. Her eyes were wide, her face as pale as milk.

"You *sold* her," she whispered. "You sold Cathy."

Tanner glanced at Heather's aunt and knew immediately that it was true.

"No!" Heather cried. She raced from the drawing room, her yellow gown bunched up in her hands.

Tanner tossed the viscountess a censuring look before taking off after Heather. He caught up with her in the yard, halfway to the stables. He slowed his strides to keep pace with hers but didn't try to speak or stop her. He felt her misery deep in his own chest.

Tanner waited in the stable doorway and watched as Heather hurried into the shadowed interior. She stopped at the third stall on the right, her hands resting on the closed half-door. The stall was empty.

A groom walked toward her from the back of the barn, a pitchfork in his hand. He wore a morose expression on his swarthy, homely face. "Miss Heather?"

"When did she sell her, Wes?" Heather's voice cracked as she fought back tears.

"Nigh on two weeks ago, miss. Her ladyship said if I was t'tell even Gram, I'd be out on my ear. I'm sorry, Miss Heather. If there'd been anything I could do ..."

" 'Tis not your fault," she whispered, turning to lay a comforting hand on his shoulder. "I made Aunt Caroline angry. I brought it on myself. Who bought her, Wes?"

"The vicar. For his little girl. Cathy'll have a good home, you needn't fear for that."

"No. No, I needn't fear for that."

Tanner was filled with an icy rage. It was plain

how much she'd loved that horse. He couldn't imagine Heather doing anything dreadful enough to deserve such a punishment. It was a good thing Lady Moredale had remained indoors. He wasn't sure what he might have said to the woman if she'd been standing next to him.

Heather turned away from the groom, her gaze rising to meet Tanner's. "It seems I shan't be able to go riding with you tomorrow after all."

"Of course you can, Miss FitzHugh. I shall bring you a horse myself. I can assure both you and your aunt that it shall be a suitable mount for a young lady." He stepped toward her. "Now, may I see you back inside before I go?"

Lord help him, perhaps it wasn't such a good thing that he could read her like a book. He felt her heartache as if it were his own.

With a tenderness he hadn't known in years— and wouldn't have welcomed if he'd recognized it—he took Heather's hand and drew her toward the house.

Chapter 10

Heather sat staring at her reflection in the mirror. She'd spent much of the night weeping, but now she'd cloaked herself in familiar anger. She mentally catalogued all the wrongs done to her by her aunt and cousin and uncle and brother and father, and by life in general. Mostly, she remembered all the reasons she had to despise the Duke of Hawksbury.

It had occurred to her during those dark hours that even losing Cathy was somewhat his fault—or at the very least, his family's. By taking GlenRoyal from the FitzHughs, Tanner's father had left Heather at the mercy of her heartless aunt. If Nicholas Montgomery hadn't stolen GlenRoyal, she and George would be living there now, and no one could have taken Cathy from her.

She frowned into the looking glass. She couldn't allow herself to be swayed by her earlier attraction to Tanner. He was a heartless, pompous buck. He'd shot George, a boy of only sixteen, in a duel. He'd left GlenRoyal to rot, along with the horses and hounds. He'd callously turned out Haskin, as loyal and trusted a servant as he'd ever find, with nary a thought about what would happen to the man. He'd lied to her from the moment they'd first met, probably laughed at her behind her back. No, she wasn't going to fall for his rare smiles or the flash in his blue eyes or the way he sat a horse or the feel of his mouth upon hers.

Her skin grew warm as the memory returned again, unbidden, to haunt her. She touched her lips with her fingertips and remembered the way the flesh had tingled as he'd kissed her.

"No!" she snapped at her reflection. "Two can play at this game of lies, your grace. I promise you shall rue the day you decided to amuse yourself at my expense."

She rose from the dresing table and ran a hand over her gray riding habit. His grace must be tired of seeing her in the dreadful thing, she thought, glancing once more at the mirror. She hoped so. But if her plan worked, she wouldn't have to wear it much longer.

A light tapping announced Mary. "The duke is here, Miss Heather. He's waiting in the hall."

"I'll be right down," she replied as she tied her bonnet at a saucy angle beneath her chin.

When she turned around, she found Annabella staring at her from the doorway, her eyes hate-filled.

"It won't work, Heather. Once the duke returns to Town, he'll forget you. A man such as he would never settle for a wife from a disgraceful family such as yours."

Heather controlled her temper. "Have you forgotten we're from the same family, *cousin*?"

Annabella's frustration was expressed in a squeak between clenched teeth. "I'll make you sorry for this, Heather," she said, then disappeared down the hallway.

Yes, you probably will, Heather thought as she started for the stairs. Annabella was not one to be thwarted without retaliation. But at the moment, Heather didn't care. She had only a short time in which to act. She had to win the duke's affections before he returned to London. She would worry about Annabella's temper only if her plan failed.

She paused at the top of the stairs and gazed down upon the man waiting in the hall. He was wearing a biscuit-colored coat, his fitted trousers and Hessian boots a deeper shade of brown. He looked terribly tall and frightfully powerful. Was it merely his physical appearance, or was it an air that came from being a duke, a result of having people hop the moment he spoke?

He glanced up as she started down the stairs. Although he didn't smile, she had the feeling he was pleased to see her.

Good, she thought, and forced herself to smile at him.

"Good day, Miss FitzHugh. We have beautiful weather awaiting our picnic."

"We do, indeed, your grace," she said as she approached him. "Wonderfully warm for May, isn't it?"

"I hope you like the horse I brought for you. Her previous owner once told me she loves to jump hedges and is a wonderful mount for a lady." He moved toward the door.

Field, the butler, promptly opened it for them.

Heather spotted the mare before she had left the hall. "Cathy?" she whispered. Surprised, she glanced at Tanner.

He nodded, offering just the hint of a smile, then shrugged.

She hurried down the steps, rushing right up to the horse and throwing her arms around her neck. "Oh, Cathy ... Cathy," she murmured. The mare bobbed her head, as if in agreement with Heather's unrestrained joy.

Tanner's voice was laced with dry amusement. "The vicar drives a hard bargain, but I felt the mare was a necessary addition to the GlenRoyal stables."

Her joy dissipated as he spoke. The GlenRoyal stables. Cathy belonged to the duke, not to her. Just one more thing he'd taken from her. Just one more reason to hate and despise him. Bitterness burned her throat.

"Allow me, Miss FitzHugh."

He lifted her onto the saddle as if she were as light as a feather. The warmth of his hands lingered on her waist long after he'd released her and turned to mount his own horse.

Try as she might, Heather couldn't hold onto her anger once they cantered away from Beckworth House. It felt too glorious to be out riding again, the sun on her face, the breeze tugging at her bonnet, the fresh fragrance of green grass and dark earth filling her nostrils.

And for today, at least, Cathy was hers again.

"You could never have done so well if you'd attended every rout and soiree in London, Hawk." Lynette watched as Edward, Celeste, Sainsbury, and Heather trotted their horses back to the blankets spread in the shade of a tall tree. "She's perfectly lovely."

"Yes, she is," he replied, listening to Heather's laughter over something Edward had said.

"She's nothing at all like Judith, and I needn't tell you how I felt about that match."

His jaw tightened as he stared at the woman.

"Pray, your grace, don't try to terrorize me with one of your icy looks. We've known each other too long, and I'm completely immune to them. Besides, I find it frightfully tedious to tiptoe around the subject all the time." She patted her abundant auburn hair, slipping an errant strand back into the bun she wore at her nape.

Tanner found it more prudent to remain silent than to reply, especially now that Heather and the others had returned.

"Splendid countryside, Hawk," Edward announced as he helped Celeste to the ground. "You must have us up again when we can stay longer. The place is teeming with wildlife."

Celeste smiled at Edward before settling gracefully onto the blanket beside Lynette. "Miss Fitz-Hugh has been sharing so many delightful stories about the area. She has kept us in stitches throughout our ride. She must tell you about the time her boat sank when she and her brother were fishing on the lake."

As Tanner helped Heather down from Cathy's back, he noticed the pleased flush on her face. He, too, was pleased. Edward and the others all seemed to like her, and Heather appeared at ease with them now, although she certainly hadn't been so at first.

That left only his mother to give her stamp of approval, and he wasn't concerned about that meeting. He knew for certain that the dowager duchess would take to Heather. He couldn't imagine anyone not finding Heather a most charming creature, just as he did.

Well, he thought, mentally shoring up his courage, he supposed there was no reason to delay speaking to her any longer. "I feel a need to stretch my legs. Will you walk with me, Miss FitzHugh?"

"If you wish, your grace," she replied softly.

He offered his arm, and she slipped her hand into place. They strolled across the meadow, always in view of the others, yet far beyond their hearing.

Tanner was surprised to find himself uncertain as to how to proceed. Once upon a time, when he was younger and foolish and yearning for love, he had spouted sonnets and sworn devotion. But he didn't mean to delude her. He was making an honest offer, based upon his regard for her. He would not promise more than he could give.

"Miss FitzHugh ..." He stopped and turned to look at her. "May I call you Heather?"

Her gaze seemed to be fastened upon his chest. "If you like, your grace."

"I should also like it if you would call me Tanner."

Her eyes flicked up to meet his. "Oh, I couldn't. It wouldn't be proper, your grace."

Damn! This wasn't going at all as he'd planned. He certainly hadn't expected to find himself tongue-tied. "It would be proper ... if we were to ..."

Her violet eyes widened, clear and deep and questioning.

He tried again. "Heather, I told you at the ball that I am seeking a wife. It has occurred to me that we have gotten on quite well together. At least until you knew I was the duke."

"I suppose my anger wasn't entirely reasonable," she said when he paused. "It was not your fault I was trespassing on your lands or that I mistook your name when I first heard it. I suppose you thought that your reasons for not revealing yourself to me sooner were sound."

"Very sensible of you." He was glad she'd come to such a logical conclusion. It only proved that he'd been right about her intelligence.

She replied with a deadpan expression. "I can be quite sensible, your grace."

"Yes. Well ..." He cleared his throat and started again. "What I'm trying to say, Heather, is that I should like to offer for you. I mean to ask your uncle for your hand in marriage, if you're agreeable."

She stepped back from him. He wasn't sure if it was simply surprise he saw on her face or something a little closer to despair. "Marriage?" she whispered.

"Yes."

"I think I should make a very poor duchess,

your grace. I'm not acquainted with Society. I'm
afraid I should embarrass you at every turn."

"I'm not interested in your acquaintance with
Society. That's one of the reasons I have chosen
you. 'Tis how well *we* get on that's important,
nothing more."

She turned her back to him and wandered a few
steps away. "You know who I am, of course. You
know that GlenRoyal was once my home."

"Yes."

"My father died in disgrace."

"The baron is not the first man to have lost his
money and lands in the clubs and gaming hells of
London. But you needn't worry. No one would
ever dare to speak ill of your father in my presence if you agree to become my bride."

"Do you remember my brother?"

Tanner shook his head, although she wasn't
looking at him. "Your brother? The brother you
said had left England?"

"He's the only brother I have." She turned
around, but her face was hidden in the shadows of
her bonnet. The silence seemed fraught with emotion. "His name is George. George FitzHugh."

"I'm sorry, I don't recall ever meeting him. Were
we supposed to know each other? Did we become
acquainted in school perhaps?" He racked his
brain for some memory of the fellow but found
none.

"No." She turned her back to him once more.
"No, George left a long time ago. I don't suppose
you would remember him, even if you'd ever
met."

Tanner waited, uncertain why she was talking
about her brother. At first, he'd thought she would
want him to apply for her hand with George. Now
he didn't know what to think.

He didn't even remember George. He'd shot the

boy and then forgotten him. How could he be so callous?

She swallowed back the urge to rage against him. Now was not the time. Not when things were going so well. She would remember the letter from the sixteen-year-old boy with a bullet wound in his leg later, when she had more time. Now she had to play her part for Tanner, and she had to play it convincingly.

She still found it hard to believe that he had proposed so soon. She'd been fairly certain of his attraction to her, but she never would have guessed he would fall so quickly into her plan for revenge. However, he'd caught her unprepared with his offer of marriage, and her response had proved it.

It was true, she would most certainly make a poor wife. She would make an even worse duchess. But she shouldn't have said so to Tanner, especially since she had no intention of becoming either.

She drew a deep breath to steady herself, then faced him once more. She looked him straight in the eye, never faltering beneath his watchful gaze. "You do not love me, your grace," she stated simply.

His brows narrowed.

"Then I should like to know what you would expect from me as your wife." She rather enjoyed the look of consternation on his face as she consciously kept her own expression as innocent as she knew how. "Besides a son, of course."

He appeared nonplussed.

"Am I to run your home? See to entertaining your guests? Will you expect me to spend time with you, or will my time be my own until you send for me? I understand you will expect me to provide you with a son, but what else will I be to you?"

"You'll be my wife, damn it!" he exclaimed. Then he pressed his lips together, as if regretting his outburst. He clasped his hands behind his back as he glared at her.

Heather lowered her eyes to the ground. "Please be patient with me, your grace," she said softly. "I've never received an offer of marriage before. I certainly never expected one from a duke."

"Heather . . ."

She glanced up as he moved toward her.

"Heather, I would expect you to behave as my wife and nothing more." He tenderly took hold of her hand. "I would be kind to you."

There was a strange tightening in her chest. She felt as if she'd been spinning in circles, arms flung wide, just as she'd done as a child. She was finding it difficult to think what her plan would require for her to say next.

"I want nothing more than your pledge to be faithful to me," he continued in a hushed voice.

She gazed up into his eyes, speaking without forethought. Speaking honestly from her heart. "I always thought I should love my husband and he should love me."

Immediately, his expression became stonelike. "This is reality, Heather. We may not love each other, but we get along well enough."

She stared at him for a moment longer, then turned and walked away, needing some distance between them. Breathing deeply as she tried to steady her reeling senses, she reminded herself once again what she had set out to accomplish.

Finally, she faced him. Her voice calm, she said, "I should like to make one request before I agree to marry you, your grace."

"And what is that?"

"I should like a Season in London before the wedding. I should like to go to routs and wear pretty clothes and meet the people I've only heard about. I should like to know that I can be a proper duchess for you. Will you allow me that? Will you provide me with a Season?"

Even when he scowled, he was handsome, she thought. It was a look she had better get used to. If her plan for revenge was successful, she would be seeing plenty of scowls.

Tanner stepped forward. His voice was low when he spoke. "Does it mean so very much to you?"

"Yes, Tanner, it does. Very much, indeed."

"Then I will see that you have your Season. I will arrange for you to stay with Lady Moberly. I believe you would find that more ... comfortable than staying with your aunt and cousin."

She wished he wasn't being so considerate. It made it difficult for her to remember how very much she despised him.

"You're frowning, my dear. Is there something else?"

"Yes. Yes, there is one more thing. I should like to keep our engagement a secret."

Hell! she swore silently, not even surprised by the uncharacteristic curse. What had possessed her to ask such a thing? Keeping their engagement a secret was not part of her original plan. Now she had to think of a plausible reason for her request.

"I'm afraid I can't agree to that," Tanner answered. "I'll not have every young swain in London fawning over my intended. Besides, I mean to see a great deal of you, and if it is not known that we're engaged, there will be talk."

The reasons came to her as if inspired. "Please, Tanner. What if I should prove a dismal failure? What if I should embarrass you terribly? I know you say you don't care about my acquaintance with Society, but I do. You are the Duke of Hawksbury, and I cannot forget that. The *ton* certainly will not. If I fail, it will be much simpler to break off the engagement if no one else knows about it. I could just return to Westmorland with no one the wiser."

There. That seemed very logical and convincing. Untrue, since she intended to break off the engagement in the most public of ways; she wanted simply *everyone* to know about it. But still, her argument sounded legitimate.

Tanner shook his head.

"There is another reason," she said quickly, not realizing immediately that she spoke the truth from her heart. "I would not want people accepting me because of you. I should like to prove to myself that I can became a part of Society." She could tell from his expression that he was wavering. "For just two weeks? Could we keep it a secret for just two weeks?"

She hated to acknowledge how much she wanted to be liked and accepted by the *ton*. To avoid facing that fact, she silently reasoned that those two weeks could be very useful to her. She could find more ways to spend his fortune. She could use that time to learn how best to humiliate him in front of his friends and peers.

Tanner let out an exasperated sigh. "All right, Heather. Two weeks. But we will begin planning the wedding at once. My mother must know our plans. The wedding will take place in July."

"July? But that's so soon."

"July. That's long enough."

Two months wasn't very long. She had so much to accomplish before then.

Tanner clasped her elbow. "I'll speak to your uncle this afternoon."

Heather didn't know how Tanner had managed it. Not only had Uncle Frederick agreed to the betrothal, but he'd also agreed to keep the matter confidential until Tanner advised him otherwise. He was not even to tell Aunt Caroline.

Three days later, Heather walked down the steps toward Lynette Moberly's phaeton, ready to begin the long trip to London. She was relieved to be on her way. She had been the recipient of many angry glances since Uncle Frederick's announcement that she had been invited to London for the Season as the guest of Lady Moberly. Her last days at Beckworth House had been more unpleasant than usual.

"Where is your abigail?" Lynette asked as Heather settled herself in the light carriage.

"I haven't an abigail."

The lady raised an eyebrow in surprise.

Heather shrugged. "I've never had need of one. I rarely attend any of Aunt Caroline's entertainments when they're here in the country. Mary, the chambermaid, has always helped me with altering and mending, and I'm perfectly capable of dressing myself."

"Oh, dear," Lynette responded. "And I sent my Emily on with Celeste so this phaeton wouldn't be overly crowded. It is uncomfortably small, but 'tis all Hawk could obtain at so late an hour. I am afraid we shall have to make do until we reach Town."

"Celeste isn't traveling with us?" Heather was not only disappointed but alarmed. She'd hoped to be able to sit quietly and listen to the two women chatter and gossip during the journey to London. She had hoped to become a little more enlightened regarding the Season and the *ton*. She had even hoped to learn a bit more about Tanner and his family through some careful questioning.

Now, without Celeste along, she feared *she* would be the one subjected to all sorts of questions. Questions about herself. Questions she didn't feel ready or willing to answer. Perhaps they could convince Celeste to join them once they met up with the other carriage.

"Celeste left with the others—" Lynette stopped suddenly as she watched a footman approach the vehicle. "Good heavens! Is that the extent of your luggage? That small trunk?"

Heather nodded and mumbled her affirmation.

"Whatever could your aunt be thinking of to send you off for the Season with so few gowns?" Lynette sounded appalled. "Well, 'tis clear our first priority will be a visit to my modiste in London."

Heather glanced out the door, her gaze fastened on the front of the house where her aunt and cousin stood watching. "I'm afraid Uncle Frederick would never authorize the expense, Lady Moberly."

"Heather . . ." The lady's voice was kind but stern.

Heather turned to look at her.

"I am perfectly aware of your arrangement with Hawksbury. He will be responsible for all your necessities and has given me carte blanche to see that you have absolutely everything you need."

Once again Heather had been caught unawares by Tanner. Even before she could ask for—or even demand—a new wardrobe, Tanner had provided it for her. Where would be the sport in spending his money if it came to her so easily? She would have to think on the matter.

"And you needn't worry," Lynette continued. "I shall not reveal your secret to anyone."

"Lady Moberly, I—"

Lynette leaned forward and laid her hand over Heather's. "My dear, I insist we dispense with the formalities. I intend for us to become great friends. I am Lynette, not Lady Moberly. And, of course, I shall call you Heather."

The phaeton jerked forward, causing Lynette to pause and steady herself. When the vehicle settled into a more comfortable rhythm, she continued speaking as if no time at all had passed.

"Also," she said, "I want you to know how very splendid I think this match will be. Tanner has needed just such a woman as you in his life. Do you know, since coming to GlenRoyal I've seen his first honest smile in years." She tilted her head to one side as she perused Heather. "And that, my dear, was when he was with you."

Heather's heart was beating an erratic cadence in her chest. She played no part when she replied, "He hasn't made such a splendid match, Lady Moberly—"

"Lynette."

"Lynette," she said. "I'm afraid I shall make a dreadful wife."

"Nonsense. All you need do is love Tanner, and he shall be the happiest man on earth."

Heather felt the blood draining from her head and feared her guilty intentions could be seen on her face. She quickly trained her eyes out the window on the passing landscape.

Love Tanner? She couldn't ever love Tanner. She didn't mean for him to be happy. She meant to make him rue the day he'd ever come to GlenRoyal and met Miss Heather FitzHugh in his gardens. If it was the last thing she did, she meant to make a fool of him before the *ton*.

She ruthlessly squelched the guilt that plagued her conscience. She would do all that she'd planned. She didn't care what happened to her after that.

Chapter 11

"**H**ere we are," Lynette announced several days later. "Albany House."

Heather followed her companion out of the light carriage. A dull lump formed in her stomach as her gaze took in the enormous edifice before her. She should have expected something so grand, but she hadn't.

Three stories tall, the exterior of Albany House was faced with Bath stone and giant pillars. The main portion of the mansion was five bays wide. A statue in the park across the street cast a long shadow over the curving marble stairway that led to the front door. Noise from the busy London street filled the air.

"*This* is your home?" she asked softly.

Lynette's laughter chimed merrily. "Oh, heavens, no! Mine is ever so much smaller. I could never have a supper party for more than one hundred, and even that would be terribly crowded. No, Heather, this is Albany House. Residence of his grace, the Duke of Hawksbury, whenever he can force himself to remain in London, and very soon to be your home."

The lump in Heather's stomach turned to lead.

"Come along, my dear. Hawk told me to bring you straight here when we arrived in Town."

There was little Heather could do but follow her companion from the phaeton.

She'd been surprised to learn that Tanner, along with Edward and Lord Sainsbury, had accompanied Celeste and Lady Moberly's abigail back to London two days before Heather left Beckworth House. Illogically, she'd also been irritated that he'd gone off without at least a word of farewell for her. She shouldn't have felt that way, of course. She shouldn't care what he chose to do. Besides, it had been much more pleasant traveling alone with Lynette, although she hadn't expected it to be so at first.

But now the journey was over, and she was about to see Tanner again.

"I should have liked to go home first to freshen up," Lynette said as they climbed the stairs side by side, "but one prefers not to cross his grace when he issues such a direct command. Hawk can be terribly grumpy." She flashed a smile at Heather. "But you know that, don't you, my dear?"

Heather nodded, then realized he'd never really been grumpy with her. He'd always been rather kind and—

The front door opened before them.

"Good day, Pengelly." Lynette glided into the hall even as she whipped off her bonnet.

"Good day, Lady Moberly."

Heather could only stare at the giant of a man who so carefully accepted the frilly bonnet from Lynette, followed by her cloak. He was close to six and a half feet tall, and his body beneath his dark suit coat and trousers resembled marble more than man. His hair was the color of ink, his eyes equally black.

"Pengelly, this is Miss FitzHugh. She's going to be staying with me until the wedding."

Heather shot the older woman a warning glance.

"Oh, my dear, you needn't worry. Pengelly knows everything about his grace and is as trustworthy as a man comes. He's been with Hawk for years. Haven't you, Pengelly?"

"Yes, my lady." He held out his hand to take Heather's cloak.

Heather had a hard time imagining this titan as anybody's butler or majordomo. Field at Beckworth House—now *he* was a butler. Even Thorpe, Tanner's valet, could pass for one. But not this man. He would more easily be mistaken for a pirate or a highwayman.

"His grace is in the drawing room," Pengelly said in his deep, gravelly voice.

Lynette drew Heather toward the stairway. She leaned her head toward her and spoke in a confidential whisper. "No one knows anything about Pengelly except that he and Hawk served together on the Continent, fighting that dreadful little Corsican. 'Tis said that if the truth were ever told, they both would be quite the heroes. But Hawk chooses not to discuss it. 'Tis my opinion that Pengelly saved his life." She shrugged. "Whatever the cause, Pengelly is far more than Hawk's servant. He is a trusted friend."

"Lady Moberly," Pengelly interrupted from the base of the stairs.

In unison with Lynette, Heather turned to look down on him. She couldn't be certain, but there seemed to be a twinkle of mischief in his black eyes, which was totally incongruous with the harshness of his features.

"You might like to know that his grace has been rather anxious about your arrival ever since he returned from Essex with the duchess. Totally out of sorts."

Lynette grinned. "Sophia is here already? Oh, how simply marvelous. Come along, Heather, dear. You're about to meet your future mother-in-law. You'll get on with her swimmingly. I just know it."

The lead in her stomach changed into a raging storm, but Heather did her best to keep it from showing on her face. Everything depended upon her ability to hide her true feelings. She hadn't come this far to fail so soon.

What sort of woman would Tanner's mother, the widow of Nicholas Montgomery, be? she wondered. Heather couldn't help but envision Sophia just as she did the woman's husband—dishonest and heartless, wicked and cruel. Surely she would have to be like that to have lived with such a man. Would she also be shrewd enough to see through Heather's ruse?

Heather unconsciously straightened her spine and lifted her chin. She refused to give in to her nervousness. She *would* fool the dowager duchess just as she had fooled her son. Heather would make Sophia believe that she was as innocent and naive as Tanner thought her, as innocent and naive as she had truly been such a short time ago.

Drawing a deep breath, she entered the room at Lynette's side, satisfied that she had concealed her trepidation.

She looked as if she were going to be sick.

Tanner was unable to tear his gaze away from Heather even long enough to welcome Lynette. Although obviously frightened and nervous, despite being weary from the long journey, regardless of the drabness of her faded brown traveling dress, she looked utterly charming, entirely beautiful.

He realized with some alarm that he'd missed her.

Tanner stepped away from the fireplace mantel and crossed the expanse of the drawing room. "Welcome to Albany House," he said as he took

Heather's hand and raise it to his lips. He continued to hold her fingers even as he straightened, staring intently down at her.

"I suppose if I simply stand here without a word, I shall never get a welcome," Lynette complained lightly.

"Welcome, Lady Moberly." He didn't bother to look at her.

The humor was gone when she continued. "Good heavens, Hawk. You order us to appear here without a moment to freshen ourselves or rest. The least you can do is allow us to sit down. We are chilled to the bone by this gray weather."

"Of course. Come over by the fire. Was it a pleasant journey?" he asked Heather.

"I enjoyed it very much." Her voice was soft and low.

Tanner had almost forgotten how much he liked the sound of her voice. Its carefree tone always warmed and soothed him.

She allowed him to guide her across the room without watching where she was going. She was too busy looking all around her, taking in the ornate decor.

He imagined Heather, the Duchess of Hawksbury, sharing tea with her guests in this room. She would smile sweetly and speak softly, and all of London would be enchanted with her. He didn't acknowledge his own enchantment.

"It's been so many years since I was in London," she said, breaking into his musings. "I'd forgotten . . . I never imagined it was this . . . *big*."

After GlenRoyal and Beckworth House, Albany House *would* seem a bit overwhelming, he supposed. He could only imagine what her reaction to Hawksbury Park would be. In fact, he could hardly wait to take her there. He was anxious to see her face as she surveyed the enormous, multilevel stone building. The Park had over a hundred rooms in its main block and family wing alone. GlenRoyal would fit into just the servants' wing.

But he would have to wait for the pleasure of taking Heather to Hawksbury Park. Right now, he wanted only to reassure her that all was well. He led her to a settee close to the fireplace, hoping that the warmth of the fire would bring some color back into her face.

"Pengelly said Sophia is here." Lynette sank gracefully into a nearby chair. "I thought she had decided to tarry at the Park until later in the Season."

He motioned to the settee and waited until Heather was likewise seated before answering. "She had a change of heart," he said to Lynette, then turned his gaze upon Heather. "The duchess should be joining us soon. Mother enjoys taking tea each afternoon about this time."

Tanner thought Heather's complexion turned a bit grayer as he spoke. So that was it. She was worried about meeting his mother. Well, she wouldn't be the first young lady to cower unnecessarily in Sophia's presence. Still, he wished he could do something to set her mind at ease.

He moved to stand behind the settee and laid his hand gently on her shoulder.

She felt his touch everywhere. Not simply on her shoulder, but throughout her body. Even her lips tingled, as if he'd just kissed her. Everything else fled from her mind: the overwhelming grandeur of this room, this house, London, everything. There was only Tanner and his hand on her shoulder, and the desire to turn her head and look up into his face and to—

It was at that moment that the dowager duchess entered the drawing room. The uproar started again in Heather's belly, and her awareness of Tanner evaporated.

Sophia Montgomery was wearing a silver gown that accentuated her tall, statuesque form. Her posture was straight and proud, her head held high. She smiled gently as she crossed the room.

"Good afternoon, Mother." Tanner stepped around the settee and kissed the woman's cheek as he took her outstretched hand, then escorted her to a chair. "You look rested."

"Of course." Her gray eyes moved quickly to Heather. "You should have informed me that we had guests. Lynette, I trust you enjoyed your sojourn in the country."

"Thoroughly, your grace." Lynette grinned. "'Twas a most satisfying experience. I shall tell you about it at length sometime."

With the attention turned from her, Heather relaxed slightly. She used the opportunity to study Tanner's mother. She certainly wasn't the gargoyle that Heather had expected.

Despite her silver hair and a few creases around her eyes and mouth, Sophia certainly didn't appear old. Nor did she seem as frightening as Heather had thought a dowager duchess would be. Sophia Montgomery bore a striking resemblance to her son with her patrician features and regal posture, but her mouth seemed more prone to smiles than Tanner's.

Heather wondered if the woman would like her. It was ridiculous, of course, but she hoped the dowager duchess would, at least a little.

Sophia returned her gaze suddenly to Heather. "So you are Tanner's Miss FitzHugh? 'Tis a pleasure to meet you, my dear. Please forgive me for ignoring you. I thought I should give you a moment to look me over, discover for yourself that I am not too insufferable or some sort of dragon lady."

"Your grace," Heather began, alarmed and

embarrassed—for those had been her thoughts before seeing her, "I never . . ."

Sophia leaned forward and patted Heather's hand. "Meeting your intended's mother is always difficult, child. I remember well enough when it happened to me. And as I recall, Nicholas's mother was most certainly a dragon lady."

Lynette and Tanner both laughed, but Heather wasn't sure if the woman was teasing or not. Besides, the comment had reminded her of why she was there—to hurt this family as they had hurt hers. She was there to take back from them a little of what had once been the FitzHughs'. She was in the lair of the enemy and must not forget it.

She would not allow herself to be beguiled by Sophia any more than she was beguiled by her lying, scheming son. If the woman had recognized her fears so easily, then Heather knew she had to work harder to disguise her feelings. She would learn the art of deceit and learn it well. She needed only to observe Tanner for lessons in dishonesty.

"Tanner, take Lynette and find something to do while this charming girl and I become acquainted." The dowager duchess flipped her fingertips at her son.

Lynette rose from her chair. She slipped her hand into Tanner's arm as she looked down at Heather, speaking in a stage whisper. "Have courage, Heather. And shout if you need my help. I'll come quickly to your rescue."

"Be gone, Lynette," Sophia snapped, but the twinkle remained in her eyes.

Heather's gaze followed Tanner and Lynette from the room.

"There. We are alone. Ever so much nicer." Sophia sighed and relaxed against the back of her chair. "Now, tell me about yourself, Heather."

"There is little to tell," she answered softly, on guard despite the woman's friendly tone.

"Nonsense. There must be a great deal to tell, or you never would have captured my son's interest. It hasn't been easy to involve him in matrimony a second time."

Heather's eyes widened. "A second time?"

"Oh, my," Sophia responded, then gave another deep sigh. "He hasn't told you about his first wife?"

Heather shook her head. Her thoughts of revenge were momentarily forgotten, replaced by curiosity. He'd been married before? Was his wife the woman who had played him the fool?

Sophia glanced toward the fire. "It should come from him, my dear, but I will tell you this. Judith died seven months after she and Tanner were wed. Theirs was not a happy union. My son still harbors resentment, not just toward his first wife but against our gender as a whole. I have great hope that you will be able to change that."

Heather thought she saw a glimmer of tears in the woman's eyes. Instinctively, she wished she could offer some comfort. Then she steeled herself against such a desire. If she had her way, if her plan succeeded, she would be causing Sophia Montgomery and her son a great deal more anxiety in the coming weeks. Heather could not allow herself to be weakened at the sight of tears.

"I hope you will give him back some faith and trust. Perhaps you can teach him to love again."

Heather's heart tightened painfully as she clenched her hands in her lap. She didn't dare meet the woman's gaze. If she did, Sophia would know instantly that Heather had no intention of giving Tanner any of the things she hoped for. Instead, Heather meant to give him even more reason to resent and distrust women.

* * *

Sophia drew a deep breath as satisfaction
warmed her. Before the girl had dropped her gaze
to her lap, she had seen what she had hoped for.
Heather was nervous and frightened and unsure
of herself, but one emotion had been clearest of all.
Heather FitzHugh was in love with Tanner.

But Sophia had also recognized a flash of hostility in Heather's beautiful eyes. Why? she wondered. Why would that be so if the girl loved her
son? And she was absolutely certain that Heather
did indeed love Tanner.

She settled against the cushions at her back.
This matter would take some study, she decided.

"Tell me about Westmorland," she encouraged
gently. "I remember that when Nicholas first went
up there he couldn't stop talking about the rugged
beauty of the place."

"It is beautiful. Very beautiful." Heather didn't
look up.

"Tanner told me you live with your aunt."

"Yes."

The girl wasn't going to make this easy, was
she? Well, Sophia Montgomery had never been
one to give up without a fight. She would find a
way to make Heather open up.

"GlenRoyal was your home, wasn't it?"

Heather's head came up and their eyes met. Her
ivory complexion was dotted with two bright
patches of pink on her cheekbones. Her violet eyes
snapped with anger. "Yes."

Ah . . . so that was it. She resented the loss of
her home to the Montgomerys. Well, it was understandable. She wondered if Tanner was aware of
Heather's feelings. She supposed he must be, but
she doubted he'd had the good sense to talk about
it with the girl.

"Let's not be coy with one another, Heather, my
dear. I'm sure it must be difficult for you, knowing
that your father lost your home to my husband in

a game of chance. I'm sure it must have been very troublesome for everyone in your family when that happened."

The color vanished from Heather's cheeks.

"I remember it all. Nicholas told me your father had taken terrible losses at the table, but he insisted on playing another game. He demanded that Nicholas accept the deed to GlenRoyal as his wager. My husband tried to reason with him, but the baron would not be dissuaded." Sophia sighed. "Of course, there was nothing Nicholas could do afterward but accept the deed. Your father's pride wouldn't have allowed Nicholas to refuse GlenRoyal. A gentleman always pays a debt of honor, and your father was a gentleman."

Heather fought the tears that welled up in her eyes. Sophia's words had been filled with kindness and compassion, but Heather wanted neither of those things from her. Nor did she want to hear that her father had recklessly gambled away GlenRoyal. She knew better. George had told her how the Duke of Hawksbury had cheated her father by using loaded dice. She knew the truth and wasn't going to be fooled by Sophia's lies. That was all they were. Just more lies.

She swallowed her hot tears. "Yes, my father *was* a gentleman," she said, her voice proud and strong.

"You were very young when he died."

"I was ten."

"I'm so sorry, my dear. I recall how sudden it was. It must have been painful for you and your family."

Heather swallowed again and nodded, fighting her reaction to the woman's sympathetic tone and the tender concern in her gray eyes.

The dowager duchess leaned forward and patted Heather's hand as she had done once before. When she straightened, she said, "Why don't we talk of something more pleasant? Tanner tells me the wedding will be in July at Hawksbury Park. We have much to accomplish in the coming weeks, my dear."

Heather nodded. The dowager duchess was right. She did have much to accomplish in the coming weeks, and she was beginning to fear it might not be as easy as she had hoped.

Tanner paced the halls and gallery of Albany House for over an hour, waiting for his mother to summon him back to the drawing room. When she finally did, he returned quickly, dragging a protesting Lynette with him.

Sophia glanced up as he entered the room. He saw the pleased look in her eyes, and some of his tension eased. He'd known his mother would like Heather.

"I wondered when you'd have the good sense to join us, Tanner," she said, amusement lingering in her voice. "I'm surprised I had to send for you. You must realize that Lynette and Heather are exhausted after their long journey. One never sleeps well in those dreadful inns." She rose from her chair, drawing Heather up with her, and kissed the girl's cheek. "It shall be my pleasure to call you daughter, my dear. I shall see you again soon." The dowager duchess said her farewell to Lynette, then patted her son's arm. "See them to their carriage, Tanner."

It was the sort of command even he didn't disobey. He felt an odd frustration. He hadn't had more than a moment alone with Heather since she'd arrived, and already she was leaving. At the very least, they should have had some time to discuss the ball the dowager duchess was going to give at Albany House the night they announced their engagement.

"Give us a few days to get organized before you

come calling, Hawk," Lynette said as he helped her into the carriage behind Heather. "We don't want you hovering around, or everyone will suspect your interest in Heather before we're ready to announce it."

"A few days?" he said.

But before he could protest further, Lynette pulled the carriage door closed and commanded the driver to move on. Tanner was left standing in front of Albany House, feeling annoyed and strangely alone.

Chapter 12

"**Z**ounds, man! You haven't heard a bloody word I've said."

Edward's sharp tone brought Tanner's attention abruptly back from the window. "Sorry, Mannington. What was it you were saying?"

"Never mind. I highly doubt it would do any good to repeat myself. Your mind's far from here."

The two men were seated near the bow window at Boodle's, No. 28 St. James's Street. Known for its sumptuous fare, the club was humming busily with the voices of men as they partook of their midday meals.

Tanner stared pointedly across the table at his friend. "You have my full attention."

"Do I?" Edward grinned. "I wouldn't put the ready on it. Why don't you spill the soup? You'd much rather be sitting in Lynette's salon than here, and you'd rather be looking at Miss FitzHugh than at me."

"I assure you, I'm perfectly content to be where I am." He frowned meaningfully at his friend, then focused upon the beefsteak on his plate.

"Hmm. Then you wouldn't care to know that three ladies of our acquaintance will be shopping in Covent Garden this afternoon. Seems a certain Miss FitzHugh is sadly lacking in the necessities, and Lady Moberly and Lady Celeste have made it their personal cause to see that this wrong is righted in due haste."

Tanner attacked his thick steak with a knife, wondering irritably how it was that Edward knew so much about Heather's activities when he'd been kept in the dark. Was Lynette playing hostess to others even though she'd told Tanner to stay away for a few days?

"Wouldn't be much out of our way to pass through Leicester Square, you know. You could do a bit of shopping yourself. Miss FitzHugh might enjoy a bauble or two that you'd picked out for her. She strikes me as being the romantic type."

Tanner grunted a response. Just what he didn't need. A romantic bride. Thank goodness Miss FitzHugh understood completely what he wanted and expected in their marriage. Romantic nonsense wasn't part of it.

"All right. You've convinced me. You're not interested in seeing Miss FitzHugh before the Haversham Ball tomorrow night. Can I interest you in a game of faro, then?"

Tanner shook his head. "I've got business to attend to this afternoon. I'm afraid you'll have to find your own diversions."

The store clerk hovered at Heather's right elbow while she perused the jewelry on the table before her.

"Might I suggest this necklace, Miss FitzHugh? The diamonds are exquisitely cut, and the emeralds are flawless. I can assure you that you won't find a finer piece anywhere in London."

"It is very lovely," Heather admitted, wondering what the necklace must cost. The price had to be exorbitant. She glanced over her left shoulder at Lynette. "What do you think?"

"I think it would be perfect with that green evening gown we ordered yesterday."

Heather turned back to the clerk. "Are there earbobs to go with it?"

"Of course. Of course. Just a moment." He scurried away.

Heather looked at Lynette again, whispering, "This must be a very costly piece. Do you think Tanner will—"

"Don't worry about Tanner. He wants you to have whatever you need."

"But do I need—"

"Of course you do." Lynette's eyebrows arched in surprise. "You're going to be his duchess."

Feeling strangely frustrated, Heather nodded as her gaze returned to the sparkling gems laid out before her.

At first it had been great fun to go shopping, knowing that the bills from the modiste and the milliner and the jeweler were adding up quickly. In the past few days, she'd spent more money than it had cost her uncle to operate his estate in the past year.

She'd waited eagerly to hear from Tanner. She'd expected him to come barging into Lynette's town house, complaining about Heather's extravagant purchases, but he hadn't come. Lynette seemed to think her expenditures ordinary and unexceptional, even when Heather chose to buy the most costly items or when she ordered far more of any one item than she would ever need.

She picked up the necklace, allowing it to slide through her fingers like a glittering waterfall. It *was* beautiful. She had never imagined wearing anything like it. But how often did a woman wear a piece like this? Four, perhaps five times a year? Certainly not more if she bought jewelry for every dress she owned.

And Heather would certainly have enough of those. Since arriving in London, she'd spent hours upon hours with Lynette's modiste. She'd ordered carriage dresses and dinner dresses, evening dresses and full evening dresses. She'd selected garden and morning and opera and promenade dresses. She'd chosen riding dresses and theater dresses and walking dresses.

And along with the multitude of gowns, there were the matching slippers, bonnets, reticules, fans, jewelry, and whatever other gimcracks, gewgaws, and fripperies Lynette insisted upon.

Surely, Heather thought, it was far more than any one woman could use in a lifetime, let alone in just a single Season.

And still the duke hadn't objected.

Heather set her jaw as the clerk returned with a pair of sparkling diamond earbobs. Her eyes narrowed.

Well, there was no fun in recklessly spending the duke's money if he didn't complain. Obviously, she would have to buy more, even if the endless shopping was losing its appeal.

"I'll take them, sir," she said to the clerk with a firm nod of her head. "And the sapphire set as well."

There. *That* should get his attention.

Tanner didn't allow himself to think about the direction his cab was taking. He hadn't lied to Edward. He did have business to attend to, and he'd meant to order the driver to take him to Albany House. Still, when he'd entered the cab moments before, he'd told the driver to take him to Leicester Square.

Now he sat on the edge of the seat, looking out the window, watching for a familiar carriage pulled by a pair of matched grays.

More importantly, he watched for Heather.

Lynette's footman struggled out of the Grafton House, his arms laden with packages. Moments later, Heather, Lynette, and Celeste stepped through the shop's doorway and onto the walk.

Lynette pointed down the street. "There's a wonderful little millinery just around the corner. They make the most divine creations. You're going to love them, Heather. I've been eyeing a little straw bonnet for two weeks now, and I think it's time I bought it before someone else does."

Heather tried to ignore her tired feet and the slight ache in the small of her back. It seemed as if they'd been shopping since sunup rather than all afternoon. Perhaps it wasn't even the shopping that had frayed her nerves as much as the people she'd met. In just a few hours, she'd been introduced to at least a dozen of Society's matrons and a few of their husbands. She'd been eyed through quizzing glasses, asked pointed questions about her family, and forced to endure speculation about why they'd never seen her before. She'd felt like a show horse at an auction. She'd fully expected someone to demand that she open her mouth so they could examine her teeth.

She glanced sideways at her companions. Both were wearing excited expressions, both obviously enjoying every minute of their outing. But Heather was tired, and her temper was growing short.

"Lynette," she said, stopping stubbornly beside the Moberly coach, "I think I'll just stay here in the carriage. You and Celeste go on."

"My dear, we couldn't possibly—"

"Please. I don't mind waiting. I am exhausted and want to catch my breath. I've already purchased three new bonnets and don't care to look at more. At least not today. I'll be perfectly content in the carriage."

Lynette looked doubtful.

"Pray," Heather insisted, "go buy that new straw bonnet, and allow me to sit and rest."

"Well . . . we won't be but a short while."

Heather waved them on. She watched the two women disappear around the corner, then turned to enter the coach with the help of the footman.

The crack of a whip and a cry of pain caused her to turn sharply. As she looked around her, the sounds carried to her again. She moved in their direction, stopping as she came abreast of an alleyway. As she did so, she saw a whip slashing across the rump of a swaybacked dray horse. The animal squealed as it strained against a heavily laden cart.

"Ya bleedin' nabob. Gi' on wi' ya, or I'll flail the hide from yer bleedin' bony back." The drayman let fly with the whip once again.

Heather turned into the alley without a thought for anything except helping the poor, beaten horse. "You, sir!" she shouted. "Stop that at once."

The drayman appeared half again as big as she and easily outweighed her by five stone. He glanced at her as if she were no more than a pesky fly, then raised the whip again. Another squeal of pain escaped the animal as the thick lash creased its matted coat.

"Stop, I said!"

The drayman's bushy dark brows arched over eyes wide with surprise. He smirked and offered a mock bow in her direction. "Pardon me, yer ladyship, but I've work t'be done. I've no time fer a coze wi' the likes o' you."

Heather bristled with anger. "Put that whip down at once, sir, or I shall summon someone to take it from you. Have you no decency? Can't you see the animal is beyond pulling such a heavy load? You'll kill him if you persist."

"Aye, I may kill 'im, but 'e's mine t'kill if I'm a mind to." He coiled the whip as he spoke, preparing to use it again.

Heather jumped forward and grabbed the end of the whip before the man could draw it to him. She held onto it tightly. "I cannot allow you to abuse this horse further, sir. What will you take for him?"

"You want t'buy this rack o' bones?" The drayman looked at her as if she were mad.

"Yes. What price do you ask for him?"

The man continued to stare at her, slowly shaking his head. She was certain he would turn her down. If he did, she didn't know what she would do.

"What price, sir?" she demanded.

"What would I do wi' me cart wi'out me 'orse?" he countered.

Without any warning, he jerked the whip from her hand, causing her to stumble forward. She nearly lost her balance, then caught herself by grabbing for the horse's harness. From the corner of her eye she saw the man take a threatening step toward her.

"Do it, and you'll not live to see nightfall."

Heather sucked in a startled breath as she turned toward the sound of Tanner's voice. He was glaring at the drayman, his arms crossed over his chest, his legs braced apart. His expression was set in a cold, calculating mask.

"Step back from the lady," he warned.

"Ye've got no right t'come in 'ere an' interfere in a man's—"

Tanner took a step forward. "The lady asked how much you wanted for the horse. Speak up, man, before I lose my temper."

The man's face reddened with anger as he glanced from Tanner to Heather and back again. "I'll take fifty guineas."

"Fifty!" Tanner snorted. "The animal's not worth two."

"Me cart's no use wi'out me 'orse. Ye'll take it all or nothin'. Ye'll not cheat me out o' me due. Either gi' me the blunt or leave me t'me work."

Without forethought, Heather stepped toward

Tanner and laid a hand on his arm. Her eyes pleaded with him, although she remained silent.

"Do you know where White's Club is?"

The drayman nodded.

"Meet me out front in one hour. I'll have your fifty guineas for you."

With a tip of his scruffy hat and a smile on his once frowning face, the man hurried out of the alley. A heartbeat later, Heather stepped back from Tanner and waited to feel the full force of his anger.

"It was a foolish thing you did," he finally said, his voice low.

"I know." Heather began to shake as the realization of just how foolish she'd been overwhelmed her. "It all happened so quickly. I couldn't let him go on striking the poor animal."

Tanner's gaze flicked to the horse. "Fifty guineas." His voice was laced with disgust. "I'll be lucky if he doesn't die before I get him to Albany House."

Heather turned to look at the animal. He stood with his head slung low. His ribs and hip bones appeared ready to poke through his hide. His coat was matted with clumps of mud. His tail was a mass of knots, tangled with straw.

"Perhaps he won't look so bad after a good brushing," she said hopefully.

There was a lengthy silence, then Tanner laughed. She stared at him, surprised by the sound. She'd been prepared for a thorough tongue-lashing.

"Come along, Heather. I'd best get you out of here before we are seen. We could never explain why we were alone in an alley. Then I'll take care of your new steed and chariot."

As his fingers closed around her arm, her pulse quickened. "Thank you for saving him," she said softly.

It made no sense, of course, but the broken-down nag meant more to her than anything else she'd purchased that day.

Tanner escorted her back to the Moberly carriage. He had a few choice words to share with the footman for allowing Heather to wander off that way, unprotected. If he hadn't been alighting from his cab at just that moment, Tanner probably wouldn't have seen her slip into the alley. He wouldn't have been there to stop that bloody drayman from threatening her with his whip, from laying his filthy hands on her, from . . .

He frowned down at her. "What was Lynette thinking, allowing you to take the carriage out alone?"

"I'm not alone. Lady Moberly and Celeste are with me. But I was tired and meant to rest in it while they went to the millinery shop. Then I heard the horse cry in pain and went to see what was wrong." Her wide eyes pleaded with him to understand.

It was difficult to remain stern when she looked at him that way, but somehow he managed. "I want your word that you won't do anything like that again, Heather," he said, his tone brooking no argument. He pulled open the carriage door before the footman could move to do so for him. He shot the servant a furious glance, then helped Heather inside. "You're not in Westmorland any longer. It isn't safe for you to wander about alone in London."

"I know. If I hadn't heard the horse scream . . ." She shook her head, gazing all the while at the carriage floor. "I give you my word I won't do it again."

He leaned against the side of the coach and regarded her. She did look repentant. He relaxed a little. Nothing untoward had happened this time, and she'd given him her word to be more careful.

She glanced up. Her violet eyes seemed enormous in her exquisite face. By gad, he'd missed looking at her.

"How did you happen to see me?"

Her question brought him up short. Irritation followed quickly upon the heels of surprise. There he stood, for all the world to see, casting sheep's eyes upon Heather in the midst of a busy London street. The next thing he knew, folks would be saying he smelled of April and May. They would think him in love with Heather FitzHugh.

"I just happened by," Tanner answered gruffly, unwilling to admit he'd been looking for her. "And now I'm late for an appointment. Good day, Miss FitzHugh." He stepped back and closed the carriage door.

"Good day, your grace." Was that disappointment he heard in her voice?

He spun on his heel and strode quickly away before he could linger long enough to find out.

Chapter 13

Could she believe her eyes? Was that girl in the mirror really Heather FitzHugh? No. It couldn't be.

Where was the unruly mop of black hair, nearly always covered by a straw bonnet with wild ribbons trailing from the brim? Where was the old, ill-fitting gown? Where was the girl who preferred the company of a chestnut mare and a big red dog to a roomful of people?

It surely wasn't the girl she saw reflected in the mirror.

Heather's hair shimmered in the lamplight, framing her face in perfect curls. The bonnet had been replaced by a spray of lavender flowers near one temple, and tiny amethysts dangled from her earlobes. The high-waisted gown was a deep purple that glistened and rustled whenever she moved. The modestly scooped neckline, trimmed with small lavender flowers and glossy ribbons, accentuated the fullness of her breasts. Matching slippers peeked from beneath the hem of the skirt, and a purple ribbon, caught with a sparkling amethyst pin, garnished her slender throat.

"Absolutely smashing!" Lynette exclaimed as she walked around Heather, her green eyes carefully assessing her from every angle. "There won't be another young lady at the Haversham Ball to equal you, my dear. What a splendid debut you shall make. Hawksbury shall be absolutely *green* when all the men are clustering about you to make your acquaintance." She laughed as she fell back into a chair. "How brilliant you were to make him keep your betrothal a secret, even for a short time. You'll have him fit for Bedlam in those two weeks."

"That wasn't why I did it," Heather responded, remembering the afternoon Tanner had proposed.

Then she thought about what Lynette had just said. No, it wasn't why she'd done it, but it *was* a brilliant idea. She tilted her head as she smiled coyly at her reflection in the mirror. Could she carry it off? Could she make Tanner jealous by flirting with other men?

She faced Lynette. "Do you suppose Tanner would really be upset if other men found me attractive?"

"Of course he will." Lynette clapped her hands together. "And it will do him good, too. Hawk is much too set on getting his own way. He *should* be brought down a notch or two. You're good for him, Heather. I've known it from the first moment I laid eyes on you."

Heather frowned as she met the other woman's gaze. "I just hope I don't embarrass everyone who's been so kind to me."

Lynette's smile changed slightly, from one of bright good humor to one of encouragement. "You needn't worry. Just be yourself, and everyone will love you."

Heather nodded even as she felt a lump forming in her throat. She'd never had a woman friend before—beyond the servants at Beckworth House—and the past week with Lynette Moberly had been a wonderful experience. The woman was a good twenty years older, but that didn't seem to matter. She was so alive, and full of zest and good will. It was such a change from Aunt Caroline and Annabella.

Heather wished she didn't have to deceive Lynette this way. The woman was going to hate her when her plan was complete, and she couldn't really blame her. She'd taken Lynette's friendship under false pretenses.

She turned away, unable to meet Lynette's eyes any longer, certain that her friend would be able to read the guilt and would know what was wrong.

"Well, I must go finish my own preparations. Thomas shall be coming for us soon. Lord Sainsbury has never been known for his patience, but 'tis all bluster."

Lynette's abigail followed her mistress from the bedchamber, closing the door behind her. Silence filled the room as Heather's gaze returned to the mirror.

Would Tanner be jealous when he saw her with other men?

No. She was letting Lynette's prattle go to her head. Tanner wasn't in love with her. He'd chosen her because he thought they should get on tolerably well, perhaps even because he thought she would give him reasonably handsome children. He'd chosen her because she was ignorant of Society's ways, and he thought he could easily control her. He'd chosen her because he was certain she would never play him for the fool.

Well, he was going to find out differently.

"I'm doing what I can, Papa," she whispered. "I hope I'm doing what's right."

A short time later, the two women climbed into Lord Sainsbury's carriage, and the matched set of palominos trotted off into the night. Heather listened while Lynette chatted with Thomas Sainsbury, but she didn't actually hear the words.

She was concentrating too hard on not breaking into nervous tears.

Tanner was standing with his back to the staircase, accepting a glass of champagne from a liveried servant. He saw the gentleman in front of him lean to one side, his gaze fastened in the distance, frankly appreciative. He heard a woman off to his left whisper, "Who is she?" and another respond, "I've never seen her before."

He knew without looking that Heather had arrived.

He turned slowly, his cool gaze sweeping over the inhabitants of the massive ballroom. By the time he was facing the staircase, it was clear there wasn't a person in the room who hadn't noticed the new arrival and who wasn't now trying to guess her identity.

It was no wonder, he thought when he saw her for himself.

Dressed in shimmering purple, she descended the stairs with an air of sublime confidence. He thought of the young lady he'd first seen, chasing a large red setter through the gardens in search of a straw bonnet. He thought of the same lady climbing a tree, her skirts tucked up at her waist, trying to rescue a kitten. There was no glimmer of that green girl in the poised beauty he saw now. Even her short curls, not really the thing, seemed unquestionably perfect.

Their eyes met above the heads of the crowd as Tanner began making his way forward. He felt a sudden need to touch her, to be certain she was real. He wanted to make it known that she belonged to him.

"Hawksbury," Lynette said as he approached, "you remember our Miss FitzHugh."

"I do, indeed. In fact, I planned to ask the lady

to reserve the waltz for me." He bowed before her. "Will you do me the honor, Miss FitzHugh?"

Heather inclined her head as her long ebony lashes brushed her cheeks, hiding her violet eyes. "Of course, your grace."

"I look forward to it," he said softly—and discovered he meant it. When they were wed, he could claim every one of her dances. By heaven, he wouldn't let another man dance with her after this night. He would insist that they let it be known they were betrothed.

Lynette was already moving away, pulling Heather with her. "There's Lord and Lady Smythe. They give the most wonderful musicales. Come along, Heather."

Tanner was left standing at the base of the stairs, feeling once again as if he'd been robbed.

As he watched, Heather was besieged by men, all of them clamoring for introductions. He saw them bowing over her hand and looking hopefully into her beautiful face. He saw her toss back her head, heard her captivating laughter in response to something one of them said. He watched as she was drawn farther and farther away from him. Then he saw her give a nod to one of her many admirers, and moments later she was led onto the dance floor.

Damnation! He didn't care for this by half. He'd finally chosen someone to be his bride, and now he was forced to keep silent while every young buck and Bond Street fribble bowed and scraped and sought her favor.

"You look in an exceedingly foul mood, Tanner."

He turned toward Edward's voice.

"Looks as though Heather is going to be the darling of the Season. Strange, I wouldn't have thought it when she swooned at your little ball at GlenRoyal. Shy as a church mouse then, but by heaven, look at her now."

Tanner didn't want to look at her. He was having enough trouble controlling his ill temper. "Let's find the Havershams' card room, shall we, Mannington?"

Heather's head was filled with a dizzying swirl of names and faces and flattering comments. She'd already danced more dances and sipped from more glasses of punch than she'd imagined possible in one night. The glittering success of her coming out left her reeling with euphoria.

To think she'd always told Annabella she wasn't interested in a Season in Town. To think she'd thought herself content to stay in Westmorland and marry a tradesman or a farmer, and never know that splendor such as this existed.

To think she owed this night to Hawksbury.

Again her eyes searched the ballroom for a glimpse of his golden head. She hadn't seen him even once since her arrival. She shouldn't have cared, but unconsciously, she recognized that her pleasure was dimmed by his absence.

"But tell us, Miss FitzHugh," said a young lady seated on her left, bringing her attention back to those around her, "what did you do when you found the fox?"

"I wrapped her in my coat and took her to safety."

"You don't mean to tell us you actually picked up that wild animal?" The expression on the girl's face was both horrified and incredulous.

"I had to. Her leg was broken. She had no way to protect herself," Heather answered. "If I hadn't acted quickly, the hunters would have found her."

"Weren't you afraid?"

Heather smiled as she remembered her panic that windy afternoon, the baying hounds drawing closer with each passing heartbeat. "Not of the fox," she answered truthfully. "I was more afraid of what the hunters would do to me if they found out I'd ruined their sport."

"Bless me, I can imagine you'd have such fears," exclaimed an indignant gentleman. "I've never heard such rot. You're lucky you weren't thrashed. Ruining a perfectly good hunt . . ."

She stiffened and faced the man with an unwavering glare. "What's so perfectly good about watching a small fox being torn limb from limb by a pack of hounds just so the first man on the scene can have its brush? 'Tis not very sporting in my opinion."

The man's face turned scarlet.

"Put that way, it does sound unfair," another man stated smoothly.

She flashed him a grateful smile, trying desperately to remember his name. Tall, thin, blond. A viscount, she thought. No, the son of a viscount. And he had a pretty sister as well. Chapman. Phillip Chapman. And his sister's name was Patricia.

"Exceedingly unfair, Mr. Chapman. And I'm happy to know you see the truth of it." She lowered her voice. "You are an exceptional gentleman, sir."

He beamed, obviously pleased by her compliment.

Flirting was much easier than she'd expected it to be, Heather thought, especially when everyone was so friendly and attentive. They actually made her feel pretty and important. She wondered if Tanner could be won with a smile, a pair of fluttering lashes, a lowered voice.

"But do tell us, Miss FitzHugh," someone else interjected, "what did you do with the creature after you wrapped it in your coat?"

She pushed thoughts of Tanner out of her head as her gaze swept over the sea of faces surrounding her. "I took her to the groundskeeper at

GlenRoyal, a neighboring estate. Mr. Haskin has a special knack with animals. He set the fox's leg and nursed her back to health."

"And did anyone ever find you out?" Mr. Chapman inquired.

Heather shook her head, grinning impishly.

A pretty brunette turned to the man at her side. "I cannot imagine doing anything so adventurous. I would never be brave enough to do such a thing on my own. Saving a fox from the hounds. Imagine!"

Her escort patted her hand. "I would never allow you to put yourself in such danger, Dorthea."

Dorthea blushed prettily, and Heather wondered if she could learn to blush at will as she suspected Dorthea did.

"I find your story as charming as I find you," a deep voice said from behind her.

She twisted on her chair and lifted her gaze to stare into a pair of black eyes capped by thick brows. She remembered the man from an earlier introduction. He was not the sort to be easily forgotten.

Aaron St. Clair, the Marquess of Stroughton, was not tall, yet he gave an impression of size. He was darkly handsome with a square, unrelenting jaw. He was stylishly attired in a red dress coat, a white waistcoat, and tight black pantaloons which clearly defined his muscular calves and thighs.

St. Clair glanced at the man seated next to Heather and, a moment later, sat down in the vacated chair. "Could I be fortunate enough to find an empty place on your dance card, Miss Fitz-Hugh?"

She shook her head. "I'm sorry, sir. There isn't a dance which is not spoken for."

From the corner of her eye she thought she saw Tanner standing on the staircase. Was he watching her? Did he see her sitting so close to another man? Was he filled with jealousy?

Just in case it was Tanner, she smiled at St. Clair as she leaned toward him. "I am surprised, my lord, that you have any free dances. I was certain you must be sought after by every young lady here."

"I dance with whomever I wish."

She wanted to turn her head. She wanted to see if Tanner was watching, but she didn't dare. She didn't want him to think she might be looking for him, that she might care what he saw.

She tilted her head and lowered her eyes, then peeked up at St. Clair through long lashes. "And you wish to dance with me? I am flattered, my lord, and disappointed that it cannot be. Perhaps at another ball?"

"I shall make it a point to see that it happens."

A shiver ran through her when he smiled. It wasn't a friendly smile, and it left her feeling cold and unsure of herself.

"Enjoy the ball, Miss FitzHugh. I will see you again soon." He rose and disappeared into the crowd.

Heather tried to hide her apprehension. There was no reason to feel this sense of distrust, yet instinctively she knew St. Clair was not the sort of man she should flirt with unless she earnestly sought his attentions.

"May I get you a glass of punch, Miss Fitz-Hugh?"

She turned to look into the florid face of a young man with an exaggerated starched collar. "Thank you, Mr.—" She searched her memory for his name.

"Higginbottom," he supplied.

"Mr. Higginbottom." She offered a polite smile. "Thank you for offering, sir, but I am not thirsty."

"At any rate, 'tis time for the waltz, and Miss FitzHugh has promised it to me."

The crush of men and women around her fell slightly away.

Another shiver ran up Heather's back, but this one didn't frighten her. It was a pleasant sensation that left her heart racing in expectation. The noise of the ballroom seemed to recede as she looked into Tanner's cool, assessing eyes.

"Miss FitzHugh?" He held out his hand to her. Hawklike, he hovered above her, candlelight captured in the golden crown of his hair, and she could do little but accept her fate. She took his hand and allowed him to pull her to her feet.

The music began. There were hundreds of guests that night at the Haversham Ball, but it seemed for now there were only two. Tanner's hand on the small of her back was warm. His gaze seemed to hold hers in a hypnotic trance. Her feet seemed only to touch lightly on air.

Here in his arms, beneath his gaze, in the glitter of this room, it was easy to forget that she'd made an oath to seek revenge upon this man and his family. It was difficult to remember that she despised everything about him. Perhaps for this one night, it wasn't so terrible that she should forget. Just for this one night.

They moved about the ballroom, gliding effortlessly, golden bird and purple flower, the hawk soaring above the heather.

Chapter 14

"**S**o you make it your cause to rescue hurt foxes as well as orphaned kittens and old workhorses." His voice was teasing.

She flushed with chagrin. She didn't know what had possessed her to tell that story to a crowd of strangers. She'd kept it a secret since she was thirteen. There certainly hadn't been a need to tell anyone now. Perhaps she'd had too much punch to drink. She wasn't used to strong spirits, and her head felt light, her feet uncertain.

"Someone had to help," she answered meekly. "Her leg was broken. She couldn't run away."

"Do all animals earn your affection so quickly, Heather?"

His eyes were a wintry blue, yet they weren't really cold at all. Just intense. They always demanded such honesty from her.

"I can't stand to see them mistreated. I suppose it seems silly to you. You and your friends must all think me a cabbagehead."

"No one who is a friend of mine would ever think you a cabbagehead, Heather. And I certainly do not."

She *had* had too much punch. Her head was spinning madly. "I think I could use some fresh air," she whispered.

Scarcely had she spoken the words before Tanner had led her through the nearest doorway and out onto the terrace. She leaned against the iron railing and drew in a deep breath, allowing the cool night air to steady her reeling senses.

Even though Tanner remained a discreet distance from her, she felt surrounded by his presence. She would have sworn she could still feel his hand on her back. She could almost believe he still guided her effortlessly around the ballroom.

She looked up at him, and her breath caught in her throat. No wonder people stepped back when he approached. There was something about his stance, about his eyes, about the determined slash of his mouth, that forbade anyone to cross him. And yet she wasn't afraid of him. She felt drawn to him. Irresistibly, uncontrollably, drawn to him.

She took a step away from the railing.

"Have I told you how lovely you look tonight?" he asked as he moved forward to meet her.

She couldn't seem to reply.

"No, I didn't think so. You do, you know. Look very beautiful."

She had to remind herself to breathe. "'Tis kind of you to say so, your grace."

"Not kind. Merely truthful."

She felt the cool night breeze against her warm flesh and could almost imagine it was his hand that caressed her. She felt mesmerized by his eyes, liked the way he was looking at her. She particularly liked the way he was staring at her mouth, as if he might decide to kiss her.

Could she *make* him want to kiss her? Was that also within her power?

"Then I should be truthful, too, your grace," she said, her voice husky and low. "I find you very handsome."

His familiar half smile curved a corner of his mouth.

She lowered her head slightly and dropped her

gaze to the floor, then glanced up at him through her lashes. "I thought perhaps you were displeased with me. I haven't seen you since I arrived."

"How could I have reached you? You've been surrounded all evening."

He'd noticed! She hid her pleased reaction by facing away from him.

"Just remember that you're to be my duchess," he said, so low she almost couldn't hear him.

He stepped closer, his chest nearly touching her back. She felt his breath near her ear. Gooseflesh rose on her arm.

"I remember, Tanner." She swallowed. "'Tis why I'm here."

Hands on her shoulders, he turned her to face him. "Don't forget," he whispered, his index fingers slowly tracing the curve of her arms, "what it is I expect from you."

His touch set her insides afire. It was all she could do not to sway forward into his embrace. All thoughts of silly flirtations—with Tanner or any other man—fled her mind. This wasn't a game. This was real. The terrible wanting inside her was powerful, and she didn't know how to fight it.

"I haven't forgotten, my lord duke," she answered breathlessly. "You expect me to be your wife. You expect me to bear your son."

There was a new look in his eyes—hot and dangerous—that left her quaking inside. He was going to kiss her. *Now* he was going to kiss her.

"Here you are, Heather," Lynette said as she sailed onto the terrace. "I've been looking for you."

Heather couldn't even turn her head to look at Lynette. It was Tanner who stepped away from her, allowing the night air to sweep around her and dispel the magic that had held her captive, making her forget everything except Tanner, making her forget her true feelings about him.

"My dear, you're as pale as a ghost. Are you feeling all right?"

She glanced at Lynette, only to discover a number of other women standing in the open doorway behind her friend.

"She became overheated in the ballroom," Tanner answered in a quick, clipped voice. "She looked about to faint, so I brought her outside for some air." He moved toward the door. "But now that you're here, I will excuse myself." He stopped and looked back at Heather. "Thank you for the waltz, Miss FitzHugh. If you will allow it, I should like to call upon you at Lady Moberly's on the morrow."

"We'll be at home, Hawk," Lynette replied before Heather could.

Tanner nodded toward the ladies gathered near the doorway, then disappeared into the house.

Even the effects of the punch didn't make Heather immune to the censuring looks exchanged among the women. She might be ignorant about many things, but she knew it bordered on scandalous for her to have been outside alone with the duke for so long.

Had it been a long time? She couldn't be sure. It seemed that they'd stood there forever, not touching yet bound together by something unseen. At the same time, it had felt far too short. Another moment and he would have held her. Another second and he would have kissed her.

Perhaps it was a good thing Lynette had come when she had. Perhaps it was a good thing that all the ladies were there. There was no telling what he might have done, what she might have allowed him to do, if they hadn't been interrupted.

Celeste stepped out of the shadows on the edge of the terrace at just that moment, interrupting the awkward silence. "I'm sorry if we worried you, Lady Moberly. 'Twas I who suggested his grace escort Miss FitzHugh and me outside. In truth, it seemed frightfully stuffy to me as well." She shifted her gaze to the onlookers. "Lady Haversham would do well to throw open all these doors, don't you think? Such a crush! 'Tis the best ball I've attended this Season. Lady Milward, I am simply in a dither over Paulette's gown. Wherever did you get such a divine thing? I must tell my modiste about it."

Heather wasn't sure how it happened, but within moments Celeste had managed to turn the women's attention from her onto the glittering crowd of guests. A short time later, she and Lynette were alone on the terrace.

Lynette stepped forward. "You must remember, my dear, there are certain rules which must never be broken in our Society. If Hawk hasn't the sense to observe them, then you must remember them for him. Perhaps it seems silly to you, all this fuss over a few minutes alone on the terrace, especially after all the time you spent with Hawk at GlenRoyal. But if you're going to get along in Society, you will be expected to follow many silly rules. Now, come with me. We'd better go back inside. We'll thank Celeste for her little charade later."

Tanner was watching from the balcony when Lynette and Heather returned to the ballroom. He was angry with himself. He should have known better than to take her outside without a chaperon. He might not give a fig for what Society thought of him, but he wouldn't want Heather hurt by the gossipmongers who gleefully spread rumors over their scandal broth each afternoon.

"She's very pretty. Pray, tell me who she is, your

grace." Althea Rathdrum waved her ivory fan in front of her face as he turned toward her.

"She's a friend of Lady Moberly's."

"From the looks of all the young bucks hanging about, she'll have no difficulty snaring a husband before the Season is over."

Tanner set his jaw and remained silent. He didn't know whether to be amused or angered by her words. Althea was right, after all. Heather would have a husband by the end of the Season, but it wasn't going to be any of those fops and fools milling about her in the ballroom below.

Althea moved a step closer to him, then another. He had a splendid view of swelling breasts and cleavage, and well she knew it as she tapped his shoulder with her fan. "You needn't feel you must avoid me any longer, Hawk. I have forgiven you for the cruel things you said to me at my party. I know Kimbell should like to have you come 'round." She fluttered her eyelashes over sultry amber eyes. "I should like it, too."

Tanner mocked her with a cynical grin. "I can't recall what you have to forgive me for, Lady Merrywood, but you may do so if you wish."

She wasn't able to hide the flash of anger that flared in her eyes, but she collected herself quickly, smoothing her mouth into an inviting smile. "You don't want a silly green girl, my lord duke, when you could have a woman who would know how to please you."

Tanner cocked an eyebrow. "You presume to know what I want?"

"I know because I am that woman, your grace. You've always known it, too. That's why I forgive you for insulting me at my rout. That's why I would forgive you anything."

"There's only one problem with your presumption, Lady Merrywood. Besides your husband, of course. I meant every word I said. It would take more than you possess to tempt me into your web. You're a very attractive spider, my dear lady, but you *are* a spider."

Her face went white with rage. "How dare you say such a thing!" she whispered. "You'll regret your words, Hawk. There'll come a day when you'll know I'm right about us, and you'll regret your words."

"I doubt that very much, Countess." He bowed as he stepped back from her. "Enjoy the ball."

He walked away without another word, not caring that he left the woman fuming at both his rejection and his insults.

Heather didn't leave the Haversham ballroom until after three-thirty in the morning, and the crowd was so great that it took Lord Sainsbury almost another hour to retrieve his carriage. It mattered little to Heather. Her head was still buzzing with the excitement of her first London ball.

She hadn't seen Tanner since he'd left her on the terrace with Lynette. She'd been nervous for a long time after that, waiting for someone to give her the cut direct, but it hadn't happened. She knew she had Lynette and Celeste to thank for much of her success that night. Their approval went a long way with other members of the *ton*.

As she climbed into Lord Sainsbury's black-and-gold carriage and leaned against the plush seats, she closed her eyes and recalled the many people she'd met throughout the evening. But they all faded beyond the memory of Tanner, looking so tall and dashing and powerful. She felt again his arms holding her as they waltzed around the ballroom. Her blood warmed as she remembered that moment on the terrace, Tanner standing so close, his gaze so intense, when she'd known he was going to kiss her. She recalled his voice, telling her he would see her on the morrow. She couldn't help wondering just how early tomorrow he would come.

She never would have guessed he'd meant five o'clock in the morning.

Tanner rose from the chair in the hall as Lynette and Heather came through the doorway. When Heather saw him, she stopped suddenly, causing Lynette to collide against her back.

"Good morning," he said, watching Heather with a hooded gaze. "I trust the remainder of your evening was enjoyable."

Heather felt a surge of renewed excitement. She smiled and nodded.

"Good heavens!" Lynette snapped, stepping around Heather. "Have you taken complete leave of your senses, Hawk? Isn't it bad enough that you exposed her to criticism on the terrace? What do you think you're doing here at such an hour?"

"I needed to speak with Heather."

"Well, you shall just have to wait until a more reasonable hour to come calling. Heather has had a long and tiring night and needs her rest. I expect several invitations to arrive in tomorrow's post." She put her hands on Heather's shoulders. "Honestly, Hawk, even you should have better manners."

His brows drew in as he scowled at Lynette. "I need to speak with Heather. If you fear she'll be compromised, you may wait in the hall." His hand darted out to grab hold of Heather's wrist. With little effort, he pulled her after him into the withdrawing room.

She didn't know what to think about his actions. She didn't have time to worry about what his visit might mean.

He closed the door firmly, then spun her around to face him, his fingers locked on her arms. "Heather, this nonsense about our engagement must—" He stopped abruptly.

The withdrawing room was cast in shades of black and gray, the faint light of dawn—now streaking the morning sky beyond the windows—unable to combat the lingering of night in the small room. Still, Heather knew his eyes were upon her, boring down in that intent way of his. She could see the white of his cravat, the gold of his tawny hair.

"Bloody hell," he muttered, and drew her up against him.

The touch of his mouth against hers was like a match to a wick. A flame sprang instantly to life, spreading heat and light to the farthest points of her body. Her hands lifted instinctively to clutch behind his neck. Were they holding her upright or keeping her from soaring away in flights of ecstasy?

With his tongue, he tasted her lips, carefully teasing the tender flesh until she couldn't help but part them as a gasp escaped her throat. The tip of his tongue slid quickly inside, invading, sampling, delighting. He was warm and tasted slightly of port.

She shivered, and he drew her closer, crushing her against him. He felt so good against her, so solid—his chest, his stomach, his muscular thighs. She instinctively wanted to meld her softness to the unrelenting hardness of his body, yet was stymied by her own lack of understanding of what that meant. She whimpered in frustration.

His right hand slid down her arm, then moved to the small of her back. He pressed her against him for a brief moment before working his fingers up her side until they skimmed the fullness of her breast. She gasped again and, this time, tried to pull away.

He wouldn't let her. With merely the strength of his kiss, he held her captive. She felt as if she were melting, going all liquid inside. Finally, she didn't care if she *could* break away from him. All sanity was gone. She would stay like this forever if he wished it.

He didn't.

As abruptly as the kiss had begun, it ended. Tanner lifted his mouth from hers and set her back from him. When he spoke, his voice sounded hoarse and winded.

"I came to tell you I want our engagement to be announced at once."

She was surprised at her own breathlessness. "But we agreed . . ."

"It doesn't signify. You have proved a great success on your first outing of the Season, and that will only be strengthened by our alliance." His fingers tightened on her arms. "I won't have other men trying to win what is already mine."

She'd convinced herself that those two weeks of secrecy were important to her and to her plan for revenge. At this exact moment, she couldn't remember why. She couldn't remember anything with him standing so close, his kisses still causing her lips to tingle. She didn't even enjoy another moment of triumph at his apparent jealousy. There seemed to be something much more important happening between them. She wished she understood what it was.

A loud pounding sounded on the door behind her.

"Hawk! Heather!" Lynette called. "I've had enough of standing out here. Come out, I say."

"All right, Tanner," Heather whispered. "You may announce the betrothal as soon as you wish."

Chapter 15

She would have to be more cautious when she was with him, Heather thought the next afternoon as she sipped her tea, staring at Tanner over the rim of her cup.

He would have to keep his lust in check, Tanner mused as he looked into a pair of hypnotic violet eyes and felt renewed desire heating his blood.

It was just part of her plan, she reflected, noting the way the sunlight glinted on his hair. The kiss had served a purpose. He would trust her all the more now.

He wasn't sorry for the kiss, he decided, watching the gentle rise and fall of her breasts—and remembering the brief caress he'd stolen last night. She knew now that she belonged to him, and she'd obeyed him when he'd told her what he wanted. It was a good beginning.

Elizabeth Sloane's laughter broke into the silence as she and her mother were shown into the Moberly salon by the butler. Tanner wasn't pleased with the intrusion. He'd hoped to find some time alone with Heather. In truth, he'd hoped to steal another kiss.

"Lynette, how very good to see you," the countess gushed.

"Good day to you, Lady Blakesley. Good day, Elizabeth. You have met Miss FitzHugh, I trust."

"Yes," Elizabeth answered. "We met at the Havershams' last night." The girl's smile seemed to crack when she saw Tanner standing in a corner of the room. "Why, your grace, I didn't think to find you here."

"Nor I you, Lady Elizabeth." He'd risen from his chair as they'd entered the room, and now he bowed his head toward the countess. "Good day, Lady Blakesley."

Elizabeth glanced at Heather, her smile firmly back in place. "Mama and I just had to call to personally invite you to the soiree we're holding on Wednesday next. It will be a small and intimate gathering with just the sort of people you should meet during your visit to Town." Her brown eyes flicked toward Tanner. "You know, of course, that you are invited, your grace." Her voice was teasing, sultry, attempting to suggest far more than a mere invitation to a party.

He felt an icy calm as he watched the girl flirt with him, not so subtly using her female charms. "Whether I come will be entirely up to Miss Fitz-Hugh. I wouldn't think of leaving the future Duchess of Hawksbury unattended her first week in Town."

Elizabeth blanched. Her mouth worked, but she seemed unable to speak. She sank swiftly into the nearest wing chair.

The countess found her voice first. "What a surprise, your grace. We could see last night that Miss FitzHugh made a splendid debut, but we never expected anyone to move so quickly to claim her hand."

"I have been an acquaintance of Miss Fitz-Hugh's for some time now, Lady Blakesley, and have visited her in her family's home. I offered for her before she came to London with Lady Moberly, but she only agreed to an announcement of our betrothal last evening." He trained his gaze on Elizabeth's mother. "I'm a fortunate man. Don't you agree, Lady Blakesley?"

Lynette poured a cup of tea and handed it to the countess. "Hawk, be a dear and don't scowl at my guests. Lady Blakesley was merely surprised. After all, Miss FitzHugh is my very dear friend. Most people must assume I would have warned her off you. I confess, it has occurred to me more than once to prevail upon her to reconsider. I shall probably live to regret my decision not to interfere."

Hidden amidst her teasing words and playful tone, Lynette's message was made clear to everyone in the salon. She'd placed careful emphasis on the words *dear friend*, intimating a long association with Heather. Tanner silently blessed her for the deception. The countess and Lady Elizabeth would be eager to spread malicious gossip if they thought they could get away with it. But they would know better than to cast any sort of aspersions upon a good friend of Lady Moberly's, a friend who would one day be the Duchess of Hawksbury.

Lady Blakesley cleared her throat and smiled helplessly. "Lady Moberly is quite right. I think it is frightfully grand that you and Miss FitzHugh have come to an understanding. Have you decided when the wedding shall take place?"

It was Heather who answered. "July." Her eyes lifted, meeting Tanner's gaze. "Sometime in July."

He was proud of the confidence in her voice. He couldn't have helped but notice that she'd been momentarily shaken. It pleased him to know she hadn't let her panic linger and take hold.

Tanner took a step toward her chair. "We'll ride in the morning, Heather." He tried to offer her encouragement with his eyes.

"I look forward to it, your grace." She smiled at him.

By gad, her smile could light up a room. He would do well to remember that she was still a woman, for all her innocence and country charm.

He turned toward the others in the room. "Good afternoon, ladies. It's been a pleasure."

Heather's gaze remained on Tanner's back until he'd disappeared through the salon doorway. She didn't want to look at her visitors. She might be a cabbagehead from the country, but she recognized hostility when she saw it. Instinctively, she knew that Elizabeth Sloane was one of the young ladies Tanner had been referring to when he'd mentioned those hoping to help him decide on a wife.

Well, there was no getting around it. Lady Blakesley and her daughter wouldn't be the first of the *ton* to wonder about Heather's engagement to the powerful Duke of Hawksbury. She might as well get used to answering their indirect questions with oblique answers of her own.

She had just turned her head toward Elizabeth when further commotion sounded in the hall. Moments later, three more ladies were shown into the salon. She'd met them all at the Haversham Ball, and their greetings were interspersed with compliments on what a splendid come-out she'd enjoyed.

No sooner were the three of them seated than more guests arrived, and the ritual began again.

It was going to be a long afternoon.

Lynette groaned as she sank onto the settee near the window. "Oh, my dear," she said in an agonized tone, "I knew you would charm Society with your face and easy laughter, but I had no idea you would accomplish it in only one night."

Heather responded with a deep sigh.

"Overwhelmed?" Lynette asked, laughing softly.

"Yes. And I'm not so certain my success is assured. There was more than one person here this afternoon who wasn't entirely pleased with me. They resent me."

"Because you managed to snare one of the most handsome and wealthiest dukes in all of England? Good heavens, they're so envious they're beside themselves, and right they should be. By the end of this evening, the news of Hawksbury's engagement will have spread through every drawing room and club in London. There won't be an unattached lady or her mama who won't be weeping and gnashing her teeth over your good fortune. But they'll recover soon enough and set their sights elsewhere."

"I fear Lady Elizabeth won't ever forgive me."

Lynette waved her fingers in the air. "Pooh! The girl doesn't signify. Lady Elizabeth is a self-centered, artificial piece of baggage, but she's harmless enough. You needn't concern yourself over that one." She rose from the settee. "Now, I do believe we should lie down before we prepare for our round of engagements tonight."

Heather wished she could remain at home this evening. She was suddenly more exhausted than ever before in her life. Of course, she was being beef-witted. The chance to enjoy herself at the duke's expense had been one of the reasons she'd come to London. She couldn't very well accomplish her goal cloistered away in Lynette Moberly's town house.

"Oh, Mama! 'Tis so unfair." Annabella threw herself across the bed. "How could Papa do this to me?"

Caroline closed the door to the bedchamber and crossed the room to sit beside her daughter. "Don't be a goose, Annabella. Your father had little choice in the matter. He couldn't very well turn down the duke's offer."

Caroline sounded much more calm than she felt.

She was still reeling from the news of Heather's engagement to the duke. If Hawksbury hadn't sent his messenger to the Beckworths' town house this afternoon, just shortly after their arrival in London, heaven only knew when Frederick would have told her. Her husband had tried to explain that the duke had demanded his silence until told otherwise, but Caroline still found his actions unforgivable.

Nearly two weeks! The duke had offered for the chit nearly two weeks ago, and only now did Caroline learn of it. She could only hope it wasn't too late to repair the damage. She might yet be able to prevail upon Hawksbury's good sense, to show him what a poor choice he was making when someone like her Annabella was still unattached.

Annabella sat up quickly, her tears forgotten. "Pray tell me why Papa couldn't turn it down! You know Heather will make a perfectly dreadful duchess. She'll make a terrible fool of herself in no time."

"We must count on that, my darling daughter." Caroline smiled as she patted Annabella's knee.

"Yes." The girl's eyes widened as she stared at the viscountess with sudden understanding. "And perhaps *we* can help her along?"

Caroline rose from the bed and walked to the window, where she pushed aside the draperies to look out on the dreary London streets. She was still seething inside over Frederick's refusal to leave Westmorland until the middle of May. It was unthinkable that her daughter hadn't been here at the start of the Season. And now this. It was too much by half!

Her temper cooled a bit when she remembered the generous settlement the duke was making upon the Beckworths. Caroline was no fool. She would have to be very careful not to jeopardize the sudden windfall. If she couldn't supplant

Annabella for Heather, then she would have to
settle for being the aunt of a duchess, rather than
the mother of one.

But, of course, Caroline would never admit as
much to her daughter. "We haven't time for hysterics, Annabella." She let the drapes fall back in
place and turned from the window. "We must
make our plans carefully. Now, see that your abigail has your clothes laid out for tonight while I
learn what routs are available for us to attend."

"But, Mama, no one even knows we're in Town
yet."

"You leave that to me, my dear. Your mother is
not without influence. I'll obtain the necessary invitations."

Annabella pushed herself off the bed and
rushed to throw her arms around Caroline's waist.
"You really will help me marry the duke, won't
you, Mama?"

"I will do what I can, my child." Caroline
stroked the girl's golden hair. "Hawksbury would
be a fool not to choose you. I have raised you to
please the most eligible men on the marriage mart.
You were born to be a duchess." She smiled as she
set Annabella back from her. "And I have raised
you to be a duchess. A very beautiful duchess."

Annabella fluttered her eyelashes as she glanced
toward the mirror. She patted her curls in a ges-
ture of approval of what she saw reflected there.

"Now, child, do as I said. Prepare yourself for
this evening's entertainments while I think upon
what must be done to rectify your father's ill-
advised decision."

"I'm so very happy for you," Celeste whispered
as she embraced Heather. "I suspected his grace
felt a strong attraction to you, but I never guessed
he had already offered."

"How did you hear about it?"

"Oh, simply everyone who called on Mother and me today seemed to know." Celeste drew Heather toward the drawing room, leaving Lynette still talking to friends near the door. "I believe Lady Merrywood was the first to tell us the news. I shall never forgive Lynette for keeping it a secret from me. She's my godmother, after all, and you're my friend."

Heather felt as if all eyes were watching her entrance. It had been that way at every gathering they'd attended tonight. Everyone was curious about the little nobody who would one day be the Duchess of Hawksbury. They all wanted to ascertain what she'd done to make such a marvelous match. She felt as if they were trying to guess whether or not she'd entrapped the elusive duke with some wonderful scheme. Heather wasn't sure if she could stand up much longer under the scrutiny, but Lynette had promised that Jeffrey and Abbie Russell's soiree would be the last for the night.

"There's Lady Merrywood now," Celeste said in a confidential tone.

The woman walking across the far end of the room was strikingly beautiful. Only a few years older than Heather, she carried herself with an air of assurance. Diamonds glittered at her throat and on her wrists. Her dark brown hair was swept back from her face, making her large eyes seem even bigger.

"How would she have known about the engagement? I don't recall meeting her," Heather whispered back to Celeste.

"If I were you, I would avoid meeting her for as long as I could. Althea spent her first Season trying to capture the Duke of Hawksbury for herself. When she failed, she settled for the Earl of Merrywood." Celeste nodded toward a gathering of gentlemen on the opposite side of the room. "That's the earl there. The tall one in the center."

Heather couldn't imagine that the man Celeste indicated was married to Althea Rathdrum. He looked old enough to be the lady's grandfather.

"Old but very, very rich," Celeste said as if she'd read Heather's thoughts. "I'm sure she was hoping the earl would turn up his toes before now so she could have another go at his grace. I heard Merrywood was rather sickly when they wed, but he doesn't look at death's door to me. Amazingly hardy for a man his age."

"Surely she wouldn't wish her husband to meet with an untimely end?"

Celeste's laughter gurgled up from her throat. "Oh, Heather! You are monstrously naive, and I'm so terribly fond of you." She sobered quickly. "Do be careful of Lady Merrywood. She's not one to forgive your interference easily."

"But I've done nothing to her."

"I'm afraid Lady Merrywood won't see it that way, Heather. You've taken what she was determined to make hers. Just be warned."

Heather turned her glance upon the Countess of Merrywood again and felt a tiny shiver pass up her spine. Why would Tanner have chosen her when he could have had a beauty like Althea? The countess certainly would never be accused of being naive, even in the affectionate tone Celeste had used. Althea Rathdrum would never be afraid she would forget the dance steps and crush her partner's toes or worry that she would embarrass herself beyond measure in a hundred other ways. She would know all the proper people and all the right things to say.

Heather gave herself a mental shake, silently scolding herself. She had to remember why she was here and what was most important to her. While she wanted to enjoy herself—for she would never be able to show her face in Polite Society again once she was finished—her purpose was to become well known and well liked among the *ton* only so that her rejection of the duke would be all the more dramatic.

"You look lovely tonight, Heather."

She whirled around, her pulse quickening at the sight of him. Why did it seem he was forever surprising her, popping up out of nowhere when she least expected him?

"I was wondering if I would chance to see you before our ride tomorrow." One corner of Tanner's mouth lifted slightly.

"I was wondering the same," she replied with feigned calm, amazed to find that her words were true. She *had* been looking for him, just as she'd done at the Haversham Ball the night before and at every mansion and town house they'd passed through this evening.

He took her hand and placed it in the crook of his arm. It seemed a natural motion, as if they'd been doing it for years. She wasn't even aware of him leading her away from Celeste.

"That's an exquisite gown you're wearing."

She found his eyes perusing the low neckline. It was almost a physical caress. She remembered all too clearly the way his fingers had brushed against her breast last night, the way her pulse had quickened and her flesh tingled.

"I'm glad you like it," she responded, willfully repressing such thoughts. "The bill for it must already be on your desk at Albany House. I hope you are not shocked by the cost."

"'Twas worth whatever the price." He stopped, turning her toward him. His voice lowered. "I'm convinced I will always like what you are wearing, Heather ... even when it's nothing at all."

She felt the blush everywhere. She wanted to turn away from his purposeful gaze but seemed unable to move. Worse yet, she realized her heated reaction was less embarrassment than a thrilled sense of expectation. She wanted all the things his blue eyes promised. She wanted Tanner Montgomery.

He smiled seductively, then stepped back from her, his expression suddenly composed and enigmatic. "Would you honor your future husband with a dance, or is your card completely filled?"

It took her a moment to find her voice. "I only just arrived, your grace," she said at last.

"Then my timing was perfect, was it not? Shall we, my lady?"

He held out his arm to her again, and she took hold, trying to ignore the rapid beating of her heart.

Why, she wondered as she looked up into his enigmatic gaze, *did fate have to set me against you?*

Chapter 16

Tanner appeared at Lady Moberly's town house the next morning, long before the fashionable hour to go riding in Hyde Park. Even so, Heather had been dressed and waiting for him for more than an hour.

Tanner's gaze remained on his companion as they rode along the quiet London street, his eyes noting every detail of her winsome appearance. Behind them, Lynette's groom followed at a discreet distance, just as propriety demanded. Tanner would have liked to have Heather all to himself, but he'd known it would be useless to suggest such a thing to Lynette, not unless he'd wanted to sit through a lengthy lecture on the scandal such action would cause. And then the groom still would have followed them.

He might not be able to have her completely to himself, but at least he could enjoy gazing at her without a dozen other swells doing the same. She did look especially lovely today.

Her light wool spencer had burgundy epaulets on the shoulders and a matching braid border around the hem. The rose-colored riding dress, a shade lighter than its short-waisted jacket, brought out the faint flush in her cheeks and fit her delightfully female figure much better than the gray one she'd been forced to wear in Westmorland.

Her ebony hair curled impudently across her forehead, peeking from beneath the wine-colored bonnet which was secured beneath her chin with a pink ribbon.

Did she grow prettier every time he saw her? he wondered.

Nary another soul was in sight when they dismounted beside the Serpentine, then led their horses as they walked near the banks of the ornamental lake.

"'Tis rather like Westmorland here," Heather said, her eyes alight with pleasure. "I could almost forget I'm in London."

"Do you not like London?"

Her eyes were wide and clear. "Oh, I like it ever so much." Then she smiled and shrugged her shoulders. "But it can get wearisome, don't you think? There are so many things to do, so many people to see. The shopping, the routs and balls, the afternoon calls, always fussing over what you'll wear, hardly getting to bed before sunrise. There never seems to be a moment of peace in Town. 'Tis nice to have a moment of peace."

He knew exactly what she meant, but he'd never met a woman who felt that way—or would admit it if she did. Heather's candor brought a smile to his lips. "You will love Hawksbury Park."

"Yes," she said softly, her gaze returning to the lake. "Yes, I suppose I will."

There was something in her voice that caused him to stop. He reached out to touch her arm, turning her to face him. "What is it, Heather? What's wrong?"

"Nothing." She managed a weak smile.

"Haven't you learned you cannot hide your feelings from me? Tell me what it is."

"Nothing important. I just thought, no matter how grand Hawksbury Park is and how much I learn to love it, I shall miss GlenRoyal."

He wanted to wipe away the wistfulness in her eyes. He could not bear to see her sad. "There's no reason for you to miss it. We can visit GlenRoyal whenever you wish. My father loved the country up there and meant to make GlenRoyal his hunting lodge, a place to escape the excesses of Town. There's no reason we cannot do the same."

"How very fortunate for you and your father." She pulled her arm free and walked briskly away from him.

For a moment he was perplexed by her sudden anger. What had he said? He'd merely sought to comfort her, assure her that she wouldn't be exiled from GlenRoyal forever. And then he understood. He'd thought her resentment forgotten simply because she'd accepted his offer of marriage. That assumption had been a foolish one.

"Heather!" He started after her, his long strides eating up the ground between them. "Heather." He caught hold of her arm, once again causing her to stop, once again forcing her to face him. "Let's talk about GlenRoyal."

"What is there to talk about, your grace? It belongs to you, and you can do with it whatever you please." A glimmer of tears mixed with the flash of ire in her eyes. "What have I to say about it?"

"Do you know how the Montgomerys came to possess GlenRoyal?" he asked patiently.

She lifted her chin, her expression as hard as granite. "I know."

"What do you know?"

Her mouth was set in a stubborn line, and she didn't reply.

"You were what? Ten, eleven years old? It is easy to misunderstand things at that age. I was there, Heather. I saw what happened."

She didn't want to hear it. She didn't want to hear his lies.

"The baron gambled rashly all that night. His losses were excessive. I suspect they were far more than he could afford. When he demanded that my father accept GlenRoyal as his wager, Father tried to convince him to reconsider, to go home, but he wouldn't. He refused. I suppose he thought it was his only hope. He'd lost too much. Perhaps he couldn't pay his debts without winning it back. He was desperate to win, Heather."

She shook her head, silently denying what he was telling her.

"Afterward, Father tried to find some acceptable way to decline the estate, but FitzHugh wouldn't hear of it. He had a lot of pride, and he insisted on paying his debts of honor."

"Papa was a very honorable man," she whispered, remembering.

Tanner stepped closer. His hands closed gently over her upper arms. "Father didn't mean to take away your home, Heather. The baron gambled and he lost. You see it nightly in the clubs. A man isn't supposed to consider what he can afford. Money should mean nothing." His forefinger lifted her chin, causing her to meet his compassionate gaze. "They don't think about the wives and children who will suffer for it later."

There was a lump the size of a plum inside her throat. It made it impossible to speak, difficult to swallow.

She didn't want his tenderness, and she didn't want to believe him. George had told her what had happened. Nicholas Montgomery had cheated their father. He'd used loaded dice to take GlenRoyal away from the baron. *That* was the truth. It had to be.

"'Tis not all bad," Tanner added. "If it hadn't happened, we never would have met."

His kiss was feather-soft, as gentle as a summer breeze. There and then gone. It left her feeling more confused than ever. Nothing seemed so crystal clear at the moment. Nothing.

Without another word, Tanner guided her to her horse and lifted her onto the saddle.

I will not forget why I came to London, she thought, steeling herself against her response to Tanner's kiss.

A FitzHugh never breaks a FitzHugh oath. Her childish voice rang clear in her memory. How simple it had seemed to her then. If only it seemed as simple to her now.

By the time Heather and Tanner reached Rotten Row, the bridle path in Hyde Park, the *ton* had stirred from their homes. They were out in force, there to see and be seen. They strolled on foot, rode on horseback, and were pulled in fine carriages.

The solitude Tanner had enjoyed with Heather was lost in the hubbub. Time and again, the couple was accosted by one person after another—most of them men. As Tanner watched, Heather seemed to change before his eyes. She flirted and blushed and laughed with each and every one of them. Tanner's mood darkened accordingly.

"I say, Hawk," Edward Kennaway said as he pulled his high-spirited bay to a halt beside the couple. "This can't be Miss FitzHugh? Not the shy girl I saw swoon at GlenRoyal?"

"You know good and well it's Heather," Tanner replied in his most unfriendly tone.

"I understand congratulations are officially in order," Edward continued. "May I say, Miss FitzHugh, that Hawksbury is a lucky man."

She grinned at Edward. "Thank you, my lord. I only hope his grace will think so after July."

"I'd wager it would be his own fault if he didn't."

Tanner directed his darkest scowl at his friend, but the earl simply regarded him as if he didn't understand.

"Received your mother's invitation to Albany House next week. I suspect she didn't much care for you spoiling her announcement. She's waited a long time for this pleasure."

"It seems to me," Tanner said, nudging Rebellion forward along the path, "that we would be a much more intelligent society if we spent less time speculating on other people's business and more time on our own concerns." He arched a brow. "Say, isn't that Lady Celeste and her mother? I believe she's waving at you, Mannington. Don't hurt her feelings on our account. Be a good fellow and say hello to her for us."

Edward's laughter trailed behind him as he cantered toward the forest-green carriage.

"Let's get away from this crowd," Tanner said abruptly. "We'll take a short canter to those trees." With that, he set his heels to Rebellion's sides, and the gelding shot forward.

Tanner allowed his horse to stretch his stride for only a minute before checking the gelding's speed, easing back on the reins while glancing over his shoulder. Heather was right behind him. In fact, she showed no indication of likewise slowing her mount. Instead, she raced past him, her horse breaking into a full gallop.

He had a brief glimpse of a determined gleam in her eyes and knew she thought it a race. She galloped down the path, suddenly disappearing around the original destination.

Tanner felt a stab of alarm. These weren't the lonely fields of northern England. This was Hyde Park, filled with the members of the haut monde.

The park was too crowded for such reckless speed. There was no telling who or what might be beyond each obscured curve in the path. And Heather's mount was not the even-tempered Cathy who responded so willingly to her mistress's commands.

Once again he set his heels to the black gelding's sides. Rebellion's response was immediate. In the open, the black could have easily overtaken the sorrel gelding Heather was riding, but Tanner had to slow his horse every time the path took another turn, his way always shielded behind green trees and shrubbery.

He heard Heather's startled scream just before he turned the corner. Then he caught sight of the sorrel racing down the path, riderless, reins trailing like ribbons in a breeze. Heather was on the ground, two gentlemen bending over her crumpled form.

Tanner yanked Rebellion to a stop, vaulting from the saddle while the horse was still sliding on his haunches. "Out of my way!" he ordered.

The men fell back at the sound of his voice.

"Heather?" He knelt beside her.

"Oh, bother," she muttered as she sat up. "I wish we'd brought Cathy from GlenRoyal. She never would have shied so easily." She pushed her bonnet back into place on her head. "This park is far too crowded for a good race."

"You should have had more sense than to run off like that," he scolded.

With his help, she got to her feet, brushing at her grass-stained skirt, then unconsciously rubbed a spot on her thigh as she grimaced in pain. "As I recall, you started it, my lord duke." She glanced down the trail. "What happened to that blasted horse?"

"Your groom's gone after him, miss," one of the gentlemen answered.

Tanner watched as she turned toward the handsome young man and flashed one of her brilliant smiles. "I thank you, sir, for what you tried to do."

"My pleasure, miss. But you must be more careful."

Cold anger spread through Tanner. He revealed it in his voice. "I, too, thank you for trying to help. It wouldn't do to have my *bride* injured so close to our wedding. If I can ever repay you, just send word to Hawksbury Park."

The swell nodded quickly, then moved toward his own horse, not needing another hint that the Duke of Hawksbury wished him to leave. Shortly thereafter, the two men were cantering away.

"Really, Tanner, I don't see why you were so short with him. It wasn't his fault I nearly ran him down. He did everything he could to avoid calamity."

She was right, of course, but it didn't erase the way he'd felt when he'd seen her smiling at the fellow. It didn't change the anger that had been building in him ever since they'd arrived at Rotten Row and she'd begun flirting with every young blood who had tipped his hat and bidden her good day.

By gad, he never should have agreed to bring her to London. He should have obtained a special license, married her quickly, and taken her to Hawksbury Park posthaste. Damnation! He wasn't going to allow her to become enamored of her own feminine charms the way all the other prime articles of the beau monde were.

His hands clutched her shoulders as he drew her close. Her head fell back, and she stared up at him with bemused eyes.

"You are to be more careful, Miss FitzHugh. Do I make myself clear?"

She'd made him angry. Good. It was what she'd wanted to do. If he was angry with her, he wouldn't treat her with tenderness. He wouldn't kiss her. He wouldn't whisper his lies and confuse her. Anger was her best defense, and she meant to use it.

Before she could answer his stern command, the groom came trotting back, leading her errant gelding behind him. Tanner quietly took her over to the lathered animal. He put his hands on her waist, then paused. From the look in his eyes, she half expected him to kiss her again. But he didn't. After staring at her for a moment, he simply lifted her onto her sidesaddle.

"We'll *walk* back," he said before heading toward Rebellion.

She fought against her disappointment. She shouldn't be wanting his kisses. He was, after all, the enemy of the FitzHughs. Why, oh, why did she have to keep reminding herself of that fact?

She looked away as he swung onto his horse. He was far too handsome in his dark blue coat and trousers. She was becoming much too fond of looking at his finely chiseled features. It would be wise for her to forget the things she liked about the duke and remember the things she disliked.

I'm glad George didn't kill him.

She stared down at her hands, realizing how traitorous her thoughts were. George could have been killed. He was the one who had been shot. Tanner had wounded a mere boy. What kind of monster would agree to a duel with a lad of sixteen?

Except, try as she might, she couldn't think of Tanner as a monster. It was even hard to think of the Montgomerys as her enemies. She was no longer certain what had happened the night

GlenRoyal had been lost. Everything was so confused.

But she *was* glad George hadn't killed Tanner.

"Heather?"

She met the blue of his gaze, feeling the familiar quickening of her pulse.

"I'll send for Cathy at once. I don't want you using an unpredictable mount again."

"Thank you, your grace," she whispered—and silently cursed him for making it so difficult for her to keep a sacred promise made long ago.

Any chance of the day being redeemed was destroyed when Heather entered Lynette's town house to find Annabella and Aunt Caroline seated in the green salon.

The moment Lynette saw Heather's dusty, grass-stained outfit, she rose from her chair. "My dear, what happened?"

"I took a little tumble from my horse. Don't worry, Lynette, I'm unharmed."

"Except," Tanner interjected, "I fear this charming riding habit may be ruined."

Heather saw the look of fury in Annabella's eyes and couldn't help the impish impulse to cause her cousin further dismay. She looked up at the duke, who stood beside her, still holding her arm. "Perhaps I should have ordered more than one from Lady Moberly's excellent dressmaker."

"I would suggest you order at least a half dozen more, Miss FitzHugh. Remember, I've seen the willy-nilly way you ride." His comment was softened by an amused glimmer in his eyes and a gentle lift of his mouth.

"I shall make haste to do so at once," she replied with an answering smile.

"For heaven's sake, Heather!" Aunt Caroline exclaimed. "Has coming to Town cost you all your manners? Come over here and welcome your aunt and cousin at once."

She did as she was bidden, kissing Aunt Caroline's cheek, then greeting Annabella before settling onto the green brocade chair next to Lynette. Tanner followed behind her with polite words to both the ladies. Then he crossed the room to stand near the mantelpiece.

Heather didn't fail to notice the way Annabella's gaze greedily followed him, visually caressing him as he lounged against the wall. Heather had the most distressing desire to scratch her cousin's eyes out.

"Heather!" Her aunt's strident voice broke into her thoughts for the second time. "Are you certain you are unharmed? You seem to have lost your senses."

"I'm quite all right, Aunt Caroline."

"Then pay attention, child. I said Annabella and I should like to have you stay with us now that we're in London. With your engagement to his grace"—she smiled at Tanner—"it seems only right that you should be with our own family until the wedding."

Heather didn't know what to say. She didn't want to leave the friendly surroundings of Lynette's home. She didn't want to be subjected to Annabella's antics day and night. But what else could she do? She'd imposed on Lady Moberly long enough, and there was no excuse to remain now that her aunt was in Town. Besides, in two months, Lynette would despise the sight of her. Heather would be back in Westmorland—*if* the Beckworths would even give her a room after she was finished in London. She refused to consider what might happen to her if they refused to take her back into their home.

"I won't hear of Heather leaving me," Lynette said in her most peremptory yet gracious tone.

"My home is far too large for just me. I rattle around in it when I'm alone, and I enjoy Heather's company far too much to give her up."

"Besides," Tanner added, "I've asked Lady Moberly's help in planning the wedding. I think it better if Heather remains here."

The color was high in Aunt Caroline's cheeks. "Of course, your grace. If that is what you wish." She cleared her throat. "Well, then ... I suppose we shall have to settle for brief visits now and then. Why don't you come to tea tomorrow, Heather?"

She should be ashamed of herself for the urge to refuse her aunt's request. After all, except for George, the Beckworths were her only remaining family. "I would love to come, Aunt Caroline," she lied.

Annabella's expression smoothed into a smile. "That *is* a beautiful riding habit, Heather. Would you mind showing me what other gowns you've had made? Perhaps I will want to see Lady Moberly's modiste myself."

"Go along, girls." Aunt Caroline gave them a dismissive wave. "I will stay and keep company with his grace and Lady Moberly."

There was no polite way for Heather to escape the inevitable. As she rose from the chair, she glanced at Tanner and found that the amused twist of his mouth had increased.

'Tis easy for you to smile, your miserable grace, she thought, staring daggers at him. *Next time I'll send you off alone with Annabella and see how you like it.*

She wasn't certain, but she thought he grimaced, just as if he'd understood her thoughts.

Annabella played true to form. Once in Heather's bedchamber, she found fault with each and every one of the new gowns Madame Pritchett had designed. Heather held her tongue and reminded herself to be grateful that her cousin hadn't said anything regarding her engagement to the duke. She just didn't feel up to discussing that particular subject with Annabella.

Chapter 17

Heather thought she might scream at any moment. This was surely her punishment for taking such pleasure in the Haversham Ball—the glitter, the music, the dancing, the laughter—and reveling in all the attention paid to her ever since.

Here in the Beckworths' salon, in the full light of day, the London Season didn't seem nearly as wonderful.

Never had she been subjected to so many conceited dandies and self-absorbed beauties. What she wouldn't give to be back in Westmorland, strolling through the gardens at GlenRoyal and throwing a stick for Strawberry. Or perhaps hiking up her skirts and climbing an old tree where she could sit and read a book. Or maybe racing Cathy across empty fields and jumping a few hedges. Or even playing a game of chess with Tanner, a fire flickering on the hearth.

Oh, for the simplicity of the country.

"I trust you have been enjoying your first Season, Miss FitzHugh."

Heather turned toward the fellow near her left elbow. Ralph Waterford, heir to the Earl of Bainburrow, had arrived only a short time before and had made his way quickly to her side. Short and slight with a long, narrow face, he was dressed to the nines in a fuchsia frock coat, tight lime-green inexpressibles, a high starched collar, and all the prerequisite gems, fobs, and watches.

Searching for a polite way to tell the truth, she settled for "It's been unlike anything I might have dreamed."

"I say, I cannot imagine being stuck in the country and missing all this excitement."

"And I cannot imagine you in the country, sir," she responded, fighting the urge to giggle as she pictured the brightly dressed man scaring the livestock. "'Tis clear to me you were born for Society life."

Pleased by her comment, Waterford puffed up and preened like a peacock.

Annabella leaned forward in her chair. "My lord, you have no idea what we had to go through to get my cousin to leave our quaint estates in the north. 'Tis positively amazing that she managed to meet anyone at all, let alone to become engaged to the duke. One might question how she arranged it, mightn't one?"

Heather wondered if anyone else could hear the acid in her cousin's words.

"'Tis a pity for us that she did," Aaron St. Clair said from her right side. "I'm not the only man in Town who wishes I'd met her first."

Heather preferred not to turn toward St. Clair. She'd felt uncomfortable beneath his admiring scrutiny ever since he'd arrived at the Beckworth town house. While men like Ralph Waterford paid compliments only so they could get the same back, she was certain that a man like St. Clair, the Marquess of Stroughton, was not the type to waste words in such a game.

"Perhaps," he added, lowering his voice, "there's a chance you would cry off should you find someone more to your liking."

There was something chilling, almost dangerous, in his voice that demanded a response. She turned to meet his dark gaze.

Heather tried to stifle her instinctive dislike for the man. "It is doubtful I would ever find anyone more to my liking than his grace."

"One can never tell." He grinned.

"Can't one?" She didn't return the smile.

St. Clair's voice was low and intimate as he leaned closer to her. "You've lived a sheltered life in the country, Miss FitzHugh. You've had no opportunity to learn what it is you really want. I would be happy to teach you."

She'd never known that a mere look could make her feel unclean, but that was what St. Clair's gaze did to her. She struggled to form a proper response.

"I am not the sort to give up when I find something I want. I can be patient. You will see that I am right."

"I will be married to the duke in two months' time," she said firmly.

St. Clair shrugged. "A minor impediment, my dear."

"La, I believe the duke should worry." Annabella's voice carried clearly across the room, causing heads to turn. "It seems you've added another heart to your collection, cousin."

Heather forced herself to remain composed as she stood. "'Tis time I returned to Lady Moberly's. Is the carriage ready, Annabella?"

"Of course, Heather. I'll see that it's brought 'round for you."

Aaron St. Clair rose from his chair. "I would be most happy to see Miss FitzHugh home."

"Thank you, my lord," Heather answered quickly, before her cousin could accept on her behalf, "but that won't be necessary. Good day to you, sir." She looked at Annabella. "Don't leave your guests. I'll summon the carriage myself." She made her way through the crowded salon, bidding farewell as quickly and briefly as possible, not unaware of the hum of conversation that followed her out of the room.

Once safely inside the town coach, Heather leaned back and closed her eyes as she began to shake. She twisted a handkerchief between her fingers, unaware that she did so.

She never should have encouraged St. Clair at the Haversham Ball. She hadn't liked him even then. If she hadn't been so foolishly trying to make Tanner jealous, she would have recognized the folly of flirting with the marquess.

And she had no doubt at all that Annabella would see that Tanner heard about St. Clair's attention to her this afternoon. Naive she might be, but even she could determine what her cousin was up to. Annabella would make it sound as if Heather and St. Clair had conducted an intimate tête-à-tête rather than sharing a salon with more than a dozen other people. What would Tanner have to say to her when he heard the gossip?

Once again she recalled how he'd looked the night of the GlenRoyal ball, his eyes like ice, his face like granite. *But I have been played the fool by a woman before, and everyone knew it. It won't happen again.*

Would he believe she'd had nothing to do with St. Clair's advances?

And what if he didn't? Hadn't she come to London to make him appear the fool? Wasn't that why she'd been spending his money so freely, ordering more gowns and hats and fripperies than she could use in a lifetime? Wasn't being a thorn in his side part of her plan?

Yes . . . yes . . . yes . . .

Then why didn't any of it feel right anymore?

* * *

Tanner entered the club and strode slowly through the crowded rooms. The gaming tables were filled, large sums of money being carelessly wagered by young bucks and old gentlemen. Within any given hour, fortunes would be made and lost. Estates would change hands. Some would never be able to make good their debts of honor. A few would take their own lives rather than live with the shame.

Never one to gamble recklessly, as was currently the height of fashion, Tanner held a dim view of those who couldn't control their addiction to the lure of the game. He need look no further than Heather to know what such carelessness could cost the families of these men.

And Heather was the reason he was here tonight. He found Aaron St. Clair observing a game of whist.

"Evening, Hawksbury," he said as Tanner approached him.

"Evening, Stroughton."

"Care for a game?"

Tanner shook his head. "I won't be staying long. I leave for the Park early in the morning."

"So suddenly?" St. Clair's gaze returned to the whist table, but there was a note of interest in his voice. "Will you be away for long?"

Tanner didn't care for the marquess's tone. He hadn't come to the club for a friendly chat, and he suspected St. Clair was aware of it. "Only a day or two. Just have some estate matters to see to."

"Well, I'm sorry you can't stay. I was anticipating some challenging play. Look at those faces." He lifted his glass toward the men gathered around the table. "You can tell who's winning and who's losing just by looking at them. No sport in the game then. You must come 'round more often. Give a bloke a run for his money."

"I've been occupied elsewhere."

St. Clair grinned as he glanced at Tanner. "Yes. I saw the lovely Miss FitzHugh this afternoon. Charming, isn't she?"

"I've always thought so."

St. Clair drank from his glass of port, his gaze returning to the nearby table. "Pity about Hadley. Did you hear? Lost it all earlier tonight at some gaming hell. Poor chap will be seeking an heiress in a hurry, or he'll be ruined for good."

Tanner had known the marquess since they were in school together. He'd thought St. Clair a rather nasty piece of work back then, and the years since hadn't improved his impression of the man. There were rumors that he'd compromised more than a few young ladies, yet he'd managed to avoid matrimony thus far. Tanner knew for a fact that he was the sort to take great satisfaction in ruining a man at the gaming tables. Some might even suspect him of cheating, but few would have the courage to say so to his face.

St. Clair took another sip of his port. "We're lucky we needn't bed a woman for the size of her dowry, eh, Hawksbury? The heiresses are seldom the beautiful ones. Take your Miss FitzHugh. Ain't got two farthings to rub together, I understand, but she's this year's Incomparable in my book."

"Mine, too." Tanner allowed his gaze to sweep over the room, his stance relaxed and casual, his voice light. "And I don't share what is mine, Stroughton." He paused for emphasis. "Fortunately, the young lady in question is loyal and incapable of duplicity. I expect we shall have a quite comfortable marriage." He brought his eyes back to St. Clair.

The man was looking at him, his mouth set in a hard line. After a lengthy silence, he shrugged. "I wish you luck, Hawksbury."

Tanner offered a bored smile. "Well, I won't

keep you. I'm sure you're eager to get into the game. Good evening." With that, he strode away.

Heather was worried. She hadn't seen Tanner in four days, not since they'd returned from their ride in Hyde Park. She'd looked for him at every rout. She'd watched for a glimpse of his black horse whenever she was shopping with Lynette. She'd waited for him to come calling when they were at home. She couldn't help wondering why he was avoiding her, although she reminded herself frequently that she should be enjoying his absence.

Still, she'd been grateful for Celeste's visit this afternoon, only too happy for any distraction that would take her mind off the duke. And when Celeste had suggested that they take the air with a carriage ride in the park, Heather had quickly agreed.

However, she was beginning to doubt the wisdom of her decision as the Andermont carriage moved through the park at a sedate pace, allowing Celeste to call out greetings to friends and acquaintances at frequent intervals. Time and again, the vehicle had come to a stop so another acquaintance could join them inside. Then they'd proceeded forward along Rotten Row until the driver was told to stop once more so the acquaintance could descend. It was another tiresome ritual of the Season that Heather was coming to despise.

"Celeste!"

Heather stifled her groan as the carriage stopped again.

Celeste leaned toward the window, wearing her brightest smile. "Teddy! When did you arrive in Town?"

"Only yesterday. Stephen and I have been in Yorkshire. His father was ill and feared dying, but the baron has made a wonderful recovery."

"Won't you join us? I'd like you to meet my friend."

The door opened, revealing the young woman Celeste had called Teddy. She couldn't have been even five feet tall. She had a fine head of bright red hair, a pair of flashing green eyes, and a pixie-ish face that immediately disarmed Heather.

As Teddy settled onto the seat next to Celeste, her friend performed the introductions. "Teddy, this is Heather FitzHugh. She's from Westmorland, and this is her first Season in Town. Heather, meet my dear friend, Theodora Elsmere. But only her husband's mother calls her Theodora. Her friends call her Teddy, and you must, too." Celeste drew a quick breath, then continued. "Now tell me, Teddy, how do you find married life?"

Teddy's eyes sparkled. "I find it very wonderful, indeed. Stephen is such a good and kind husband." She wrinkled her nose. "If it weren't for the baroness, my life would be perfect."

"Teddy's mother-in-law would have preferred another choice for her son," Celeste explained to Heather.

"Luckily for me, my Stephen has a mind of his own. Besides, I think the baroness will change her opinion of me soon enough." Her voice dropped to a whisper. "Can you keep a secret, Celeste?"

She nodded.

"I'm increasing."

Celeste squealed for joy and threw her arms around her friend's neck. "Oh, Teddy, how marvelous! When is the next heir to the barony due?"

"Not until December. So I intend to enjoy every moment of this Season, for next year I'll be an old matron."

Heather couldn't imagine the redheaded elf across from her ever being considered matronly.

Teddy glanced out the carriage window. "The park is so busy today. Simply everyone must be here. Look! There's the Duke of Hawksbury." She pointed a finger. "Mama would have loved it if he'd offered for me, and I was so afraid she might somehow arrange it. Can you imagine me married to such a man? He's frightfully handsome, of course, and terribly rich, but I would have been terrified whenever he looked at me."

"Teddy . . ." Celeste's fingers closed on her friend's arm, but she was ignored.

Teddy's voice lowered to a confidential tone. "Celeste, do you know who that is he's talking to? That's Harriette Morton. 'Tis scandalous the way those women meet their lovers in public, flaunting themselves before decent folk."

Heather sat forward to look out the window. There was Tanner, seated astride Rebellion, looking splendid in a black coat and trousers, his Hessians gleaming in the afternoon sun. He was leaning down, talking with a woman in a gilded white carriage. Heather couldn't see her face.

"Who is she?" she asked, unaware of the way her voice trembled.

"Why, only one of the most famous cyprians in London. 'Tis said she's as rich as Croesus, thanks to her wealthy patrons. Everyone knows she's been the duke's mistress since last Season. Some say he is inordinately fond of her and that he might not ever marry since he can't have her for a wife."

Heather continued to stare out the window. The slight buzzing in her ears covered up Celeste's quick whispers to the girl beside her.

The duke's mistress . . . Harriette Morton, the Duke of Hawksbury's mistress . . . Everyone knows . . . Couldn't have her for a wife . . . As rich as Croesus . . . Most famous cyprian in London . . . The duke's mistress . . . Everyone knows . . .

"Miss FitzHugh," Teddy said softly, "I'm so sorry. You mustn't pay any attention to what I said. Everyone can tell you that I have a terrible habit of rattling on about just anything and not making any sense or knowing what it is I'm saying. I'm sure the duke ..."

Heather straightened as they drew closer to the white-and-gold carriage and the handsome duke on the black horse. She forced a calm expression onto her face. "You needn't apologize, Lady Elsmere. I am not so naive that I don't know that men have mistresses."

Celeste and Teddy both murmured comforting words, but Heather didn't hear them. She was trying not to shatter into a thousand pieces, just as her heart had done only moments before.

Chapter 18

Heather saw Tanner coming down the stairway that same evening at the Mannington rout. A sense of panic swept through her, not because he was there, but because of the ache in her heart. She couldn't allow herself to feel this way. It was foolish and dangerous.

She scanned the faces nearby, looking for someone to ask to escort her in to supper before Tanner found her. Her gaze fell upon Aaron St. Clair just as he glanced her way. Her action was instinctive, born of desperation and pain.

She smiled at St. Clair and inclined her head in invitation. He nodded in understanding, excused himself from those he'd been standing with, then walked in her direction.

"Miss FitzHugh." He bowed over her hand. "'Tis a pleasure to see you again."

"Thank you, my lord. 'Tis a pleasure for me as well," she lied, hoping he wouldn't hear the slight hesitation in her voice. "I'm feeling a trifle lost this evening, and I was just wondering whom I might have for my supper companion. I'm afraid I still know so few people." It was another bald-faced lie, and this time she knew they were both aware of it.

"Would you do me the honor of allowing me to

escort you?" St. Clair asked with a smile, then held out his arm.

She attempted a return smile as she placed her fingers around his elbow. She fluttered her eyelashes and tried to think of something interesting to talk about as she mentally urged him toward the dining room and out of Tanner's view. "I believe I heard that you have a marvelous stable at your estate in Surrey." She took the first step, hoping he would take the hint.

"Are you interested in bloodstock, Miss Fitz-Hugh?"

A sixth sense told her that Tanner had spotted her and that even now his eyes were trained on her back.

St. Clair started forward. "Miss FitzHugh?"

"I'm sorry. What did you say, my lord?"

"Horses, Miss FitzHugh. Are you interested in horses?"

"Oh, yes. I love horses." She thought of Cathy, so well mannered and big-hearted. And then she thought of Tanner's Rebellion, sleek and tall, flowing mane and tail, neck arched and nostrils flared. Glorious. Rather like his master. "Yes, I do love them," she repeated.

"I spend a good deal of time at Tattersall's, acquiring the best for Ridgemont. Have you been to the horse auction?"

She repressed the urge to glance behind her. "No, my lord, I haven't."

"Perhaps you will do me the honor of accompanying me one day." His hand covered hers in the crook of his arm. "We might find we have a number of things in common."

There was a dangerously seductive gleam in his black eyes that caused her stomach to quake. She should have expected it after the afternoon at her aunt's. She should have known she would regret tricking him into offering to escort her to supper.

There must have been a dozen other available men, if only she'd taken the time to look. Oh, why had she allowed her own fear and hurt to replace common sense?

"Will Hawksbury be here this evening?" he asked as he pulled out a velvet-covered chair for her.

"I really couldn't say. The crush is always so great at these events, it can be hard to find anyone. Don't you agree?"

The need to know if Tanner was watching her was too great. She glanced over her shoulder.

He was there, framed in the doorway to the dining hall. His face was hidden in shadows, yet she would swear she could see a predatory gleam in his eyes. She could feel his displeasure.

She'd known he would hear about her encounter with St. Clair at Annabella's. And she'd known he wouldn't approve of the man. Perhaps that was why she hadn't seen him these past four days. He was angry with her because of St. Clair.

Or perhaps, her mutinous thoughts suggested, he'd spent the past four days with his mistress.

He started forward, his expression one of mild indifference. He gave her a sardonic smile before turning to St. Clair. "Surprised to see you here, Stroughton."

St. Clair's features hardened, and there was a look of challenge in his black eyes. His words, however, were polite, almost conciliatory. "I hadn't intended to stay, but Miss FitzHugh was without a supper companion. However, now that you're here . . ."

Tanner nodded once.

St. Clair looked at Heather. "Enjoy your evening, Miss FitzHugh. Perhaps we shall see one another again soon. At Tattersall's?"

"Perhaps, my lord."

Tanner waited until the marquess had moved

down the table before taking his seat beside Heather. His glance drifted lazily over the dining hall, watching as the guests filled the room, the noise level increasing as laughter punctuated the conversations going on all around them.

Without looking at her, he said, "I realize 'tis bad form for a man and a woman, even though engaged, to appear too close. I understand there will be times when I am not with you that you will need a supper companion." His head turned suddenly. Their gazes collided. His voice dropped even lower without dimming the warning in his words. "But you are not to spend time with the likes of St. Clair."

She clenched her hands beneath the table. "Why not, your grace?" she asked perversely, knowing all the while that she would prefer to avoid the marquess.

"My reasons are my own. Suffice that I have expressed my wishes and expect you to follow them."

"I see." Her meekly spoken response belied her sudden flare of anger. "Are you to choose all my friends, my lord duke?"

One golden-brown eyebrow rose, as did one corner of his mouth. There was a hint of amusement in his voice when he answered. "Only if you choose poorly, Heather."

The overbearing, egotistical, conceited, arrogant ass! She was tempted to pick up the china plate set before her and smash it over his head.

"Heather, you cannot know about men like St. Clair, but I do. You would never meet his sort at Lady Moberly's. She cannot abide him. This is Annabella's doing. She hopes to cause trouble between us."

The truth of his words—echoing her own thoughts four days before—did nothing to stem the fury brewing inside. She hated his condescending tone. She despised his duplicity.

Her chin lifted in a show of defiance. "Tell me, your grace, should I ever see *you* make a poor choice in companions, may I speak up, or does that privilege belong only to you?"

"I hope our marriage shall be one in which we always speak freely."

"Need I wait until marriage, your grace?"

The expression on his face turned to one of puzzlement, mixed with a slight wariness. "No, Heather. Is there something you wish to say to me now?"

"Only that I shall gladly avoid Lord Stroughton when you no longer are seen with Harriette Morton." She nearly spat the woman's name at him.

"I believe," he said stiffly, "we should discuss this matter when we can enjoy more privacy."

"Why is that, your grace? You seem to have no such compunction about being seen in public with your mistress. Why should a little squabble with your intended cause you any embarrassment?" Heather rose from her chair as she fought to keep her voice low. "You have made it clear what you want from me in marriage, your grace, but you don't seem to care what I might want from you. Well, I demand the same faithfulness as you do. You will *not* see that woman again." She fought to control the shaking that threatened to overwhelm her. "Please excuse me. I am overcome from the heat of this room. I believe I need some air."

Walking with as much grace as she could muster, forcing herself not to flee at a run, Heather moved against the crowd of revelers pushing into the dining hall. She didn't know where she was going. She just wanted to get away from Tanner and the image that remained in her mind from her afternoon in Hyde Park.

* * *

A moment later, Tanner rose and followed her, the determination in his blue eyes enough to part the throng of guests before him. Just as he left the dining hall, he saw Heather slipping through the doors leading to the courtyard.

Little fool. Didn't she know it wasn't wise to go out into the dark alone?

What nerve she had, telling him she wouldn't see St. Clair if he avoided Harriette. It wasn't the same thing. For one, Harriette—as much a friend as a lover—wasn't seeking to ruin his reputation. The same couldn't be said of St. Clair's intentions toward Heather. The marquess was only looking for a challenging amusement, and despoiling Hawksbury's intended would be just the sort of thing he would enjoy. For another thing, Tanner had only chanced to see Harriette in the park. He was innocent of Heather's insinuations.

He yanked open the door and followed her outside, his righteous indignation adding speed to his forceful steps.

Confounded woman! He'd spent the past three days at Hawksbury Park, seeing to the affairs of his estate, but she hadn't ever been far from his thoughts. It was with the hope of seeing Heather in the park that he'd gone there first. It was merely coincidence that he'd met Harriette, and the words they had exchanged were the first since the night he'd visited her after the Rathdrum rout over two months before.

By heaven, he shouldn't have to justify his actions! He had a right to express his wishes to Heather and expect them to be followed.

He knew he never should have brought her to Town. He should have married her and hidden her away at Hawksbury and sired that blasted heir immediately. London was changing her, just as he'd feared.

The soft sound of weeping stopped him in his

tracks. He listened, turning his head slowly, then left the footpath, walking off into the darkened gardens.

Heather choked back a sob as she dashed the tears away. She didn't know why she was crying. She didn't care what Tanner did with his time or whom he consorted with or whether or not she ever saw him again. She'd come to London only to get even with him. She had to stop this foolishness and stop it right now.

She dabbed her eyes with a lace-edged handkerchief, then drew in a deep breath. She sat up a little straighter on the cool stone bench.

There. She was feeling better. She wasn't going to give in to hysterics again.

"Heather?"

His voice made her eyes swim with tears once more.

"Heather?" He stepped out of the shadows of the tall shrubbery. The quarter moon cast a pale light across his face as he knelt beside her. "I'm sorry. I should have chosen my words more carefully."

She swallowed and tried not to sniff as she looked away from him.

"Heather . . ." His fingers closed around her wrists. "I only seek to protect you when I forbid you to see Lord Stroughton. If you cannot believe me, ask Lady Moberly's opinion of the marquess."

She nodded sharply.

Tanner's fingers tightened on her wrists as the silence lengthened between them. When he finally spoke again, his words came in a hushed voice. "Harriette has nothing to do with us, Heather. It was a chance encounter this afternoon. I won't be seeing her again. You have my word on it."

The gentleness of his promise caused the tears to spill over and course down her cheeks.

"Please don't cry anymore, my sweet."

She tried her best to obey him. "You needn't explain or apologize. I have no right to make demands upon you. Ours is not a love match. I understand the reasons you chose to wed me."

"Do you?" he asked softly.

"Yes, I do." More tears traced damp paths over the apples of her cheeks, then splattered against her bodice.

Tanner took the handkerchief from her fingers and tenderly dried her face. "Perhaps you understand it better than I," he whispered. Then he slipped onto the bench beside her and drew her into his arms.

Althea Rathdrum saw them reenter the house from the terrace. Tanner glanced down at the girl on his arm and spoke softly to her, his expression tender and concerned.

Althea saw red.

She couldn't believe the duke had turned down all she'd offered to him and was now going to marry that stupid little chit. Even after she'd married Kendall, Althea had made it clear she was open to a friendly liaison, but again he had rejected her. Still, she wasn't about to give up hope. Not yet anyway. After all, her husband couldn't possibly live much longer. The old curmudgeon should have gone aloft long before now, and she secretly cursed him for each day he lingered.

Althea knew she must make sure the duke wasn't caught in another marriage before she was free. She just wasn't certain how best to accomplish it. She must do something before it was too late.

She smiled to herself, knowing that this room must contain a dozen or more young ladies who had hoped to snare Hawksbury for a husband. She knew many of them had spent hours weeping into their pillows and hating Heather FitzHugh when they had first heard the news of the engagement. The difference, of course, between Althea and the others was that she meant to do something about it, while they turned their attention to other eligible men.

She watched as Tanner and Heather were joined by the Earl of Mannington and Lady Celeste Andermont. Moments later, the gentlemen made their way across the drawing room and into the hall. From her vantage point, she saw them turn and climb the stairs, no doubt headed for the card room.

She quickly looked back at Heather. The girl was staring after Tanner, a bittersweet expression on her face. It was obvious that all was not well between those two. Heather looked as if she might even have been crying. Good. It would make Althea's job much more difficult if everything was rosy between them.

Heather went through the motions of having a good time, but it was all pretense. She couldn't rid herself of the confusing emotions that threatened to overwhelm her. No matter whom she danced with, no matter who brought her a glass of punch or shared some plump *on-dit*, she was thinking of Tanner.

It couldn't be, of course. She mustn't let herself care for the duke. He was ruthless, heartless, unfeeling. She couldn't possibly care for such a man. She mentally catalogued all the things he'd done which made him unlovable. Strangely, none of them seemed so terrible now.

He was a Montgomery. That should have been a good enough reason by itself.

Only it wasn't.

He'd lied to her from the moment they'd first met.

It still wasn't enough.

He *was* an overbearing, egotistical, conceited, arrogant ass, but he was also kind and gentle and giving. He had a wonderful laugh and a powerful walk, and when he kissed her ...

She stopped herself from thinking of his kisses. Perhaps she couldn't deny all the things that made her want to care for him, that made her want to be with him, but neither could she deny her loyalty to her family. She owed it to her father and her brother to remain firm. She had a promise to keep. George had tried. Now it was up to her.

George. He was the reason she couldn't give in to her treasonous feelings. Maybe she could have forgiven Tanner everything else, but never could she forgive him for shooting George. If not for that one cruel act, George never would have left England, and she wouldn't have spent all those years alone and unloved.

No, she couldn't forgive or forget, and she couldn't care for him. No matter what he said, no matter what he did, she wouldn't allow herself to care for Tanner Montgomery.

"Heather ..." Celeste squeezed her arm.

"I'm sorry. What were you saying?"

"I said I should like to see Edward before Mama decides it is time for us to leave. Will you come with me?"

She almost refused. After all, it would mean seeing Tanner again, and she had only just now settled things in her mind. She wasn't sure she was ready to see him and stir up the confusion so soon.

She remembered his tenderness to her in the garden, the way he'd apologized, the feel of his arms as he'd embraced her. She recalled the way he'd called her "my sweet." It was the first endearment he'd ever spoken to her, and even now it threatened to bring tears to her eyes.

Traitorous heart.

"Please come, Heather. It would be much too bold of me to go alone, but Mama couldn't object if I'm with you. After all, you're engaged to the duke. No one could think it improper for you to bid him good evening before leaving."

Celeste's expression was so hopeful, Heather couldn't resist her friend's plea. She nodded, and the two wove their way through the crowded room to the hall and up the stairs.

She could feel the spark of excitement as she stepped through the doorway into the crowded card room. A smoky haze hovered in the air. There were a few women gathered around to watch the action, but most of the occupants were men.

Heather located Tanner immediately. He was seated at the center table, his expression cool and slightly bored as he observed his opponents. Seated to his right was Edward Kennaway. Across from him was Aaron St. Clair. She supposed she'd met the other men at one time or another, but their identities were unimportant to her. It was clear that only two men were left in the game.

She moved slowly around the table, Celeste behind her, until she had a clear view of Tanner's face. She'd been wrong to think he looked cool and bored. She knew him too well, she realized, to be fooled as others might. She caught the determined gleam in his eyes. She saw the set of his mouth. Something told her this was more than just a card game. This was a duel of sorts between Tanner and St. Clair.

"Perhaps we could make this more interesting, Hawksbury."

She was standing behind St. Clair and couldn't see his face, but there was something about the tone of his voice that filled her with dread.

"How is that, Stroughton?" Tanner replied evenly.

"I hear you're rather fond of that hunting lodge of yours. The one in Westmorland. How 'bout that against my finest stallion and your pick of any three of my mares? They're worth a fortune, you know. Far more than any crumbling estate in the north."

Heather gripped Celeste's hand.

Tanner leaned back in his chair. "If you think it's crumbling, why risk your fine bloodstock for it?"

"Because ..." He gave a throaty laugh. "I don't plan to lose."

Was this how it had happened to her father? she wondered. A simple game of chance. A sudden challenge. And then everything was gone.

"It's tempting, St. Clair." Tanner's smile was chilling. "But it would be a foolish move on your part. Very foolish. I don't intend to lose, either. Another time, perhaps. But not tonight."

A lengthy silence followed.

Heather gasped for air, unaware that she'd been holding her breath. Tanner looked up at the sound, and their eyes met briefly. Although his expression didn't alter, she knew he was surprised to see her standing there. Then he dismissed her presence with a glance, returning his gaze to his cards.

She felt cold all over. He could have gambled away GlenRoyal. It could have been lost to St. Clair with the turn of a card. Although Tanner had turned him down, it could still happen. He'd said he might consider it another time. Her beloved GlenRoyal. So meaningless to him.

She whirled away, dragging Celeste with her, not slowing until she was outside the card room.

"Heather, I didn't get to speak to Edward," her friend complained. "We didn't even get to see what happened."

"I don't want to see," Heather said hoarsely. "I'm going home. I don't feel well."

She meant it, too. She didn't feel well.

She was sick at heart.

Chapter 19

Tanner leaned forward in his chair as he stared down at the paper on his desk. Was he mad? he wondered as he picked up the pen and dunked it in the inkwell. Before he could consider his silent question, he signed his name to the document with a bold flourish.

A sense of peace immediately flooded him. He knew he could have waited. Their wedding day would have been the appropriate time for such a gift. But after seeing Heather's face last night, he'd known he couldn't wait any longer.

He picked up the paper, waved it in the air to make sure the ink was dry, then folded it and placed it in his pocket before pushing back his chair and rising. Hands clasped behind his back, he strode purposefully from his study, a bemused expression creeping onto his face.

By Jove! How had she managed to do this to him?

He'd had every right to demand that she avoid St. Clair, yet within minutes of his doing so, she'd had him on his knees offering apologies. Now he was about to give her the deed to GlenRoyal. Free and clear. Forever hers, to do with as she pleased.

How had she managed it?

He paused in front of his father's portrait and looked up at the familiar face. *This is your fault*, he silently accused. *If you hadn't accepted the baron's wager, I never would have met her, and I wouldn't be wondering if I was doing the right thing now.*

"Tanner, there you are." His mother greeted him with a kiss on his cheek. "We haven't had a moment to speak since you returned from the Park," the dowager duchess said as she stepped back from him. "How did you find things?"

"Clatworthy is as thorough as ever," he replied, referring to the steward at Hawksbury Park. He raised an eyebrow as he gazed down at his mother. He knew she wasn't concerned about the condition of the ducal estates. She knew as well as he did what went on there.

Sophia hooked her arm through his and began walking. "Our Miss FitzHugh has caused quite a sensation in her first week in London. Not only is she an incomparable beauty, but she was unknown to the *ton* and nonetheless became engaged to a duke. Even better, my dear boy, I hear she has enchanted young and old alike. I was right in thinking you'd made a wise choice for your duchess."

As he nodded, he wondered when his mother was going to get to the point. She usually wasn't one to mince words.

The dowager duchess stopped abruptly, turning a shrewd gaze upon him. "Why is it I hear you're still seeing that woman from York Place? Really, Tanner! If you feel you must continue this liaison, at least be more discreet. Have a care for Heather. Would you crush the dear girl?"

She hadn't minced words this time either, he realized as his jaw tensed. "I am *not* still seeing Miss Morton," he replied tersely, "but if I chose to, it would be my concern and no one else's."

Sophia gave him an imperious look that could have quelled the great majority of the haut monde in an instant.

In return, he gave her a wry grin. "Don't try to terrorize me, Mother. It won't work."

"Really, Tanner . . ."

His grin vanished. "Don't worry. I have no intention of hurting Heather or disgracing the family name. I did speak with Miss Morton in Hyde Park, which, as I look back, probably showed a lack of judgment. I assure you, Miss FitzHugh has already taken me to task for the error of my ways. It won't happen again."

Sophia looked surprised and then laughed. "I knew I was going to like that girl. There is more to Heather FitzHugh than mere beauty, Tanner. You would do well to remember it." She took hold of his shoulders and drew him close for another kiss on the cheek, then started off down the hall. "Tell her I'm looking forward to seeing her at the Hawksbury Ball."

"I'll do that."

He looked back toward his father's portrait and found himself wearing a genuine smile. He wasn't surprised that his mother liked the idea of Heather scolding him. After all, Sophia had defied Nicholas on more than one occasion during their long marriage.

Tanner shook his head as he started off toward his bedchamber, the rare smile gone as quickly as it had come. His parents' marriage was not the issue. He wasn't about to be bullied—by his mother or anyone else—into behaving differently than he thought he should. He meant to take care of Heather and protect her, and he hoped he would be able to give her some measure of contentment. One only had to witness his gift of GlenRoyal to know how generous and tolerant he would be.

But contentment was all they would ever share. By heaven, he would not allow there to be more than that between them.

* * *

"Truly, Lynette, I am all right." Heather straightened against the pillows at her back. "I just have a headache and would rather remain home tonight. Please don't cancel your plans because of me."

"I don't know, dear. If you're not well, I shouldn't leave you ..."

"Honestly, Lynette! I have a headache, not consumption. Please go and quit fussing over me. I've spent months at a time at Beckworth House with no one else there but the servants. I can certainly manage being alone for one night here in Town."

Lynette drew back in surprise at Heather's sharp tone.

Heather groaned as she closed her eyes. "I'm sorry. I didn't mean to act ungrateful."

"Well, I must admit, if you have the energy to snap at me that way, you must not be too ill." Heather opened her eyes to find Lynette smiling patiently down at her.

"You are quite right, Heather. I *have* been fussing. And I don't doubt a fig that you are in need of more rest. We have been constantly busy since we arrived in London." She walked toward the bedchamber door. "We can't have you feeling poorly for Sophia's ball on Friday. After all, the dowager duchess is giving it in your honor. You get a good night's sleep, and we'll see how you feel on the morrow."

"Good night, Lynette. Have a wonderful evening."

The moment the door clicked shut, Heather sank down on the bed, burrowing her way beneath the covers and pillows, trying to hide from the thoughts and feelings that had pestered her throughout the day.

What a muddle everything had become. If only she could push back time. If that were possible, she would choose never to go to GlenRoyal that fateful April day, seven weeks ago. Then she would never have met Tanner, and she wouldn't be feeling this terrible confusion now. She wouldn't be engaged, wouldn't be in London, wouldn't be in love.

In love . . .

There it was. She'd finally admitted it. That was the crux of all her problems. Try though she might to deny it, she'd never stopped loving Tanner, not even when she'd learned his true identity.

Heaven help her, what was she to do about it?

Tanner arrived at the Andermonts' musicale a little after ten. Standing in the doorway to the rose salon, he glanced quickly over the crowd for the familiar black curls. He listened for her special lilting laughter but failed to find Heather among the guests seated throughout the room.

As he turned toward the dining room, he spied Lynette Moberly near a far wall. She was deep in conversation with Lord Sainsbury and hadn't noticed him. He moved purposefully in her direction.

When he stopped before her, Lynette looked up and smiled. "Good evening, Hawk. I was wondering if we were to have the pleasure of your company tonight. You've been rather neglectful of late."

Tanner bobbed his head in greeting. "Lynette. Sainsbury." He swiveled for one more quick glance about the room. "Just returned from Essex yesterday." He paused, then added, "I can't seem to find Heather."

"She's not here."

He looked back at Lynette, frowning.

"She remained at home this evening. Poor thing is exhausted, I fear. Not used to our particular brand of living. I dare say, she still rises long before noon, even when we don't return home until dawn. I doubt we shall ever break her of that dreadful habit."

"Is she ill?"

"Good heavens, no. A slight headache, perhaps, but don't let her know I told you so. She's already accused me of fussing over her too much. Who knows what she might say if you became overset because of something I said." Lynette patted the seat of the chair next to her. "Do sit down and tell me how you found things at Hawksbury Park. I trust it was nothing urgent that called you there."

"No. Nothing urgent." The last thing he wanted was to sit and chat with Lynette. He felt a great need to see Heather for himself, just to make certain she was all right. "I'm afraid I can't stay, Lynette. I'd only intended to drop in for a moment. I have a previous engagement at my club."

She shook her head, her tone scolding. "I suppose we cannot hope to see you become more sociable simply because you're engaged, but you should try to call upon Heather more often. She misses you when you don't come."

"I'll try." He bowed. "Good evening, Lynette. Good to see you, Sainsbury."

He didn't bother to speak to anyone else as he left the salon. He had come to the Andermonts' only to see Heather. With her not there, he saw no point in remaining.

When his carriage was brought around, he instructed the driver to take him to his club, then climbed inside. They were approaching St. James's Street before he realized he'd lied to Lynette. He'd never had any intention of going to his club.

Moments later, the Hawksbury coach was speeding along in another direction, headed for Lynette Moberly's town house.

Tanner told himself he merely wanted to present the deed to Heather so that he needn't bother with it later. After all, it was in his coat pocket now.

Why trouble himself with having to reschedule his plans? He realized that the lateness of the hour and Lady Moberly's absence from home constituted a problem of propriety, but at the moment, he didn't give a damn. He was going to see Heather, and he was going to see her tonight.

Still, as he alighted from his carriage in front of the stately house, he decided some discretion would be wise. It didn't much matter to him. He'd flown in the face of convention before and had never catered to the whims of Society. But he'd seen Heather's face as she danced at balls and routs. She was loving her Season, and he had no wish to destroy it for her.

"Take the coach back to Albany House, Crandall," he told the driver. "I'll summon a cab when I'm ready to leave."

"Yes, your grace."

As the clip-clop of the horses' hooves faded into the night, Tanner headed toward the front door, wondering over his actions and why it had seemed so urgent that he see her tonight.

Heather paced the perimeters of her large bedchamber. Her headache was forgotten, replaced by an increasing restlessness.

She would have to call off her engagement to the duke immediately. It had been easy to deceive Tanner when she sought only revenge, when she thought she despised and detested him. Now everything had changed. She couldn't follow through with her plan to hurt and humiliate him. She loved him too much.

But she still couldn't marry him. Her love didn't change the past, couldn't alter the events that stood so resolutely between them. She was bound by an oath to her father and brother. She owed her first allegiance to them, didn't she? The FitzHughs had always stood united against adversity. She had loved and adored her father. And no girl could have had a better brother than George. He'd even fought a duel to try to give her a home again. She couldn't betray her father or George.

She sank onto the stool of her dressing table and stared at her reflection in the mirror.

It wasn't just her family that stood between them, she realized. She couldn't marry Tanner because she wasn't the woman he thought she was. He believed she was sweet and naive, and all the while she'd been plotting shamelessly against him. She'd been spending his money on useless items, and on trunkfuls and closetfuls of clothes, without a word of complaint from him. He had indulged her every whim since she'd asked him to bring her to London, and she'd repaid him with deception and intrigue. She'd even sought to make him desire her, had demanded that he not see his mistress, when all the while she never intended to be his compliant wife.

Any affection he might feel for her was based upon lies.

She could confess all. She could tell him the truth about herself—what she'd planned to do, what she'd already done. She could tell him she loved him and hope that he might care for her enough to . . .

To what? To marry her still?

She rose from the stool and began pacing again.

No, she couldn't marry him. How could she tell George when he returned for her that she had married the man who had shot him? How could she give herself to a man who didn't love her, betraying everything she'd ever wanted, ever hoped for?

No, she couldn't marry him, no matter what, and she couldn't confess the truth either. She hadn't the courage. It would be better if she simply left him a note, telling him she'd changed her mind. She would just slip out of London, unnoticed, and he could choose someone else for his duchess. There were plenty of women anxious to take her place.

After all, it wasn't as if he loved her. Tanner would find someone else to marry, someone more suitable who hadn't used and deceived him as she had. Besides, he was only marrying to provide an heir. Any debutante of the Season could fulfill that requirement.

A sharp pain pierced her chest, causing her to sit suddenly on the edge of her bed.

His son. How she would have loved to give him a son.

"Why did it have to be Hawksbury, Papa?" she asked aloud. "Why couldn't you have lost GlenRoyal to someone else?"

A mixture of anger and despair filled her. Anger that her father's reckless gambling had cost her not only her home but also the man she loved. Despair that she was helpless to change the events of the past.

She would have to go away, and soon.

"Excuse me, miss." Mrs. Harwood, Lynette's housekeeper, stood in the open doorway. "His grace the duke is waiting below to see you."

Her pulse jumped. "He's here?"

"I told him it was late for visitors, but he insisted I announce him. He said it is important that he sees you."

Heather's stomach tightened. "Tell him I'll be down shortly," she whispered.

No, she couldn't marry him, she thought as she rose from the bed. She would have to leave London and never see him again. But she didn't have to leave tonight. Perhaps not even tomorrow.

What would it matter if she allowed herself a little longer to be with him? Once she returned to Beckworth House, she would never see him again.

A few days would have to last her a lifetime.

Chapter 20

T anner heard her footfall and turned toward the door.

Heather paused just inside the salon entrance. Candlelight cast a soft, flickering light across her pale complexion. There was a sadness in the curve of her mouth, a pain in her violet eyes that disturbed him.

He felt a jolt of concern as he stepped toward her. "You're not well," he said.

"I'm fine." She closed the door behind her.

"Lynette said you were too ill to join her."

"I had a headache, but it's gone now."

He took her by the hand and led her to the nearest settee. "I should have waited until tomorrow and not interfered with your rest."

"I'm glad you came." She looked at him as she sank onto the small sofa, continuing to hold his hand.

Tanner felt a strange stirring within himself, a feeling more than desire and yet that, too. A feeling poignant and passionate. He sat down beside her.

She continued to watch him, her gaze moving slowly over the contours of his face. It was almost as if she'd never seen him before, as if she were trying to memorize each feature. He felt a curious disquiet.

Finally, her gaze returned to meet his. "I hope you did not spoil your evening because of me, your grace."

"Not at all. Coming here was the best part of my evening."

A tiny smile lifted the corners of her heart-shaped mouth.

In that instant, Tanner knew he wanted to see genuine joy in her eyes. He wanted to hear her laugh the way she had the first time he'd seen her, chasing Strawberry. He wanted to taste the sweetness of her lips.

He squeezed her fingers, trying not to think about holding her and kissing her. That wasn't why he'd come. "I had something important to discuss with you, Heather. About last night."

She stiffened beside him. "What is it, your grace?"

"I know how much you love GlenRoyal. Would you believe me if I promised you I would never do anything so reckless as to gamble it away?"

He read the uncertainty in her eyes even as she replied, "If you told me so, Tanner, I would believe you."

Her words weren't enough, he realized. He wanted her to trust him. He wanted her to believe in him without question. He wanted . . .

He wanted to kiss her. He wanted to see her looking at him with surprise and passion, the way she always did after he'd tasted her mouth. That was the problem. He hadn't kissed her often enough.

By heaven, he couldn't deny it any longer. Kissing Heather wouldn't be enough to satisfy him now. He wanted to possess her completely. He'd wanted it for weeks. Instinctively, he knew she would be a glorious lover, that she would put all her zest for life into her lovemaking.

He rose from the settee and walked toward the

fireplace, controlling his desire with a will of iron. He drew in a deep breath, then faced her once again. Looking at her, he felt his will nearly falter.

Heather watched him uncertainly as she stood. "What is it, your grace? What's wrong?"

Tanner shook his head. "Nothing is wrong. I came here to put your mind to rest about GlenRoyal. I want you to know it shall never be lost." He reached into his coat pocket and withdrew the signed deed. "This is for you."

Heather stepped forward and took the paper from his hand. Casting him a questioning gaze, she turned toward the nearest light. She read it once, then again, and yet again. Still, she couldn't believe she understood it.

"It's mine?" she said at last, her voice barely audible. She glanced at him.

Tanner was wearing a stern expression, his blue eyes intense, watchful.

"You're giving GlenRoyal to me?" she asked, louder this time. "It's really mine?"

"Yes. It belongs to you. It's no longer part of the Hawksbury estates. It is yours to do with as you please. If you like, we shall place it in trust before the wedding so that it's protected for our children. No one, not even I, can sell or gamble it away from you."

She couldn't believe it. He had given her back her home. It was hers! She wouldn't have to go back to Beckworth House and live with Aunt Caroline and Uncle Frederick and Annabella ever again. She could go home, and Tanner had done it for her.

Tears welled up in her eyes. He didn't know what he'd given her. By his generous gift, he'd made her deception all the more painful, made her departure even more difficult to bear.

She'd fulfilled her FitzHugh oath. She'd regained GlenRoyal for the family. She'd done everything in her power, albeit unwittingly. And in doing so, she'd betrayed the man she loved. She knew he would never believe that this hadn't been her goal all along. He would never believe she loved him, had *ever* loved him.

"I thought it would make you happy," he said as he came to stand before her.

"It has." Teardrops slipped from her eyes and trickled down her cheeks. "I will never be able to thank you enough. Never." She stood on tiptoe, her hands on his shoulders, and kissed him, silently giving him her heart.

She felt the change in him almost instantly. Her gentle expression of thanks and appreciation had turned into something much more. The fury of his passion ignited a fire within her. The deed drifted to the floor as she tangled her fingers through his tawny-colored hair, drawn ever closer to him like a moth to a flame.

I love him, she thought as his hand on the small of her back pressed her close, so close that the heat of his body became her heat.

His tongue parted her lips and sparred with hers, darting, sliding, teasing. The action made her skin tingle. Her head felt light, her body weak.

I will always love him.

His hands began to move, exploring her body, only the flimsy silk of her gown preventing a more intimate touch. As his hand cupped her breast, kneading the sensitive flesh, she gasped, feeling a mixture of alarm, surprise, and a wish for him to continue.

She held his head between her hands and deepened the kiss, silently asking for more, her body speaking in a language all its own, conveying her desire.

She wasn't aware of them moving from where they'd once stood, yet suddenly she was being lowered onto the thick carpet before the fire. His kisses continued to batter her senses, sending her thoughts reeling.

His fingers pushed her gown free from her shoulders and slid the capped sleeves down her arms. As the dress moved, so did his lips. He trailed kisses along the length of her neck, pausing for a moment to press against the racing pulsebeat at the base of her throat.

Heather groaned. A wave of restlessness and impatience washed over her, plunging her into a sea of wanting. She whispered his name.

His lips moved on, following his hands as they pushed the low neckline farther downward until her breasts were exposed. She hadn't time to realize what he had done, what he was doing, before he'd captured the rosy flesh of her nipple into his mouth.

She arched suddenly, her hands once again entangled in his hair, holding him to her as a white-hot heat seared the length of her body.

Once again his name slipped from her lips on a whisper of air. "Tanner . . ."

He released her nipple, rising above her, braced on one arm. His blue eyes smoldered with desire as he gazed down at her. "You're so very beautiful, my sweet." His voice sounded hoarse. "You make me forget that we must—"

"Make me yours, Tanner," she pleaded quickly, before he said that they must stop. She knew that was what he was about to say, sensed that he was trying to restore reason where none existed. "Please . . ."

Let me belong to you before I lose you forever, she added silently. *Make me yours, my love.*

His whole body throbbed with desire. It gripped him, shook him, overpowered him. He could see his own passion mirrored in her violet eyes, eyes wide with revelation as new emotions stormed through her. He was helpless against her plea. It had been years since he'd felt like this with a woman. Perhaps he'd never felt this way. The need for her was devastating.

"My sweet Heather . . ." he whispered as he lowered his lips to hers once more.

He knew there was no turning of the tide. He would make her his this very night, and Society be damned.

Her skin was as soft and delicate as the fabric of her gown. He ran his fingers along her arms, then trailed them down her side to her thigh. Slowly, he drew up her skirt until her legs were exposed, the pale flesh turned golden by the dancing firelight.

As his hands traced tiny circles over her thigh, he released her mouth, then dropped light kisses over her cheeks, her temples, her forehead, her earlobes. When he heard the tiny moan deep in her throat, another surge of wanting shot through him, leaving him shaken, his control nearly shattered. He wanted her now. He wanted to be buried inside her, sheathed in the warmth of her body.

He set his jaw and forced himself to take a long, slow breath. "Your bedchamber, Heather," he said softly near her ear. "We cannot stay here. Where is your bedchamber?"

"I . . . I will show you," she whispered in return.

He rose to his feet, grasping her hands and pulling her up with him. She swayed, as if unable to stand. He glanced once more at her full breasts, then slid the fabric of her bodice over them, hiding them once again from his hungry gaze. Sweeping her into his arms, he looked down into her face. "Point the way."

The sultry look in her eyes was one he'd never seen there before. He suddenly wondered if he would be able to carry her to her bedchamber. The urgency of wanting had drained the strength from his legs.

"Upstairs," she told him, her voice quivering. "To the right."

The urgency turned to action as he strode quickly across the salon, pausing only long enough to yank open the door. He gave no thought to any servants and, luckily, encountered none. He moved like a man possessed.

Perhaps he was.

Heather felt a warmth deep in the innermost part of her. It was almost a pain, yet not so undesirable. She didn't want to be rid of it so much as to become a part of it.

"This room," she whispered huskily as he neared her bedchamber.

In the moment it took him to open the door, their eyes met again. She knew this was her last chance to stop him. She knew that what she was about to do would ruin her forever in the eyes of Society. She didn't care. She would have this night. She would have these minutes, these hours in his arms. She would love him for this moment in time.

She smiled tremulously, silently telling him her decision.

Tanner stepped into the bedchamber and closed the door with the heel of his boot.

Moments later, the feather mattress sank beneath her as he lowered her onto the center of the bed. She shivered as she waited for him to join her. Her heart was pounding in her chest, the rapid beat echoing in her ears. She could hear his movements but could see nothing in the darkness. The strange aching in her loins increased, and she lifted her arms.

"Tanner?" she whispered.

Then he was beside her, gathering her to him. She slipped into his embrace as naturally as if she'd been doing it all her life. Her fingers slid over the bare skin of his back. She sucked in her breath, startled by the magnificent feel of his muscles beneath her fingertips.

She was vaguely aware of his hands slowly divesting her of her clothes, each movement accompanied by kisses and caresses. He didn't seem to be rushing, yet it wasn't long before she lay beside him, as naked as he. She was thankful for the darkness. Fear mingled with anticipation.

His gentle hands stroked and tutored, slowly building the aching need inside her to an undeniable desire. She raised toward his skillful touch, wanting more, demanding more.

"Tanner!" she cried as a burst of strange sensations exploded within her.

Then he rose, her glorious golden hawk. She opened her eyes to see his shadowed form hovering above her.

"Tanner?" she said again, her voice softened by the sense of wonder that warmed her blood.

Like the hawk, he seemed to swoop earthward, and she, his prey, became his willing captive.

When he plunged inside her, the brief pain was scarcely noticed, overshadowed by her heart's flight of joy.

His release came quickly, but not before he heard her enraptured cry and felt her body shuddering beneath him. His own climax followed hers; explosive, intense.

Breathing raggedly, his forehead pressed into a pillow, he supported his weight on his forearms. He was shaking, completely sapped of strength. He felt her muscles contract around him again, heard her contented sigh.

It was as if he were awakening from a dream. He felt strangely disoriented, not quite sure what had happened to him. Cool. Controlled. That was how he lived his life. Even when he was making love to a woman, he always remained in control. But not this time. He'd been carried by some unseen force, whipping him about like a tiny ship in a hurricane.

He rolled onto his side, taking her with him, holding her in a tight embrace. He had no strength left with which to speak, let alone move. He could only hold her and listen to the rapid beating of his heart.

His thought before drifting into sated slumber was of her eyes and the way she'd looked at him as he'd carried her into this room. As he'd always known, she could never lie to him. She wore her emotions openly—on her face, in her eyes. Remembering that look now, he felt a strange peace warming his heart, a peace he hadn't known in many, many years.

Heather listened to the gentle sound of his breathing and knew he slept. It was soothing, comforting, just lying here in his arms, remembering their lovemaking and everything she'd felt. She couldn't believe it yet, the explosive reality of their joining. She hadn't had any idea it would be like this. Even yet, the longing for him threatened to overwhelm her.

She was truly a woman now, *his* woman. She would always belong to Tanner.

Sadness drove the lingering sense of wonder from her heart. She wasn't lying in his bed, sheltered in his arms, because she'd won his love. She was there under false pretenses. As surely as he had lied to her about his identity when first they'd met, she had been living a lie from the moment she knew he was the duke.

I have been played the fool by a woman before . . .

What did she do to you, Tanner, that woman who hurt you so? Who was she? Was it your wife, the one you never speak of, the one you pretend never existed? Tell me what happened between you. If you tell me, perhaps we could find a way . . .

I have been played the fool by a woman before . . . It won't happen again.

She had to face the truth. Tanner would never forgive her. No matter what her reasons for lying, he would never forgive her. And she couldn't continue to deceive him anymore. She loved him too much for that.

Heather moved closer to him, fitting her body against the length of his, her head still on his shoulder. She laid her hand on his chest and felt the warmth of his skin.

She would give herself just a little while longer, she decided. She would wait until after the Hawksbury Ball. She would allow herself that one night, and then she would do what she had to do.

Half asleep, his body still lethargic, Tanner drew Heather close against him. He nuzzled her ear, then brushed his lips through her short tangle of curls.

And then reality struck. What had he done? If he should be discovered here . . . He tossed back the covers and searched for his clothes.

"Tanner?" Heather mumbled sleepily. "Where are you going?"

"I must leave before Lady Moberly arrives home. There'll be the devil to pay if she ever finds out what's gone on here."

He heard a match strike, saw the flare of light coming from behind him. He grabbed his trousers from the floor, turning as he slipped into them. He looked up to find Heather watching him with wide, sad eyes, the bedclothes clutched to her breasts. She seemed frightened and uncertain.

No matter how great his feeling of urgency to be gone before he was discovered, he had to reassure her. Placing one knee on the bed, he leaned forward to kiss her lips.

"We're to be married, Heather."

It was a simple statement, meant to keep her from feeling ashamed for what had happened. He could only assume that remorse was what had brought the heart-wrenching look to her face. Yet instead of giving her comfort, his words made tears spring suddenly to her eyes. Her lower lip trembled.

"I will treasure your gift of innocence always," he said.

She flushed and dropped her gaze.

He felt a tightening in his chest. "Heather . . ." he said softly.

She looked up again.

"Don't ever be ashamed of what we shared this night."

He knew she would never understand how he felt. He'd been fooled before, but not this time. He'd judged Heather a sweet innocent, and that she had been. He knew without a doubt that he was the first man ever to lie with her, ever to awaken the passion within her. He knew there were no secret lovers in her past. He hadn't meant for their lovemaking to happen before the wedding, but now that it had, he couldn't help but feel glad to know he hadn't been duped by another pretty face.

"I must go."

He kissed the tip of her nose, then pushed himself off the bed and quickly continued to dress. Just as he was shrugging on his coat, he heard voices in the hall.

He glanced about for any means of concealment, then darted toward the window. He raised the glass and stepped out onto the ledge just as the door to the bedchamber opened.

"You *are* up," he heard Lynette say. "I thought

you'd fallen asleep without dousing the light. Are you feeling better?"

"Yes. Yes, my headache is gone," Heather replied. "But I'm terribly tired. I think I'll put out the light and go to sleep now."

"All right, my dear. We'll talk in the morning. Good night."

"Good night, Lynette."

The candlelight was extinguished. Tanner heard the door close. Still, he didn't move.

"Tanner?" Heather's head appeared at the window.

"I'm here."

"What are we going to do?" she whispered.

"I'll climb down that tree and go over the garden wall."

Pale light from the first quarter moon spilled over her face as she turned her attention toward the young oak outside her window. "It's not a very big tree. Doesn't look very strong."

She was right. It didn't look strong, but he didn't seem to have any other options.

Heather leaned forward. She was wearing a nightgown now, and the thin fabric was pulled tight across her generous breasts. It was hard for Tanner to think about climbing trees when she was so near and looked so fetching.

Was there an impish gleam in her eye, or was it merely moonlight?

"You'd better try for that branch there." She pointed. "It looks to be the strongest."

"You're the tree-climbing expert," he replied dryly.

She muffled her laughter with her hand.

"Get back into bed, Heather, and if I'm found out, deny that you ever saw me tonight."

She hesitated for a moment. The smile faded from her sweet mouth. Finally, she called a soft

"Good-bye," then disappeared into her darkened bedchamber.

Tanner studied the tall tree several feet out from the side of the house. He wondered if he would still think the lovemaking so extraordinary if he fell and broke his neck.

He shook his head and chuckled with self-deprecation. The little filly had done it to him again. Not even his closest friends would believe he'd found himself in such a predicament, even if he told them himself.

Chapter 21

Heather remained in bed with her eyes closed long after she was fully awake. Bittersweet, the images of their lovemaking returned to taunt her, reminding her of what she had lost, what she would never experience again. She longed to be able to lie with him just one more time. For just an hour. For just one night. For just one lifetime. If only ...

But she had been through it time and again. No matter how long she thought about it, there was no changing the past. She couldn't change what had happened to her father, or the oath she had sworn to uphold, or that George had been shot. She couldn't erase the lies she'd told or the ones she'd been told. Her marriage to Tanner was never meant to be, and she could not fool herself into thinking otherwise.

She couldn't even console herself that the deed to GlenRoyal was now hers, for it had come to her at far too high a price. Had she given herself to Tanner in exchange for the deed? she wondered guiltily, then answered herself with a resounding No!

Fearing that she would give in to tears if she remained in her chamber much longer, she got out of bed and pulled on a wrapper, then went to the door.

A rapping sounded before she reached it, followed by Lynette's voice. "Heather, dear, are you awake?" The door opened to admit the woman. "You're up? Then you must be feeling better." Her green gaze moved slowly around the bedchamber as she strolled into the room.

"Yes. Much better." Heather took a step backward.

She wondered if Lynette could see the changes that she felt must show on her face. In one night, she'd left all innocence behind. In a few hours in Tanner's arms, she'd become a woman. Surely the difference could be seen.

Lynette's gaze returned to Heather as she raised her arm. Rolled up in her grasp was the GlenRoyal deed. "I found this on the floor of the salon."

"I . . . I must have dropped it. How careless of me." Heather's fingers closed around the cherished paper with the bold signature at the bottom.

"Hawk came here last night?"

Heather nodded.

"The man has no sense of acceptable behavior. Has he no idea of the gossip he might cause, coming so late when there was no one here to chaperon?"

"We weren't alone. The servants were here," Heather responded defensively. Fighting the flush that threatened to color her cheeks, she added, "Besides, he only wanted to give this to me."

Lynette's eyes narrowed a fraction as she studied the young woman before her. "Are you certain you're feeling all right, Heather?"

She nodded even as another headache began to throb in her temples.

Once again Lynette's gaze moved over the room. A tiny frown made a crease between her eyebrows as she looked at the bed, then shifted her focus suddenly back to Heather. "My dear, you may not think it necessary, but I feel a great responsibility for you. I have gladly sponsored you for the Season because you have no mother, no family as far as I'm concerned." She flicked her fingers at the air. "I don't count your aunt. Lady Beckworth is more liability than asset. Be that as it may, I am terribly fond of you, Heather, and I want to see your success in Society continue long after your marriage to the duke. I shouldn't want a scandal to mar things for you. It wouldn't matter much to Hawk. He is oblivious to it all. But you could be hurt, my dear."

"There will be no scandal," Heather said around the lump in her throat.

"Of course not." Lynette offered a smile as she reached out to pat Heather's cheek. "Well, I must see to some business before our busy day begins. Remember, we have an appointment with Madame Pritchett this afternoon. Your gown for the Hawksbury Ball is ready for its final fitting." Then she breezed out of the room as quickly as she'd arrived.

Heather stared at the closed door for a long time before going to stand at the window. She stared out at the backyard and the high garden wall that closed out the noisy London street.

They were all going to hate her when she left. All of them. Lynette, Celeste, the dowager duchess, Tanner. Especially Tanner.

She leaned her forehead against the glass and closed her eyes, finding the weight of her deceit unbearable.

"It's outrageous! Simply outrageous!" Caroline tossed the cards and envelopes onto the table as she faced her husband. "We get invitations from absolute nobodies. Nobodies, I tell you. I'm surprised we're even invited to the Hawksbury Ball." She picked up one of the cards, then dropped it again in a show of disgust. "But Heather is absolutely everywhere. I understand she's even to receive a voucher to Almack's. *I'm* her aunt! *I* should be going with her, not Lady Moberly!"

Frederick laid his paper aside. "Shouldn't you be glad of her success in her first Season in London? Besides, she'll be married in a couple of months, and then you needn't worry about her any longer."

"You're such a fool. Don't you realize that if she'd fallen on her face, the duke might have found an acceptable way out of the engagement? Annabella might have won his attentions then. Our daughter could have been the next Duchess of Hawksbury."

Her husband shook his head, his mouth set in a tense line. "Well, she didn't fall on her face. Our niece is one of the darlings of the Season, and I doubt very much that the duke will cry off. Even if he did, I see no reason for you to expect he would then offer for Annabella. He's scarcely noticed her existence, from what I've seen."

Caroline continued to fume, but she knew it was useless to argue with her husband. He simply refused to understand the disaster that had befallen them.

She rose from the table and left the dining room, frowning thoughtfully. Frederick was right about two things, she feared. Hawksbury didn't know Annabella existed, and Heather was truly the darling of the Season. How either of those things could possibly be was beyond her.

Annabella had better breeding and was the daughter of a respected viscount. Heather was a penniless orphan, daughter of a wastrel baron who hadn't been able to hold his liquor. Caroline's daughter had style and beauty. Her niece was more at ease on the back of a horse than in a ballroom. Annabella had been an enormous success in her first Season. It was only because she hadn't wanted to accept any offer too hastily that she hadn't captured a husband last year. Heather was—

Oh, bother! There was no point dwelling on this. They simply couldn't waste any more time on the duke. If Annabella didn't end this Season with an acceptable offer, it would become more and more difficult to find her well married. Caroline certainly hadn't seen the signs of any truly desirable men calling upon her daughter. With the possible exception of the Marquess of Stroughton, there hadn't been any with a significant title—or even the prospect of one. Next year there would be another batch of fresh-faced beauties vying for the available men on the marriage mart. Annabella must make her match before the Season's end.

Caroline climbed the stairs, her mind made up. They would begin their new strategy at the Hawksbury Ball. Annabella and Heather would simply have to become good friends. No matter what she had to do, Annabella would ingratiate herself with Heather so that she received the same invitations as her cousin.

She eyed her daughter's door with dread. Annabella was not going to appreciate her mother's advice. She had set her foolish heart on being a duchess. Perhaps it was still possible, just not with this particular duke.

"But you are early, Lady Moberly. I was not expecting the young lady until two." Madame Pritchett wore a harried expression as she regarded the two women in her waiting room.

Lynette frowned. "Oh, dear. And I have another appointment to keep at two. However did I confuse the times?"

Heather touched Lynette's arm. "I don't mind waiting here alone. Go on to your appointment.

By the time you return, Madame Pritchett will be finished with me."

"Very well, but I am sorry to leave you like this. I did want to see your ball gown." With a parting wave, Lynette swept out of the shop.

"If you will sit here, Miss FitzHugh, I shall return to you as quickly as possible. I must complete my fitting in the other room. Here is a pattern book you might care to look through. Perhaps you will see something you just cannot live without."

Heather took the book from the modiste's hand and watched as the birdlike woman scurried off toward the back of the shop, disappearing behind some heavy brocade curtains. She glanced down at the book in her lap and began to idly turn the pages. It wasn't long before her thoughts had drifted back to the previous night, and soon she was lost in the memories once again.

"Good day, Miss FitzHugh."

Startled from her thoughts, Heather jumped, and the pattern book fell to the floor. She looked up into the amused face of Althea Rathdrum.

"I'm sorry," Althea said. "I didn't mean to alarm you."

"I'm afraid I was daydreaming, Lady Merrywood. I didn't hear you come in."

The woman smiled. "I do the same thing in a dress shop. I do love to buy new things. Don't you?"

Althea strolled around the outer room of the shop, looking at bolts of fabric and spindles of thread, running her fingers over the colorful display of feathers and bonnets that lined one wall.

Heather watched each and every movement, for she remembered what Celeste had told her about the Countess of Merrywood. Here was another woman who'd been determined to marry Tanner. Why hadn't he chosen Althea? She was beautiful beyond compare, elegant, self-assured—everything Heather was not.

Finally, Althea turned back to Heather again. "You must be excited about your upcoming marriage to the duke," she said as she crossed the room. She settled onto a nearby chair. "You must know that you are the envy of many a single young woman."

Heather remained silent, cautiously observing the woman.

The countess picked a stray thread from her tangerine-colored walking dress. "Of course, there was so much talk after Judith died. Terrible." She clucked her tongue. "Simply terrible."

"Judith?"

Althea's amber eyes widened. "Surely you know about Hawk's wife?" Her voice softened, conciliatory in tone. "No, I can see that you don't. However have you managed to remain so ignorant?"

A flash of anger warmed Heather's chest, but she managed to bite back a retort. She'd wondered about this Judith—though she hadn't known her name—from the moment the dowager duchess had mentioned her. She'd planned several times to ask Tanner about his first wife, but the timing had never seemed right. They were so seldom alone together, and when they were . . .

She felt her cheeks grow warm as she thought of last night, the two of them lying on the carpet beside the fireplace, flickering light glowing upon her breasts as he kissed her bared flesh.

She swallowed and pushed the memory away. Last night had certainly not been the time to ask him about another woman.

"It was very sad," Althea continued, fastening her gaze upon her hands in her lap. "Everyone thought it was the love match of the Season. Hawk was positively besotted, I am told. Of course, I didn't see him myself. I hadn't come out yet. It wasn't long after they were married that we heard the duchess was increasing. Naturally, we expected the duke to be thrilled about it."

Heather was scarcely breathing. *Love match of the Season ... positively besotted ... the duchess was increasing.* Why did Althea's words hurt so much?

Althea lowered her voice to a confidential tone. "We heard he beat her in a fit of rage and sent her away to one of his remote estates. She died in childbirth. Very mysterious, don't you think?"

Heather couldn't believe it. She'd experienced Tanner's temper, seen the cold disdain in his icy blue eyes, but she couldn't believe he would ever beat a woman. Not the Tanner who had kissed and caressed her and held her tenderly in his arms. Not the Tanner who had introduced her to true passion. Not the Tanner she loved.

Althea glanced at Heather again, her head cocked slightly to one side, her gaze assessing. "Of course, I'm sure you can't believe such a thing is true, since you are to marry the man soon, but the whispers kept many a young woman from accepting the duke's offer of matrimony. Who would want to suffer the same fate as poor Judith?" She rose from the chair, her expression troubled. "They're only rumors, of course. No one ever dared accuse a man as rich and powerful as the Duke of Hawksbury of brutality. Only ... do be mindful of it, Miss FitzHugh, and guard yourself. You seem terribly naive. All those years in the country, no doubt."

With a flick of her head in an abbreviated wave of farewell, she crossed the modiste's shop room and disappeared into the London street, leaving Heather with added trouble for an already troubled heart.

* * *

Tanner was in his study when Pengelly announced that Lady Moberly wished to speak with him in private. He had a bad feeling about such an audience, but he told the majordomo to show the lady in.

While he waited, he pushed his chair back from the large desk, then rose and walked over to the window. There were flowers blooming in the Albany House gardens, and birds were singing in the trees. He smiled, thinking how Heather would look, ribbons flapping, curls bouncing, as she raced after a large red dog. He'd been thinking such thoughts ever since he'd jumped from the ledge outside her bedchamber and climbed down that tree very early this morning.

"I'm glad one of us has something to grin about, Hawk."

He turned as the door closed behind Lynette. She was wearing a thunderous expression on her usually composed face.

"You know why I've come," she said as she walked toward him.

"Do I?" He arched an eyebrow.

"Of course you do." Lynette stopped beside the large oak desk. "You have not only abused my friendship, you have jeopardized Heather's place in Society. I am appalled."

Tanner schooled his face to reveal no emotion. "Just what is it I've done that has caused you such distress, Lady Moberly?"

"Don't play the fool with me, Hawk. Heather may be naive, but I am not. You not only came to see her when you knew I wasn't home, you took advantage of my absence."

"What makes you think so?"

Lynette made a frustrated sound in her throat as she turned away from him. She paced the length of the study, then returned. "How like you to force me to speak of such things."

It seemed that he'd been found out, but he wasn't going to admit to anything until he was pushed to. He wanted to know if Heather had been reckless enough to speak of the night they'd shared. He wanted most of all to protect her. He waited for Lynette to continue.

With a sigh, she sank into the nearest chair. "I am not an innocent Bath miss with a head full of romantic notions and no knowledge of what goes on in the real world, my friend. You knew my husband. Lord Moberly was a rather ... lusty man, and I am not unfamiliar with the art of love." She paused long enough to allow herself a secretive smile, then sobered quickly as she pulled her attention back to the matter at hand. "Believe me, Hawk, I know the signs. You were there in her bedchamber last night. Heather didn't destroy her bedding during a nightmare, nor did she stain her bedsheets without your help. Pray, have I said enough, or must I continue?"

Tanner faced the window, hiding from Lynette's shrewd gaze. The sudden memory of Heather lying naked and willing beneath him struck him with force, and left him aching to be with her again.

"Servants do gossip, Hawk. Even mine. Should this get out . . ." Lynette let her unspoken warning hang in the air.

His reply was abrupt, gruff. "No one will hear of it."

"You can't control everything with the same iron will you use on your emotions, my friend. Did you stop to consider what would happen if she should end up carrying your child as a result of last night? Your wedding is still many weeks away."

"We'll move it forward," he answered stubbornly.

"Look at me, your grace."

He turned around. The anger and frustration had faded from her face, tender concern left in their place.

"You must promise me you won't compromise her any further. She won't be able to stop you, you know. She loves you too much to deny you anything."

He stiffened. "Nonsense."

"Is it?"

He shifted uncomfortably. Of course it was nonsense. Neither of them had ever pretended there was anything beyond a mutual fondness and admiration between them. Take the other night, for example, when they were at the Mannington rout. Heather herself had stated that theirs wasn't a love match. She couldn't possibly love him any more than he loved her. Last night had been merely a moment of reckless passion. That was all.

"I assure you, it won't happen again," he stated.

Amidst a soft rustle of silky skirts, Lynette rose and circumvented his desk. She reached forward, laying her hand on his arm. "'Tis bad enough you are blind to Heather's feelings. 'Tis sadder still that you are blind to your own. You have been more content these past weeks than I have seen you in years, your grace. Don't risk losing it because you refuse to recognize it."

She crossed the study, pausing to look behind her when she reached the door. She opened her mouth as if to speak, then closed it again, shaking her head as she left the room.

Blasted interfering female! Tanner raked the fingers of his hand through his hair. What right had she to waltz in here and demand that he behave like a gentleman? What right had she to try to tell him his own feelings?

"Bloody hell!" he muttered as he sat down at his desk, jerking the account books toward him and staring at the entries.

He'd be damned if he would let a woman—*any* woman—turn his life upside down again. He'd be damned if he would.

Madame Pritchett scurried into the fitting room. "There is a message for you, Miss FitzHugh," she said as she held out a slip of paper.

Heather turned from the mirror to accept the missive. She unfolded it and studied the flowery handwriting, a cold knot forming in her stomach.

Must speak with you about Judith, the Duchess of Hawksbury, and his grace the duke. My carriage awaits in back of Madame Pritchett's shop. Please use discretion.

H.M.

She didn't know what to make of the message, but she knew she couldn't ignore it.

"Help me change, Madame Pritchett. I must be going."

H.M. Who was H.M.? Why would someone send her a note here, wanting to tell her about Tanner and his first wife?

Althea's words echoed in her head, but she shoved them aside. She refused to believe such gossip. Tanner wasn't capable of mistreating a woman, no matter what she did to provoke him. With all her being, Heather knew he would never do such a thing.

But she still wanted to know who had sent the note and why. It was too much of a coincidence that Althea should tell her those things and then for the note to arrive. The two had to be somehow related. Curiosity demanded that she discover the link between them.

Within a short time, Heather was back in her own clothes. She left the shop, barely glancing up and down the street before hurrying along the walk toward the narrow alley behind Madame Pritchett's shop. As she stepped around the corner and into the alley, she saw a pair of fancy grays standing before a burgundy-and-black carriage. The door opened in silent welcome. She walked toward it, then hesitated while still several feet away.

"Please get in before you're seen, Miss Fitz-Hugh," a cultured feminine voice said from within.

Bolstering her courage with a deep breath, Heather stepped forward just as the driver hopped down from his seat. As she paused before the open carriage door, he offered his hand to assist her inside. She took hold and stepped into the ornate coach. The door was closed quickly behind her.

It took her eyes a moment to adjust to the interior of the closed carriage. By the time she'd settled herself on the plush velvet seat, the vehicle had snapped into motion.

"Thank you for meeting me," said the woman across from her.

Heather stared at her companion. She was strikingly beautiful. Her honey-brown hair was piled in a mass of curls atop her head, accentuating her long neck. Wide brown eyes were the focal point of an arresting face. Her nose was petite, her mouth full, her complexion like porcelain. The cut of her dress revealed the generous swell of her bosom, and she was surrounded by a seductive cloud of perfume.

"I am Miss Morton. Harriette Morton." She paused, as if awaiting Heather's reaction.

Heather tried to hide her surprise while she searched for some response to the woman's announcement. She found none.

Harriette smiled. "You know who I am, then." It wasn't a question.

"Yes." Heather drew herself erect, holding her chin high and proud. "You're Tanner's mistress."

Harriette's laughter filled the coach. "La! Is that who I am?" It took her a moment more to control herself.

Finally, dabbing at her eyes with a handkerchief, she said, "The duke would never do anything so permanent as to have his own mistress, Miss Fitz-Hugh. I may have shared his bed on occasion, but I think it more accurate to describe us as friends." She lifted an eyebrow. "Does that shock you?"

No, Heather wasn't shocked. She couldn't imagine any woman not wanting to share Tanner's bed. She'd discovered that last night. But there was no denying the surge of jealousy that shot through her as she looked at the woman. She hated the thought of Tanner ever choosing to be with Harriette rather than with her. He'd promised Heather that he wouldn't see Harriette again. Would he return to Harriette once Heather broke the engagement?

"No, it doesn't shock me," Heather answered with a shake of her head.

"Good. Now, I must speak quickly. It would never do for us to be seen together."

"Why *did* you send the note, Miss Morton?"

"Because I heard what Lady Merrywood said to you inside the shop. I was on the other side of that curtain. Madame Pritchett is my modiste."

Not only the same man but the same dressmaker, Heather thought. What else did they share in common, the country chit and the London courtesan?

"The gossip about his grace and Lady Hawksbury has been around a long time, but you mustn't believe it. I know of the woman."

Heather felt a tightness in her belly. "He discussed her with you?"

"I don't suppose he meant to, but I have

gleaned bits of information here and there. Let me tell you what I know. Then it will be up to you how you use that knowledge." Harriette glanced at the closed curtains of the carriage door. "Judith Montgomery was pregnant with another man's child when she married the duke. She fooled him into believing she was a virgin when they were wed and that the child was his. Perhaps she would have succeeded in the deception if she'd not been imprudent in her affair." The cyprian returned her gaze to Heather.

"She foolishly took her lover, an artist from the streets of London, to one of the duke's own estates in the north."

GlenRoyal? Heather wondered. Surely it could not be. But hadn't he once told her, when he was merely Mr. Tanner, that the duke associated unpleasant memories with GlenRoyal?

"A few weeks later, the duke learned of her affair and confronted her. She confessed the truth and told him she was leaving him once the baby was born and they were well enough to travel. He told her she would never leave with his child. That was when she admitted the child wasn't his, and accused him of being a fool ever to believe it was." Harriette shook her head sadly. "But her lover deserted her before the birth of the child. He found a wealthy widow and married her."

Heather bit her lower lip and twisted her hands in her lap. Her heart felt as if it were breaking. She didn't want to hear any more, yet she couldn't tell the woman to stop.

"Judith died in childbirth, along with her son."

The noises of London receded to a dull buzz. Heather's eyes blurred with hot tears. She felt Harriette's hand upon hers.

"The duke has kept his heart cloaked in ice all these years, Miss FitzHugh. I believe you are the one who can thaw it."

Heather's throat felt tight, and her voice came out in a hoarse whisper. "Why did he tell you this? Was he in love with you?"

"A man often speaks freely when he's had too much claret. And no, Miss FitzHugh, his grace was never in love with me. He would be angry to learn what I have told you. I hope you will use the knowledge wisely."

What could *she* do? She was leaving London soon. She wished she'd never heard the story. His pain had become her pain, and she already had more than she could bear.

Harriette tapped on the top of the carriage. "Return to Madame Pritchett's, John," she called to the driver. "Miss FitzHugh?"

Heather swallowed back her tears.

"I told him once that not all women are like Judith. They do not all lie and cheat and deceive to gain wealth and power. I can see in your eyes that I was right. You love him. You will be able to help him."

Lie and cheat and deceive. The cyprian's words found the most vulnerable part of Heather's heart, cutting deeply. Her own guilt was like salt in the open wound left behind.

The carriage rolled to a stop. The door opened, and the driver offered Heather his hand once again. Numbly, she took it and stepped down from the carriage.

"Miss FitzHugh?"

She stopped but didn't look back.

"The duke hasn't come to see me since he met you. We talked once in the park, but he has never visited my home again. He cares for you, my dear. Do take care of him in return."

"And then, Mama, what do you suppose we saw?" Annabella removed her bonnet and tossed it onto a nearby settee. Her face was flushed with excitement, her brown eyes sparkling. "*Heather* got out of a carriage in the alley behind Madame Pritchett's shop. The windows were curtained, and I couldn't see who was inside, but it most certainly wasn't the duke's coach."

Caroline listened to Annabella with interest.

"Prudence thinks it could be she was with another man. She said only lovers rendezvous in closed carriages, and that if it had been anyone respectable, she wouldn't have alighted in an alley. Do you suppose it's true, Mama?"

"It does give one pause to think," Caroline murmured even as a slow smile curved her lips. "Perhaps it could be true. I don't suppose the duke would like it if she were keeping assignations. I wonder how he might hear of it?" She cocked an eyebrow at her daughter.

"Not I!" Annabella exclaimed. "I couldn't possibly tell the duke that Heather was ... well ... Mama, I couldn't."

"Heavens, no. No ... we could never be so direct. Hmm." She tapped her fingernails on the table. "I'll have to give the matter some thought."

"Perhaps, if he were angry enough with Heather, he might turn to me?" Annabella's expression was hopeful.

Caroline wanted nothing more than to tell her daughter she thought it might work, but she had to remain practical. Frederick had made it clear that if something didn't happen soon, they would be forced back to Beckworth House. The family coffers were in dire straights. Heather's betrothal to the duke had helped them obtain more credit, but it still wasn't enough. No, her darling Annabella couldn't wait for the duke. She had to make another match, and soon.

Caroline shook her head as she rose from her chair and went to stand beside her daughter. She stroked the golden hair back from her child's face, then dropped a kiss upon the crown of the girl's head. "No, my dearest, I don't think that will happen. But there are plenty of other eligible men who will want you for their bride. We must select the right one to make my angel happy."

And in the meantime, if she could cause that niece of hers a bit of the same anguish Heather had caused the Beckworths, all the better.

Yes, she would have to give the matter more thought.

Chapter 22

Tanner slipped his arms through the sleeves of the white waistcoat, then waited as Thorpe brought him his jacket. The burgundy dress coat was made of fine kerseymere, and the cutaway style revealed both the breadth of his shoulders and his slim, athletic waist. Likewise, the formfitting trousers defined his muscular thighs and calves. Shiny black kid pumps completed the fashionable ensemble. Tanner glanced in the mirror as his valet fussed with the snowy white cravat, but he was only vaguely aware of his reflection.

"Her grace asked that you join her in her chamber when you are ready, your grace." Thorpe stepped back and admired his handiwork.

Tanner grunted a noncommittal response, his thoughts far from this chamber at Albany House. He'd received a note in the morning post from Hawksbury Park, filled with bad news. His steward had died suddenly in his sleep two nights before, and the very next day, his butler had fallen down a flight of stairs and broken his leg. His groom of the chambers had written to request that the duke return to the Park as soon as conveniently possible.

"Miss FitzHugh and Lady Moberly are expected momentarily," Thorpe continued.

Tanner would have to leave London soon, but

he was reluctant to do so. This couldn't have happened at a worse time, what with his engagement and Heather and—

His valet cleared his throat. "Shall I tell her grace that you'll join her shortly?"

Tanner shook his head as if to clear it. "Yes. Do that, Thorpe."

The valet nodded and turned away, leaving the duke still gazing into the mirror.

Damn inconvenient, he thought, recalling the problems at Hawksbury Park, and then immediately felt a twinge of guilt. His steward, Roger Clatworthy, had been at the Park for over thirty years. He would be sorely missed by everyone there, most of all by Tanner, who had always known he could trust the man implicitly. As for the butler, they didn't come any better than Murray, and Tanner truly hoped the man's leg would mend quickly and completely.

But then Heather's image swam before him, her face flushed with passion, her eyes glimmering with desire. By gad, he wanted to see her like that again.

He glowered at his reflection. It wasn't like him, this daydreaming. He'd always taken care of his responsibilities before pursuing pleasures. Such behavior had been second nature to him. But for the past two weeks, he'd found his desk cluttered with business papers that he'd ignored while he dashed from rout to ball to soiree in hopes of seeing Heather.

Tanner strode across the vast bedchamber toward the open window. A gentle rain had begun to fall, bringing with it a fresh breeze. The darkening sky hinted that evening was drawing nigh. Soon the crush of guests would begin to arrive.

It was no secret, of course, that the duke was engaged to Miss FitzHugh, but tonight's ball was their official and most public announcement of their impending nuptials. Perhaps that was why he felt so tense. Perhaps that was why he couldn't decide when to go to Hawksbury Park. He'd made a ghastly mistake before. With this engagement, could he be embarking on another?

Even as he asked himself the question, he knew that wasn't the reason for his dark mood. He silently admitted he was still brooding over Lynette's upbraiding of two days before. Begrudgingly, he'd been forced to acknowledge the truth of what she'd said. He had endangered Heather's place in Society by his recklessness. He was bound and determined not to repeat his mistake. He would keep his passion in check until after they were wed. If that meant he had to avoid seeing her so frequently, so be it. That was why he hadn't called upon her for the past two days.

Only there was one problem with his decision. He missed her. He'd been missing her ever since he'd climbed down that blasted tree and over that miserable wall.

"I'll be damned," he whispered, bemused by the realization.

The clatter of horses' hooves mingled with the soft melody of raindrops spattering against the windowpanes, and his attention was drawn to the carriage in the street below. Lady Moberly's carriage. It stopped in front of the curved staircase leading to the front entrance of Albany House. A moment later, two ladies were helped from the carriage, a footman holding an umbrella over their heads to protect their evening finery from the rain.

Lord, he wished the fool would move the blasted thing so he could see her face.

As had happened often since their night together, he recalled her innocent smile, her instinctive response to his lovemaking. His nostrils seemed filled with her sweet scent, a heady, seductive aroma that was uniquely hers. The desire to hold her, to possess her, gripped him like a merciless vice.

By Jove, it wasn't supposed to be like this. He'd outgrown such silly schoolboy yearnings. An heir: that was the only reason he'd chosen to wed again. His concern was for the Hawksbury estates, nothing more. He was not a man who would allow himself to be ruled by passion. He'd learned long ago it was better not to care too much for any woman who shared his bed.

He watched as the elegantly clad ladies climbed the sweeping marble stairway. The umbrella continued to obscure his view of Heather, and his frustration mounted.

He swore beneath his breath even as he turned from the window and stalked resolutely toward the door, the promise to join his mother in her chamber forgotten.

Heather unfastened the shoulder brooch that held her Poland mantle in place and let the silk wrap fall into the hands of the waiting groom of the chambers. She felt the cool air slide over her bare flesh above the deep, square-cut neckline of her pale lavender gown.

She'd dressed for him tonight; there was no denying it. She'd chosen the pattern from Madame Pritchett's book because she thought he would like it. From the purple ribbons in her hair to the soft lavender slippers on her feet, she'd selected each item to please Tanner Montgomery.

Her heart seemed to be thumping against her ribs, and she felt a trifle light-headed. Nervously, she ran her fingers over her high-waisted ensemble, smoothing the transparent silver dress worn over an opaque lavender slip. Would Tanner like the way she looked? Would he approve of her gown? Would he think her lovely?

Her hands balled into tight fists at her sides as

she reminded herself not to think such things. Better instead to remember that she would soon leave London—and Tanner. He would never break the engagement on his own, no matter how outrageous she might behave—and she'd considered any number of outrageous things she could do to convince him of his poor choice in a bride—but she knew that once the formal announcement had been made, there would be no honorable way for a gentleman like Tanner to withdraw his offer. She would have to be the one to cry off. She didn't much care that she would carry the label of jilt. She cared only that she wouldn't ever see him again.

She should have ended it long ago, should have broken with him the moment she first suspected she might truly care. She shouldn't have let the engagement be announced in the *Morning Post* and the *Gazette* and *The Times*. She should have prevented the dowager duchess from holding this ball in their honor. She never should have allowed Lynette to help her select the pattern for her wedding gown. Above all, she shouldn't have permitted Tanner into her heart or her bed.

She heard the sharp clip of his heels on the tiled floor and drew in a quick breath at the sight of him, so handsome in his burgundy attire. He exuded strength and ruggedness of character. As appealing as that could be, she saw even deeper to the tenderness and good humor he hid beneath the surface. She saw the Hawksbury no one else saw.

How cruel that she should love him so.

"Heather . . ." His voice speaking her name was like a gentle caress. He took her hand as he gazed down into her eyes. "You look beautiful."

She felt a flush warming her cheeks. They were

the words she'd longed to hear. "Thank you, your grace."

She realized how frightened she'd been for the past two days. She hadn't known why he'd stayed away after their night of lovemaking. All manner of reasons had raised their ugly heads, taunting and tormenting her. But as she looked up at him, she forgot her fears, forgot the reasons why she shouldn't love him and couldn't marry him. There was only Tanner and this night. She would worry about the rest tomorrow.

Wordlessly, he offered his arm to her. She placed her fingertips on his wrist and allowed him to guide her into the rose salon. Lynette followed unnoticed.

"You've scarcely taken your eyes off the girl all evening, my lord. Tell me, what is her appeal?"

Aaron St. Clair turned to gaze upon the lovely woman at his side, who had spoken. Althea Rathdrum was a rare beauty and a fiery paramour, as he'd discovered recently.

Taking a married woman for a lover was a change for him. He rather preferred the careful and slow seduction required with the green girls in their first Season. The challenge was to woo them into bed but avoid the scandal that would force him into marriage, and he'd become quite adept at it through the years. He wasn't certain how his liaison with Lady Merrywood had come about, but he meant to enjoy it while it lasted.

St. Clair shrugged in answer to her question as he looked toward the dance floor again, his gaze quickly finding Heather FitzHugh in her shimmering lavender raiment. "I'm not sure. Perhaps it's her innocence." His smile didn't hide the dangerous gleam in his eyes. "Or perhaps it's because she belongs to Hawksbury."

"You haven't any particular fondness for his grace, do you?" Althea sidled closer.

"Why should I?"

"No reason, I suppose."

St. Clair gave his companion a sidelong glance. She was wearing a curious smile, a look that was suspiciously smug. "What are you thinking in that insidious little head of yours?"

The smile grew as she turned to look at him. "Nothing in particular. Except 'tis no secret about his first wife's infidelity. 'Tis a shame he seems to have chosen no better the second time."

"What are you talking about?"

Althea fluttered the fan in front of her face as she leaned closer to him, lowering her voice to a confidential tone. "Only that Miss FitzHugh may not be as innocent as you and Hawksbury think. Yesterday I made a call on Lady Beckworth, and she confided to me that she is concerned Miss FitzHugh has formed a *tendre* for another man. She didn't know who. And only today I heard a rumor that the young lady was seen disembarking from a mysterious carriage—and it wasn't the duke's. Obviously, she was with someone she didn't want to be seen with, because she kept her rendezvous in an alley. Pity whoever saw them didn't recognize the carriage. I would *love* to know whom she met there. Wouldn't you?" Whatever would Hawk think should he hear of it? His fury would be frightening to behold."

St. Clair's gaze found Heather once again. "And how would he hear of it?"

"Such things have a way of getting 'round. Some people are frightful gossips, you know. But, of course, *I* would never be the one to tell him."

It was the marquess's turn to laugh. "Of course not, *chère amie*. You would never be so foolish."

* * *

They clustered around her like bees to honey.
Men and women, young and old, she drew them
irresistibly to her.

Tanner watched from across the room as
Heather charmed the Albany House guests, from a
duchess to a lady of the manor, from a duke to the
youngest son of a baronet. Even the servants
seemed enchanted by her. She smiled and laughed
when she should. She answered their questions
with patience and refreshing honesty, never trying
to make herself seem more important or more
wealthy or more anything than what she was.

Time and again, whether he was beside her or
across the room, her gaze would lift and meet his.
Then her face would light with a secret smile, and
he would find himself smiling, too.

Of course, he didn't much care for the way the
dandies and bucks looked at her with longing.
Even his frequent frowns and meaningful glares
didn't drive them away fast enough to suit him.

Well, by heaven, he'd jolly well remind them
whom she was going to marry. He was tired of
sharing her with everyone in this place. He was
going to have a moment alone with her. He was
going to hold her in his arms and kiss her. He
was going to look into those beautiful eyes of hers
and see his passion mirrored in their violet depths.

He set his glass on a passing servant's tray and
strode toward Heather.

Tanner was smiling at her. His smiles had always been rare and unexpected, but tonight,
whenever he looked at her, the smile returned,
warm and secret and just for her. It made her heart
want to sing. It made her heart want to break.

Just a moment before, he had returned to her
side and taken hold of her arm. Mumbling some
excuse, he'd escorted her away from a group of
people, guiding her along a wall lined with enor-

mous oil paintings and gilded mirrors. Now, suddenly, he slipped through an open doorway, pulling her with him. She found herself in a dimly lit
hallway.

Tanner placed an index finger over his pursed
lips. "Shh."

Then, his expression as mischievous as a little
boy's, he led her away from the crowded salons
and ballroom and down a narrow stairway. Moments later, they were standing beside the open
door leading out to the Albany House gardens.
The rain was still falling, and the air had the clean,
freshly washed fragrance that Heather loved. It reminded her of the country and of home.

"I was tired of the crowd," he said softly, as if
not wanting to disturb the gentle sounds of the
rain.

"Me, too," she whispered.

"You look beautiful."

"Thank you, your grace."

"I was tired of everyone else admiring you."

She felt strangely warm as she looked out at the
night.

"I wanted you to myself."

With those words, he pulled her into his embrace, drawing her up against his chest. Even before his mouth covered hers, she felt the searing
heat of desire streaking through her, weakening
her limbs. She clasped her hands behind his neck
to keep from falling helplessly to the floor.

But he held her too securely for that. She was
molded to him, fitting the contours of his body as
if made for him. Perhaps she had been. Perhaps it
was destiny that they should be lovers. She could
feel his desire as strongly as her own.

She heard him draw a ragged breath as he released her lips. His hands moved to her upper

arms and gripped her tightly as he set her away from him. Was she mistaken, or did she feel a tremor pass through him?

"I don't think this is the time or place," he said. His voice sounded gravelly. He cleared his throat. "I was wrong to have jeopardized your reputation the other night, Heather. It would have been disastrous if I'd been discovered with you. I don't mean for it to happen again."

His image swam before her, blurred by unshed tears. How could she tell him she wished she could lie with him just one more time before she left him? Only one more time before she ran away and left behind her heart.

Was it so terrible to want another night in his arms? Just one before she had to go.

Again, Tanner drew her toward him, this time hugging her gently. "I didn't mean to make you cry," he whispered. "I'm sorry. I shouldn't have mentioned the other night."

" 'Tis all right."

"I have a surprise which I think will make you smile again."

She sniffed. "A surprise?" She stepped back from him.

Tanner gave her a handkerchief. "There's someone waiting out in the stables to see you."

Heather wore a puzzled frown.

"Haskin arrived today with Cathy."

"They're here? They're here now?"

He nodded.

She clutched his hand. "Oh, Tanner, may we see them?"

"I thought you might want to. Wait here."

He was gone for only a moment. When he returned, he was carrying an umbrella and a long black cloak. He placed the cloak over her shoul-

ders and opened the umbrella as they stepped outside.

"Mind where you walk. We don't want to spoil
your slippers with mud."

Chapter 23

Tanner watched Heather throw her arms around Haskin's shoulders and kiss him on the cheek. All signs of tears were gone. Her face was animated and filled with joy.

"Look at you, Miss Heather," Haskin said as the two released each other. "You've blossomed into a real lady since I seen you last. I don't reckon I'll ever find you climbin' trees again."

"I haven't changed so very much, Mr. Haskin," Heather protested with a laugh. She glanced over her shoulder at Tanner. "In fact, I was tempted to climb a tree just a couple of days ago."

Tanner knew exactly the moment to which she referred, and he had a sudden vision of her, her nightgown flowing in the evening breeze, her feet bare, following him down the tree outside her bedchamber. He repressed an amused smile.

"Look who I brought with me, Miss Heather." Haskin turned toward a nearby stall. "She's missed you."

"And I've missed her." Heather opened the gate and, mindless of her fancy ball gown, hugged the mare around the neck and pressed her forehead against the sleek coat. "Wait until you see Hyde Park, Cathy. There are people everywhere."

Tanner walked to the center of the stables. "Perhaps you'd be interested in seeing this horse also,

Heather. He's one of my newer acquisitions. I wouldn't mind your opinion, too, Haskin."

Heather gave Cathy's neck a few more strokes before leaving the mare's stall. Tanner watched her carefully, waiting for the moment of recognition.

Her face was so delightfully open. First there was the tiny frown between her brows. Then there was the sudden widening of her eyes. Next came the slight pursing of her mouth as she silently denied what she saw before her. And finally, her whole face lit up with pleasure.

"This can't be," she said with a laugh.

Tanner nodded smugly.

"Not that broken-down nag you paid fifty guineas for?"

Again he nodded, then followed her gaze back to the old dray horse. Eleven days of good food and plenty of rest, not to mention a thorough grooming, had done wonders for the animal. The horse wouldn't ever be considered a beauty, but at least he no longer looked as if he would drop dead at any moment.

"Pardon me, your grace," Haskin said, his tone skeptical. "Did I hear Miss Heather say you paid fifty guineas for this animal?"

Heather laughed, her violet eyes twinkling with merriment. " 'Twas my fault, Mr. Haskin. I found him in an alley being terribly mistreated. I couldn't bear to see it." She lightly touched Tanner's arm, her gaze meeting his briefly before she turned back to Haskin. "The duke bought the horse at my insistence."

Tanner felt his chest swelling with something akin to pride. And it was at that moment that the truth hit him.

He loved her!

He took a step backward, almost as if he'd suffered a physical blow. The groundskeeper's comment and Heather's response faded into a hum.

He loved her.

"Excuse me. I'll leave the two of you alone to talk." He didn't even glance at Heather as he whirled about and walked out into the rainy night.

How had it happened? How had he allowed himself to fall in love with her? When had he dropped his guard and let her into his heart?

He stood stock-still, rivulets of rainwater running down from his head and over his face.

Zounds! He was *glad* he loved her.

No one would believe it. The Duke of Hawksbury, impatient to be leg-shackled. The Duke of Hawksbury, moon-eyed over a girl who berated her future husband for wasting his hounds while at the same time rescuing foxes from the hunters. The Duke of Hawksbury, totty-headed over a girl who faced down burly draymen in alleys for the sake of a swaybacked rack of bones she called a horse.

No, no one would believe it. He couldn't believe it himself.

He began walking again, still mindless of the rain soaking him from head to toe. Looking back, he was filled with amazement at his memories of the weeks since he'd met Heather. Why hadn't he recognized it? How could he not have seen? She'd made him enjoy life again. She'd given him a fresh outlook. He no longer met each day with cynicism or greeted everyone with a jaundiced eye. Heather had made him feel warm and alive for the first time in many years.

And she'd made him want her. Not just to relieve his passions. Not just to sire his heirs. He wanted Heather because she was Heather— beautiful, naive, bright, honest, reckless, wonderful Heather.

Suddenly he laughed at himself. There was no question about it. He was completely addlepated—standing there in the rain, soaked to the skin, acting like an unlicked cub. And enjoying every minute of it!

There was a new spring in his step as he headed for the house and his bedchamber. He would change and then return for her, and then he would decide what to do with his new discovery of love.

"I couldn't believe it when I heard," Haskin said as he leaned against the stall door. "Your betrothal, I mean."

Heather stroked Cathy's nose. "I should have told you before I left Westmorland, but I . . . I just couldn't."

"Who'd have thought it? You and the duke himself."

Her lighthearted mood vanished in an instant.

"Oh, Mr. Haskin," she said quickly over a sob, "I can't marry him. What am I to do?" She threw herself into his arms, almost knocking the man off his feet.

"Here, now. What's this?" His gnarled hand stroked her head. "What's brought on these tears, Miss Heather?"

She used Tanner's handkerchief to blow her nose and dry her eyes. "I've never really intended to marry him, Mr. Haskin. I only accepted his offer to keep a promise I made to my father and brother. You see, I thought if I agreed to marry him and then showed everyone . . . Oh, 'tis too hard to explain." She choked on another sob. "I just know I can't go through with it. I can't intentionally hurt Tanner, but I can't marry him either. He shot my brother, Mr. Haskin. Tanner could have killed George. I can't marry the man who did that. I can't." She tipped her head back to look into the older man's eyes, hoping he could understand when she herself wasn't even sure she did.

"His grace shot George?"

Heather nodded. "In a duel."

"An' that's why the boy never come back?"

She nodded again.

"Lor', miss, 'tis my fault. If I'd known, I never would've kept silent 'bout his bein' the duke when you first met. But I had no way of knowin'. An' when I saw you losin' your heart to him and—"

"You knew I loved him?" she asked in a small voice, tears welling once again.

"Aye. I knew it." He cupped her chin. "An' from the looks of you, you love him still."

"What am I to do, Mr. Haskin? What am I to do?"

The groundskeeper laid her cheek against his chest and patted her hair. "I wish I could help you, miss, but I fear 'tis somethin' you must decide for yourself. This ain't a fox with a broken leg I can set and nurse back to health. I'm afraid I'm better at tendin' the animals an' the roses than givin' answers to you, Miss Heather."

She shook her head against him. "You're a good friend, Mr. Haskin. You've always been a good friend to me. Always."

She let him hold her for a long, long time, hiding for this short while from the troubles that plagued her.

St. Clair leaned negligently against the doorjamb, waiting for Heather to leave the stables and return to the ball. It had taken him a while to locate her once he'd realized she was missing, and he never would have counted on finding her in the arms of that old man. When he'd seen the two in their warm embrace, he had quietly retreated to wait patiently by the back door of the mansion. His turn with Miss FitzHugh would come, and he was looking forward to it.

He stared through the rain at the barn, remembering how he'd seen them, Heather's head pressed tightly against the groom's chest, the old man's hand stroking her hair as he whispered softly in her ear. A very touching scene, indeed. Why, he'd been tempted to shed a few tears himself, just looking at them.

St. Clair chuckled to himself. Of course, *he* knew the old groom wasn't Heather's lover, but he wasn't one to let such an opportunity pass him by. And he knew just how to best use the information. He had only to wait for Heather.

It was a wonder he'd seen them at all. He'd checked the barn on a whim, knowing that it was secluded and warm and the last place most members of the *ton* would think to look. But he'd thought of it because he'd taken a few ladies to the stables himself in his younger days.

He grinned as the door opened and Heather headed toward him, holding the umbrella over her head. Her eyes were cast downward as she carefully skirted puddles and breaks in the stone walkway. She was almost upon him when she stopped suddenly, her gaze darting up to meet his.

"Lord Stroughton," she said, her voice wary.

"Have a nice walk in the rain, Miss FitzHugh?" He took a step to the side, effectively blocking the door.

Heather held the umbrella a little higher over her head. Her expression was apprehensive. "I've been to the stables to see my horse. Tanner had her brought down from GlenRoyal."

"Your horse?" St. Clair chuckled. "Or your groom? I heard you'd been seen stepping in and out of strange carriages, but I never would have guessed your preference would be for a simple stablehand. But surely it wasn't this man you met in an alley for a private rendezvous? Surely your secret beloved is a nobleman?"

Heather gasped.

So it *is* true, he thought.

Euphoria filled him. "If you're so eager to know other men, my dear, I'm sure you would find more pleasure with someone like me. And I would make certain you weren't so easily seen. Hawksbury would never hear of it." He moved toward her, enjoying the fear in her eyes, violet eyes turned ebony by the dark and rainy night. "I could teach you things no other man could."

"If you touch her, Stroughton, I will gladly break your neck."

Damn! Hawksbury *would* choose just this moment to come looking for his errant fiancée. How much had he heard?

St. Clair turned slowly, his expression carefully composed, prepared to bluff his way out. "Well, well. Seems I was mistaken. I thought Miss Fitz-Hugh had wandered outside alone. I was just going to escort her back to the ballroom."

Tanner moved through the doorway. "Let's not play games with each other. Who Miss FitzHugh sees and where Miss FitzHugh goes is my business, not yours. If I choose to leave her alone to talk to an old friend in the barn, 'tis my concern and no one else's."

Tanner took another step closer, close enough for St. Clair to see the cold fury in his icy blue eyes, close enough for him to see the steely set of the duke's jaw, close enough to cause apprehension to swamp him.

"And by heaven, if you repeat your filthy lies or ever so much as speak to her again, we'll settle things between us with pistols. Do I make myself clear, Stroughton?"

St. Clair's dread escalated to true fear. Hawksbury was known to be a crack shot. "You would call me out over this—this—" He choked on the rest of his sentence as something in the duke's eyes warned him that he'd already gone too far.

"Heather." Her name was a command. "It's time we returned. Our guests will be looking for us." Tanner held out his arm for her.

She scurried quickly around St. Clair, never even giving him a sideways glance. Within moments, the pair had disappeared indoors, leaving St. Clair standing in the rain.

"Damn you to hell, Hawksbury," he muttered. "We'll settle this, all right, but it will be on my terms, my way."

Tanner had never felt such fury. Just thinking what might have happened if he'd returned for Heather only a moment later made him want to follow his first instincts and beat St. Clair to a bloody pulp. If the bastard had laid a hand on her, there would have been no stopping him. He'd come dangerously close to losing control as it was. It would have been much too easy for him to kill the marquess where he'd stood.

He moved in rigid silence, trying to block out the blackguard's words, trying to ignore the nasty insinuations he'd made.

Halfway up the stairs, Heather paused, her hand on his arm stopping his forward motion. "Tanner, please. What the marquess said. It isn't ..."

"We won't discuss it, Heather."

"But ..." Her eyes narrowed determinedly. "You never want to discuss things. You keep everything shut up inside you. You always have. Just once, I wish—"

"I meant what I said," he interrupted in a clipped voice. "We won't discuss it. It's over. And if St. Clair even so much as speaks to you, I'll call him out."

"A duel?" she asked in a whisper, her face as white as a sheet.

He imagined St. Clair lying wounded on a field

of honor. The mental picture made him smile thinly. "Don't worry, my dear. I'm an excellent shot, and Stroughton is at heart a coward. He wouldn't stand a chance."

If possible, she seemed to grow even more pale. "I know."

Her obvious concern helped to ease his anger. His voice softened. "Don't be frightened. He won't dare spread his lies about you."

But even as he reassured her, a troublesome voice whispered in his ear. What strange carriages had Heather been seen stepping into? Whom had she met in an alley? Just what had St. Clair been talking about?

"Tanner?"

He looked down into her eyes.

"No duels. Promise me."

" 'Tis a matter between men. Don't concern yourself with it."

She opened her mouth, then closed it, her gaze dropping to his chest.

Determinedly, he cast aside the ugly suspicions St. Clair had raised. Heather wasn't like Judith. She wasn't capable of lying to him. He was the only man who'd ever lain with her, and she loved him. He knew she loved him, although she'd never told him so. He could trust her.

"Let's get back to the ball," he told her softly, clasping her arm once again.

Caroline sat on a satin upholstered chair, listening with half an ear to the conversations going on around her as her gaze swept the rich decor of the Albany House ballroom. She could scarcely contain her envy over the beauty of it.

The entire room was decorated in various shades of blue and accented with silver. Bishop's blue draperies framed enormous windows. Spanish blue settees and chairs lined the walls. Silver candelabra stood on tables, and refreshments were offered from glittering silver trays. Three walls were lined with ceiling-to-floor mirrors, reflecting the dancers as they whirled about the room in a kaleidoscope of colors. In the center of the intricately decorated, domed ceiling hung a huge silver hawk, and held in its claws was a massive chandelier, shedding its flickering light over all.

It galled her to think all this might have been Annabella's, if only they had known the duke would be at GlenRoyal, if only they had done something differently.

She quelled her anger. This was not a night for wishing for what couldn't be. The very pink of the *ton* were here tonight, and it was her duty to make sure Annabella caught the eye of the right man.

Caroline had briefly considered Aaron St. Clair but had changed her mind this evening. One would have to be as blind as old Merrywood himself not to guess that the countess had taken the marquess for her latest lover. Perhaps that wouldn't have been enough on its own to dissuade Caroline from encouraging a permanent liaison between St. Clair and her daughter, but she suspected the marquess was not likely to go easily into wedded bliss.

As if conjured up by her thoughts, St. Clair reentered the ballroom. His black hair looked damp, as did the shoulders of his dress coat. She wondered where he'd been.

Then she followed the direction of his gaze. It led to Heather.

Hmm. Interesting. Althea had always coveted the duke. Now she was St. Clair's paramour. Heather was engaged to Hawksbury, yet St. Clair's interest in Caroline's niece was obvious.

Interesting. Very interesting, indeed.

Caroline smiled to herself, glad that she'd followed her instincts yesterday when Lady Merrywood had paid her a call. It had been so easy to express an aunt's concern. With any luck, Althea hadn't seen fit to keep the information to herself. Once Hawksbury heard of it . . .

At that moment, the music stopped and the Scotch reel ended. Soon after, she caught sight of Annabella being escorted toward her mama. Caroline hid a smile, her musings about her niece momentarily forgotten. She found it much more intriguing to note whose arm Annabella was holding.

The heir to an earl. And, according to the rumors passed over the scandal broth, a very wealthy earl at that.

Heather went through the motions of smiling and pretending to have a good time, but nothing could bring back her earlier enjoyment. What St. Clair's ugly insinuations hadn't destroyed, Tanner's remarks about a duel had. It was another painful reminder that every moment she remained with Tanner, every kiss she shared with him, every embrace she cherished, was a betrayal of George. No matter how hard she tried, she couldn't shake the image of George lying wounded, felled by Tanner's pistol.

There'd been just a moment on the staircase when she'd thought she could say something to Tanner about her brother, when she could have confronted him about it. There'd been an instant when she'd thought she might be able to tell him why she couldn't love him, couldn't marry him, had to leave him.

And then she'd realized it wouldn't have made any difference. Tanner would still be the man who'd shot her brother, and Heather would still be the woman who'd lied to him. Nothing would change those truths. Nothing.

A gentle hand touched her arm, and she turned to find Celeste standing beside her.

"Heather, I must speak with you." The girl's eyes were bright, almost feverish-looking.

"Is something wrong?" Heather asked quietly, her dark thoughts making her expect the worst.

Celeste shook her head. "Come with me. Just for a moment."

Heather excused herself from Tanner, then followed her friend out of the ballroom and into a secluded alcove. "What is it, Celeste?"

"I just had to tell you first. Edward ... Lord Mannington ... he's going to ask Papa for my hand. Oh, Heather, I'm so happy! Just think. We'll both be married before the year is out, and our husbands are the very best of friends, and Kennaway Hall isn't far from the Park. We can see each other often. I'm so glad we've become friends." She threw her arms around Heather's neck.

Heather hugged Celeste back, her emotions soaring and plunging like a gull over the ocean. She was happy for her friend and heartbroken for herself. They wouldn't both be married this year. She wouldn't have a husband to be Edward's dearest friend, nor would it matter to her how close Kennaway Hall was to Hawksbury Park. She wouldn't be seeing Celeste often. Soon, she wouldn't be seeing her at all.

"I'm very happy for you," she whispered. "Very, very happy."

Chapter 24

Tonight would be her last night with Tanner. She couldn't delay her departure any longer, or she would never be able to leave. Even now it was nearly impossible.

Heather huddled in a chair in her bedchamber, staring sightlessly out the window.

A week had passed since the Hawksbury Ball at Albany House. A whole week, and still she remained in London, promising herself she would leave soon, telling herself she wanted only one more day—and then one more and then one more.

Tanner had called on her daily. He'd taken her riding on Cathy in the park during the fashionable part of the afternoon. He'd escorted her to Vauxhall Gardens, where they'd listened to Haydn, Handel, and Hook, and indulged on chicken, ham, pastries, and wine while watching the fabulous display of fireworks. They'd danced together at countless balls and routs and soirees. And tonight he was taking her to Covent Garden to see *Macbeth*.

He knew something was wrong, of course, even though she'd tried so hard to act lighthearted. She'd seen the questioning way he looked at her when she pulled away from his embrace. It wasn't that she didn't long for his touch, for the taste of his mouth upon hers. She did. Heaven help her, she ached for it, ached until she thought she might die from the pain of wanting. But she knew if she allowed him to hold and kiss her, she would be lost forever. She would forget her oath, her honor, George, everything except Tanner, and she couldn't allow that to happen.

She'd dreamed of George last night. He'd regarded her with sad, accusing eyes and said, "You forgot, Heather. You forgot."

No, she hadn't forgotten. She was bound to that fateful oath as surely as she was bound to George and her father. She couldn't escape it or them. She'd been forced to choose between those she loved. She couldn't turn her back on her own family, no matter how much she loved Tanner.

One more night, she thought as she closed her eyes. *I have just this one, final night.*

Tanner had helped her decide to leave tomorrow. He'd told her yesterday that he had to go to Hawksbury Park to replace his steward, who had recently died. He'd wanted her to go with him, with Lynnette accompanying them as chaperon, of course. Oh, how she'd longed to accept his invitation, but she'd refused. She'd told him she had too many things to do in London before the wedding, and a host of obligations to members of the *ton*. Besides, Lynette couldn't go with them. She and Lord Sainsbury were leaving for the Fretwells' house party in two days.

No, Heather couldn't go with him to the Park. She couldn't see him again after tonight. This would be the last evening they spent together. She sat quietly, feeling the finality of her decision fall around her like a heavy curtain. It was a bit like death, she thought. Quite a bit like death.

She pushed herself up from the chair and went to her closet, where she searched through the dozens upon dozens of gowns there.

I'm not in mourning yet, she thought as she pulled a cranberry-colored gown from among the others.

She'd given herself one last night to share with him. Well, then, she would make it a night they would always remember. She would laugh, and she would make him laugh, too. Perhaps, because she knew this was to be their last evening together, she would even allow him to kiss her.

Perhaps . . .

At four-thirty, Tanner climbed into his carriage and instructed Crandall to take him to Lady Moberly's. He sat back against the plush seat, unaware of the frown he was wearing.

Something was amiss, and he was uncertain how to set it right. He'd been trying for the past week to tell Heather how he felt about her. He had hoped she would tell him the same in return, but nothing had gone as he'd planned. At every turn she seemed to be drawing away from him rather than moving closer. She'd deftly repelled his every attempt to kiss her.

And every time she'd pushed him away, that nagging voice had returned to whisper in his ear. Why did she no longer come willingly into his embrace? Was he wrong to think she loved him, to think she could never lie to him? Was he wrong about Heather? He'd heard the rumors. Could they possibly be true? Was she meeting with another lover?

Well, tonight would bloody well be different. Before he left for the Park, he would know what she felt for him. Tonight he would hold her and kiss her and know the truth. So help him, he would.

The carriage slowed to a stop, and he realized they'd arrived at Lynette's town house while he'd been lost in thought. As the footman opened the carriage door, Tanner picked up the pouch on the seat next to him and stuffed it into his coat pocket, then climbed from the vehicle and headed for the door with a decisive step.

"Her ladyship is expecting you," the butler said as he took Tanner's hat and gloves. "She's waiting in the salon, your grace."

Tanner nodded and hurried in that direction. He came to an abrupt halt the moment he stepped into the room.

Heather rose gracefully from the settee. The satin finish of her red gown shimmered in the late afternoon light spilling through the large salon windows. She smiled at him, a genuine smile that tugged at his heartstrings.

"Good day, your grace."

She looked dazzling. The neckline of her gown gave him an alluring glimpse of her pale, voluptuous breasts. The skirt surrounded her in gentle folds, hinting at the feminine curves hidden beneath the silky fabric but revealing little to his hungry gaze. Tiny diamonds dressed her earlobes, and a matching teardrop necklace rested at the base of her throat.

"How did you know?" he asked, half teasing, half serious.

"Know what?"

He moved toward her. "About the Hawksbury jewels."

Her expression became bemused.

He really didn't give a fig about the blasted rubies. What he wanted was to crush her against him and kiss that beautiful mouth of hers.

"What are you talking about, your grace?"

"I always think of you in lavender. 'Tis your color. Your eyes are the same color as the amethysts you so often wear."

"You don't like my gown," she said sadly. "I'll change at once. It won't take but a moment."

"No." He grabbed her wrist. "I do like your gown. You look lovely."

The frown returned to pinch her forehead.

" 'Tis only that the color surprised me. I didn't know you'd be ready to wear the Hawksbury jewels tonight." Tanner reached into his pocket and pulled out the velvet pouch he'd brought with him. Turning her right hand palm up, he poured out the contents.

Heather gasped as the ruby necklace and earrings fell into her hand. She'd never seen anything so beautiful. The gems seemed to glow with a light of their own.

Tanner placed his hands on her shoulders and slowly turned her away from him. She felt his fingers working the clasp of the diamond necklace. A moment later, it was lifted away from her throat and over her head. Then Tanner reached for the gold-and-ruby necklace still lying in the palm of her hand. She followed it with her left hand as it slid over her bare flesh above the bodice of her gown, waiting almost breathlessly as he fastened the clasp behind her neck.

"There." His hands returned to her shoulders, and he drew her toward the mirror hanging between two windows. "This necklace has graced the neck of every Duchess of Hawksbury for the past two hundred years. And they never looked more beautiful than you do. I'm glad I brought them to show to you. They are perfect with that dress."

She met his gaze in the mirror. "But I'm not the duchess. I can't wear them tonight. It wouldn't . . . it wouldn't be right."

"You'll be the duchess soon. I see no harm in your wearing them for this one night."

Heather felt the hot burn of tears in the back of her throat. She closed her eyes as she moved away from the mirror—and from his touch. She clenched her hands into fists, the facets of the ruby earrings pressing into her flesh.

One night. Just one last night. She would smile and laugh and make merry. She would find every moment of joy she could, and she would take the memories with her when she left.

"I will wear them," she said finally in a small voice, her back still toward him. She removed the diamond earbobs and replaced them with the rubies. "Thank you, Tanner."

She heard voices in the hall and looked toward the doorway as Lynette and Thomas Sainsbury entered the salon.

Lynette was resplendent in a green-and-gold gown. Her auburn hair was hidden beneath a Turkish turban, the entwined emerald-green gauze and shimmering golden silk adorned with strings of pearls, an ostrich feather, and gold fringe. She was laughing at something Lord Sainsbury had said to her just as they'd entered the room, and there was a delightful flush of color in her cheeks.

"Hawk," Lynette said, laughter still lingering in her voice, "I had no idea you'd arrived. I feared you were to make us late to the theater." She turned to Heather and stopped dead still. "Lord-a-mercy," she whispered at last.

Heather glanced down at her theater dress. "Is something wrong?"

"Heavens no, dear," Lynette replied as she moved across the room. " 'Tis the rubies. I haven't seen them since before Nicholas died. Sophia never wore them again. I'd forgotten how spectacular they are." She glanced at Tanner. "I didn't expect to see them until after the wedding."

"Devilishly beautiful on her, aren't they?" he said. He stepped forward, offering his hand to Heather. "Shall we go? We don't want to miss the curtain going up."

* * *

Covent Garden was one of only two theaters licensed to perform legitimate drama, Tanner told her as the carriage moved down Bow Street. This night, John Kemble, the Covent Garden manager, and his actors were performing a one-act play, followed by the Shakespearean tragedy *Macbeth*, and ending with a farce that featured Mr. Bailey, a popular vocalist.

Despite the turmoil that had troubled her days and disturbed her nights, Heather made good her promise to herself. It was easy to enjoy herself as she listened to Tanner tell about the evening's program. Her natural enthusiasm rose to the surface, and she realized how excited she was to get there. She'd never been to the theater before. Having read a number of Shakespeare's plays, she couldn't curb her eagerness to see one performed.

The carriage drew to a halt before the magnificent building which the architect had modeled after the Temple of Minerva at Athens. Heather stared at the Greek Doric portico as Tanner helped her from the carriage. She'd seen the theater before, of course. In her three weeks in London, she'd driven down Bow Street countless times. But tonight was different. Tonight she was going inside, and it was as if she were seeing the spectacular building for the very first time.

Behind them, Lynette and her escort alighted from the Sainsbury carriage and joined them.

"We mustn't dawdle," Lynette said. "We want to be in our box before the curtain goes up, and 'tis nearly six already."

Heather claimed Tanner's arm as they followed Lynette and Lord Sainsbury.

The elegant interior of the theater nearly took Heather's breath away. She knew she was staring like some goosecap just arrived from the country, but she couldn't seem to help herself.

The staircase ascended between two rows of Ionic columns, the way lit by Grecian lamps. At the head of the staircase was an antechamber surrounded with pilasters, and there, on a pedestal of yellow marble, stood a statue of Shakespeare himself. They passed through a lobby divided by arched recesses filled with paintings of various Shakespearean scenes, and moments later, entered their theater box.

A general hubbub filled the theater from the pit to the boxes to the two-shilling gallery. Heather's eyes moved quickly around the horseshoe-shaped interior, watching as the most elegant in Society settled into their private boxes, separated by slender pillars and adorned by chandeliers of cut glass.

Her wandering gaze stopped suddenly, resting upon a familiar figure. Harriette Morton was wearing a confection of ivory-colored lace and satin, simple and classic in design. She wore no jewelry except for a tiara in her honey-brown hair, a cluster of ringlets gathered at the back of her head. She was laughing at something her young companion had said to her when her attention turned upon Heather. The laughter faded. She gave only the most subtle of nods in Heather's direction before immediately looking away.

"Heather?"

Tanner was motioning her toward a chair covered with light blue cloth.

"We'd best be seated. It's almost time for the curtain to go up."

She nodded and slipped quickly into place. She glanced at Tanner as he sat down on the chair beside her, wondering if he'd seen Harriette, if he wished he could talk to her, if he would be jealous of the fellow sharing her box. But his gaze didn't move from Heather, except to look at the large stage with its crimson drapery as the music started and the curtain began to rise.

Heather quickly forgot all about Harriette Morton when the evening's performance began.

It was like nothing she'd ever experienced before. Actors were applauded as they entered through the stage door, but if the audience didn't like what they saw, which happened with the one-act play that opened the evening's performance, they terrorized the actors with hisses and boos, rooster crows and dog howls, not to mention high-flying missiles—orange peelings, apples, and sticks—provided by the orange girls circulating through the house.

The howling, maddened audience was finally quieted by profuse apologies from the actors. The lead actor, a tall, bean-pole-slim fellow with thinning brown hair, begged the crowd to forgive him for performing in a role which did not suit him. He promised they should not be disappointed with the play that followed and beseeched them to give the players an opportunity to entertain them.

Heather couldn't help wondering at the deportment of the audience. It didn't seem to matter if they were the commoners in the pits or the wealthy courtesans and members of nobility in the boxes. They all showed an appalling lack of manners.

"Why don't they let them continue?" she asked Tanner in a whisper.

He merely grinned and shrugged his shoulders.

Gradually, as the story of *Macbeth* began, the theater quieted, and before long, an enthralled audience was caught up in the suspense and tragedy of Shakespeare's play.

Heather leaned forward in her seat and forgot all else but what appeared upon the stage.

* * *

Tanner studied Heather in the dim light. Her violet eyes swirled with a confusion of emotion. Her heart-shaped mouth was pressed together, revealing her consternation over Macbeth's dilemma. Her hands were folded in her lap, nearly crushing her fan.

It was enjoyable watching her reactions to everything—the theater, the audience, the play— but it was dashed inconvenient for taking her in his arms, as he wanted to do. At least he felt that tonight she would allow him to kiss her. Whatever had been troubling her apparently was settled or forgotten.

He felt the tension drain from him. The rumors couldn't possibly be true. Heather would never be able to lie to him, to play him false. Whatever doubts he'd harbored were banished from his thoughts. He would go to Hawksbury Park tomorrow and take care of the business of hiring a new steward, and then he would return to the woman he loved.

As if she'd known he was watching her, she turned her head to meet his gaze. She gave him a warm smile, then looked back at the stage, leaving him even more impatient than before for the play to end.

"Oh, Tanner, it was wonderful! Truly wonderful." Heather sank back against the cushions of the ducal coach, a dreamy expression on her face.

"Lady Moberly's, Crandall. Slowly." The carriage door closed as Tanner settled onto the seat beside her.

"The theater was so utterly beautiful. So very big. I never imagined it would be so big! And the actors! They made me feel as if I were right there, in the middle of the story. Almost as if it were happening to me. Oh, it was truly wonderful."

"I'm glad you enjoyed it," he said as he stretched his arm behind her. Just as she turned her head to look at him, his arm dropped to her shoulder and he drew her close against his side. "Very glad you enjoyed it," he whispered.

One night, she reminded herself. Just this one last night.

"Did I tell you how very beautiful you look? There wasn't a woman in that theater who was your equal, Heather." His lips brushed her forehead. "Even the Hawksbury rubies looked like common stones in comparison."

She eagerly lifted her lips to meet his. The moment they touched, a sweet pleasure washed through her veins, making her skin tingle and leaving a warm glow in its wake.

Deftly, he turned her in his arms until she was facing him, lying partially across his lap, her knees pulled up onto the seat. He supported her back with one arm while his free hand glided over the slick surface of her gown until it came to rest upon one breast.

Heather moaned softly, enjoying the light pressure as he gently kneaded the tender flesh. She'd almost managed to forget how wonderful his caresses could feel. But the memories came back in a rush, bringing with them a surge of wanting. How desperately she needed him.

She belonged here in his arms. From the first moment she'd seen him, she'd been his, though she hadn't known it then.

One night . . .

She pressed herself against him, offering her lips, and through them, all her love. There was nothing tender about the kiss. It was demanding, thirsting, afire with passion. She held nothing

back. She couldn't have done so even if she'd
wanted to.

One night. Just one last night . . .

His hand slid from her breast and trailed to her
thigh. Her skin prickled and seemed to burn.
Slowly, ever so slowly, he inched the fiery red fabric of her gown up from her ankles, over her
calves, above her knees. And then he was tracing
circles on the bare flesh of her legs.

She groaned again and strained toward him. He
answered with a groan of his own. His kisses grew
ever more demanding. His tongue moved over the
flesh of her lower lip, and in response, shivers of
delight ran the length of her body.

Suddenly, he was caressing her in the most intimate of fashions. A tiny sound escaped her throat
as she gasped in surprise at the overwhelming
pleasure that invaded her body. Heat, slow and
molten, spread from the place he touched to the
tips of her fingers and toes. Yet, despite the ec-
static sensations, she was equally frustrated, wanting more, wanting all.

Somewhere in the back of her mind, she remembered briefly that this was the last time she
would enjoy his embrace, the last time she could
revel in the desire that seared her flesh, the last
time . . .

One final night . . .

And then a burst of light seemed to fill her
head. She felt herself battered by wave after wave
of exquisite bliss until, at last, she lay exhausted in
his arms, her head against his chest, unable to
move, unable to think.

"Heather . . . my sweet Heather . . ." Tanner
whispered into her hair. "How shall I wait until
we're wed?"

The carriage slowed.

"I'm afraid we're home," he said softly, his voice sad.

But not as sad as she.

Her one last night was over.

Chapter 25

Heather stared up at the ceiling of her bed-chamber. Lethargy held her captive. She didn't want to get out of bed. Once she did, she would have to set things in motion for her departure from London, from Tanner.

She heard a soft tapping at her door and was tempted to ignore it.

"Excuse me, miss," she heard Emily say. "You've got a letter in the post."

"A letter?" She sat up. "Come in."

Lynette's abigail opened the door and crossed the room, holding out the envelope toward Heather. "Lady Moberly thought it might be important and had me bring it directly to you, miss."

"Thank you, Emily." She looked at the nearly illegible writing. "George," she whispered. Then louder, "It's from my brother."

Emily smiled. "Well, then, 'tis right nice to hear from family. I'll leave you to read it, Miss Heather."

The envelope was open before the door had closed behind the abigail. Heather smoothed the smudged sheet of paper and began reading.

My dearest sister,
I have arrived in England and am now at GlenRoyal. Mr. Haskin has told me of your engage-

*ment to the Duke of Hawksbury and why you plan
to cry off. Please, I beg of you, Heather. Do nothing
and say nothing to the duke until I can speak with
you in person. Ship's business keeps me from you
only a few days longer. Meet me in Portsmouth on
Tuesday next at the Knight's Inn. Public coach will
get you there in six or seven hours. I will wait at the
Knight's Inn for you until you are able to come.*

> *Your loving brother,*
> *George*

George was here! George was in England! She
would see him on Tuesday. That was only three
days away. She would see George in just three
days.

The joy diminished somewhat with her next
thought. George knew of her engagement to the
duke. He must think she'd betrayed him and their
FitzHugh oath. How would he ever be able to forgive her? Just as in her dream, she imagined his
sad, accusing eyes and felt sick at heart.

Another thought occurred to her, this one even
worse than the first. George wanted her to do
nothing and say nothing until he'd spoken to her.
What did that mean? What was he planning?
Would he call Tanner out, as he'd done once before? Would he challenge the duke to another
duel, perhaps get himself killed this time?

She read the letter once more and then a third
time, but she could make it say no more than it already did. She would have to wait until Tuesday
to see what George had to say.

But at least George was home again! Home in
England. She would be able to pour out her troubles, and he would help ease the pain in her heart.
He would help her do what she must. Her beloved George was home.

* * *

"Heather, dear, why don't you come with us? Your fittings can wait, and we'll return before Tanner gets back from the Park." Lynette poked through her jewelry box as she spoke. Behind her, Emily was busily packing a large portmanteau with suitable clothing. "Won't you please join us? The Fretwell parties are always frightfully fun. This time there's going to be a treasure hunt with clues to solve. You'd love it. We won't even be gone a week."

"Honestly I don't want to go. I'm quite content to stay here. I'll be glad for a moment of peace and quiet all to myself." Heather clasped her friend's shoulders and leaned forward to kiss her cheek. "Besides, the dowager duchess has invited me to Albany House for supper tomorrow night. I can't disappoint her. You have a wonderful time, and you can tell me all about the treasure hunt when you get back."

Lynette frowned at her. "I never quite know what to do with you, Heather FitzHugh." Then she smiled. "But I'm terribly fond of you just as you are, so I don't suppose I'd want you to change a thing."

"I'm terribly fond of you, too."

"Oh, no, Emily. Not that one. I wore it to the Russell soiree, and nearly all the same people will be at the Fretwells."

Heather smiled as Lynette hurried to a closet filled with dozens of gowns of every conceivable hue and design. Unnoticed, she slipped out of the room and made her way to her own bedchamber.

A sudden onset of tears caused her to pause as the door closed behind her. She was going to miss Lynette so very much. Most likely, Heather would never see her again. She wished she could have said a proper good-bye. She wished she could have told Lynette how sorry she was for deceiving her, for using her friendship so despicably. She wished . . .

But wishing changed nothing. Even thoughts of George could not erase the sorrow she felt for the loss of this good and true friend.

Sophia wore a frown as she read the note.

Your grace,

I ask your forgiveness, but I am unable to dine with you this evening. I must be away from London on a family matter. I am sorry I could not notify you sooner, but word only just arrived that I am needed elsewhere.

> *Regards,*
> *Miss FitzHugh*

The dowager duchess wasn't certain why the note left her with a sense of unease. She only knew she would be glad when Tanner returned from the Park.

Heather supposed she should have felt guilty about using the Moberly carriage to take her to Portsmouth to meet her brother. Perhaps she would later. For now, she could just be thankful that she hadn't had to be crowded into a public coach with all manner of people, and jerked and bounced about while the horses were driven, neck or nothing, toward their destination.

The hours alone had given her time to contemplate her upcoming meeting with George. Excitement mingled with nervousness. It had been seven years since she'd seen her brother last. Seven very long, very lonely years with only memories and his sporadic letters to keep them close. He'd been a boy on the threshold of manhood when he'd gone away; she'd been a girl of twelve.

What changes would they see in each other

when she stepped from the coach at the Knight's Inn? Would he recognize her? Would she recognize him?

They'd been inseparable as children. George had always tried to protect and care for her, and she'd idolized him. Would it be the same now? Heather checked the small watch suspended around her neck on a gold chain. It was well after two o'clock. They should arrive in Portsmouth in another half hour or so.

She closed her eyes and leaned her head against the seat, trying to calm the jitters in her stomach.

"Well, what is it you have to tell me?"

The scullery maid nervously shifted her weight from one foot to another.

"Speak up, girl. I haven't forever."

"Miss FitzHugh got 'erself a letter in the post a few days back. Miss Emily says she ain't never 'ad a letter before."

"Who was it from?"

"I don't know, your ladyship. Miss Emily didn't say an' I can't read, so it don't matter that I couldn't see it."

The woman tapped her fingers impatiently against the mahogany desk. "Is that *all* you've managed to come up with? If you think I'd give you even a farthing for that information, you're sadly mistaken."

"That's *not* all, your ladyship. I come t'tell you Miss FitzHugh left London early this mornin'."

The woman straightened in her chair. Her amber eyes gleamed with interest. "Left London? Where did she go?"

"I 'eard 'er tell the driver t'take 'er t'Portsmouth, your ladyship. She was bein' most careful abou' it, too. Like she didn't want a soul t'over'ear what she was sayin'."

"Did she take much baggage with her?"

"Nay, your ladyship. She didn't take 'ardly a thing."

"Hardly a thing," Althea Rathdrum repeated softly, a smile beginning to curve her lips as she pulled open a desk drawer. When she closed it again, she was holding several coins. "You've done well," she said as she dropped the money into the maid's outstretched hand. "If you learn anything you think I should know, come to me." Her voice hardened. "But if I ever hear that you've told anyone of our arrangement, I will see that you end up at the bottom of the Thames. Do you understand me?"

"Aye, your ladyship," the maid said, her voice quivering.

"Good. Then you may go. Use the back way again."

Althea turned toward the window as the study door closed behind the maid. Her thoughts were racing madly, and excitement surged through her veins.

It could be nothing, of course. Heather's trip to Portsmouth could be entirely innocent, but Althea didn't think so. St. Clair had described Heather's guilty expression when he had accused her of having a lover the night of the Hawksbury Ball, and Caroline Beckworth had confided her own concern about her niece's behavior. Then there were the rumors of Heather having been seen disembarking from a mysterious carriage in an alley. And now this.

Hmm. It was interesting, to say the least. And how very convenient for Heather. Tanner Montgomery had left London three days ago for the Park. Althea had learned of it at the Andermont rout. Lynette Moberly and Thomas Sainsbury had gone to the Fretwell house party and wouldn't return until the end of the week. Althea had been invited as well but had turned down the invitation at the last minute.

Thank goodness, or she would never have been home to hear from her little spy. The girl wasn't terribly bright, but she was eager enough for the coins Althea had offered her for information regarding Heather FitzHugh's comings and goings.

Althea pushed herself up from her chair and wandered across the room to the opposite window, but she wasn't interested in what was going on in the street below. She was too busy mulling over the possibilities suggested by Heather's sudden trip to Portsmouth. Why would she go there? And why would she wait until Tanner and Lynette were both out of town? The most logical answer was another man.

Another smile graced Althea's mouth.

How positively delightful! Another man. Tanner would be most unhappy to hear of it. Unhappy? He would be furious. And he would most certainly end his alliance with Heather FitzHugh without delay. A pity, too. They'd made such a lovely couple.

Of course, the duke, having been burned twice, would most likely be reluctant to consider marriage again, which would be for the best until the Earl of Merrywood finally turned up his toes. In the meantime, Tanner might be persuaded to take a sympathetic lover.

And Althea Rathdrum could be a marvelous lover. She credited it to some wonderful advice she'd received from an elderly aunt many years before.

"Never let a love affair interfere with more important matters, such as advancing your social status," the old woman had counseled. "Be discreet, and when the affair has run its course, break it off with the minimum of recrimination. Remember, my dear, however irregular one's private life may be, it is important to appear guiltless." Her aunt had smiled wisely. "And one more thing, Althea. Remember that it is more important to be faithful to your lover than to your husband."

Remembering, Althea laughed aloud as she left the study.

Heather leaned forward to look out the open carriage door, glancing first to the right, then to the left, and finally up at the boldly lettered sign hanging above the door of the establishment on the edge of Portsmouth. "Knight's Inn," it proclaimed. There wasn't another soul in sight, nor did the inn look particularly reputable.

With the driver's help, she stepped down from the carriage.

"Are you certain this was where you were to meet your party, Miss FitzHugh?" the man asked, eyebrows raised in doubt.

"Yes," she replied softly. "Unless there's another Knight's Inn in Portsmouth."

"Not that I've ever heard of, m'lady."

"Then this is where I'm to be. Wait here please, Logan."

The man's eyebrows darted even higher on his forehead as his chest puffed with indignation. "I'll not do it, m'lady. Beggin' your pardon, but you ain't goin' in such a place without a proper escort."

Heather sighed. "Really, Logan, you don't understand. I must—"

The door to the inn opened with a squeak, drawing her gaze toward the sound. There, standing in the opening, was an extremely tall man with chestnut-brown hair and eyes the color of an Irish meadow. Gone was the thin lad she'd remembered, replaced by a man with a broad chest and muscular arms and legs. His face—more handsome, somewhat older, perhaps even wiser—

had been darkened by sun and wind. He wore a striped guernsey wool shirt and blue dungarees that fit him snugly at the hips, and he carried a tarpaulin hat in his left hand.

"George?" she whispered.

His face broke into an old, familiar smile.

"George!" She raced forward and thrust herself into his waiting embrace.

"Here, let me look at you." He set her back from him, the fingers of his right hand cupping her chin.

She found herself smiling beneath his scrutiny. She knew she had changed from the tree-climbing tomboy in pigtails and scraped knees he would remember best.

"Aye," he said as if reading her thoughts. "You're not the girl I saw last. What a beauty you've become." He glanced toward Logan and the Moberly carriage. "You didn't come by public coach?"

Heather shook her head.

"Come inside. We must speak in private."

She stayed her brother with an upheld hand, then looked back at the driver. "Logan, I'll be inside with my brother. Please take care of the horses."

A relieved expression crossed Logan's face. She knew it was because he now knew that George was her blood relative. Nodding, he said, "I'll see to 'em, m'lady."

George took her arm and guided her into the shadowy interior of the inn. "I've taken a dining room for us," he told her as he led her through the taproom.

Heather was surprised by the fine accouterments of the private eating room. A vibrantly colored rug adorned the floor, and the furniture was upholstered in luxurious fabrics. The table was

covered with a white cloth and set with bone
china and fine crystal.

George motioned toward a blue wing chair. "By
evening, the Knight's Inn will be full to overflow-
ing. The food is the best in all Portsmouth, and the
beds are clean. I suppose the landlord does so well
as is, he doesn't need to make the exterior look
prosperous." She took the seat indicated, and he
sat beside her in the chair's mate. "I never would
have believed it," he whispered as he studied her
once again.

She leaned forward and clasped his hand. "I
can't believe it either. I don't think I'd have known
you on the street, George. You're another head
taller and half again as wide." She squeezed his
fingers. "Why didn't you let me know you were
coming? When did you arrive in England? Can
you stay long? Tell me about where you've been
and what you've seen. There's so much I want to
know."

"Whoa. Wait a minute. One question at a time."
His smile faded. "Besides, it's answers from you
I've come for, dear sister."

He rose from his chair and walked over to the
window. It was then that she noticed the slight
limp. Seeing it, knowing who had given him that
limp, her joy vanished and she began to weep. She
hid her face in her hands, sobbing quietly.

She heard his footsteps bringing him back
across the room. A moment later, she felt his
hands upon her shoulders but shook her head, unable to look at him. She felt her betrayal too
keenly. She loved her brother. She loved the man
who'd shot him. How could she be so double-
minded?

Kneeling beside her chair, George removed her
hands from her face, then pulled a handkerchief
from his pocket and dried her cheeks. "Before you
waste anymore tears on me, Heather, you must

hear me out." 'Tis not a pretty tale I've come to tell."

"But, George, you don't understand. 'Tis I who've done a terrible thing. When I found out who the duke was, I thought I could keep our FitzHugh oath in part. I thought I could get even with the Montgomerys for taking GlenRoyal, at least just a little. So I told Tanner I'd marry him, but I didn't ever mean to go through with it. Only then . . ." Tears welled up in her eyes again.

"Only then you fell in love with him," George finished for her.

Miserably, she nodded.

Once again he cupped her chin in one of his large hands. The look in his green eyes was tender. "And you love him more than life itself, am I right?"

She swallowed the lump in her throat, then whispered, "It doesn't matter. I can't change what happened, can I?"

"No. You can't change it. But you don't know all that happened, Heather, and that's my fault."

What was he talking about? Of course she knew what had happened.

"No, you don't," he said forcefully, rising suddenly to his feet. There was fury in his voice when he continued. "I'm going to tell you a story, Heather, and I don't want you interrupting me while I'm about it. 'Tis hard enough for me to tell." He glared down at her. "Do you understand? Not a word."

Heather nodded, feeling suddenly alarmed at the angry young man looming over her, a man more stranger to her than brother.

George clasped his hands behind his back and stalked across the room to the window once again. She watched his fingers flex and release, flex and release. Silence filled the room. An uncomfortable silence, fraught with tension.

"I suppose I knew right from the start that Nicholas Montgomery didn't cheat Father. It was just my way of trying to save face. Father had already lost nearly everything else, including Mama's property, before he ever gambled away GlenRoyal." He paused, drawing a deep breath. "It was foolish of me to go off the way I did, but I was so tired of Aunt Caroline treating us like beggars. I thought maybe I could get GlenRoyal back and give you a home. I thought I could prove what a man I was, and then things would be all right for us both."

"I knew that, George."

Suddenly she thought he looked much older than his twenty-three years. And tired. He seemed so terribly tired. Within the depths of his eyes, she saw a weariness of the soul. Then, as if he couldn't bear to look at her any longer, he turned back to the window.

His voice was low when he continued his story. "I tried to see the duke at Hawksbury Park, but he wasn't there, and I didn't have the blunt to get me into the London clubs where I might meet up with him. So I decided to waylay him on the road to Hawksbury one afternoon. I was going to confront him about his father and demand he return GlenRoyal to the FitzHughs. If he didn't, I was going to call him out, challenge him to a duel of honor. I even had my own pistol with me."

Heather closed her eyes. *Don't worry, my dear. I'm a very good shot.* Tanner's words left her feeling cold and clammy as they echoed in her memory.

"Heather . . ."

She opened her eyes again to find George staring at her.

"I was sixteen and tired of living on Aunt Caroline's charity and being made to acknowledge how grateful I was for every miserly bite of food I ate."

"I know, George." Heather stood and took a step toward him.

He raised his hand to stop her. "The Duke of Hawksbury didn't shoot me, Heather."

"What?"

"He didn't shoot me. I shot myself. I was holding the pistol, planning what I was going to do when he approached, and it went off. I shot myself in the leg. If Hawksbury hadn't come when he did, I probably would have bled to death."

Heather sank back into the wing chair, a confused numbness spreading through her.

"The duke took me to the Park and saw that I was attended to by his personal physician. I didn't tell him my real name. I hadn't the courage."

"He didn't know you," Heather whispered to herself. "He said he'd never met you."

Her brother walked slowly toward her. "I came to admire the duke while I was there, despite not wanting to. Of course, I didn't see him much. He had his own problems. He was a busy man with his newly inherited estates, and there was his wife . . ."

Her eyes widened. "You met her? The duchess?"

"No." He shook his head. "I only heard about her from the servants." He sat down in the chair beside Heather and held her hand. "When I was well enough to leave, I knew I couldn't go back to Beckworth House. So I signed on with Captain MacGruder. Then I wrote you that letter."

She remembered the letter well enough.

George's fingers tightened around hers. "I was ashamed. I couldn't bear to tell you the only reason I wasn't returning was because of Aunt Caroline. So I let you think it was the duke who had wounded me. It made me feel less of a coward." The words poured out of him, rapid-fire, one on top of another. "I thought I would go with Captain

MacGruder to the East and make my fortune and return for you. I never meant for it to be seven years before I saw you again. And I never thought it would matter what you thought of the duke. I didn't think you would ever meet him." He stopped suddenly.

She heard him, and yet she could scarcely believe what he was telling her. It wasn't Tanner's fault. None of it was Tanner's fault.

She supposed she should be angry with George for letting her believe the duke had shot him, but she wasn't. She could only be glad that Tanner wasn't so heartless. She'd known it, of course. Deep down inside, she'd known Tanner wouldn't have dueled with a boy, shot him, and then forgotten him. Not her Tanner.

"If you love him, Heather, marry him. There's nothing to stop you. You'll make a grand duchess."

Suddenly she felt like smiling, laughing. "Yes," she said, a wellspring of joy bubbling over in that one word. "Yes, I can marry him."

The day sped quickly by as brother and sister became reacquainted. Heather plied George with questions about the ships he'd sailed, about the countries he'd seen. She was disappointed to learn how short his visit was to be, but he promised his business on the Continent would take only a few weeks, and he would come back in time for her wedding. She was saddened that he had no desire to return to the life of the landed nobility but, instead, thrived on his life at sea.

George was just as eager to ask questions, and it wasn't long before Heather had told him the entire story of how she'd met Tanner and everything that had happened to her since then. She saw fury in his eyes when she talked about Aunt Caroline and

Cousin Annabella, but she told him it didn't matter. Not anymore.

"You must return to London with me," Heather said as George walked her to her bedchamber late that evening.

"I can't. I received word from MacGruder that we have a meeting with another merchant in Dover. That's why he didn't arrive today as planned. I'll take the coach early in the morning and meet him there tomorrow night."

"Then you must ride with me in my carriage as far as London. You can catch the public coach from there. At least that will give us a few more hours together." She stood on tiptoe and kissed his cheek. "I wish you could meet Tanner before you go," she repeated.

George shook his head. "There's no time. Besides, I rather like the notion of surprising him when I come for your wedding. It'll be interesting to see if he recognizes me as the foolish youth he found on the side of the road." He chuckled, then returned her kiss. "You'd best get some sleep."

But how could she sleep when there was so much to be happy about? She wouldn't have to tell Tanner she couldn't marry him. She wouldn't have to leave him or Lynette or the dowager duchess or Celeste or Edward or anyone else who mattered to her. She would marry Tanner and spend wondrous nights in his bed, in his arms. She would bear his children. She would go on loving him until she was an old, old woman. And then she would love him in eternity, too.

Oh, how could she sleep when she felt so wonderful?

Chapter 26

Tanner paced the length of his study.

"I'm sure there's nothing to be distraught about," Sophia said as she watched him. "Heather will return to London in a day or two, and will explain where she's been, and the matter will be closed."

He shot her an impatient glance. He didn't want to listen to his mother's assurances. Besides, she didn't sound the least bit certain that what she said was true.

He tried to ignore the niggling doubts in the back of his mind, but it was hard to do when Heather had up and disappeared so completely. He'd finished his business at the Park with extra speed, just so he could hurry back and see her again. Instead, his mother had shown him Heather's note that claimed a family matter had called her away.

Naturally, he'd immediately ridden over to the Beckworths' house to inquire into the matter, only no one there had known where Heather was or what her note might mean. Her aunt, uncle, and cousin were all in good health and quite happily settled in London for the rest of the Season. They were certainly not the reason Heather had left Town.

He'd checked next at Lynette's, but all the ser-

vants had been able to tell him was that Heather
had left early the day before without telling anyone where she was going. The housekeeper had
said she took only one small bag with her, so no
doubt she would return soon. Tanner had told the
woman to notify him the moment Heather got
back, then had stormed out of the town house.

He would have checked with Haskin, but the
old groundskeeper had already returned to Westmorland. Could Haskin have sent for Heather?
Did it have something to do with GlenRoyal? Just
what did she mean by "family matter"? She had
no family other than the Beckworths, and they
were all here.

Pengelly walked into the study at that moment.
"This just arrived for you, your grace." He held
out a small white envelope. "I thought it might be
from Miss FitzHugh."

Tanner grabbed the envelope and tore it open.
Quickly, his eyes scanned the message.

Your grace,
  If you care to know with whom Miss FitzHugh
meets in private when you're not in Town, look for
Lady Moberly's carriage in Portsmouth.
                                                A friend

No! No, it wasn't true.

He turned and strode to the door.

"Tanner? Tanner, what is it?" Sophia called after
him, but he didn't stop to answer her.

Within minutes, he was galloping Rebellion
away from the Albany House stables, racing recklessly through the London streets, headed south-
west toward Portsmouth.

He had no concept of how long he'd ridden or
how far he'd gone before he became aware of the
thick lather on his gelding's neck and heard the

animal's labored breathing. He immediately
slowed the horse to a walk.

It was almost as if the thoughts had been galloping at his heels, just waiting for a chance to catch
up with him. Suspicion smote him with a fury.

Could what the note implied be true?

Tanner forced back the ugly question. He would
not think the worst. He would not condemn her
until he'd seen for himself. He would not—

Tanner reined in his horse as a landau pulled by
a matched set of grays rounded the bend in the
road up ahead. He turned Rebellion off the high-
way and waited in a grove of trees for the vehicle
to draw closer. As it whisked by, he caught a
glimpse of a lavender gown and black curls from
inside the carriage. He also heard deep male
laughter.

The fury didn't rage through him. It seeped.
Cold and treacherous, it spread from the place in
his heart that had once known love. Carefully,
skillfully, he closed out the memories of Heather
in his arms, Heather's violet eyes, Heather's
mouth upon his, Heather's delightful body curled
against him. He closed his heart and mind to anything beyond callous indifference.

Then, and only then, did he spur Rebellion forward, following at a judicious distance behind the
landau.

The journey back to London had seemed much
faster than the one to Portsmouth the day before.
All too quickly, the Moberly carriage was travers-
ing the streets of London, taking George to the
General Post Office, where he would catch the
next coach to Dover.

Heather clasped her brother's hands. "You'll
come to me the moment you return to London,"
she said, her eyes questioning.

"I'll be knocking on your door before the ship's even docked."

The carriage slowed to a stop.

"Oh, George, I wish you didn't have to go. We've been apart for so long."

"I know, love, but 'tis only for a few weeks. You'll hardly know I'm gone. There must be dozens of things a girl must do before her wedding day."

She smiled and nodded.

George opened the door and stepped out. "I said it before. I'll say it again. You'll make a grand duchess, Heather. The duke's a lucky bloke."

"Thank you," she whispered before following him from the carriage. She was trying desperately not to burst into tears. Finally, she couldn't help herself any longer. She threw her arms around his neck and pressed her face against her chest. " 'Tis hard to let you go."

He pulled back from her and cupped her face in his hands. "I don't deserve such devotion, Heather, but I'm grateful for it. You could have hated me for leaving you all these years, and for lying to you as well." He took out a handkerchief and wiped the tears from her eyes.

Heather sniffed. "FitzHughs don't ever stop loving each other."

"You're proof of that, dear sister. You're proof enough." He bent low and kissed her.

She swallowed the lump in her throat and tried to smile. "God keep you, George. Hurry back to England."

"I will." He grabbed his canvas bag from the floor of the landau and walked swiftly into the General Post.

Heather stared sadly at the building for a moment before climbing back into the landau and calling to Logan to take her home. She leaned back against the cushions, her eyes closed, and slowly the sadness left her. After seven years, George had come back to her, and he had brought her the most wonderful gift in the world. He had given her the freedom to love Tanner.

She looked out at the busy London streets, wondering when Tanner would return from the Park. Would he come to see her right away? Had he missed her as much as she'd missed him? She hoped so. Oh, she hoped so. She hoped he would hold her and kiss her and make love to her in all those deliciously wonderful ways of his. And then she would tell him how much she loved him.

She could hardly wait to see him again.

"Excuse me, Miss Heather. His grace the duke is here and asking to see you."

Her heart skipped with excitement. So soon? She hadn't dared hope she would see him today. She hadn't expected him until the end of the week. "Thank you, Mrs. Harwood," she said to the housekeeper. "Please tell him I'll be down momentarily."

Heather jumped up from her chair and hurried across the room to stand before the mirror. The rose-colored walking dress she'd changed into upon her return still looked crisp and fresh. Her excitement had brought a warm flush to her cheeks which complimented the color of the gown. Her short curls framed her face, their dark color in sharp contrast to her fair complexion.

But despite the things she saw in the reflection that were right, she saw a dozen more that were all wrong. She wished she had time to change her clothes. She wished her hair were longer, or perhaps shorter. She wished she were half a head again taller. She wished she were thinner, or perhaps plumper. She wished her nose were a little longer or her lips not quite so full or . . .

She turned from the mirror. It didn't matter.

He'd told her before that he found her beautiful. All that mattered today was that she was free to tell him she loved him.

Her heart in her throat, she left her bedchamber and made her way down to the salon. She paused in the doorway, her gaze finding him standing near the front window, his tall body silhouetted by the late afternoon sun, light gleaming off his golden-brown hair.

"Tanner . . ."

He turned slowly toward her. The glare of sunlight at his back hid his face from her view.

"Is all well at the Park?" she asked as she entered the salon, moving toward him, her stomach fluttering nervously.

"As well as can be expected. Murray's leg should heal up right enough. Replacing Clatworthy will be more difficult."

His words seemed normal, yet there was something about his reply that made her stop before she reached him. She could feel his gaze upon her, though the sun's glare continued to obscure his face.

She shivered, feeling suddenly cold and strangely bereft. She sat down in the nearest chair. "Lynette and Lord Sainsbury haven't returned from the Fretwell party. They'll probably have many stories to tell when they get back."

"Are you sorry you didn't go with them, Heather? I know you were invited."

Again she shivered, an automatic response to the tone of his voice. She lifted her chin and glanced in his direction. "No . . . I'm not sorry. Tanner, there's something I must tell you."

"Mother tells me you canceled your supper together. Nothing untoward, I presume."

"No. I was sorry not to see her, but in truth—"

"What was it she said called you away?"

She couldn't seem to answer him. The look in

his blue eyes had stolen her voice from her, had robbed the strength from every part of her body. She was scarcely able to breathe beneath the icy glare. This cold and distant man wasn't Tanner. He was a stranger to her.

"Oh, yes. A *family* matter."

Heather rose from the chair, her heart pumping madly, and took a step toward him. *What's wrong?* her mind screamed as she looked into eyes devoid of emotion. *What's happened, Tanner?*

"And is everything all right now?"

Everything is all right, Tanner. I love you. She moved across the distance that separated them. *Let me tell you I love you.*

His gaze remained hard and remote.

She placed her palms upon his chest. "We're alone," she whispered. "Wouldn't you ... wouldn't you like to kiss me?"

What he wanted was to put his hands around her throat and choke the very life from her, to squeeze until she could never utter another lie again.

He'd seen her kiss her lover, seen him wipe the tears from her cheek, seen the look of sadness on her face as the man walked away from her. If he'd kept his wits about him, he would have paid more attention to the sailor. He would have gone inside the General Post and found him and called him out. He would have blown the man's head from his body.

Only he hadn't been able to think of anything except Heather and the look of sadness on her lovely face. He hadn't been able to do anything except follow the carriage back to Lady Moberly's. After he'd seen her alight from the landau and enter the town house, he'd turned Rebellion around and ridden, unseeing, through London. He didn't know for how long. Finally, he'd gone back to Al-

bany House, changed his clothes, and then come
to see her.

He'd come to see if he'd been right. He'd always
thought he could read her so well. He'd been certain he would be able to tell if she lied to him.
He'd been partly right, at least. He could see the
fear of discovery written on her face.

The lying bit of muslin. The cheating doxy.

He grabbed her suddenly by the upper arms
and jerked her against him. His mouth claimed
hers in a savage kiss. The instant their lips
touched, he felt the surge of emotions, the torrent
of desire. It infuriated him beyond measure. He
would feel nothing for her. The devil take him if
he would. Abruptly, he set her away.

Tears welled up in her eyes. "Tanner?" she whispered. "What's wrong?"

By gad, he almost believed the tears were real.
"Tell me where you were," he answered, relieved
that his voice was calm and steady. "Tell me who
you went to see in Portsmouth."

She sucked in a surprised breath of air. "You
know I went to Portsmouth?"

And then she did something that caught him totally off guard. She smiled.

"Oh, Tanner, I've the most wonderful news. My
brother is back in England. George sent word for
me to meet him in Portsmouth. And he approves
of our marriage. He gave us his blessing."

A brother. How unoriginal. Perhaps her powers
of deception weren't as perfect as he'd begun to
think them. "Very decent of him," Tanner replied
dryly. "To give us his blessing, I mean."

"But it is. Don't you see? Now it doesn't matter
that your father took GlenRoyal from the Fitz-
Hughs. Oh, there's so much I need to explain, so
much to tell you. I didn't understand it all myself
until I saw George."

GlenRoyal. He should have known. He felt the fury building inside him as he stared down at her.

That innocent, beguiling face of hers. How much scheming had she hidden behind it? Had she known from that first day in the garden that he was the duke? Had she set out even then to snare him for her husband? Had she tricked him into her bed, lost her virginity before the wedding on purpose, and left him feeling guilty of doing the seducing? Was it GlenRoyal she'd been after all along? Had she known he would give her the deed if only she pleaded with those wonderful eyes? Had her kisses, her passion, been pure contrivance, mere diversions to get back the FitzHugh estate?

What wiles had she practiced upon him, the simple male? What deceptive, feminine wiles?

"Well, my dear, GlenRoyal is yours. Why wouldn't your *brother* be happy?"

Her smile had disappeared, replaced by confusion.

"GlenRoyal was, after all, what you were after. Isn't that right, my dear?"

She laid her fingertips on his forearm. "Tanner, please let me explain. Yes, perhaps at first it was about GlenRoyal. I never meant to hurt you."

"Hurt me?" He turned and walked toward the door. "You give yourself too much credit. We made a bargain, you and I. I suppose an heir is worth a small estate in Westmorland."

"Tanner, wait!"

He stopped and looked behind him.

She took several steps forward. Her right arm came up from her side, reaching beseechingly toward him. "Tanner, I ..." Tears swam in her exquisite violet eyes. "Tanner, there is something else I must tell you."

His vitals tightened reflexively, waiting for the blow. Would she now tell him the truth about this sailor, this commoner, with whom she'd spent the night in Portsmouth?

Her voice was nearly inaudible. "Tanner, I . . . I love you."

He'd been dead wrong. He'd thought she couldn't lie and him not know it, but he'd been wrong. Looking into her beautiful face, he could still almost believe her. If he hadn't seen her deception for himself, he *would* have believed her.

"Love, my dear?" he replied, his icy control firmly back in place. One corner of his mouth curled. "What a purely ludicrous emotion. You would do well to learn that while you're still young."

He left the town house without another backward glance.

Chapter 27

A bouquet of delicate pink roses arrived before noon the next day, along with a note from Tanner, asking Heather to join him for a private supper. His note said he would send his carriage for her at eight.

She supposed, as she admired the flowers, that they were meant as an apology. Only it didn't *feel* like an apology, especially when his words continued to replay over and over in her head. *Love, my dear? What a purely ludicrous emotion.*

"Oh, Tanner," she whispered as she pressed her nose into the fragrant bouquet. "How do I make you listen to me? How do I make you believe me now? I love you."

She climbed the stairs. Her footsteps seemed to echo in the empty house. She'd never felt so alone in her life. She wished George hadn't gone to Dover. She wished Lynette would return from the country. She wished she had someone to talk to, someone who could help her understand what to say to Tanner.

Perhaps he'd been tired and saddened from his trip, and that was why he hadn't listened to her. After all, he'd lost a trusted servant, and his butler was badly injured. Perhaps things would be different tonight. Perhaps he would be more himself. Perhaps then she could explain everything.

338

Love, my dear? What a purely ludicrous emotion.

She closed her eyes momentarily while she drew a deep breath. There, she thought as she opened them once more. That was better.

She wouldn't dwell on his strange behavior any longer. She would prepare for tonight's supper. Tonight he would be more ready to hear her declaration of love. She would make certain he understood her, that he believed her.

Quickly, she searched through her dresses, discarding first one, then another. At last her eyes fell upon the cranberry silk. She recalled the way he'd looked at her the night she'd worn it to the theater. His voice had been deep and husky as he'd fastened the ruby necklace around her throat, saying, "And they never looked more beautiful than you do." She remembered the way he'd held her, kissed her, touched her in the carriage as they returned home.

She would wear the dress again tonight, and hope for the same results.

She rang for the chambermaid and ordered a bath drawn at once. She would need plenty of time to prepare for the evening ahead. Everything must be perfect. She wanted Tanner to look at her and see her love and love her in return.

And surely, if she wanted it badly enough, she could make it come true.

"Your grace!" Harriette Morton looked up in surprise as Tanner was shown into her salon.

"Hello, Harriette." Tanner offered one of his sardonic grins.

She was reclining on a chaise longue near the cold fireplace. As he walked toward her, she straightened the satiny hem of her gown over her calves. "I wasn't expecting you this evening, or I would have dressed for the occasion."

"I didn't expect to come either, but I was in the

neighborhood." He crossed to the sideboard where a crystal decanter had been set out, surrounded by several glasses.

When he turned, holding a glass filled with claret, he found her watching him with attentive brown eyes. Her mouth was slightly pursed, giving her an air of consternation.

He lifted the glass in her direction. "You look as lovely as I've ever seen you. I've missed you, my sweet."

Harriette slid her legs over the edge of the chaise longue and sat up. "What's happened, your grace?"

"Not a thing." His laugh was sharp and humorless, even to his own ears. "Perhaps I've missed you."

"Perhaps." She rose artfully and walked across the salon to stand beside him. Her doelike gaze moved slowly up the length of him, stopping when she was staring directly into his eyes. "Perhaps, but I think not," she added, then poured herself a drink as well.

Tanner gulped down half the claret in his glass. The courtesan was correct, of course. He hadn't missed her. Bloody hell, he hadn't even thought of her since he'd met Heather. Heather had wormed her way beneath his skin, into his heart. She'd blotted all reason from his mind. She'd made him forget the hard lesson he'd learned, made him think himself in love again.

Angrily, he swallowed the remainder of his drink.

"Getting foxed won't help matters, my friend."

He stiffened. Damn her! He hadn't come here to be preached to.

Harriette laid her hand on his arm. "Why not tell me what's really troubling you?"

Tanner laughed again as he pulled away and crossed the room. "Nothing that I shouldn't have expected when I was forced to take a bride to save Hawksbury."

"So it's Miss FitzHugh who has you tied in knots." It was Harriette's turn to laugh, the sound light and merry. "Sit down, Hawk, and tell me your troubles."

Tanner didn't want to laugh or tell anyone his troubles. He wanted to stay angry. He wanted to remain alert to the dangerous wiles of women. Any woman. Even this one.

"Tell me, Harriette," he said as he turned to look at her across the room, "how did you come to this life?"

It wasn't often that anyone surprised the famed cyprian, but he saw that his question had.

"Did you always intend to become a courtesan, or was there a time when you wanted to be a man's wife? Is there more freedom as a man's mistress than as his beloved bride? More wealth even? Tell me, Harriette. Was it for just one man you came down this path, or did you hunger to know many men?"

Harriette set her glass on the table. Her back was straight, her head held high. She leveled a particularly sharp gaze in his direction. "I'm sorry, your grace, but I believe you should go."

"Aren't you going to answer my questions?"

"No, Hawk, I'm not. I think, after you leave, I shall cry. I had thought we were friends. I see that I was wrong. I'm sorry for you, and I'm sorry for your Miss FitzHugh because she loves you and will only be hurt far worse than I."

"The devil she does!" he exclaimed as he stalked out of the salon.

Heather was surprised to find Pengelly standing inside the doorway, rather than Crandall, when she descended the stairs. She was further surprised to find a simple black gig waiting at the

curb rather than the stately Hawksbury town
coach with its ornate coat of arms emblazoned on
the doors.

Despite Lynette's earlier assurances that
Pengelly was Tanner's trusted friend, the giant's
sheer size, let alone the rest of his daunting appearance, was enough to make her nervous. She
longed to ask him why Crandall wasn't driving or
where the usual carriage was, but she hadn't the
courage to speak. She simply took his hand and
allowed him to assist her into the small vehicle.

As the horse trotted away from the Moberly
town house, Heather folded her hands in her lap,
unconsciously squeezing them together until her
knuckles turned white. The butterflies in her stomach were all aflutter, and she felt slightly nause-
ated. A sixth sense warned her that all was not
right.

After nearly a month in Town, spending much
of it shopping in the Great Wren or strolling the
pleasure gardens at Vauxhall or gallivanting
through the streets from one rout to another,
Heather knew London well enough to realize they
weren't on their way to Albany House. Nothing
looked at all familiar as they wound their way up
and down narrow streets and byways. She began
to wonder if Pengelly knew where he was going
when suddenly he stopped the gig before a mod-
est town house.

The big man jumped to the ground, then as-
sisted her from the carriage. Wordlessly, he motioned toward the front door. She looked up at the
narrow, two-story house, then back at Pengelly.

"His grace is waiting inside," the man answered
in his gravelly voice. He stepped forward and
opened the door for her.

Curiosity overrode trepidation. She glanced
once more at her guide, then entered the house.
She stopped just inside and stared about her.

The entry was ablaze with candlelight, flickering in silver candelabra and in chandeliers and in sconces on the walls. The golden light danced on the wallpaper, on the shiny wood floors, and on the thick carpets.

Tanner's voice called to her from the room on her right. "Come in, Heather."

She moved forward, hesitating briefly just before she reached the doorway. For some reason, she was terribly afraid.

"Come in. I've been waiting."

Swallowing the lump of fear that had formed in her throat, she entered the small salon.

Like the entry, this room was also aglow in candlelight. Brocade-covered sofas and settees were set in an intimate arrangement near the fireplace. At the other end of the room stood a black table with two high-backed chairs. The table was set with crystal and fine china. Tanner was standing beside one of the ebony chairs.

"What do you think?" He waved his hand around the salon. "Do you like it?"

She didn't look at the room. She kept her eyes on Tanner. "It's ... charming."

He smiled, but it was merely a reflex action of his mouth. It didn't reach his eyes. "Come sit down, Heather. The cook has prepared something very special for us tonight." He held out his hand.

She moved forward, placing the tips of her fingers in his. His hand was cold. So were his eyes.

Cold. So very cold.

She shivered.

"Shall I have Pengelly light a fire?" Tanner asked as he led her to her chair, holding it out for her as she settled onto the seat, then pushing it toward the table.

"No," she replied softly. "I'll be fine."

Again he smiled. Again it left her cold.

Tanner rang a small bell, and within moments, a

footman appeared carrying a silver tray. Delicious odors filled the room.

But Heather wasn't hungry.

Supper seemed to take forever. Course followed course, but Heather tasted little of what was set before her. She kept staring at Tanner, trying to understand what was happening, but she couldn't. She wanted to ask him what they were doing there, but again she seemed unable to do what she wanted. She could only wait.

Tanner, however, smiled often and appeared to be having a good time. His words were few, most of them having to do with the quality of the food or the wine. The turtle soup was delicious. The salmon nearly melted in his mouth. The mutton was prime. The cauliflower was crisp. The rich dessert would surely add an inch to his waist.

Finally, when the last dish had been cleared away, Tanner leaned back in his chair and showed one of his half smiles. "Did I tell you how lovely you look? No, I'm afraid I didn't. Well, you do, my dear. Of course, the Hawksbury rubies are missing. A shame you can't wear them. But you're lovely, all the same."

She tried to smile in acknowledgment of his compliment, but found she couldn't. Perhaps because he hadn't made it sound like a compliment.

He sipped claret from a crystal glass. "I'm glad you like my little place. I own a number of properties in Town which I let. This one has been empty for several weeks. Young fool who rented it eloped to Gretna Green. I was going to find a new tenant, but I have a better use for it now."

"It . . . it seems very nice." She glanced about the small room, thinking of the grand salons—several of them—at Albany House. "But why would you—"

"Come with me. I want to show you the rest of

the house." He pushed back his chair and rose from the table. A few steps brought him to her side.

She glanced up at him, fear lying like lead in her stomach.

"My lady," he said with a mock bow, holding out his hand to her.

She took it and was drawn up from her chair.

Tanner tucked her fingers into the crook of his arm and led her from the salon. He moved slowly, pointing out quaint items in each room, listing the many small comforts. Finally, they arrived at the master bedchamber on the second floor.

From top to bottom, the room was decorated in shades of lavender and purple, the theme broken only with touches of stark white. Even the air seemed to be scented with lavender. It was overwhelming, cloying, and somehow quite frightening.

"What do you think?" he asked as he drew her forward. "Do you like the room?"

"Tanner, what is this about? Why does it matter if I like this room or not? Why would you need such a place when you have Albany House?"

"Oh, but it isn't for me, my sweet. 'Tis for you."

"For me?" she repeated breathlessly.

He let go of her arm and walked to the bed. He ran his hand over the lavender-and-white spread that covered the mattress. His voice seemed to come from a remote distance. "You see, I realized that you couldn't go on staying with Lynette forever. It is unfair, especially now that we would both like more privacy to pursue our pleasures." Heather shook her head as she took a step backward.

"Aren't you pleased with your new home? It wasn't easy to get this chamber decorated for you so quickly."

"Tanner, don't," she whispered. "You're frightening me."

His voice turned suddenly harsh. "Surely you knew I wouldn't actually marry you. Surely you knew I would see through you in time."

She groped for a chair, a table, anything to steady herself.

"But then, perhaps you thought you would leave London, go back to GlenRoyal. Ah, yes, GlenRoyal." He seemed to stalk her. "You do *own* GlenRoyal, don't you, Miss FitzHugh? However did you become so clever, stuck out there in the country? You manipulated me so easily, didn't you?" He frowned thoughtfully. "But there is one problem about GlenRoyal. You don't own the lands to support it. Those still belong to Hawksbury. You would quickly starve in that house all alone, wouldn't you, my sweet?"

She felt sick to her stomach. "Why are you doing this? If you would only let me explain. I'm so very sorry for what I've done, but I love you. I was wrong. I was wrong about you and your father and George and my father. I was wrong and I ..." Her words faded into nothing. His handsome face was set like granite. The blue of his eyes was as frosty as a winter day. He loomed over her, her beloved Hawk, and prepared to destroy his prey.

"I may not choose to marry you, Heather, but I will arrange for your welfare. I will give you the use of this house in Town, and a generous allowance. In time, if you are careful and continue to please me, you will have enough to support GlenRoyal. Or perhaps you will find yourself another gullible male to propose marriage."

A blessed numbness had spread over her, momentarily shielding her from the cruelty of his words. "I am to be your ... your *whore*?"

"Such a vulgar word. I prefer something more

delicate. My bird of paradise, perhaps." He stroked her hair, pushing the curls back from her face. "Yes, that's much better."

Tears streaked her cheeks, but she wasn't aware that she was crying. She looked up at this man, the man she loved, and saw only a stranger. It was her own fault. She had brought this upon herself. She had set out to make him a fool, to hurt and humiliate him in the worst way. It seemed she had succeeded.

But she didn't want to succeed. She didn't want this stranger. This wasn't Tanner. This wasn't the man who had held her and kissed her and made love to her. Where was the man she loved? What could she do or say to bring him back to her?

"Please." She choked out the word. "Why won't you listen to me?"

He felt himself weakening at the sight of her, tears rolling down her pale face, lips quivering. Her strangled question was nearly his undoing.

He stepped quickly back from her, reminding himself of her duplicity, of how easily she could lie to him, use him. His only defense was to use her as well.

"I do it because I'm the Duke of Hawksbury and I choose to. I do it to help provide for you, Heather. Do you think the Beckworths will take you back once they know that we are no longer to be wed? What do you think will happen to you once the whispers begin that you are not so innocent after all? In truth, they've already begun."

And, he added silently, *I do it because I find myself wanting you despite knowing I shouldn't. Because I cannot bear to give you up. Because I love you even more than I hate you for what you've done.*

He turned his back on her before she could see the confusion in his eyes, his own love and fear.

"You must need some time to think about it, my dear. Pengelly will take you home. He will be very careful to make sure you are not seen and recognized, coming and going from this place. When you are ready to move in, you need only send word, and he will come for you."

Suddenly he swung around and pulled her into his arms. He could feel the rapid flutter of her heart. He could smell the sweet freshness of her cologne.

"You are *mine*, Heather FitzHugh," he whispered in a ragged breath. "You will remain mine."

He kissed her then, with all the passion and rage that filled him. He kissed her and placed his brand upon her. He would not let her go. If his threats and reasoning didn't persuade her to become his mistress, then he would bring her here by force. He wouldn't let her go.

Not yet. Perhaps not ever.

Heather drew back from his embrace. "I do not need to think about it, your grace. I will stay."

She turned away from him, unable to bear the harshness of his gaze. She walked over to the bed and wrapped her fingers around one of the posts, holding on for dear life.

"I will stay because I love you."

She wanted so desperately to believe that she could make him love her simply by staying with him, simply by loving him first. She had made so many mistakes, perhaps she could somehow make up for them. Surely the strength of her love could overcome the hurt that stood between them. Surely once she could talk calmly, once she could explain fully, he would forgive her for what she'd set out to do.

She was guilty of many things, but she'd never lied to him, except by omission. Surely he knew that. Surely . . .

"You needn't lie about your feelings, Heather. We aren't man and wife. Don't pretend what you don't feel."

She resisted the pain his words caused and tried to remember her belief that her love for him would see them through this dark time. "I will stay because I hope by doing so I can prove my love. If this is what you want, if this is what I must do, then I will do it." She drew a deep breath as she turned to face him. "But first you must hear me out. I must tell you the truth."

"The truth?" Something inside him snapped. Several long strides carried him to her side. "If you're so fond of the truth, Heather, begin by telling me why you decided to marry me. Was it because of GlenRoyal?"

She stared up at him for what seemed a very long time before she replied, "Yes, Tanner, it was because of GlenRoyal. At least at first. Until I knew I loved you." Another lengthy pause followed, and then she continued, her voice strong and sure. "Before my father died, I made an oath to do anything I could to get back GlenRoyal for the FitzHughs. My brother even planned to fight a duel with you to keep that same oath, but I didn't know what I could do. I was just a child when I made the promise. I never dreamed I would have an opportunity to meet you. I was so angry for the way GlenRoyal had sat empty and fallen into ruin. I was so angry for what you'd done to my brother." Her voice softened again. Her gaze faltered. "I never intended to marry you. I was going to spend your money and experience all the things I'd never experienced. I was going to make friends with your friends. I was going to flirt and make you want me and make you jealous when others wanted me, too. And then, at the last moment, I was going to refuse to marry you. I was going to make a fool of you in front of everyone, the one thing you'd sworn would never happen to you again. I intended to make it happen."

She turned her back on him once again. "Only

I never thought I would fall in love with you. I realized too late that I was wrong about so many things, most of all you. You didn't shoot a foolish young boy. It wasn't your fault Papa gambled away my home. You were kind and infuriating, and tender and frustrating. How could I help but love you?" Her voice lowered slightly. "I thought I would have to run away, that I would be betraying George and my father if I married you. And then ... then George told me the truth. Your father didn't cheat at hazards. You didn't fight a duel with George. I knew then it was all right for me to love you."

Tanner didn't care what she said. It was all a jumble in his head. He'd heard her say it was for GlenRoyal, and then he'd heard her say she loved him, and after that he'd stopped listening. He couldn't stand to have her tell him again that she loved him. He didn't want to listen to any more of her lies. He had to stop her from saying those words again.

"What about your lover, Heather? What about the man you've been seeing?"

She spun to face him, her eyes wide and clear. "There was never anyone but you, Tanner. Never. I love you. I—"

He reached out and pulled her into his embrace. "Stop it, Heather," he whispered gruffly. "No more lies. GlenRoyal is yours. You needn't deceive me anymore."

He silenced her with kisses.

Her love welled up and overflowed. He could stop her words, but he couldn't stop her emotions. She willed her love to be in her kiss as her mouth responded to his. She willed it to be in her fingertips as she moved them up his arms to clasp behind his neck. She willed it to be in her body as she pressed herself closer to him.

He might not listen to her or believe the truth, but surely he would feel her love as she gave herself to him. And maybe—maybe when their passion was spent—he would believe her declaration of love.

Instinctively, Heather knew when his anger was replaced by desire. His grip on her arms gentled; then he released her. One hand slid up and he tangled his fingers through her ebony curls. The other moved to the small of her back, applying faint pressure, drawing her all the closer to him. She heard a frustrated groan deep in his throat and felt her own need for him flare, white-hot and resolute, scorching her to her very soul.

He swept her suddenly up from the floor. She dared to open her eyes, to look at him. She saw the warring emotions written on his handsome features, knew that even still, he fought the desire to possess her, to love her.

"Tanner," she whispered.

"Don't, Heather," he responded. "Don't say anything."

He laid her on the bed, then knelt beside her on the mattress, his hands gently disrobing her, his hawklike eyes staring down at her, a fire in their blue depths. His movements were unhurried, and she responded with impatience. She wanted him to take her, enter her, fill her. She wanted to belong to him forever.

At last, she lay beneath his gaze, her naked body aching for his touch. He didn't disappoint her. His hands gently kneaded her breasts until the nipples were hard and erect. He traced tiny circles on her skin, gently and slowly moving his hands over her body.

She moaned and closed her eyes, wriggling as the need for a more intimate touch assailed her. He didn't oblige. Instead, he leaned forward and kissed her, starting with her mouth, then moving from her lips to the tender spot on her throat, to her breasts, even to the flat plane of her stomach and back again. And all the time his hands teased her, promised her more but never quite delivered.

The wanting became unbearable. She saw her passion mirrored on his face. She fumbled with his cravat, the need to feel his skin upon hers devastating, irresistible. His hands followed her arms until he was covering her hands with his.

He stood and began to undress. His actions were no longer slow and deliberate. They were hasty, jerky, urgent. His shirt dropped to the floor, and she glimpsed the light, golden furring on his chest, a slender path of hair dipping beneath the waistband of his trousers. A moment more and he stood naked before her, gloriously male.

Silently, she reached for him.

Their joining was abrupt and furious. She wrapped her legs around his hips and rose to meet him. She heard the mingled sounds of their rapid breathing, felt the moisture gathering on their flesh. And within, she was buffeted by winds of passion that rushed her toward a zenith of desire. The need, the wanting, it all came together in a blinding heat that possessed her, body and soul.

She cried his name as sudden release exploded within her. She shook and quivered beneath its power. Before her emotions could plummet her back to reality, she felt his body go rigid as he drove one last time inside her. She clutched him to her breasts, felt the warmth of his seed filling her.

For the longest time, the only sound in the bedchamber was that of ragged breathing. Neither of them moved. Their bodies remained joined, their sweat mingling.

Then Tanner rolled onto his side, taking her with him. She pressed her cheek against his chest, her eyes closed, her body and mind languid. Exhaustion and satisfaction beckoned her toward sleep.

Then, into the silence of the room, she heard his whisper.

"Damn you, Heather."

Chapter 28

Sleep had been long in coming, and now consciousness returned slowly. Lethargy held him in its grasp, reluctant to release him. It tempted him to surrender to slumber, enticed him to remain in bed.

Keeping his eyes closed against the certain daylight, he reached out, searching for another warm body to curl against him. He found only bedsheets.

Tanner opened his eyes as he sat up. He'd been right. Golden rays streamed into the bedchamber through the double windows. He scanned the room but found it empty. Disappointed, he realized he'd been thinking of making love to her in the morning light, perhaps even staying in bed and possessing her again and again throughout the day.

He raked his fingers through his tousled hair, pushing it back from his face, then dropped his legs over the side of the bed and reached for his trousers. They'd been moved from the floor where he'd left them last night and were now neatly folded and waiting for him atop the bedside stand.

He lifted the tight breeches over his legs and hips before reaching for his shirt, which he didn't bother to button or tuck into his waistband. He was in a hurry to find Heather. He wanted to kiss her good morning.

Why not admit it? He wanted to hear her tell him again that she loved him.

He sank onto the mattress and hid his face in his hands. Last night, as he'd held her in his arms, drained by their lovemaking, he'd cursed her for making him love her. But even still, he wanted to be with her.

Bits and pieces of what she'd told him last night flitted through his head. Things about her brother and her father and GlenRoyal. Something about a promise and a duel and a fool. The words were confusing, disjointed. He tried to make sense of them but couldn't.

He saw again the clear honesty of her eyes, heard the earnest whisper. *There was never anyone but you, Tanner. Never. I love you.*

Could he possibly be wrong? Was the sailor from Portsmouth really her brother?

Confound it, he would get the truth from her if it was the last thing he ever did.

Tanner headed for the door. He would speak to her now. In the harsh light of day, he would face her and know the truth.

The small town house was silent. Dead silent. No sounds drifted to him from the kitchen or the servants' quarters. Had everyone slept as late as he?

Tanner descended the stairs. He glanced first into the small dining chamber, then went to the salon. It, too, was empty.

Where could she—

He heard a door close at the back of the house and turned toward the sound, expecting to see Heather in the hall. Instead, Pengelly stood there.

As the big man walked toward him, Tanner asked, "Pen, have you seen Miss FitzHugh? I can't seem to find her anywhere."

"I haven't seen her, your grace. I thought she was upstairs with you." His expression was clearly disapproving.

"Search the house," Tanner ordered, filled suddenly with alarm. "Find her, damn it!"

He turned and raced up to the second floor. He threw open the doors to each and every room. She was nowhere to be found. She'd left him. Sometime in the wee hours of the morning, she had slipped from the bedchamber and out of the house. Didn't she know the streets weren't safe for a woman alone? If anything had happened to her . . .

"Pen!" he shouted toward the door. "Harness the horse to the gig!"

The public coach bounced and jounced its way along the road. Heather—squeezed between the ample girth of an elderly matron and the snoring figure of a country vicar—closed her eyes and tried to ignore the pain that tore at her heart. She was determined not to weep before these strangers.

She wondered if Tanner had discovered she was missing yet. Had he gone to Lynette's to demand she return to the hideaway he'd made for his mistress?

She'd thought she could do it. She'd thought she could stay and be his paramour. She'd thought she could prove her love to him.

Damn you, Heather.

But it wasn't any use. He hated her. She'd hoped he simply hadn't heard, hadn't understood what she'd tried to tell him. But it didn't matter. He despised her. She'd done what she'd set out to do. She'd made him appear the fool, and now he hated her for it. He would never forgive her. Could she blame him?

Damn you, Heather.

She swallowed back salty tears and folded her hands in her lap. She wouldn't think about it. She wouldn't think of Tanner. She wouldn't allow a picture of him to form in her mind—his wide forehead and aquiline nose, his rare but wonderful smile, the golden highlights of his tawny hair, the cool, clear blue of his eyes. She wouldn't remember his tall physique, the breadth of his shoulders, the muscles of his thighs, the golden furring on his chest, the red-gold stubble that appeared on his face in the early hours of morning. She wouldn't think of the way he kissed her or the special taste of him. She wouldn't remember the unique melody his hands played upon her body.

No, she wouldn't think of any of it. Not ever again.

"No, yer lordship," Lynette's maidservant said as she closed the door behind Tanner. "Miss 'Eather never come 'ome that I know of. I 'aven't seen 'ide nor 'air of 'er since she went out last night, I 'aven't."

Tanner brushed past the girl and headed toward the stairs. He took them three at a time as he made a beeline for Heather's bedchamber door. He pushed it open, shouting her name.

The room stared silently back at him.

What if some ruffian had grabbed her while she was out looking for a cab? What if she'd come to harm because of him? He'd done this to her. He'd been intentionally cruel. He'd struck out, wanting to wound and hurt her as deeply as he'd been wounded and hurt.

His gaze roved over the chamber, stopping when he spied a sheet of paper on the bed. He crossed the room, a sense of foreboding growing in his chest. He knew what the document was before he picked it up.

The GlenRoyal deed.

And at the bottom, in petite, flowing letters, were the words "I'm sorry. H."

He knew it then. He knew that everything she'd told him, everything she'd tried to tell him, was true. She hadn't taken a lover. The sailor from Portsmouth was her brother. And she loved him, Tanner.

He didn't understand all the things she'd done or all the reasons for them, but he knew she loved him as much as he loved her. He also knew that he'd hurt her far more than he'd been hurt. And he knew that she would try to hide from him, would seek a safe place where she could work through the pain. He knew what it was like. He'd been there.

He had to find her. He had to find her, and tell her he loved her and was sorry, and she'd never needed to make him appear a fool. He *was* one.

"She went out and didn't come home, you say? How very interesting." Althea closed the door to the withdrawing room and regarded the scullery maid. "And where did she go?"

"I don't know, m'lady. Dulcie didn't tell me. I tried t'follow the carriage, I did, but I lost it. Mrs. 'Arwood, she thought she was goin' t'the duke's 'ouse, but she didn't. I know that much."

"Why didn't you ask the carriage driver when he returned where he took her?" Althea asked impatiently.

"Wasn't our carriage she took, m'lady. Was another come 'round for 'er."

"The duke's, perhaps?"

"No, ma'am. I've seen the duke's carriage often enough since Miss FitzHugh's been wi us, an' it weren't 'is." The girl puffed up with importance. "Besides, 'is grace come by this mornin' in a terrible state. Lookin' for 'er, 'e was. 'E don't know where she is either."

"Well, well," the countess muttered as she retrieved some coins from her desk drawer. "Keep your ears and eyes open, girl, and let me know if you learn anything else." She dropped the coins into the scullery maid's open hands. "Now go on with you."

Althea waited until the girl had slipped out the servants' entrance, then strolled slowly back to the blue salon.

"Anything important?" St. Clair asked as he looked up.

"Perhaps," Althea replied, smiling slyly. "Perhaps."

For three weeks he searched for her. He went all over London. He went to Westmorland. He talked to the staff at Beckworth House and to Albert Haskin at GlenRoyal. He even rode to Portsmouth and inquired about a lady in lavender and a tall, dark-haired sailor. But there was no news of Heather anywhere to be found. It was as if she'd disappeared from the face of the earth.

It wasn't long before talk was flying about Town. It was rumored that Heather FitzHugh had jilted the Duke of Hawksbury, then disappeared. Tanner cared little for what was being said in the salons and ballrooms of London. He cared only about finding Heather. He was obsessed with finding the woman he loved.

Edward Kennaway sat back in his chair and stared at the dark liquid in his glass. He swirled the port several times, then glanced across the rim of the glass at Tanner.

"You know, Hawk, one more thing we don't know is who sent you the note, telling you to look for Heather in Portsmouth. Seems to me someone was dead set on causing trouble between you two. Seems to me it worked."

"Why should I care who sent it?" Tanner grumbled. "She isn't with whoever it was."

Edward leaned forward. "But if they were interested enough in Heather to know her comings and goings to Portsmouth, perhaps they'd also know where she went when she left your town house."

Tanner straightened in his chair, intrigued.

"Who might have wanted to stop your marriage to Heather?"

He considered Edward's question, adding a few of his own. Why *would* someone have sent that note? What *was* the purpose? It had been signed "A friend." But would a true friend have sent it?

The earl sipped his port. "Seems you have only two logical choices. One would be a woman who'd hoped for her own alliance with you. Perhaps someone you've scorned in the past. The other would be a man who wanted Heather for himself."

The last suggestion rang a cold, angry bell inside Tanner's head. "Stroughton," he whispered, remembering the marquess's advances toward Heather at Albany House.

"Really?" Edward swirled the glass again, watching the port with an air of indifference. "Interesting. 'Tis whispered he's Lady Merrywood's latest lover. And wasn't there a time not long ago when she fancied herself a duchess?"

Tanner felt himself growing as taut as a bowstring. He remembered the many times Althea had thrown herself at him. He also remembered her white-hot anger the night of the Haversham Ball. She'd promised him then that he would regret his insults.

With a sudden certainty, he knew Althea had sent the note. It would be more her style than St. Clair's, but beyond that, she was the one who was interested in matrimony. St. Clair wouldn't have cared if Heather had married Tanner or not. He was interested only in the conquest. Althea, on the other hand, had always made it clear she wanted to be his next wife as well as his current lover.

Edward seemed to know what Tanner was thinking. "Go easy, Hawk. You have no proof of the lady's involvement."

"Not yet," he replied tersely.

St. Clair leaned close to Althea in her opera box and whispered in her ear. She struck him with her fan.

"Do be quiet, Stroughton," she snapped at him, "or else find another box so that I might enjoy the evening."

Even in the dim light of the theater, she knew his face had darkened with anger. St. Clair didn't take rejection well. She didn't particularly care. She wished he would simply go away and leave her alone. He'd been an amusing distraction from her humdrum existence as the wife of the elderly earl, as well as a quite adequate lover. But he'd served his purpose, and she was tired of him.

Besides, her campaign against Miss FitzHugh seemed to have been successful. Although nothing was confirmed, rumors said the duke had been jilted. Althea was certain the truth was the other way around. It was the duke who'd cried off. Hawksbury had doubted the girl's purity—and, if what Althea had been told was true, with good reason. Miss FitzHugh would have been unable to proclaim her innocence when the duke went looking for her in Portsmouth, and Hawksbury would have been forced to throw her aside.

Althea smiled thoughtfully. Heather hadn't been seen for weeks, leaving the duke unattached and lonely. Althea meant to have that vacated spot in his life. She couldn't do so with St. Clair nipping at her heels.

She gave no thought to her husband, the Earl of

Merrywood, even now lying in his bed at home. After all, he was well past sixty years old. He hadn't been hale when she'd married him. Surely he would be dead before the year was out. Heaven knew, she hadn't expected him to live this long when she'd agreed to be his bride. She'd expected to be a very wealthy widow long before now.

And she intended to be an even wealthier duchess.

She returned her attention to St. Clair. "Do you suppose Hawk knows where Miss FitzHugh is staying? Odd, how she just seemed to disappear into thin air. I've heard it whispered the wedding will never take place, and 'tis only a matter of time before that fact is announced. Strange that she would disappear like that. Hawk must not have been man enough to keep her." She tapped St. Clair's breeches suggestively with her fan. "If you were in the duke's place, my dear, you would know how to hold her, wouldn't you?"

She saw a flash of white teeth.

"Of course you would. Pity you don't know where she's staying. Such a pity." She leaned closer to him, brushing her breast against his arm. "But then, you're not the type to stop until you get what you want, are you, Stroughton?"

She smiled inwardly, feeling the thrill of success. She'd planted a seed in his mind, one he wasn't likely to let go of. He'd always wanted Miss Fitz-Hugh. Now he would go looking for her, leaving Althea to her own pursuits.

Tanner didn't care that it was damned unfashionable to show up on the Earl of Merrywood's doorstep so early in the day. Throughout the night, he'd thought about nothing but the likelihood of Althea's authoring the anonymous note, and he wasn't about to wait any longer to confront her.

Having bullied the majordomo into announcing his presence to the countess, Tanner spent better than half an hour wearing a line in the Aubusson carpet as he paced from one end of the small salon to the other.

"Hawk," Althea called as she swept into the room, meticulously dressed and coiffed. "How frightfully naughty of you to disturb a woman's beauty sleep. Are you always up at this ungodly hour of the day?" She stopped only a few feet away from him.

He stared at her in silence, trying to cool the rage that swelled and crashed within him at the sight of her.

Althea's seductive smile faltered ever so slightly. "Won't you sit down, your grace?" She waved toward a sofa.

Tanner ignored her question as he stepped toward her. "I'd like to know who you had spying on Heather."

"Spying?" Althea's eyes widened, and he would have sworn she lost a bit of color in her cheeks. "I don't know what you're talking about, Hawk. Why would I bother spying on Miss FitzHugh?"

"You needn't pretend, Lady Merrywood. I know you sent the note, telling me to look for Heather in Portsmouth. I know you hoped to cause trouble between us, to put suspicions in my mind. What you didn't realize was that when two people love each other, there's a certain amount of trust that goes with it." He felt a pang of guilt, knowing that he was condemning himself with his own words, but he shoved the emotion aside. He couldn't allow Althea to see that her machinations had succeeded. He decided that one lie deserved another. "I knew she planned to go to Portsmouth. She went with my blessing." He was convinced his next words weren't a lie. "She went to meet her brother."

The countess turned away from him and moved to a chair. She settled gracefully into it, smoothing the skirt of her elegant morning gown. Finally, her features more composed, she looked up at him again. "I still don't know what it is you're talking about, Hawk. I have no interest in where Miss FitzHugh goes or whom she sees."

Lord, how he wanted to strangle a confession from her lips. He wanted to know who'd been watching Heather so he could learn if they would know where she'd gone. But instinct told him Althea didn't know where Heather was. He was wasting his time here.

He took two steps toward her. "You know, Althea, you're much like my first wife. She could rarely tell the truth either."

She rose from her chair, her hands closed in fists at her sides. "How dare you come into my home and insult me."

"Have I insulted you? How bothersome of me. Well, if I've gone that far, there's no reason why I shouldn't say more." His eyes narrowed. "If I ever suspect that you've said an ill word about Heather, if you ever so much as breathe a hint of scandal, I shall see that you are ruined. Most of London is aware of your many lovers. You're not selective, are you, Althea? You are merely biding your time until Merrywood obliges and turns up his toes, leaving you a widow. Well, it won't be as pleasant as you think if you persist in harassing Heather. I'll see that the earl has nothing left to leave you when he goes. The Dowager Countess of Merrywood will be a pauper when I'm through."

Althea gasped.

He took another step closer. His voice lowered. "I have the ability to do it, Althea. Those funds and properties that don't go to his heir—a cousin, isn't it—are heavily mortgaged. Your earl isn't as plum as you think. Persist, and I'll see he has nothing to leave you. I can do it."

"Hawk, you wouldn't," she whispered, her face as white as a sheet. "You wouldn't do that to me." She reached forward but stopped short of touching him. "You know I've always loved you, always wanted to be your wife. You know I would have gladly been your lover, anytime you would have had me. The others meant nothing to me. Kimbell won't live forever. He's an old man. God knows, I thought he'd be gone by now. You don't want to throw your life away on that girl when you could have a woman like me. You can't turn me away. You can't!"

"What an impassioned speech from my devoted wife."

Althea gasped as she spun around to face her husband, standing in the doorway. "Kimbell . . ."

The earl's gaze lifted from Althea to Tanner. "I believe, your grace, that I should prefer to be alone with my countess. We have much to discuss."

Tanner nodded and stepped around Althea as he headed for the exit.

Merrywood stopped him. "Your grace?" Their eyes met again. "I assure you that Lady Merrywood shall not trouble you or Miss Fitz-Hugh again. Since I intend to live for many years yet, I believe I can keep such a promise."

Hearing a new strength in the old man's voice, Tanner found that he believed the earl.

"Good day, Lord Stroughton," Caroline Beckworth said as she entered the room. "I hadn't expected callers today. As you can see, the house is in quite an uproar. We are packing to return to the country."

"Leaving Town so soon, Lady Moredale?" St. Clair asked. "But the Season still has weeks to go."

"Perhaps you haven't heard. Annabella is to be married. Viscount Covillon has offered for her. The wedding is to take place in only a matter of a few weeks, and since the earl's estates are much closer to Beckworth House, we are retiring there for the duration." She waved absently toward a grouping of chairs.

"I hadn't heard," St. Clair answered as he obeyed the silent command, taking his place on a blue brocade chair while Caroline settled onto a white settee. "Covillon, you say."

Caroline's eyes were alight with victory. "Yes. My husband and I couldn't be more pleased. Covillon was introduced to Annabella at the Hawksbury Ball, and he was completely taken with her from that moment on. Of course, I always knew my daughter would make a brilliant match. Just think, she'll be a countess one day."

St. Clair hid his smile. He knew what Lady Moredale was thinking. She was counting the days until her daughter would be a *wealthy* countess. But he knew Covillon and his father, the Earl of Chilton. Oh, yes. They were extremely plummy, all right, but it took a veritable miracle to pry any of the blunt free from their pockets. Two more tight-fisted niggards St. Clair had never known. Covillon avoided the Season because of the cost. Only the search for a bride would have brought him here, and St. Clair would happily wager that the skinflint wouldn't be back until, should he be blessed with children, his own daughter's Season. If then.

"That's two brilliant matches in your family, my lady," he said, leaning back in his chair. "Your daughter marrying the heir to Chilton and your niece marrying a duke."

He noticed a slight thinning of her lips as she pressed them together.

"Of course," he continued, "there are rumors in Town that Heather has cried off and that the wedding won't take place, though nothing has officially been said. Still, 'tis strange no one has seen her in weeks. Hawksbury has been acting dreadfully strange. Why doesn't he do something to stop the gossip?"

"How should I know?" Caroline retorted angrily. "The ungrateful chit. After all I've done for her. Taking her in and giving her a good home after that drunken fool of a brother of mine left her orphaned on my doorstep without a farthing to her name."

"Do you know where she's staying now that she's left Lady Moberly's?"

"Why would you expect her to have the good grace to tell her own aunt? I haven't the foggiest notion where she is."

"Surely she's not still in London?" he persisted. "Does she have friends in the country she might be staying with?"

Caroline waved her hand in irritation. "The girl's never known anyone outside of a few of the neighbors in Westmorland. Common folk mostly. Until she came to Town, she knew no one among the *ton*, which was just as well. See how she's deported herself in just a short time. To tell you the truth, Lord Stroughton, 'tis her lack of good breeding that brought this shadow over us in the first place. If she wasn't forever sneaking over to GlenRoyal to trespass on the duke's property, they should never have met, and I wouldn't be worrying about scandal now."

"GlenRoyal? Are you referring to Hawksbury's hunting lodge, which Mannington has talked about so often?"

"Yes. It belonged to Heather's father before he

gambled it away. Now it belongs to the duke. But my niece ignored my warnings. She continued to walk through the gardens as if they belonged to her. The duke heard about her trespassing and insisted on meeting her. I tell you, 'twas a terrible time of worry for me. I knew we should all be ruined." She pulled a fan from her pocket and waved it dramatically in front of her face. "I only pray I can get through Annabella's wedding before Heather does something to shame us for good."

GlenRoyal . . . Hmm.

St. Clair rose to his feet. "I am most sorry for causing you this distress, Lady Moredale. I shouldn't have inquired about Heather. I can see you have more than enough to occupy your mind without sitting here passing the time of day with me. Please give my best wishes to your lovely daughter on her marriage to Covillon."

Caroline smiled up at him. "I shall do so, my lord."

He bowed. "Good day, my lady."

"Good day, Lord Stroughton."

Moments later, as St. Clair stepped into his town coach and commanded the driver to take him home, he pondered what he'd learned. Lady Moredale was clearly expecting disaster and scandal. That meant there definitely was trouble between Heather and Hawksbury, which in turn confirmed the rumors about the girl leaving London. It confirmed a lot of things except where she'd gone.

GlenRoyal? It made sense. If nothing else, it was a place to start.

Chapter 29

Heather sat in the shade of a tall willow, gazing across the pond without seeing anything. A blessed cool breeze was stirring the branches above her head, but she was oblivious to it. Strawberry whined and inched across the grass on her belly until she could place her head on Heather's lap.

"What's the matter, girl?" Heather whispered, her hand falling to the dog's head. She scratched the animal behind the ear. "Do you feel it, too?"

She glanced toward the house. She'd always dreamed of coming home to GlenRoyal. It had meant everything to her. Now, too late, she had discovered that it was just brick and wood and paint. Why didn't it feel like home anymore? What had changed?

She knew the answer, of course. Everything had changed because of Tanner. Nothing was the same without him.

She sighed as she stroked the dog's head. She wouldn't be staying here much longer. George would come for her soon, and she would leave England, probably for America. She would never see GlenRoyal again, never see Strawberry or Cathy, never eat scones in Mrs. Osmond's kitchen, never watch Haskin set an injured animal's leg, never see Tanner.

Tanner . . .

She closed her eyes as twin tears burned their way down her cheeks. Would the pain ever lessen? she wondered. Would it ever go away?

She thought back over the weeks she'd been at GlenRoyal. The day Tanner had come looking for her here, she'd hidden in Mr. Haskin's room above the stables. She'd been able to hear his voice but could not understand his words. She'd heard the anger, however. After he'd gone, Mr. Haskin had tried to tell her she was making a mistake, that the duke truly wanted her back for his bride, but she knew she wasn't wrong.

Damn you, Heather.

She could still hear the bitterness, the cold rage in his words. No. Mr. Haskin was wrong. No matter what Tanner had told the groundskeeper, she knew she was doing the right thing. She had to leave.

Strawberry whined again.

She glanced down at the dog. "When I'm gone, you'll love him for me, won't you, girl?" she whispered.

The setter's ears lifted, then flattened against her head.

"Sure you will. Someone has to keep on loving him. He needs it so very much."

Tears threatened again, but she blinked them away. She had to remain strong until she left here. She couldn't allow herself to weaken and think about how much he needed her and her love.

She turned her thoughts to George again. In America she would make a home for him. A warm place to rest between voyages. She would be very happy doing that for George. After all, even through the long years of separation, she'd always known he loved her. He'd always tried to take care of her. With him, she would be happy and content. She would be . . . she would be . . .

She rubbed her forehead as she bit her lower lip, trying to staunch the pain in her heart with a different pain.

She would never see Tanner again. Or be his bride. Or lie in his arms, replete from his lovemaking. She would never bear his children.

Tears came suddenly once again. Perhaps she was saddest for that. She'd hoped . . . But it wasn't to be. She wasn't carrying his baby.

When will it stop hurting so? she wondered as she closed her eyes. *When will it stop?*

Tanner put down the report, then dropped his head into his hands, his elbows resting on the shiny dark surface. Mr. Markum, the Bow Street runner he'd hired, hadn't been able to turn up any new clues. And with each passing day, Tanner's hope of finding Heather diminished, replaced by despair.

"You need to rest," the dowager duchess said from the doorway of his study.

He watched wearily as she entered the room.

"You haven't slept more than a few hours this week. You aren't eating properly. My son, I'm worried about you."

"You don't understand, Mother. I drove her away. I pushed her into hiding. If anything untoward has happened to her, it is my fault."

Sophia came around the edge of the desk and placed her hand on Tanner's head, gently stroking the hair away from his face. "I know you blame yourself, Tanner, and from what you've told me, you've good reason to, but killing yourself with worry won't find the girl. Come. Luncheon is about to be served."

Tanner shook his head. "I need to write some instructions to Mr. Markum."

"It can wait, my dear."

Tanner was about to reply when Pengelly

stepped into the study. "Excuse me, your grace. There is a gentleman downstairs who insists upon seeing you."

"Not now, Pen. Tell him to come another time."

"Sir ... I think you should see him."

Tanner raised a brow in question.

"He claims to be Miss FitzHugh's brother."

The duke rose swiftly from his chair.

"The gentleman is waiting in the rose salon, sir," Pengelly supplied as Tanner strode purposefully past him.

He took the stairs two at a time and crossed the hall with due haste, then paused in the open doorway.

The man's back was toward him. He was staring up at a portrait of Tanner's father which hung above the fireplace. But that wasn't what caught Tanner's attention. It was the color of his collar-length hair, caught back in a ribbon at the nape of his neck. It was the striped guernsey shirt and the slightly flared trousers. It was the tree-stump-thick biceps and the sailor-strong thighs.

This was the man from Portsmouth.

As if sensing Tanner's presence, the man turned around. His green eyes assessed the duke with a harsh gaze. There was a slight resemblance to Heather in the shape of his face, but something else was familiar about him as well. Tanner searched his memory for where he'd seen the man before.

"I didn't think you'd remember. It's been a long time." He stepped forward and held out his hand. "I'm George FitzHugh." He grinned. "But the name I gave you back then was Walter Alberts. I'm the boy who couldn't hold a pistol without shooting himself."

"I remember, but ... I didn't know you're Heather's brother."

The smile disappeared from George's face almost as quickly as it had appeared. "Heather's the reason I've come. I've been to Lady Moberly's. She was very evasive and would only tell me that Heather isn't staying with her any longer. Is she here with you?"

Tanner shook his head.

"Where is she?"

"I'm afraid I don't know."

"Don't know?" George frowned.

"She left London over three weeks ago. I haven't heard from her since then. I don't know where she's gone."

George ran a hand over his slicked-back hair. "I'm afraid I'm a bit confused. Shouldn't she be here getting ready for the wedding? Isn't the ceremony being held next week at Hawksbury Park?"

Tanner felt a terrible ache in his chest. His stomach seemed twisted into grotesque knots. "It was, until I accused her of taking a lover, of being unfaithful to me."

"Heather? But she loves you."

"I know that now." Tanner crossed the room, pushed aside the curtain to gaze out the window at the garden below, then let it drop back into place as he turned to face her brother once more. "But I was too angry to believe it then. Besides, I saw her with the other man."

George moved toward him, a scowl furrowing his brows. "You saw her?"

"With a sailor at the General Post Office. She kissed him."

"But that was . . ."

"You," Tanner finished for him.

"What happened?"

Tanner swallowed as another wave of hot shame washed over him. "I offered to set her up as my courtesan instead of as my wife."

He didn't see it coming. The fist seemed to come out of nowhere, slamming into his face with incredible force. It knocked him back against the wall. The room tipped precariously, and he was only vaguely aware of George moving toward him as he slid down the wall until he was seated on the floor, his knees up close to his chest.

He held up a hand. "Wait. Before you give me what I deserve, I want you to know I already realized my mistake. Heather tried to tell me what had happened in Portsmouth, but I wouldn't listen to her. I always believed she couldn't be dishonest with me, that I would see through her, but when it really counted, I forgot how completely candid she is. By the time I remembered, it was too late. She was already gone." Tanner took a deep breath and let it out. "She took nothing with her. Not her clothes or her jewels. She didn't take anything I gave her. Not even the GlenRoyal deed." He paused again, then whispered, "I love her. I never told her I love her."

George's expression didn't change much. He was glaring down at Tanner as if he intended to tear him limb from limb. And from the looks of the sailor's burly arms and the white-hot pain in Tanner's eye, he knew George could do it, too.

Tanner didn't even attempt to rise, certain he would only be knocked down again. "I've been looking for her ever since she left," he said, futility filling his voice. "I've been to Westmorland and talked to Haskin and the staff at Beckworth House. I've been every conceivable place here in Town. I even went to Portsmouth. No one has seen her. Not even her aunt knows where she's gone. I've got Bow Street runners looking for her, but they've found no clues either."

George's meaty fists remained clenched at his sides. "You mean to marry my sister when you find her, Hawksbury?"

"Drat it all! Haven't you heard a word I've said? Of course I mean to marry her. That is, if she'll still have me. God knows, I wouldn't be surprised if she never forgave me for what I've done."

"She'll forgive you."

"I wish I were so certain. But at the moment, I only want to find her and make sure she's all right."

"Do you have a couple of swift horses?" George asked.

Tanner nodded.

"Then we'd better be on our way." George offered his hand to Tanner.

He looked at it for a moment, then met the man's gaze. Finally, he grasped the proferred hand and was yanked to his feet. They continued to stare at each other in silence for a long time before Tanner asked, "Where are we going?"

"GlenRoyal," George answered as he swiveled on his heel and headed toward the door.

"But I told you, I've been there. Haskin hasn't seen her."

George glanced over his shoulder. "I may have been gone a long time, but I know one thing must still be true about my sister. The servants love her. There isn't a one of them who wouldn't lie for her. Especially Haskin. Heather knew I was coming back in time for the wedding. She'll know I'll look for her there when I can't find her in London. She'll be waiting."

Tanner recognized the logic of what George was saying.

"Hawksbury." George's tone was grave. "If you're not telling me the truth—if you don't marry her, if you don't love her and treat her well and make her happy—so help me, I'll kill you."

"If I don't do all of those things, I'll deserve it."

Heather glanced around the small quarters above the stables before she met the grounds-keeper's solemn gaze. "George should be here any day, Mr. Haskin, and then you can have your own room back. I feel so guilty, having you sleeping down in that empty stall."

"Don't be silly, miss. 'Tis not hard on me to make do with the cot, though I think you're wrong for bein' here at all. You should send for his grace afore it's too late."

She didn't answer. She couldn't.

"Well, you'd best eat some of that breakfast. You've grown a mite too thin for my likin', eatin' next to nothin', day in and day out."

Dutifully, she sipped at her cup of morning chocolate, then nibbled on some hot bread and honey.

"Maybe you'd like to go for a ride this afternoon," Haskin suggested, his voice hopeful. "His grace had several new hunters sent up from the Park more'n a month ago now. 'Bout the time he lost his steward, I think it was. Mighty fine horseflesh, they are. They could use a bit of exercise. More'n what me an' my old bones can give 'em."

"No, thank you, Mr. Haskin. I think I'll just walk in the gardens. The roses are all in bloom, and the air smells so sweet."

Haskin shook his head. "As you wish, Miss Heather." Mumbling to himself, he left the table in the corner of his quarters and descended the steps to the stables below.

Heather glanced out the dingy square of a window. She wondered how much longer she would have to wait for George. The wedding was to have taken place within the next week. Surely he'd come back from the Continent by this time and knew she'd broken off with Tanner. Surely all of London knew she'd run away. George must also know that she would come here to Mr. Haskin to wait for him.

She went to the window and with the heel of her hand, rubbed away the dirt and peered out toward the house. How many years had she come here, wishing it were her home again? Well, it had been. For just a little while, it had been hers. She'd held the deed in her hands. But the price had been too high.

She sighed and turned back from the window. Slowly, she cleared away the breakfast plates and carried them to the small kitchen àrea behind Mr. Haskin's sleeping room. She put away the leftover food, then washed and dried the dishes. Finally, she returned to the bedchamber, where she stripped out of her worn and faded dress, and donned the togs of a stablehand. She pulled a cap firmly over her black curls, hiding them from view.

Heather and Mr. Haskin had decided the disguise was wise. Although the recently hired household staff was small and hadn't had much communication with the duke, there was always the chance Tanner had told them to send for him if they saw her. Just to be safe, Heather stayed out of sight as much as possible, and when she couldn't bear the restrictions any further, she dressed in boy's clothes. So far, the disguise seemed to be working.

She climbed down the narrow steps to the stables and went outside to the kennels. One by one, she opened the gates, allowing the hounds their freedom. Strawberry bounded joyously around her, causing a small smile to curl her mouth.

"Come on, girl," she said, and started off toward the gardens. "Let's go to the maze."

St. Clair wasn't sure what made him stop his horse in the middle of the drive and take a second look at the stableboy out exercising the dogs. A sixth sense told him something wasn't quite what it appeared, although from this distance he couldn't be certain what it was.

He glanced toward the house but saw no other servants about, no one who might question his presence there. So he dismounted and headed toward the thick green maze that covered the grounds off to the side of the house.

He stopped when the "stableboy" came into view again. It was hard to believe that it was Miss FitzHugh, the one-time, would-be duchess, but it was. The loose shirt couldn't hide the lush fullness of her breasts. The floppy cap couldn't shade enough to hide the uniquely feminine beauty that adorned the heart-shaped face. Grinning to himself, the marquess followed the girl and dogs into the maze.

He'd been right to trust his instincts. He'd found her. And he wouldn't be as foolish as the duke. He knew how to please and keep a woman. Keep them until he tired of them. Keep them until the conquest was his and his interest waned.

Heather FitzHugh might even be different from the others. He might want to keep her around longer. There was something special about her that had always intrigued him. Not enough for marriage, of course. He had no interest in that dreaded institution, and he really didn't care whom his title passed to when he was gone. Devil take it. Why *should* he care? He'd be dead. The only duty he cared about was seeing that he enjoyed life while he was here.

And Miss FitzHugh would definitely make a man enjoy it, he thought as he watched her walking, the gentle sway of her hips easily visible in the trousers she wore.

Whatever had made her run from the duke, he meant to see that she now became his.

Strawberry stopped hopping around Heather. Her ears shot up, head lowered slightly, and she growled in her throat.

"What is it, girl?" Heather asked as she turned in the direction the dog was staring. Her heart nearly stopped.

"I always did find you charming, no matter what delightful thing you chose to wear. But this is beyond the pale, even for you, Miss FitzHugh. Still, you'd put many a girl at her come-out to shame, even as you are."

Heather tried to find something to say but was unable to do so.

St. Clair walked closer. Strawberry's growls grew louder.

"Please, Miss FitzHugh. Call off your dog. I am not here to cause you any harm."

Heather placed her hand atop the setter's head. "Shh, Strawberry," she whispered. To St. Clair, she added, "Why is it you've come, my lord?"

"Why, to make sure you are all right, of course. You have caused some stir in Town, I assure you. Everyone is wondering what has happened to the duke's bride."

"Tanner hasn't announced that the wedding is off?"

"Is it? Well, that's good to know. I never thought him right for you. He never would have understood your penchant for excitement. That is why you sought out other men, isn't it? For the excitement. I'm much like that myself."

St. Clair took another step forward.

Heather took a step back.

"Return to London with me, Heather. You are a diamond of the first water and could have any man you want. You were wasted on Hawksbury. He doesn't know what to do with a woman like you. Let me squire you around. I would see that you have your own town house. My visits to you would be most discreet so that we wouldn't scare off the eligible males who will surely be swarming about you now that you're unencumbered by the duke. I promise, you would know great pleasure with me. And when you settle on a husband, I will bow graciously out of the picture."

Heather felt the blood rushing from her head. Did he know about Tanner's proposition? Was that why he was offering to make her his *fille de joie*? She moved swiftly toward a stone bench set against the high hedge.

Her reply was spoken breathlessly as she sank onto the cool stone. "I'm afraid I have no interest in your offer, Lord Stroughton. Now, if you would please go." She stared down at the ground, unable to look at him.

"Go? After coming all this way to find you?" His voice had hardened. "Don't be mistaken about me, Heather. I mean to take you back with me, one way or another."

There was no misunderstanding the threat in his words. Fear leaped to life in her heart. She kept her eyes closed and hoped he would simply disappear.

St. Clair's voice carried clear and cruel over the top of the maze. Seeing red and wanting blood, Tanner started toward an opening in the hedge, but George's hand on his arm stopped him.

"Let me," he said in a soft but deadly tone. "I abdicated my duty to Heather a long time ago. Let me make it up to her now."

Reluctantly, Tanner nodded.

George rounded the corner with Tanner on his heels.

Tanner's gaze shot past St. Clair's back to the small form seated on the bench, a cap shading her face. She looked thin and pale, forlorn and frightened. Her eyes were closed, as if to shut out the world—or at least St. Clair.

George's voice broke the silence. "You're not taking my sister anywhere."

Heather's eyes shot open at the same time St. Clair whirled around. Before he could react, George was upon him. A swift upper cut caught St. Clair under the chin. Having been on the receiving end himself, Tanner winced as he watched the marquess fall to the ground. George grabbed St. Clair by the collar and dragged him to his feet, then punched him in the belly one more time for good measure. There was no real fight in the dandy. St. Clair turned a ghastly shade as he tried to protect himself from another speeding fist.

George hauled the marquess with him toward Tanner. "I think you and my sister need some time alone. Just remember something, Hawksbury. I will see that Heather is well taken care of from this moment on, and no one but her husband will ever take that right from me again."

"I'll remember."

George glanced at his sister. "I won't be going anywhere until things are settled, Heather. I'll be in the stables if you need me."

Tanner watched George and St. Clair disappear through the opening in the maze, then turned once again toward Heather. She was standing now, rubbing her palms nervously over her trouser legs.

Please, God, let her forgive me.

He started forward.

"You shouldn't have come," she said when he was halfway to her.

"I had to come. You left before I had a chance to say some things that needed to be said."

"There is nothing more to say."

"You're wrong, Heather." He halted before her.

There were dark circles beneath her beautiful eyes, a terrible sadness in their violet depths, one he'd put there. His guilt burned like a hot knife in his heart.

"I can't do it, Tanner. I can't be your mistress."

"I know." He had to touch her. He couldn't bear not to touch her. Standing there in those ridiculous clothes, she looked as beautiful as any woman he'd ever seen. "I don't want you for my mistress. I want you for my wife, for my duchess."

Her eyes widened.

"Nothing I say can ever excuse the terrible things I said to you, the terrible things I did. I made a bloody fool of myself because . . . because I was afraid to believe you were different, that you might truly love me. I didn't know how to trust a woman." He reached slowly forward and took hold of her left hand. "I'm asking you to forgive me, Heather. You have no reason to, of course. But if you do forgive me, if you'll marry me, I give you my solemn word you'll never have reason to hate me again. I'll love you until the day I die."

Winded by his long speech, he gulped in a breath of air, then held it as he waited tensely for her reply.

She stared at him in silence for what seemed an eternity. Her eyes seemed to bore their way into his soul. Finally, she raised her right hand and touched the corner of his eye. "How did you get that bruise?" she asked softly.

"George. He didn't like it when I told him what I'd done to you."

A very small smile appeared. "My brother *hit* you?"

"*You* should have hit me," he whispered.

"I know." Her smile grew a little wider.

"I do love you, Heather. I think I fell in love with you the night you beat me at chess, only I was too stubborn or stupid to recognize it." He drew another tentative breath. "Is it too late? Have I been so cruel that you can never forgive me?"

In that moment, she knew that whatever demons had once tortured his soul had been exorcised. There would be time later for a full explanation, to sort through the lies and deceptions on both sides, to discover what had brought them to this moment. For now, only one thing was important.

"I love you, too," she whispered as she moved into his arms. "I think I must have fallen in love with you the first day I saw you."

"Can you forgive me?" he asked, his head near hers.

"Forgiving is a part of loving."

He pushed the cap from her head and ran his fingers through her curls. "I don't deserve you, Heather."

"I like to think we deserve each other, your grace." Then she stood on tiptoe and offered him her mouth.

As their lips touched, she knew her heart had brought her home. Not to GlenRoyal but here. Here to Tanner's arms.

Epilogue

Hawksbury Park, July 1817

"Zounds, man! Have you listened to a word I've said?"

"Hmm. Oh, sorry, Mannington."

Edward laughed. "Never mind, Hawk. I can see you've no interest in what's happening in Town this Season."

"What? Oh, the Season." Tanner shook his head, his gaze still locked on the gardens beneath his study window. "No, I don't know when we'll get to London."

Edward slapped him on the back as he came to stand beside his friend. "The odds at White's are for a boy by the first of August. Brooks's is leaning toward a girl. I've placed my wager at Brooks's and intend to get a very good return on my money."

Tanner grinned, only vaguely aware of what Edward was saying. Below him, Heather strolled amidst the bright flowers and green shrubs and grass, surrounded by a red setter and her rambunctious pups. "Stroll" wasn't a particularly accurate word for his wife's movements, he thought as he watched her stop and press her hand to the small of her back. Perhaps "waddle" was more appropriate.

The high waist of her lavender gown couldn't hide the fact that she was large with child. Even so, he'd never seen a more beautiful woman. He supposed the odds at White's or Brooks's would also be good that he was unquestionably besotted with his wife.

"You know, Hawk, you're lucky you found her."

He knew how lucky he was. It was still hard to believe that she'd forgiven him, that she loved him. Every day, he thanked God for giving him another chance.

"Well," Edward said as he moved away, "I can see there'll be no intelligent conversation with you today. I'd best take myself back to Kennaway Hall. Celeste will be wondering where I am. Good day, Hawk."

Tanner mumbled something appropriate as he watched Heather lean as far forward as her swollen abdomen would allow to stroke Strawberry's head. Through the glass, he could hear her laughter as two of the puppies tumbled head over heels near her feet.

Love welled up in his chest, a familiar feeling. Who would have thought he could ever know such happiness? The cynical man who'd viewed women through jaundiced eyes seemed like a stranger to him. To think one slight girl could have changed his life, could have changed *him* so.

He remembered their wedding day. A year ago this very day . . .

The Chapel, Hawksbury Park, July 1816

"Can you imagine, letting us come all this way? I heard she was seen in another man's carriage and that she eloped with him to Gretna Green."

"I cannot credit Sophia Montgomery not coming clean about the matter. The scandal will be terrible if you're right."

"I heard the odds at White's were extremely high last night that the bride won't appear for the wedding."

"Isn't that what I told you? There'll be no wedding. Miss FitzHugh disappeared weeks ago. I heard she was seen in . . ."

The groomsman, Edward Kennaway, closed the door on the whispers and murmurs that filled the interior of the Hawksbury Chapel. He looked at Tanner with a grin. "You're going to make me a very rich fellow, my friend."

"How's that?" Tanner asked.

"I took the odds at White's. They should have realized your best friend would surely know the truth, but apparently they thought I was merely being loyal. As if I'd throw away good money for loyalty." He laughed.

Tanner echoed the laugh, then pulled anxiously at his collar. "Here now," Edward protested, "leave that collar alone. If Thorpe comes in and finds I've allowed you to make a mess of yourself, there'll be the devil to pay."

Tanner nodded as he began pacing the small antechamber, his hands clasped behind his back to keep them out of trouble. He couldn't believe he was so nervous. He wasn't a schoolboy, after all. He was two and thirty. It wasn't even the first time he'd been married.

Only this time he was marrying Heather, and she made all the difference in the world.

The vicar stepped into the antechamber. "Are you ready, my boy?"

Suddenly, the case of nerves vanished. He was more than anxious, he realized. He was impatient. "Yes. I'm ready."

Hawksbury Park, July 1817

Heather glanced up at the window. She'd known he would be watching her. Even from this distance, she could tell he was smiling. It brought a warm glow to her chest. He smiled so often now. She remembered the sardonic grimace that had passed for a smile when she'd first met him. That, along with his bitterness and distrust, had disappeared.

She felt the baby kick and placed her hand on the spot. The Hawksbury heir was very active today.

The sudden joy that burst upon her was almost overwhelming. That she should have found such a love. To think how close she'd come to throwing her happiness away for the sake of revenge. Sometimes it still frightened her to think how near she'd been to losing Tanner and the child she carried so close to her heart, a child made by love.

But she hadn't lost them. A year ago this very day, this happiness had become hers forever ...

The Chapel, Hawksbury Park, July 1816

The traditional white-and-silver dress was fashionably high-waisted, making Heather appear all skirt and shoulders. The bridal gown seemed to glow with a light of its own, shimmering in the late morning sunlight streaming through the windows.

A floral wreath of violets and heather garnished her ebony hair, and from it flowed a trailing scarf of white lace. The veil fell in gentle folds down her back to the hem of her gown.

"Heather," Celeste said softly from behind her, "you look so very beautiful. I hope I'll look as lovely when it's my turn."

She turned to her bridesmaid. "You will, Celeste."

Her friend held out the posy of violets. "I think it's time."

Heather nodded but didn't start toward the door. Instead, she walked over to the window and glanced out at the morning light bathing the great lawns of Hawksbury Park in its golden glow.

Who would have ever thought this day would come? she wondered. Was it really only a little more than three months since she'd turned in the maze at GlenRoyal to find Tanner watching her as she played with Strawberry? It was hard to believe how that one chance meeting had changed her life. Now she was about to become the Duchess of Hawksbury. She, a simple country miss.

A tremor of doubt and fear shook her confidence. Could she make him proud of her, or would she forever be blundering into scandal? She was nothing like Sophia. She would make a terrible duchess.

"I've told you before, sister, you'll make a grand duchess."

"George! Can you read my mind? What are you doing in here?"

Her brother walked slowly toward her. His eyes swept over her gown, and she read his approval. She didn't fail to note how handsome he looked in his dark green suit.

"I couldn't send you off without one more chance to have you all to myself." He stopped before her, taking her proferred hand in his and squeezing it. "It was cowardly of me to have left you all those years ago. I should have come back and taken care of you, as I'd promised. I'll always regret my neglect."

"We've already been through this, George. It doesn't matter anymore."

"Your duke had better know what he's getting,

Heather. You were a princess at heart long before he made you a duchess."

"Thank you, dear brother," she whispered as she kissed his cheek. Then she turned to Celeste. "I'm ready now."

Hawksbury Park, July 1817

"You're deep in thought."

Heather looked up as Tanner strode across the lawn. "I was remembering our wedding day."

He nodded, and somehow she knew he'd been remembering it, too. It was like that often between them.

"Edward was here," he said as he drew near. He smiled, his once cool eyes filled with warmth. "He's made another wager on us. A son by August first. He's counting on us to increase his fortune."

Her heart did its usual little hiccup as he touched her cheek, then smoothed curling tendrils of hair back from her face. "I don't suppose we dare disappoint him," she responded softly. "He did so well after our wedding."

"I realize, since an heir was what I was after when I went looking for a bride, I should be dead set on a son." He drew her close to him, her protruding abdomen pressing against his own flat belly. "But I must confess, I wouldn't mind a little violet-eyed daughter with short black curls. No, I wouldn't mind that at all. We could always try for a boy next time."

She smiled secretly, thinking of the nights of "trying" she would spend in Tanner's arms.

Once again her husband seemed to read her thoughts. "That day at GlenRoyal, when I decided to propose marriage—I thought then that it would neither be difficult to spend time in your company nor be unpleasant to sire a child with you. I was right on both accounts."

"And did I ever tell you how *wrong* I was? The duke is neither a cheeseparing care-for-nobody nor a rakeshame." She reached up and traced his lips with a fingertip. "He is my laughter and my strength. He is my heart and my home. He is my life and my love."

They stared at each other for a long time, the two of them bathed in golden sunlight, both aware of the treasure they'd found in the other.

And then, as had happened so often in the past, the hawk dipped low to kiss the heather, holding his prey in gentle talons of love.

America Loves Lindsey!

The Timeless Romances
of #1 Bestselling Author

PRISONER OF MY DESIRE 75627-7/$5.99 US/$6.99 Ca
Spirited Rowena Belleme *must* produce an heir, and the mag
nificent Warrick deChaville is the perfect choice to sire he
child—though it means imprisoning the handsome knight.

ONCE A PRINCESS 75625-0/$5.95 US/$6.95 Ca
From a far off land, a bold and brazen prince came t
America to claim his promised bride. But the spirited vixe
spurned his affections while inflaming his royal blood wit
passion's fire.

GENTLE ROGUE 75302-2/$4.95 US/$5.95 Ca
On the high seas, the irrepressible rake Captain James Malo
is bested by a high-spirited beauty whose love of freedom ar
adventure rivaled his own.

WARRIOR'S WOMAN 75301-4/$4.95 US/$5.95 Ca
In the year 2139, Tedra De Arr, a fearless beautiful Amazo
unwittingly flies into the arms of the one man she can ne
hope to vanquish: the bronzed barbarian Challen Ly-San-T

SAVAGE THUNDER 75300-6/$4.95 US/$5.95 C
Feisty, flame-haired aristocrat Jocelyn Fleming's wor
collides with that of Colt Thunder, an impossibly handso
rebel of the American West. Together they ignite an unsto
pable firestorm of frontier passion.